Forg

Danielle Driver

First published in 2023 by Blossom Spring Publishing
Forgotten © 2023 Danielle Driver
ISBN 978-1-7394532-8-2
E: admin@blossomspringpublishing.com
W: www.blossomspringpublishing.com

1

"See you soon." – Chris.

Becky knew he was looking at her and although she wouldn't have admitted it, it was distracting her. It was a Thursday evening and she was sitting alone in a bar with a glass of wine, revising for a job interview she had tomorrow at the Fairview Care Home. It was a job Becky was desperate for. Working as a carer for people with learning disabilities had been something she had wanted to do for as long as she could remember. She did not need distractions. She had just taken the leap and given up the two jobs that she had been working simultaneously for the past seven years to focus completely on getting this one role. It meant so much to her.

Against her will, though, she looked up again, catching his eye, wondering why her heart started beating at an accelerated pace when their eyes met. He was staring at her, a smile playing on his lips. They were the bluest eyes she had ever seen – she could see that even from this distance. He wasn't her type at all, his dark blond hair was a bit too long for her liking, but those eyes! Becky usually liked her men tall, dark, handsome – and older. This guy looked about the same age as her, twenty-three, maybe twenty-four. She looked away again, annoyed with herself.

*

"I'm going to marry that girl," Chris announced to his friends as he finally stood up to walk over to the girl he had been watching at the other side of the bar.

*

Becky saw him approaching and to her surprise felt her heartbeat quicken. He was definitely not her type. She tried to convince herself she didn't like his confident walk, his self-assurance and obvious ease. He didn't take his eyes off her the whole way over, and when she finally looked up and their eyes met there was electricity in the air.

His eyes were boring into hers, she could still feel it even when she looked down at the papers on the table, surprised when she saw them laying there in front of her as if she had forgotten her reason for going in there in the first place.

He slid onto the bench on the opposite side of her table, his head tilted slightly to the left, still smiling. She noticed he had slight dimples in his cheeks.

"Hi," he said, and his gentle voice surprised her. Becky looked up, trying to look indifferent, unruffled, cool. She did not answer him. It was silent for a period of time that could have been an hour, but was probably more like ten seconds. His eyes were still on hers, his smile still there. It unnerved her.

Chris was taking her in. Her gorgeous, thick, dark brown hair that hung down past her shoulders, her strikingly beautiful face filled with huge brown eyes. There was no hint of a smile on her face though as she looked up at him, staring, impatient, waiting. Chris' smile eased wider. He felt as if he knew the look she was giving him, had seen it a hundred, even a thousand times before, knew exactly what it meant – even though he'd never *actually* seen her before. Becky saw his smile change and get even bigger. It was as if he was silently laughing, as if he had a secret no-one else knew. For a fleeting second, she wanted to know what it was, wanted to share it with him.

"You're going to marry me," Chris said, and, if it was possible, his smile grew even bigger. The silent laugh was there, dancing in his eyes – was it challenging her to say differently? Becky could not help it, she laughed.

Whatever she had been expecting from this boy, that had not been it.

Chris did not take his eyes off her face. He had thought she was beautiful while he'd watched her from a distance, sitting on her own, chewing on her lip, intently looking over the papers she had in front of her. When her face suddenly changed to a smile, she blew him away.

"You're not my type," Becky said, speaking the truth, but she wondered why she felt a knot in her chest as soon as she'd said it. What if he got up and left? *Okay, sorry to bother you.* But somehow, she knew he wouldn't. She was getting flustered and annoyed with herself. What did it matter if he did? She was being stupid. She had so much more to think about at the moment. This interview tomorrow was so important. She had not been without a job since she had left school and she was still so worried that she'd made a hasty decision to quit her jobs and put everything on the line to try for this dream. She didn't even want to think of what the consequences would be if she didn't actually get offered the job at the care home after tomorrow's interview. She wouldn't be able to get by, how would she afford her rent? Afford to live? It made her feel sick every time she thought about it. Chris' words broke through her train of thought.

"Of course I am," he said confidently. "Why would you marry me if I'm not your type?"

As Becky looked up at him, she was surprised at how sincere he was being and it threw her off guard. "I'm sorry... now is really not a good time," she said carefully. "I've got stuff to do, I've got an interview tomorrow-"

Chris stood up. "Okay," he said, and Becky's heart sank slightly. He *was* going to leave. Again, she was annoyed with herself. This *is* what she had wanted.

"What's your name?" he asked as he stood up.

"Becky."

"Becky." The smile. "I'm Chris. See you soon."

*

As Becky lay in bed that night before finally drifting off to sleep, the thoughts that flew around her head were not of the interview tomorrow, of the job that she was desperate for, or of all the research that she had been doing for the past few months. It was of the pair of blue eyes, which somehow seemed so familiar, that she had seen for the first time that evening.

"I want to help people who cannot help the way that they are." – Becky, aged eleven.

Becky was a very lonely young woman. Her father had left suddenly one day when she was young and her once doting mother, Maria, fell into a crushing depression and, like so many before her, had turned to alcohol. Becky was still at primary school when she first noticed the drastic change in her mother that was brought on when she started drinking. At first, the low points would only last for a few days at a time, then Maria would pull herself together, clean herself and the house, and take Becky out for the day.

They would go shopping or to the park, as if it made up for the last few days of neglect. Maria would buy Becky pretty clothes or treats in Woolworths, telling her that everything would get better from now on. But they never did. Eventually, the times that Maria spent drunk became more and more frequent and the trips out together as mother and daughter happened less and less until they finally ceased altogether.

Becky watched all this unfold before her in horror, knowing, despite her age, that she was powerless to stop it. She resolved that no-one would ever find out what was happening at home and took it upon herself to look after herself and her mother as best she could. She would run home from school every night to see how her mother was that day. Some days she would still be in bed, some days passed out on the sofa with a pool of vomit next to her. Other days, the worst days, Becky would find her weeping in the armchair that her father used to sit in with a framed photo of their wedding day on her lap. On these days, Becky would climb up on the chair and sit with her mother, also staring at the picture. Never crying, just thinking, *I'm still here, Mum.*

*

Becky didn't remember much from the years before her father died, but she could at least remember that they were happy. She had adored school and making friends. She had been a typical girly girl who loved to chatter and gossip and ignore the boys. She had been surrounded by friends at this point and the thought had never crossed her mind that her life may change, as is the way with children. But it did change, and once her father had left and her mother had started drinking, Becky started to pull away from the circle of friends that she'd had at school. She would no longer walk to and from school with them. She was unable to, she was constantly rushing around on her own schedule depending on her mother's mood that day.

In the playground, she now had no time for gossip and games; she just sat and worried. With her knees pulled up under her chin and her arms wrapped around them, she would rest her head on her knees and shut everything else out. Becky never cried. She just sat away from the other children, locked in her own misery. Eventually, the other girls stopped trying to be friends with her and Becky became an outsider. She would hear her old friends go quiet as they walked past, or see them point at her in the dining room.

At the time, her teachers did notice a change in her, but as her schoolwork did not seem affected, they didn't think too much into it. On the contrary, Becky's schoolwork and her grades flourished. She threw herself into each subject, seizing the opportunity to think of anything else except what was going on at home.

The years dragged past for Becky in a blur of school, fending for herself, and looking after her mum. She couldn't see a way out and worried constantly that this was going to be her life forever. Until one day, just after she had turned sixteen, Becky was called out of a GCSE exam moments before the other students were dismissed and was taken directly to the headmaster's office. He broke the news, looking at her kindly and sadly over his glasses that her mother had died. Maria had been very drunk and had fallen. She had managed to call an ambulance for help, but by the time the paramedics arrived it was too late, she had choked on her own vomit. Becky listened, detached and sad but not overcome with grief. If anything, she felt relieved, although she would never have admitted this to anyone out loud.

Becky didn't dwell on her mother's death. She was already hardened to what life threw at her. She had no friends, no family, and no-one to turn to, but that didn't stop her from wanting more. She had already accepted a full-time waitressing job for when she left school, which she was due to start the day after her last exam finished, and after she left the headmaster's office that day she went straight out and got an evening job four nights a week, too.

With the help of her headmaster, she managed to find a small flat for rent. It would cost her a fortune, nearly all the wages she got from her two jobs put together, but it was her own place and it meant that she wouldn't get placed into a hostel, which would have been the only other choice for her now that she was sixteen with no family to live with. The landlady of the flat was an older lady named Edna who had recently lost her husband. Becky was not aware that Edna was a good friend of her headmaster and, on hearing Becky's story, she had told him that Becky could move in without putting down the usual required deposit.

Becky moved into the flat and adored finally having

her own space. She threw herself into her two jobs the way she had with her work at school. At first, colleagues tried to befriend her and she was invited out on numerous occasions, but not having the luxury of spare cash once again pushed her further and further away from her peers until they finally stopped asking her. Becky fell into a pattern of work, sleep, and loneliness.

*

When Becky was still in primary school, a while after her mum had started drinking, she was asked by a teacher what she wanted to be when she grew up. Becky had thought about it for a second, wrinkling her nose in concentration.

"I want to help people," she said simply. The teacher raised her eyebrows at the response.

"Do you mean like a doctor or a nurse?" the teacher had asked, and Becky went quiet, thinking again before she replied, "I want to help people who cannot help the way that they are, like disabled people. Because they don't choose to be disabled, they are just born that way and that's not fair." The teacher told her it was a lovely idea and wasn't she a nice girl.

3

"I'll be here." – Chris.

Becky was on the way to her interview, and she was beyond nervous. She was annoyed that her interview was at three o'clock. She wished that she'd had a morning slot so that she hadn't had all day to worry. She got off the bus and walked the final few hundred metres along the busy pathway to the agency where she was being seen, cringing against the cold winter's day. She looked up at the dark clouds gathering in the sky, praying that the rain that had been threatening all day held off, at least until she was inside the building. People pushed past her in both directions, and she struggled to make her way forwards. As the crowd in front of her thinned, she darted through a gap and hurried towards the agency door.

Becky stopped dead in her tracks, almost rooted to the spot, when she realised with a tingle that Chris was lounging against the wall next to the door that she was about to walk through. He was casually watching the crowd of people filing past him down the busy pavement, struggling with their bags of Christmas shopping and trying to avoid puddles at the same time. He held a red rose lightly in one hand and his head nodded very slightly to music that Becky supposed only he could hear.

As if he knew she was there, he turned his head and caught her eye. It was as if his eyes were drawn to hers like a magnet. Their eyes met and for moment it seemed as if time stood still for both of them. The crowds of people moving around them may as well have not been there. Becky walked towards him, feeling as if she was in slow motion. She didn't know what she was going to say, didn't know how or why he was there – though, it didn't seem crazy or weird or amazing, it just made sense completely.

"Hey," he said, his crisp blue eyes roaming her face. He lifted the rose up briefly, pausing very close to her face, for a second almost touching her nose. She could smell its sweet aroma even through the London fog.

"This is for you. Good luck with the interview, I'll be here when you get out."

Becky nodded, managed a shaky smile, and walked into the building, leaving the traffic, the crowds, and Chris behind.

*

For years to come, Becky would always tell people that the reason she so confidently breezed through the interview that day and eventually got offered the job was because she knew that Chris was there, waiting for her.

4

BECKY

"There was no question." – Becky.

The day Chris turned up at my interview was without a doubt the day I fell in love with him. When I saw him standing outside the agency, the old saying *my heart skipped a beat* didn't even cover it. It was like my heart stopped beating and just exploded in my chest. I felt such a longing to be near him that it scared me. All thoughts of the interview I was about to go into suddenly seemed completely insignificant – what had I been worried about for weeks... months? All that mattered was that Chris was there.

I don't think I had allowed myself to realise how much he had affected me the night before, even though he had been all I could think about for the entire evening and all through the night as I lay tossing and turning in bed. I had even pushed it to the back of my mind when his face was the first thing I thought about when I opened my eyes that morning.

The shock of seeing him standing there in front of me, when I had never expected to see him again, brought all my feelings crashing down. It was as if a ton of emotion and longing had hit me like a physical heaviness, but at the same time I'd felt as if a weight had been lifted off my shoulders. It was indescribable.

I can't really remember anything specific about my interview with the people from the care home. I can remember chatting away and laughing a lot (completely unlike me); everything seemed so entertaining. I do remember wanting to tell the people doing my interview that Chris was downstairs waiting for me, but I had to keep reminding myself that they didn't care! I knew I had the job before I even left the building. I just had a good feeling about it – which, again, is completely unheard of for me. Renowned as a pessimist, I would usually have stressed from the second I walked out of the interview, convinced that I had said or done something wrong.

After the interview, I ran down the stairs towards the main entrance of the building where Chris was waiting when nervousness hit me briefly. What was I doing? I didn't know anything about this person outside waiting for me. But there was something there, a reason I wanted to be with him. There was not one moment of concern that he wouldn't be there, I just knew he would be. There was no question.

As I stepped outside onto the pavement it was still a typical gloomy London afternoon, and now it was starting to get dark. Our eyes met quickly and without even speaking we were walking along the street together as if we had been doing it for years. I didn't know where we were going, and I didn't really care.

The street was getting even busier, as it was rush-hour almost a week before Christmas, but we didn't move from each other's side. We weaved around people, never breaking apart. As we rounded a corner onto a quiet side street, Chris pulled me into a pub I hadn't even noticed named the 'The Arthur'.

It was the kind of place you would expect to see in a small country village, not off a main street in Central London.

The walls were covered in wooden panelling, on which hung an odd assortment of horse brasses, yellowing country paintings of shire horses ploughing fields and of racing greyhounds, and some signed photos of football players I didn't recognise. The carpet and upholstery I guess would have been canary yellow when the bar opened but now looked filthy and had turned a sickly colour I can't describe. There was a very small, extremely old TV mounted on the wall in one corner, playing a football game you could barely see through the static. There were two elderly men sitting at a table close to the bar looking over the racing pages, surrounded by empty pint glasses in a companionable silence. Other than them, we were the only customers, which I thought was unusual for a Friday evening.

"Drink?" Chris smiled at me, and, as I looked into his eyes again, the lump where my heart had been hurt in my chest.

"A glass of red wine, please." *Large.*

"Large?" he asked.

"Please," I smiled. Chris ordered the drinks from the dejected looking, balding barman who was miserable and rude, something that would usually irritate me, but Chris flashed his smile and joked with him, seeming completely unaware. He turned to look at me every spare second and he seemed to be drinking me in as much as I was him. He even managed to get a smile out of the miserable barman as he handed Chris his change. Chris' cheerfulness was all encompassing.

He steered me to a booth table in the furthest corner of the room and we sat down opposite each other. Chris laid the rose down on the table between us and leaned back in his seat for a second, briefly stretching with his hands behind his head before he sank back into the cushions, instantly comfortable. I realised I was perched on the edge of my seat and shifted back, trying to look at ease. After a few moments of silence, getting unnerved by how comfortable Chris seemed to be just sitting looking at me, I finally spoke.

"So, how did you know where I would be today?" I asked, trying to seem casual. I didn't really care how he had known, I was just happy he was there! I was so happy to see him again after the way I had dismissed him yesterday.

"You said your interview was today," he said slowly and casually while smiling at me. "I saw that the brochures you were looking at in the bar last night were for the Fairfield Care Home... I presumed it had something to do with your interview.... So, I called them this morning and said that I had an interview with them today and asked if they could reconfirm the address that I needed to go to..." His smile widened into the grin I had seen yesterday; the dimples were back in his cheeks and his eyes shone with mischief. He looked around the room, briefly taking everything in, and then his eyes were straight back on mine. "I've been waiting since eight-thirty this morning, you know! If I'd known you weren't in until the afternoon, I could have had a lie in." He laughed to himself and had a mouthful of his drink. I didn't know what to say.

5

CHRIS

"I even considered following her home!" – *Chris.*

It sounds cliché to say that I knew I was going to be with Becky for the rest of my life the first time I saw her, but call it what you like, love at first sight, whatever. When I first saw her, I just wanted to be near her, look after her, know everything about her. Before that moment, I wouldn't have thought of myself as a 'romantic' kind of guy. I'd never had a serious girlfriend. I mean, I'd had girlfriends; girls like me, and I enjoyed their company, but after the first few hours I'd spent with Becky in the pub, I knew that this was different and that we were really going to be something.

When I first saw her sitting across the bar from me the night before, I literally couldn't take my eyes off her beautiful face. She was exquisite, tall and slim with long, thick, dark brown hair hanging down to her shoulder blades. She was casual in jeans and a jumper but wore a pair of very high heels. She really caught my eye. I knew that she didn't really want to dismiss me the way she did. It seemed as if it was just a habit, and I thought that she may have been nervous, so I let it go, already knowing I would have to find a way to see her again – I even considered following her home, I was that desperate not to miss out on her!

The idea of finding out about the interview came to me as I was leaving the bar with my friends and I'll admit it, I did lie awake for most of the night, worrying that my plan wasn't going to work out. I worried I wouldn't be able to find out where her interview was being held and that it would mean I never got to see her again.

I found the phone number online for the care home that Becky had been looking at in the brochures in the bar as soon as I got home. Then I had tossed and turned all night, waiting until it was morning and a time that I could finally ring them.

When morning arrived at last, I used a little bit of charm whilst talking to the female secretary who answered, and she finally gave me the details I wanted. She confirmed that the Fairfield Care Home were interviewing for new staff and that interviews were being held today at a recruitment agency near Leicester Square.

I thanked God that it was the school holidays. I had just started my first year of teaching as a PE teacher at a local primary school. It was my dream job, and I particularly loved all the school holidays, but I had never appreciated having a day off as much as I did that day! I cancelled the plans I had with my friends and headed into town to find the agency.

*

When I finally saw Becky walking down the pavement towards me, the whole day of waiting was worth it. I felt like I had been holding my breath for twenty-four hours and could now finally breathe! The hour or so I waited outside while she was in the building having her interview was the worst. It made it so much harder knowing that she was so close.

When I saw her walk out of the building when it was over, our eyes locked and I had to stop myself from embracing her, touching her, kissing her. It was as if there was an irresistible force at work that I was completely powerless to resist. I led her to a pub up the road, somewhere quiet off the main street so I could finally talk to her properly.

It was amazing. We sat for hours talking and staring at each other, I couldn't get enough of her. I wanted to listen to her talk all night long. Her voice was low, musical, and elegant. She was very passionate about getting the job at the care home that she had just interviewed for, telling me she had always wanted to work with people with disabilities.

She told me about her life. Her mum, who had raised her on her own, had suffered from depression and died when Becky was sixteen. Becky had cared for her for years before she'd died, and suddenly found herself with no-one around her and nowhere to go. She had gotten two jobs and rented her own place from the age of sixteen! I couldn't believe it. I didn't know how someone could cope with all the things that she had been through, especially at that age. I hadn't even had a paper round when I was sixteen! I listened to her tell her story while she looked down at her wine glass. She occasionally glanced up at me, defiantly, as if daring me to feel sorry for her (which I did, but I didn't want to let it show). My heart ached for her. I inched closer to her while she talked and being so close to her filled me with such an intense longing, I didn't know it was physically possible to want another human being as much as I wanted her! In return, I told her a little bit about my life, almost feeling guilty that I had had it so easy.

"I live with my mum," I said. "My dad died when I was very young, I don't remember him at all. But my mum has always been amazing, and we're very close. I've always had everything I could ever want. I never really went without anything. I think she's worked hard to make me feel as if I wasn't missing out from not having a dad. Even from a young age I had the 'cool Mum'! Everyone always wanted to hang out at my house!" I paused. "I can't wait for you to meet her," I added. Becky was surprised. I could see the unease on her face, but also, I think, delight.

6

"Now you're my responsibility." – Chris.

Becky and Chris were still sitting in 'The Arthur' when the two men who had been hunched over the racing pages finished up the last of their pints, folded up their newspapers, and left. The football match that was playing on the TV reached half time, then full time. They didn't even notice when the rain finally started outside, although it fell incessantly against the roof and windows.

When the barman eventually approached them and told them it was time to leave, they realised with a jolt that it was nearing eleven p.m. They had sat and talked for nearly seven hours.

Becky had not been even remotely aware of the time and had no idea how long they had been sat there. She felt desolate at the thought of this being it and having to leave him already. Chris grinned at the barman and thanked him. He stood up and finished the last mouthful of his drink before reaching his hand out to Becky, pulling her to her feet.

"Dinner time!" he said. "You like Chinese?" Becky smiled, grateful that she didn't have to leave him just yet, and she followed him to the door. As Chris led her outside, he noticed that she was clutching the rose he had given her tightly in her hand. He wondered how she managed to grip so tightly and still avoid the thorns.

*

Becky followed Chris as he ducked out into the pouring rain and ran in the direction of the tube station. She ran after him, her jacket held over her head, attempting to keep up with him through the downpour. She was no match for his speed, though, and he was already waiting for her when she got there, sheltered in the doorway, smirking. Becky laughed and flicked her soaking wet hair over her shoulder as she playfully took a swing at him with her handbag for leaving her out in the rain.

Before she knew what was happening, Chris caught her wrist and pulled her in close to him, pressing himself up against her soaking-wet body, kissing her firmly on the mouth. It was the most passionate moment of Becky's life. The surge of adrenalin she felt when Chris was pulling her towards him exploded inside her as their bodies touched. One of his hands pressed into the small of her back and the other reached out in front of him in the direction he was pushing her until they were kissing up against the graffiti covered wall of Leicester Square tube station. Chris moaned slightly as he kissed her, and Becky's body seemed to respond to the sound. She had never wanted anyone as much as she wanted him, and she knew that she never would again. He pulled away from her and looked deep into her warm brown eyes. He leant his nose against hers and sighed, a sound of contentment. Becky knew she was in love.

*

Chris took Becky to China Town, which was vibrant and full of people now that the rain had finally subsided. Although Becky had lived in London all her life, she had never been to China Town before. Chris was shocked when she told him and he watched as she wandered around, amazed by the sights and smells, the scent of vegetables and spices on the air, the Chinese style street furniture and the unique pagoda style telephone boxes that lined the street.

Chris took Becky to a small restaurant that she would never have known was there, up a flight of stairs above a small massage shop. It was packed full of people, brightly lit, and barely furnished, but Chris insisted it offered the best Chinese food outside of China and, overhearing their conversation, so did the waiter that came to take their order!

Becky and Chris were both starving, as neither had eaten all day. Becky out of nerves for her interview, and Chris, from fear of missing Becky, had not moved from his position outside of the agency since first thing that morning. They devoured four courses and drank several bottles of wine. Both of them were starting to feel the effect of the alcohol.

As the night wore on, they talked even more. There was never an awkward moment. Becky opened-up and elaborated on her life before her mum had died. It had always been a struggle after her dad had left, she told Chris, and her mum had never gotten over him leaving. She had pined for him for the rest of her life. Once the depression hit, she had found most daily tasks difficult, sometimes not getting out of bed for days at a time.

Becky had grown up very quickly, getting herself ready for school, getting there and back every day by herself, making all her own meals, doing her homework, and keeping the house clean as best she could. She became very independent, but also very isolated.

"I didn't really have any friends," she confided. "At first it was because I didn't want anybody to come to the house. I didn't want anyone to see what Mum was like, and even if I got invited to go to somebody else's house I never accepted the invitation because I always wanted to get back home as soon as I could to see how Mum was that day. My whole life revolved around seeing what mood she would be in, or even if she was out of bed or not. I felt like she was my responsibility." Becky looked up at Chris with a watery smile.

"Now you're my responsibility," he said.

*

A few hours later they asked for the bill, paid, and left.

It was the early hours of the morning, and the tubes were no longer running. Chris led Becky down the now quiet street, and they found a cab parked around the corner relatively quickly. They climbed into the back seat, rubbing their hands together trying to get rid of the cold, as Chris leaned forward to give the driver the address.

"Are we staying at mine?" he asked, looking at Becky over his shoulder. The question came naturally, as if they had this conversation every night on their way home. Becky didn't feel uncomfortable. She didn't know at which point during the night she had realised she wouldn't be leaving him, but she knew they were not ready to be apart yet.

"No, mine," she said, a shy hint to her voice. She gave the driver her address and settled back on the seat next to Chris. He pulled her close to him, settling his arm around her, kissing the top of her head. The heaters started to warm them up once the car was moving, and they watched the damp city pass by through the window, the Friday night masses walking home, leaving bars, queuing for cabs, and piling into fast food places. But neither of them were really taking it in, they were both sat in awe of just being near each other.

*

They got out of the cab onto a long, quiet street lit up by streetlamps and lined with huge white buildings. Chris followed Becky to a set of steps leading down to the front door of a basement apartment. Becky took the keys from her bag, and as she was putting the key in the lock she turned to him, as if to say something, but stopped before she did, changing her mind. She opened the door, and they walked inside.

She flicked on the light and Chris looked around at the inside of Becky's flat. The door opened into a small living room that opened-up to a small kitchen on the right-hand side, separated by a breakfast bar. Chris could see a small bedroom off to the right just past the kitchen. The whole place was small but cosy and filled with missmatched furniture. Becky hesitated and looked up at Chris as if she was about to justify her home to him, but before she could say anything Chris strode forward into the living room, looked around, and turned to Becky, smiling.

"It's brilliant," he said. "I love it!"

Becky smiled, finally relaxing and walked behind him, fingering some furniture as she walked past.

"I love it, too," she said. "I've been here ever since I left home. It was a real struggle paying the rent when I first got here, and the place was pretty empty because I couldn't afford any furniture. I used to just have a mattress on the floor in there," she smiled and nodded towards the bedroom, "and a chair and TV in here. Over time I've managed to collect more furniture and make it more of a home. Most of the stuff is from charity shops and markets." Chris sat down on the sofa at the back of the room in amongst an array of coloured cushions.

Becky went into her bedroom to get out of her interview clothes. She pulled on some tracksuit bottoms and an oversized woollen jumper, and piled her hair on top of her head in a messy bun. Chris thought she looked stunning when she walked back into the room.

She went into the kitchen and picked up a bottle of red wine with two assorted wine glasses and put them on the coffee table in front of Chris before going back to the kitchen to put her rose into a glass with some water. She brought it into the living room and placed it next to the wine on the table, switched on the TV, and sat next to Chris on the sofa. The TV went unwatched.

7

BECKY

"Once again his lips found mine." – Becky.

Having Chris in my flat just felt right. As soon as he walked in and plonked himself down on my sofa, it was as if he belonged there. I actually wondered how I hadn't noticed before that there had always been something missing. How it had been so empty. As we got out of the cab and walked towards my front door, I had another momentary flash of nervousness. The same feeling I'd had as I'd walked down the stairs earlier after my interview when I knew that Chris was waiting for me, but the moment passed and once we were inside it was completely forgotten.

I got changed, thankful to be out of my smart clothes and into something comfy. I carried some wine into the living room and sat down on the sofa next to him. We talked even more, still unable to take our eyes off each other, and the memory of our kiss in the tube station made my heartbeat quicken every time I thought about it.

We laughed a lot. I can't remember ever laughing as much in my entire life as I did with Chris that night. He just had this contagious way about him. He was always so happy, and it made me feel happy.

The sun was starting to come up when Chris finally leant towards me and kissed me again. Any tiredness I had been feeling completely vanished. My body was suddenly wide awake and alert as Chris' lips found mine, and before I even had a chance to kiss him back he had scooped me up and was carrying me towards the bedroom. He laid me down in the dark bedroom and kissed me with such an intensity I didn't know was possible. My body arched into him and before either of us knew it, we were finally making love.

We eventually fell asleep when the sun was up hours later, exhausted, entwined in each other, sleeping nose to nose.

*

When I woke up in the morning, Chris was already awake and was lying there watching me. When our eyes met, he closed his eyes and pretended to be asleep, his huge smile giving him away.

"Hey!" I said. "Don't watch me sleep!"

"Why? You're so beautiful, I can't help it!" he said, his face plastered with a grin as he jumped out of bed, giving me the chance to look at his gorgeous body in the daylight that streamed in through my bedroom windows. *He* was beautiful.

"Where are you going?" I asked, missing him the second he left my side.

"Breakfast," he replied, smiling. He started picking his clothes up off the floor and I watched, mesmerised by him as he pulled his jeans on. When he was dressed, he leant in and kissed me on the forehead.

"I'll be back in a minute," he mumbled against my skin. I heard him walk across the living room, scoop up my keys from the table, and shut the front door behind him. I dragged myself out of bed and walked to the kitchen. I switched on the kettle and headed back into my bedroom and through to my little en-suite bathroom. I jumped in the shower, standing under the boiling hot water, unable to stop smiling. I was still there a while later when I heard the front door open. I was about to shut the water off when Chris poked his head around the bathroom door.

"What are you doing!?" he cried, and he started pulling off his clothes in an exaggerated fashion. "No more secret showers!" He jumped into the cubicle with me and once again his lips found mine instantly.

He kissed me under the water, running his hands over my soaked body, pressing me up against the tiles.

Both distracted from the thought of breakfast, we stayed in the shower until the water ran cold.

It was early afternoon by the time Chris and I made it back out of the bedroom again. I sat on a stool by the breakfast bar and leant my head in my hands, watching him move around the kitchen in just his jeans, his body still damp from the shower and his wet hair falling into his eyes. He flicked the kettle back on and started opening and closing the cupboards, looking for things. I dragged my eyes away from him and started to pull items out of the plastic bags that he had dumped on the side before joining me in the shower. There was a beautiful smelling, no longer warm, loaf of tiger bread, a packet of bacon, a box of eggs, and two containers of juice – one apple and one orange. Chris slid over to me, grinning, and started taking the items out of my hands as I took them out of the bag, moving around the kitchen gracefully, getting things ready, nodding his head slightly and humming under his breath. I could have sat and watched him for hours and hours and never get bored.

*

We didn't leave the house that day. After an amazing breakfast of bacon and egg sandwiches that Chris made for us, we moved to the sofa, wrapped up in my big brown woollen blanket, and talked and talked even more. I found it impossible that we hadn't run out of things to talk about yet and impossible that we ever would. Chris never took his hands off me, he was constantly holding me, stroking me, touching me. I have never, ever seen a person laugh so much before and I was amazed that the smile never left his face. I had never felt so light and carefree in my entire life.

In the evening we ordered food to be delivered and drank the last of my wine as rain fell outside, listening to it lashing against the windows. I had never felt more content.

*

Later that night, Chris' mobile phone started to ring. The shrill noise surprised us both and he shuffled around on the sofa, trying to free the phone from his jeans pocket while holding my feet on his lap at the same time. I was shocked, it was the first time in well over twenty-four hours that I had thought of anything but him and it seemed weird that someone outside of this flat was trying to get hold of him. He looked at the screen briefly before lazily holding the phone to his ear, his head cocked to the side. He didn't take his eyes off my face and continued smiling at me and massaging my feet with his free hand.

"Hello?" he said, and I could hear a high-pitched voice on the other end of the phone, although I couldn't make out the words. "I know, I know, sorry Mum… I know… No, I wasn't with him… I know… I'll text him. I know… I'm sorry… look, Mum!" He shifted in his seat and raised his eyebrows at me. "I met a girl on Thursday night, fell instantly in love with her, spent the whole day yesterday searching London for her, found her, and ended up staying at hers last night!" Silence on the other end of the phone. Chris winked at me and squeezed my foot, making my heart hurt with love for him. The voice on the other end started again and his eyes shot up and met mine. He grinned. "Erm… tomorrow?" he said and looked at me sheepishly, still smiling. I instantly knew what they were talking about and felt a stab of panic. "Yes, yes, okay… will do. Okay. Lunchtime. Yes, Mum! Okay, see you then, yes, yes, I'll text him! Okay! Bye."

8

CHRIS

"You are cordially invited..." – Chris.

I threw my phone onto the coffee table and looked over at Becky. She was chewing her lip and looking at me nervously. I grinned at her.

"You are cordially invited to Sunday lunch at the McNulty household tomorrow afternoon," I said, looking at her questioningly. She attempted a smile, but I could see she was terrified. "My mum is very excited! I've never brought a girl home before. She won't be able to sleep tonight, she'll be so worried about impressing you!"

At that moment, my phone beeped. I leant over to pick it back up and sure enough it was a text message from my mum asking if Becky was a vegetarian, then another one asking if there was anything that she didn't eat, then another asking what her favourite dessert was. I showed Becky the messages and she seemed to relax a bit. She smiled up at me. I leant over and kissed her beautiful, apprehensive face.

*

The next afternoon I watched Becky closely as we sat in the back of a taxi on the way to my house. I still couldn't believe how beautiful she was. She looked stunning in a baby blue polka dot dress with flat ankle boots and a big oversized woollen cardigan. Her gorgeous long hair had dried in a natural wave around her face, emphasising her huge brown eyes. She was, as usual, chewing her lip and looking nervously out of the window. As if she could sense me staring at her, she turned and caught my eye, attempting to smile. I leant forward and pulled her into me, finally making a smile spread across her face. I kissed the top of her head and breathed in the natural sweet smell that radiated from her and drove me wild.

I well was aware of how nervous Becky was, and I wasn't surprised. As I'd listened to the story of her life growing up, and even when I realised what her life was like now, I began to understand how secluded she'd been. She put it down to working all the time and admitted that she didn't really have any friends, as well as having no family to speak of. I knew that being thrown into the limelight like this and meeting new people was really difficult for her. For some reason, this made me love her even more and I felt a genuine need to look after her.

The taxi finally pulled up against the pavement outside my mum's red brick, three storey townhouse and we both got out. I paid the taxi driver through his window and noticed him watch Becky as she walked around to my side of the car. She was oblivious to him watching her, though, and she didn't take her eyes off me for a second. She looked like a lost animal that could take flight at any moment as she looked up at me with her dark brown eyes. I held my hand out to her and she clasped onto it, causing another surge of love to shoot through me, almost taking my breath away.

I could hear the usual noise and hustle and bustle coming from inside my house as we approached the front door. Pots and pans were clattering and banging in the kitchen, drowned out slightly by the sound of the blaring TV, and all this on top of the continuous barks of my two dogs coming incessantly from the back garden. I slipped my key into the door and squeezed Becky's hand as it opened.

Before it had even reached half-way, my mum appeared, all five feet of her. Her long, bristling, greying hair was pulled back into a bun at the back of her head and frizzy strands escaped everywhere. As usual, she had an apron tied around her waist and she wore a moth-eaten old pair of slippers on her feet. I picked a piece of grated cheese out of her hair and stooped down to give her a kiss, but she pushed me out of the way and held her hands out to Becky.

"Oh, my dear!" she cried, looking up at me and then back to Becky. "Aren't you gorgeous!" She embraced a mortified Becky in a huge bear hug, and then stepped back to look at her again. She clasped her hand and led her towards the kitchen door, swiping at me as she went past, mumbling something about terrible sons who stayed out for days on end without informing their mothers.

*

My mum's kitchen is her pride and joy, and considering we live in a tall townhouse in London, it is more like a kitchen that you would find in a country farmhouse. It takes up most of the ground floor and is long, thin, and warmly decorated. There are worktops along the left-hand-side with a huge, old-fashioned AGA almost halfway down, which currently had pots and pans bubbling away on top of it. Below, the oven seemed full to bursting with trays of food. The smells and the heat hit us as soon as we walked in.

Mum's friend Tom was sitting reading the newspaper at the big heavy wooden table to the right-hand-side of the kitchen. He also looked as if he would be more suited in a country farmhouse, wearing scruffy jeans, a filthy white shirt and a tweed flat cap. His iron-grey hair and beard were both unruly around his extremely tanned face. How he managed to have a tan in the middle of an English winter I'd never worked out. He looked up and nodded at me briefly before burying his head back in the paper again.

I strode through the kitchen and pulled open the patio doors, allowing my two dogs to come flying into the kitchen.

"*Chris!*" my mum shrieked at me as Toby, my chocolate brown Labrador, and Scoobie, my Jack Russell Terrier, flew past her legs and into the kitchen, jumping up at me, barking and whining.

"*Chris! Get those dogs back out in the garden, NOW, or I swear to God I will kill you, Becky or no Becky!*"

The noise in the kitchen had reached an almost deafening pitch now, with an old re-run of *Cash in the Attic* blaring at an unnecessarily loud level from the small TV that sat on the kitchen side, the dogs barking, and now the sound of my mum shouting and shooing Toby towards the patio doors. She grabbed Scoobie by the collar before he could dash through to the rest of the house and bent down to pick him up. I grabbed him off her, burying my face in his coat as I walked out to the garden with Toby leaping up at me, desperately wanting to be able to get up into my arms, too.

As I stepped into the garden, I put Scoobie back down on the floor and turned to look back into the kitchen through the patio doors that my mum had slammed shut behind me. Becky was still standing at the entrance of the kitchen, shifting from one foot to the other looking petrified!

9

BECKY

"You must be very special!" – Sue.

The patio door slammed shut behind Chris and I watched him squat down on the floor as the dogs scrambled to climb all over him. Chris' mum turned towards me, wiping her hands on her apron with a look of disgust.

"That boy, bloody dogs… always barking… he comes in here, opens the door while I'm trying to cook, running around the kitchen… such a mess," she was mumbling. She shot a look towards the man at the kitchen table. "Doesn't he, Tom?" she said. I glanced from her to him.

"Hmmm," he agreed without looking up from his paper. She nodded curtly as if ending the conversation.

"Right, dear!" she exclaimed, as if just realising I was there. She bustled over and gave me another huge hug, taking me by surprise once again, before leading me to the kitchen table.

"Sit down!" She beamed at me, pulling out a chair from underneath the table and lifting a stack of magazines off it while gesturing for me to sit. She turned around as if looking for somewhere to put the pile of magazines, but gave up and dumped them on the table, pushing them to the side. "I'm Sue, and it is so lovely to have you here!" she said as she sat down in the chair opposite me, next to Tom. I sat nervously in front of her, embarrassed at the attention, not knowing where to put my hands. I caught a glimpse of Chris out in the garden throwing a ball for the dogs whose tails were wagging back and forth in excitement, causing their whole bodies to vibrate.

"Tom!" She looked sharply at the man to her left. He

glanced up from his paper briefly and nodded at me. I wasn't sure if I heard a faint, "'Ello," under his breath.

"So, my dear!" Sue continued, still beaming at me. "This is all very unexpected! Chris has never brought a girl home before!" She leapt up from her chair suddenly as a pot on top of the stove boiled over, causing the flame underneath to hiss and spit. "Where did you meet?" she asked over her shoulder while bustling around the oven. I was thrown by the question and suddenly felt very embarrassed that I had met her son in a bar three nights ago and he had slept in my bed for the previous two. I could feel my face flush and didn't quite know how to respond. I saw out of the corner of my eye that Tom had lowered his paper slightly and was looking at me over the top of it.

"Well... er... I was in a bar a few nights ago and Chris came over and introduced himself," I started, flushing even more as I remembered how Chris had walked over to me in the bar and declared that he was going to marry me.

"I was quite busy, I had a job interview the next day and I was doing some last minute research for it. I told him that I was busy, and he said goodbye and left... but then the next day he was waiting for me outside the agency where I had my interview. He'd figured out where I was going to be and was there waiting for me when I turned up..." I trailed off and paused, looking up at Sue, embarrassed.

"We've been together ever since, really." Sue raised her eyebrows and a look passed between her and Tom.

"Well!" she said. "I was worried that I was never going to see the day, lovey. You must be very special! I thought that he was going to be single for the rest of his life. Like I say, he's never brought a girl home before." Sue trailed off and I looked up and noticed that Tom was still looking at me over his paper, quickly glancing back down at it when I caught his eye.

Sue was still busy lifting lids off the different pots and pans on the stove, stirring them and mumbling to herself as she turned the heat up or down as well as glancing through the glass of the oven door, checking the food inside. When she was satisfied, she came back over and settled into the chair opposite me again. I thought I saw her briefly touch Tom's knee as she sat down, but I couldn't be sure. She pulled her chair right under the table and crossed her arms in front of her, leaning towards me, smiling.

"So, tell me about yourself," she said, and as I looked into her kind face I started to talk and, for once, I actually found it quite easy.

*

A little while later, Sue and I were still deep in conversation when there was a loud banging at the front door, making me jump. It sounded as if the door was going to come off its hinges. Sue got up to answer it, and I could hear a male voice booming in from the hall. A young guy, around the same age as Chris, appeared in the kitchen doorway followed closely by Sue. He was tall, with extremely dark wavy hair that had grown long enough to curl at the ends around his face. It looked as if it had taken him hours to perfect the look, but when he dragged his hands through it, it fell exactly back into exactly the same place. He was wearing a huge, easy smile that reminded me of Chris' as he talked to Sue, but he point-blank refused to look in my direction. He was gorgeous – exactly the kind of man I would have found attractive before, the typical 'tall, dark, and handsome' type.

He was very loud and overbearing, and seemed to take over the kitchen the second he walked in. Sue fussed around him as he strode past us. He greeted Tom loudly, not acknowledging me, before reaching the end of the kitchen and clumsily yanking the patio door open to step outside.

"Alright then, mate?" he yelled to Chris as he crashed the patio door closed behind him.

"That boy is like having a herd of elephants in the house," Sue scolded to no-one in particular, but I could see that she had a twinkle in her eye as she said it.

"Who was that?" I asked.

"That's Chris' best friend Simon," Sue replied, although I had already known the answer. Chris had told me all about Simon and his other friends over the last couple of days. Chris and Simon had grown up together and had been best friends since primary school. They had stayed friends all through secondary school and college and they even went to the same university together, living together for the entire time they were there. From the way Chris talked about Simon, I got the impression that they were more like brothers than friends. They were part of a large social group, but it was the two of them that seemed to have a real bond.

I could hear the dogs going mad outside again now that Simon had joined them, and they barked wildly. I could hear Simon's booming voice, shouting and winding the dogs up even more between bouts of laughter from both him and Chris. I realised that although Chris had only been outside for about fifteen minutes, I really missed him. Stranger than that, I felt completely comfortable with his mum and this silent man as I sat at their kitchen table.

*

Sue got up again while we were talking and started to serve dinner. I got up to give her a hand and between us we moved around the kitchen, perfectly in unison with each other, getting out plates and serving dishes and setting up the table. The boys came crashing back into the kitchen just as Sue was pouring gravy over the huge plates of food. My heart skipped a beat as Chris walked in. He was behind Simon who bounded in like an oversized puppy, looking like a model with his perfect features and dark hair. But I only had eyes for Chris. He seemed so graceful behind Simon, his dirty blond hair falling over his blue eyes. He pulled the patio door shut, bending down at the last second to scratch Scoobie on the head through the gap before closing it. I wanted those hands on me.

He turned and looked at me, his eyes boring into mine, and my insides clenched up. I had to breathe deeply to steady myself. As I watched him walk towards me it was as if it was just the two of us in the room, and he seemed to be moving in slow motion. When he was finally next to me, he put his arms around my waist and buried his head into my hair, nuzzling my shoulder.

"I missed you," he mumbled, and I sighed, feeling like I could breathe again. I pulled back and looked up into his eyes.

"I missed you, too," I whispered, and smiled at him.

"Sit!" Sue ordered, breaking the spell, dragging chairs across the kitchen floor, causing even more noise. Simon had sat himself down next to Tom who had, begrudgingly, put his paper down after he was ordered to by Sue. He looked naked and exposed without it.

As Chris and I sat down next to each other, I still couldn't take my eyes off him. I felt as if we had been apart for a week. He turned to look at me as he pulled his chair in under the table, his usual smile in place, and as we caught each other's eye I knew beyond a shadow of a doubt that this was the person I would spend the rest of my life with, and that these people were going to be my family.

10

CHRIS

"It made me realise how one small moment really can change your life. Mine was never going to be the same again." – Chris.

I had just started to get the dogs settled and they were finally starting to look worn out when I heard Simon enter the kitchen in his usual clamorous way. Before I knew it, the patio doors were being dragged open and Simon had yelled a greeting at me before appearing next to me in the garden. The dogs took this as a cue to start going wild again. Simon, in his usual boisterous fashion, wound them up while playing with them, causing them to start barking and jumping around all over again.

"I'm good," I said, smiling, responding to his greeting, and we both grinned at each other. I bent down to stroke Toby's head as it went quiet.

"Well, she's hot," Simon said begrudgingly, which caused me to laugh out loud. The dogs stood at our feet, looking up at us expectantly, wagging their tails slowly, desperate for one of us to throw their ball.

I had finally gotten around to texting Simon last night to apologise for dropping off the face of the earth for the last few days. I told him that I had met a girl who he would get to meet when he came for dinner today. I didn't know where to begin or how to even start explaining the situation or how I felt about Becky to him. I didn't know how to tell him that I knew my life had changed forever and that from now on it would always centre around the girl who was now sitting in my kitchen. I didn't know how I could begin to tell him that I was in love after such a short amount of time and that I knew for certain I would spend the rest of my life with her.

We kicked the dogs' ball back and forth between us for a while, causing them to run to each of us in turn as I tried to put the last few days into words. He looked sceptical and uninterested, obviously thinking it was a passing fad.

"I love her," I said, smiling, and I looked over at him, waiting for a reaction. I saw him falter for a second and pause before he kicked the ball back to me, not replying. We carried on for a few minutes in silence before Simon changed the subject.

*

I could see my mum and Becky starting to serve dinner through the patio doors. Watching them together and seeing Becky looking so relaxed made me smile. I'd known that my mum was going to adore Becky and absolutely love having her around, relishing having another female in the house after the usual house full of boys, but I hadn't thought that they would get so comfortable so quickly.

Simon and I headed inside and, as usual, he bounded off in front of me through the doors. He made his way straight over to the table, towards a very weary looking Tom, who he plonked himself down next to, engaging him instantly in a very one-way conversation, oblivious to the fact that Tom looked like he was being tortured.

I looked up and caught Becky's eye. She was hovering between the kitchen side and the table, standing completely still, watching me fixedly. Once again, she reminded me of an animal that stood ready to take flight at one wrong movement. As usual our eyes locked and I felt a tug at my heart. I walked over to her, pulling her close, breathing her in and savouring being so close to her.

"I missed you," I said, and meant it.

"I missed you, too," she replied. We looked at each other and smiled before my mum ordered us to sit down. We sat down next to each other on one side of the table with my mum and Tom opposite us. Simon was perched on the end to my left. Without realising it, Becky and I both pulled our chairs closer together, and I reached out and rested my hand on her leg. She laid her hand over the top of mine and squeezed.

*

Dinner was a complete success, and my mum's food was perfect, as usual. We devoured the pork and stuffing roast dinner, as well as the piles of vegetables that were placed around the table in separate dishes. We ate and talked, and the wine flowed between Becky, Mum, Simon, and me. Tom had one beer and stayed silent, observing as usual.

I couldn't believe how animated Becky became when she was talking to my mum, she even seemed more comfortable with her than she did when it was just the two of us! Mum was listening intently as Becky told her, filled with passion, all about the job she had just interviewed for and how excited she was at the prospect of becoming a carer. She had always been worried that without any qualifications she would not be able to get into the kind of role that she wanted, and because she'd had to start working straight from school to enable herself to afford somewhere to live she'd not had time for any further education or qualifications.

Mum sat and listened to her talk and she handled listening to Becky's story perfectly. I knew that Becky did not receive sympathy very well, hating to think that people pitied her, and although I could tell my mum felt sorry for her and was feeling her usual need to mother her, she listened with empathy, nodding along and saying all of the right things, which actually seemed to encourage Becky to open up even more.

Simon and I had plenty of time to catch up while they were talking, and he told me about his weekend with our two friends Charlie and Frankie. They were twin brothers who we had known since we first started primary school. Although they were twins, they were polar opposites: Charlie was very competitive, feisty and almost a bit aggressive, whereas Frankie was very chilled and laid back – he never took anything seriously. But when they were together, they were like a double act that bounced off one another and it was difficult not to love them.

While Simon and I were talking, I started to sense that he was aware of the interaction between Becky and my mum, and I got the impression that he didn't like it. No-one else would have noticed the subtle differences in him, but I could tell that they were there. I almost felt as if he had had taken a disliking towards Becky. I tried to put it to the back of my mind and concentrated on listening to the story of their drunken night out on Saturday, my mind wandering while he was talking. It struck me as he spoke, how strange life was. If I hadn't gone to the bar for a drink with them on Thursday and seen Becky for the first time, I too would have been out with them on Saturday night as usual, and this Sunday dinner would just be the same as always, the three or four of us, discussing the same old things. It made me realise how one small moment really can change your life. Mine was never going to be the same again.

*

A few hours later after dinner and pudding had been eaten (apple and blackberry crumble with custard – Becky's favourite!), wine had been drunk, and everything had been cleared away, we all sat around the table with the TV now playing quietly in the background. Everything was winding down, it was getting late, and it was almost pitch-black outside. The dogs were sitting staring at me through the patio doors, longing to come into the warm kitchen. Tom caught me looking at them.

"I'll walk them for you tonight," he said in his gruff voice, "so you can head back with Becky."

We all looked up at him in surprise, as we do almost every time Tom speaks. For Becky it was probably the first time she'd heard his voice. I was surprised, I felt as if he'd read my mind. I had just been thinking that I would really prefer for me and Becky to go back to hers tonight instead of staying here; I really didn't want to throw her into the deep and make her feel uncomfortable by staying the night after such a lovely afternoon.

My mum looked slightly put out that Tom had suggested that we may not stay – I knew she would love it if we did, but although I didn't want to hurt her feelings, I took up Tom's offer, knowing Becky would be much more relaxed if we went back to hers. I thanked him and smiled, and he nodded briefly back at me.

I had never really understood the relationship between my mum and Tom. He had just appeared one day like a stray dog. I had come home from school when I was about eleven years old and walked in to find him in the kitchen, sitting in the exact same spot at the table as he was now. My mum had introduced him to me, explaining that he had just moved into a house a few doors down from ours. He had nodded at me, and I had carried on to the garden, not taking much notice of the silent man, and since then things had never changed. He'd spent more and more time at our house until he was almost a permanent fixture. As far as I could tell, he never stayed the night, but other than that he was here all the time. He shared Christmases and birthdays with us, and I couldn't work out if he was more like a husband or a brother to my mum. They didn't seem to have any relationship past companionship as far as I could tell.

It made me sad for my mum that she had never met anyone else after my father had passed away, and I did worry that having Tom there as a companion stopped her from looking for someone, but their relationship seemed to work for both of them, and, on the other hand, I was glad that she always had someone around.

*

A little while later, Tom had gone to take the dogs out for their walk and Becky, Simon, and I were standing in the hallway saying goodbye to my mum. She looked desolate that we were all leaving. She gave me and Simon a huge hug each before embracing Becky, holding on to her as if she would never see her again. As they said their goodbyes, Simon and I walked out of the front door and down the icy steps to the pavement. The street was completely empty of people, there were only the cars that lined the street, crammed together, parked bumper to bumper, already covered with a layer of frost. I had ordered another taxi to take me and Becky back to her flat. I'd had too much to drink to be able to drive, and Becky's wasn't that far from here.

Simon and I stood on the dark street, hunched against the cold with our hands in our pockets, not saying a word. Condensation made clouds appear out of our mouths that lit up like ghosts under the streetlights. Simon only lived a few minutes' walk away from here and it was unusual for him to hang around like this once the goodbyes had been said, and I had a feeling that he wanted to say something to me. He was hovering in a most un-Simon like way.

"You love her," he said finally, matter-of-factly. I wasn't sure if it was a statement or a question, and I didn't reply straight away, the tone of his voice caught me off guard. He sounded so bleak. We looked at each other in the dark and I thought I saw him shake his head slightly. He looked as if someone had died. He mumbled, "Goodbye," and turned to walk up the road, leaving me staring after him, confused.

Becky suddenly appeared at my side and grasped my arm, looking up at me brightly, shivering in her dress and cardigan. I forgot about Simon's weird behaviour and pulled her in close to me, wrapping my arms around her to warm her up as I gave her a kiss on the top of her head. She moved her face towards me to kiss me back and the world shrank around us until it could have been just the two of us left on earth. The taxi pulled up next to us, its headlights throwing long black shadows over the road, and we had to drag ourselves apart to jump into the back seat, rubbing our hands together, relishing the warmth. We sat as close to each other as possible, content in each other's company, travelling along in silence.

11

"Have you ever been in one of those dreams... when you've been in such a deep sleep... you wake up and don't even know what day it is?"– Chris.

The next couple of weeks were bliss for Becky and Chris. At 9:30a.m. the following morning after they'd had Sunday dinner with Sue, Becky received the call she had been waiting for: the care home telling her that she was being offered the job. They had loved her in the interview and wanted her to start straight after the New Year on the second of January, a day before Chris' new term started at school. It meant that both of them had two weeks free before they had to be at work.

Becky was elated when she put the phone down. She had been in bed when her phone had started ringing, with Chris pressed up against her back, one arm thrown protectively over her, his face buried in her neck, so close she could feel his breath on her skin. She had slipped out from under his arm to grab the phone from the bedside table, her heart in her mouth when she recognised the number.

She ran lightly to the kitchen, closing the bedroom door quietly behind her. Relief and happiness flooded through her as they told her the news, and after thanking them profusely Becky put the phone down, feeling close to tears with happiness.

Chris opened the bedroom door, looking like a little boy standing in his boxers with his hair flopping into his eyes, squinting against the light, wondering what she was doing up.

"I got the job!" Becky cried, her voice catching with emotion. Chris' face lit up and he held out his arms to her. Becky danced into them and he gave her a huge bear hug, lifting her off her feet and spinning her around.

"I knew you would!" he said, and she was laughing, nearly crying, overwhelmed with emotion and a happiness she had never ever felt before. She couldn't believe how much her life had changed in a matter of days. She had this man in her home who she loved with all her heart, a future to look forward to sharing with another person, – something she had never thought would happen to her – and now a new job that she had been dreaming of for years. She felt ecstatic, lucky, and completely overwhelmed. A sob escaped her lips and Chris dropped her to the floor, looking into her eyes.

"What's wrong?" he asked, his eyes flicking around her face. Becky looked up at him.

"I'm just so happy!" she said, and stood on her tiptoes to kiss him, putting her arms around his neck. He lifted her and carried her back towards the bed.

"Let's celebrate," he whispered between kisses, pressing his mouth hungrily to hers. She moaned in response and, in that moment, she forgot everything else in the world but him.

*

A while later, Becky and Chris were lying nose to nose in bed, wrapped up in the bed sheets, smiling and talking.

"I've got an idea," Chris said conspiratorially, looking around the room exaggeratedly as if he was checking that no-one could overhear them, as if he were about to suggest something sordid. He lowered his voice and leant in to whisper in Becky's ear.

"Let's venture outside today!" he said, grinning. "I'm going to take you out to celebrate your new job."

Becky was full of excitement. Apart from the first night after her interview when they had gone into China Town, and then had dinner at Sue's, they hadn't actually left the flat. They were like excited children as they showered and brushed their teeth together, getting ready to go out. Chris sat on the end of the bed, damp from his shower, wearing only a towel, and watched as Becky sat on the floor in front of the mirror, putting her make-up on and brushing her hair. An arrow of pure love hit him as he watched her concentrating face, and he leapt onto the floor and crawled up behind her, running his hands over her, stroking her long hair over one shoulder and kissing her neck, causing her to squeal.

"Get off! I thought you wanted to go out!" she cried, knowing where his kisses would lead, as she tried to wriggle away from him.

*

Eventually they were both ready and left the flat, wrapped up against the cold. Chris thought Becky looked as pretty as a picture wrapped up in jeans, boots, and a fur-lined parker jacket with mittens threaded through her sleeves like a small child. They walked down the street towards the tube station, hand-in-hand. It was a gorgeous, crisp winter's day, the sun was shining and everything looked crystal clear. Becky followed Chris, not knowing or caring where they were going.

They entered the underground and after a while got off the tube at Leicester Square tube station. Becky blushed as they walked out of the entrance and past the spot where they had shared their first kiss only a few days ago. It seemed like a million years ago now. She looked up at Chris out of the corner of her eye and saw that he was smiling down at her too, knowingly raising an eyebrow. Before she knew what was happening, he had scooped her up, spun her around, and pushed her up against the same wall, kissing her exaggeratedly, but briefly, on the mouth, before pulling away, knowing she would be embarrassed in front of the passing foot traffic. Becky was mortified and delighted at the same time, and grabbed his hand to pull him away from the station entrance and out onto the pavement, laughing.

*

Chris took Becky to a small café down a side street not far from the tube station, and they sat at a table outside in the winter sunshine with their hands wrapped around cappuccinos while talking. They sat this way for a couple of hours, still enthralled with each other. Many people walking past looked over at the laughing, good looking young couple, although they were oblivious to anyone but themselves. They spent a lazy lunch there, sharing a bottle of wine before Chris paid the bill and they walked hand-in-hand down towards Covent Garden.

"I'll take you to one of my favourite bars around here," Chris said, smiling down at Becky. "It's got a huge balcony where you can watch some of the best buskers and street entertainers performing right outside the bar. We usually go a lot in the summer, but as today's not too cold, we could still try it?" Becky nodded, happy to follow him anywhere.

*

Covent Garden was busy for a Monday. They approached the market square as Christmas shoppers laden with bags poured out of the indoor market and out onto the street. Smartly dressed office workers were sitting out on the steps opposite St Paul's Church enjoying the winter sunshine, eating sandwiches, salads, and sushi off their laps, gossiping about work and the up-and-coming Christmas parties.

Children enjoying their Christmas holidays ran up and down the West Piazza whilst waiting for the next street entertainer to start. Their parents kept an eye on them, enjoying a glass of wine in the restaurant situated under the bar that Chris was about to take Becky into. He pulled her through the crowd, stepping over the office workers, avoiding the running, screaming children, and over to a pub called 'Punch & Judy', situated above the market, opposite the church. They entered and pushed through the hordes of people inside, attempting to approach the crowded bar. Chris ordered a beer for himself and a glass of wine for Becky, which they then carried up the steep steps that led upstairs and out onto the large balcony. It looked directly down onto the street where the next street entertainer was now preparing his show, tying a rope around one column of the church and stringing it to the next column, tying it around that one, too. Becky looked down at the street below and watched as the crowd thickened. A group of young boys were pushing through a group of Chinese tourists clinging onto their huge cameras, eager to get to the front, impatiently waiting for the next show. Chris and Becky stood leaning over the side of the balcony, looking down at the gathering crowd which was getting bigger by the second.

A few minutes later the street performer finally spoke into his crackling microphone, introducing himself as 'Aziz the Amazing' and the children below squealed with delight and excitement. Becky got completely caught up in the atmosphere and watched, enthralled as Aziz charmed the crowd, first on his unicycle juggling knives whilst singing, then walking across the rope he had strung between the two columns of the church as if it were a tightrope, before back flipping again and again around the gap in front of the children who were squealing with delight. Chris was laughing and cheering like a child and Becky found it hard not to get wrapped up in his enthusiasm and soon began cheering and chanting along with him.

The afternoon slipped away as Becky and Chris watched the afternoon's performances, continuing to drink throughout. By late afternoon it had started to get cooler, and by the time it was dark and the crowd below had dispersed they decided to move inside. The bar was full and there was nowhere left for them to sit, so they huddled in a corner trying to warm their hands, balancing their drinks on a shelf next to them. They stood amongst a pile of shopping bags on the floor that belonged to a group of women at the table next to them who were talking loudly of writing cards and wrapping presents, and the conversation between Becky and Chris turned to Christmas.

It was something that Chris had been wanting to talk about, but he hadn't known how to bring the subject up. He knew that Becky would spend Christmas with him and his family this year, although they hadn't actually spoken about it yet. He just didn't know how to go about actually asking her. Ordinarily, he would start the conversation by asking what she usually did at Christmas and go from there, but he didn't want to hear the words that he knew she was going to say – that she usually spent them alone.

"Will you spend Christmas day with me?" he blurted out all of a sudden, spurred on by the afternoon of drinking. Becky, who had been watching the group of women next to them over his shoulder, faltered for a second, looking embarrassed, shocked, and pleased all at once. She looked up at his face and saw uncertainty in it for the first time since she'd known him, and she instantly replied, "Yes," before she could even protest that she didn't want to intrude. Seeing Chris' face light up and the smile back in place made it worth it, though, and he started talking at a million miles per hour at how pleased his mum would be and how excited he was to spend their first Christmas together. He leant over and grabbed her hand, squeezing it as he looked at her. Becky felt a lurch of delight as he touched her.

"I love you," he said, looking deep into her eyes.

"I love you, too," she whispered back.

*

The following days that led up to Christmas were just as pleasurable for Becky and Chris. They were constantly busy and blissfully happy in each other's company. As if sensing that Becky had not seen much of London, Chris took it upon himself to take her out each day to try and share with her the city that he loved. Each morning he would wake her up with a suggestion of what they should do that day. They spent one day visiting the museums, starting off early at the Natural History Museum, wandering around, exploring like children as they spent hours looking at dinosaur skeletons and wildlife exhibitions. In the afternoon they headed to the Science Museum, where Chris headed straight to the Sports Science area. He walked from section to section, engrossed and fascinated, explaining details to Becky passionately, his eyes alert with interest and excitement. She saw the teacher in him come out properly for the first time and it made her smile as she listened to him. Later on in the afternoon, they ended up wandering hand-in-hand around the Tate Modern, the controversial art museum, where Chris' silly comments on the 'artwork' kept causing Becky to laugh out loud. By the time they had walked around Damien Hirst's exhibit, the original Young British Artist who uses death as a central theme in his works, Becky was laughing so much she had to hold back from Chris while he walked ahead, trying to regain control of herself. Finally composed, she started to walk back towards him, and she could hear his voice ringing from around the corner, reading the plaques dramatically out loud.

He turned and looked at her, raising his eyebrows, and as she looked over at the piece he was looking at – a sheep in what resembled a large fish tank – Becky snorted and fell about laughing once more, earning several dirty looks from other visitors.

*

They spent one day braving the crowds on Oxford Street, making their way down the packed pavement, wandering in and out of the shops and marvelling at the Christmas lights. They somehow spent hours wandering around inside the John Lewis department store and, at one point while Chris was trying on some clothes in the changing rooms, Becky managed to slip away from him. She ran around as quickly as she could, picking up presents for Chris, Sue, Tom, and Simon, confident that she was concealed by the crowds if Chris started to look for her. She ignored her phone when it began to vibrate inside her bag. With the presents bought and paid for in record time, she hid them away in the bottom of her shopping bags before finally answering her phone. Chris had phoned constantly since he'd realised she was missing.

"Where are you?" he asked, and she could hear the strain and anxiety in his voice. She started walking back in the direction that she had left him while trying to explain where she was. A few moments later, when she saw him approach through the crowds at full speed, she could see the worry etched across his face. He grabbed her in a bear hug.

"I've been so worried!" he said, looking down at her. Becky felt guilty and mumbled that she was looking for some new shoes. He took a step back and looked her in the eye.

"I don't know what I would do if I lost you," he said, pulling her close again as he rested his head against hers.

*

Becky and Chris spent their evenings inside the flat with the dark, windy, and cold nights trapped outside. One or the other would cook – it was something that they both enjoyed. If Chris was cooking, Becky would sit at the breakfast bar and watch him move around the kitchen, his jogging bottoms hanging from his hips, his smile firmly in place, listening to him as he chatted away, constantly entertaining her. If Becky was cooking, Chris would sit himself down on the sofa with a beer in front of him and plan his lessons for the new term or watch some form of sport on the TV – usually football. Chris was an avid football fan and had grown up supporting Tottenham Hotspur, the team his dad had supported before he had died. Simon was also a Tottenham fan and for the last few years, after years of being on the waiting list, both of them had finally been lucky enough to buy season tickets, scraping cash from their student loans and part time jobs through university for the luxury.

Tonight, Becky was cooking a lasagne, which was a lengthy process as she cooked it from scratch. She stood inside the kitchen at the breakfast bar with all the ingredients spread out in front of her. She looked up between layering pasta and mince into a baking dish, watching Chris who was fixed intently on the football match on the TV in front of him. It was the only time she ever saw him lose his temper, and she had been shocked the first time he'd leapt up screaming at the TV. Today was a similar story, and he was huffing and puffing and throwing his arms around, causing Becky to smile as she listened to him.

When the final whistle blew and the match was finished, Becky had just put the lasagne into the oven and was now washing salad before putting it into a large bowl. Chris came over and sat at the breakfast bar, looking downcast.

"Arsenal won," he said, and Becky looked up at him, amused. "We really need to win tomorrow." Becky presumed that by 'we' he meant Tottenham Hotspur and she tried to think of a response, but she had no idea what to say, not having the faintest clue about football. Chris suddenly hopped off the stool and scooped his phone off the coffee table without saying a word. He headed into the bedroom and closed the door behind him, leaving Becky smiling and shaking her head with confusion in the kitchen. He emerged a few minutes later, looking a bit brighter.

"Do you want to come and watch Tottenham play with me tomorrow?" he asked, looking more nervous asking her this than he had done approaching her for the first time in the bar. Becky paused, looking up from the cucumber she was slicing.

"How much are the tickets?" she asked slowly, wiping her hands on a tea towel and leaning over the breakfast bar to look at him.

"You can use Simon's season ticket," he said. Becky knew that Simon was away with his family, visiting relatives in Cornwall, and wasn't due back until Christmas Eve in two days' time.

"I just asked him if it was okay, I hadn't planned on going because he was away and I couldn't be bothered to go on my own, but now you can come!" he said, as if he were offering her a trip around the world. Becky sensed she should be very grateful for this invite, although she couldn't think of anything worse than sitting in the cold watching football for nearly two hours, but she wanted to make Chris happy, especially as he'd taken her to some lovely places over the last few days.

"Okay," she heard herself saying. "If you're sure Simon's okay with me using his ticket?"

Chris assured her that he was, not adding that Simon had sounded very not okay when Chris had asked if he could borrow his pass for Becky to use tomorrow. In fact,

Chris had never heard him sound as moody as he just had on the phone and he felt guilty, although he didn't know why. He thought back to the odd moment they had shared outside of his house on Sunday when Simon had walked away from him. He decided he would make a real effort with him when he got back.

Becky was pleased that she had agreed to go with Chris, if just for the level of excitement in him that evening. He was like a child bouncing around on his seat, talking to her between mouthfuls as they ate their lasagne. He talked about the team, how they were doing in the league, the players and team tactics. Becky watched him light up again as he spoke about it, the way he had in the museum when he was talking to her in the section about sport science. She loved seeing him speak so passionately about something and was flattered that he was sharing it with her. She was actually starting to look forward to the match tomorrow so she could be a part of something that he loved so much and share some of this excitement with him.

*

The next morning, Chris was just as excitable. He woke Becky up with a kiss as he put a steaming mug of coffee on the bedside table for her. He climbed onto the bed next to her, almost bouncing up and down with excitement, talking non-stop, firing more football facts at her. When Becky buried her head under the covers to escape from him, he lifted them up and put his head under to sing at her.

"Oh, when the Spurs! Oh, when the Spurs! Oh, when the Spurs come marching in!" He laughed as she groaned at him in response. This was not the Chris that she knew and loved! The Chris she knew would lie in bed and sleep all morning if he had the chance, moaning, groaning, and complaining whenever he had to get up. Becky had never

understood it. She had always been a light sleeper and an early riser, and she hated lying in bed when she could be up and doing something. They were total opposites in that sense; Chris was a really deep sleeper. She remembered something he'd said to her a couple of mornings ago after she had woken him up from a particularly deep sleep.

"Have you ever had one of those dreams," he'd said, sleepily and genuinely confused, "when you've been in such a deep sleep… you genuinely believe your dream is real? And as you wake up you don't even know what day it is?" She had laughed at him, because she was such a light sleeper and rarely ever had dreams; she had not understood him at all.

*

Kick off for the match wasn't until three o'clock that afternoon, and Becky was mystified when Chris started getting ready at ten o'clock in the morning. She went along with it, though, and it didn't take long until she started getting caught up in the excitement, too. It was impossible not to, Chris' moods were always so infectious. They showered together before getting ready, both choosing their thick winter coats to protect them against the freezing weather.

They left the flat hand-in-hand, locking the door behind them before they walked up the steps to the pavement and started heading in the direction of Simon's house, which they needed to detour via before they got on the tube so that Chris could pick up Simon's season ticket for Becky. She had asked him last night how he was going to get hold of it with Simon and his family away in Cornwall.

"With my key," Chris had replied flippantly, and Becky marvelled at a friendship where you had the keys to each other's family homes and could let yourself in whenever you wanted, even if the other person was away.

It was not something she could ever fathom having. She wondered fleetingly if Simon had a key to Chris' house.

They walked through the quiet, frosty roads in silence, and it didn't take long until they approached a house very similar to Chris', although it wasn't on the same road – another tall, red brick building with steps leading up to the front door, with black iron railings separating it from the matching houses attached on both sides. Chris darted confidently up the steps to the front door and slipped his key into the lock. He let himself in and the door opened into a beautifully decorated dark hallway. A polished wooden staircase stood directly in front of them and ran up against the left-hand wall. Chris headed straight for it and dashed up the steps two steps at a time, humming under his breath. Becky hovered behind, still on the concrete step outside of the front door, feeling awkward about entering the house of someone that she didn't really know.

"Come on!" Chris called down to her as he reached the top of the staircase and turned the corner, disappearing out of sight. Becky hesitated for a split second before she stepped inside and pulled the heavy front door closed behind her. She took off her shoes, leaving them on the doormat, and ran up the stairs after him, her sock-covered feet thumping against the polished wooden steps as she went.

She could hear Chris moving around in the first bedroom that she came across and she stood in the doorway watching him as he rummaged through a bedside table. Becky looked away from him and glanced around the room that he stood in; she presumed it was Simon's. She was taken aback at how meticulously neat it was. The walls were painted alternatively blue and white, and it took her a moment to realise that this was probably because they were the Tottenham Hotspur colours.

Not a thing in the room was out of place. The bed was made so perfectly it would have fit in in a five-star hotel. All the sides and surfaces were clear and clean and there was not a speck of dust to be seen anywhere – even the large window that looked down onto the street below was so crystal clear that for a moment Becky actually wondered if it had been left open. As she stood taking it all in, she suddenly realised that she hadn't even seen Chris' bedroom yet. They hadn't ventured out of the kitchen when they had been at his house at the weekend. Chris suddenly stood up and it stopped her train of thought as she looked back over at him. He had found what he needed, and he closed the draw with an unnecessary slam before grinning at her.

"Got it. Let's go!" he said, but instead of walking straight over to the door where she stood, he walked over to a bookshelf that stood in the corner of the room and began to move books around, re-arranging the order and switching which shelves they stood on. He then swapped the deodorant and aftershave bottles around on a desk in the corner, before finally pushing a photo on the wall to a slight angle. Becky raised an eyebrow at him questioningly, looking puzzled. Chris shrugged, still smiling.

"I do it to wind him up, it's like he's got OCD or something. He really hates it when things are moved out of their original places!" he said, and grinned wildly while chuckling to himself as he strode past her out of the door, slapping her bum before he thundered down the stairs, singing the football song from this morning again at the top of his voice, which echoed around the large empty house. Becky wondered how this person could possibly be a teacher when he could so easily act like a child himself! Shaking her head and smiling to herself, she followed him downstairs.

*

It wasn't long until they were crammed up against each other on the busy tube heading up to Seven Sisters station. The carriage was packed, and they were squashed in amongst the huge crowd. Chris chatted happily away to the people next to him with a protective hand around Becky's waist.

It was just gone midday by the time they eventually pulled into the station and the doors opened with a hiss. The crowd of people all tried to fight their way out of the doors at the same time, causing nothing but a backlog. Chris' hand tightened on Becky, holding her back as he shot her a look as if to say, "What's the rush?" Becky smiled and rolled her eyes at him in return, loving the way they were able to communicate with each other now without using words.

When they were finally off the tube and out of the station, they followed the huge mass of people along the street in the direction of the stadium.

They walked for about fifteen minutes, stopping off momentarily so that Chris could buy Becky a Tottenham Hotspur scarf from a makeshift stall at the side of the road before they walked to a pub called 'The Elmhurst' on Lordship Lane, a large mock Tudor style pub with four big screens mounted on the walls – all of which had the football on. Becky was getting quite caught up in the atmosphere and began to relax as they settled into comfy chairs with their drinks. They ordered some food and chatted away happily as they ate and drank over the noise in the pub. More and more people were entering now and the queue for the bar was huge, but the atmosphere was good, and the sounds of cheers and laugher rang out every few minutes. Becky realised that she was actually enjoying herself.

A couple of hours later, the crowd inside the pub

started to thin as drinks were finished and empty glasses were left on the bar. The whole pub it seemed started heading to the stadium. Chris paid their bill, and they left the pub, once again following the crowd towards White Hart Lane.

*

Inside the stadium, the atmosphere was even more electric than it had been in the pub, and Becky's head swung from side-to-side as she looked around and attempted to take everything in. She stood behind Chris as he queued for a drink at the bar, ignoring the stares she was getting from other men as her eyes darted from the crowd, to the big screens, to the pitch. Chris eventually bought two pints of freezing cold beer, which were served in condensation covered plastic pint glasses. Becky struggled to balance hers as they made their way through the thick horde of people and headed in the direction of their seats.

They eventually approached the correct block and walked down the concrete steps, drinks still held aloft. Becky followed Chris until he spotted their row and squeezed along towards their two empty seats, thanking everyone that stood up to let them through. Becky was concentrating on not spilling her beer over anyone as she passed when she noticed two young boys in the row in front of theirs. They had spotted Chris as he walked along the row and their faces lit up, pure excitement radiating from them. Before Chris could even sit down the two boys had spun around in their seats, sitting up on their knees, almost climbing over the back of their chairs as they leaned over, desperately trying to catch his attention.

"Hi, Mr. McNulty!"

"Hi, sir!"

They squealed in unison at Chris, staring at him in awe and admiration. Becky smiled as she realised that they must be two of his students.

"Hello, boys, are you having a good holiday?" Chris asked, sitting down in his chair, leaning back, relaxed in his easy way, smiling his huge smile at each of them in turn.

"Leave Mr. McNulty alone, Jack, Billy," one boy's father said, turning around to smile at Chris and roll his eyes. "I bet you rue the day your season tickets came up so close to two of your students!" he said to Chris, but Chris shook his head and smiled.

"Where's Simon?" one of the boys asked, looking at Becky in distaste as if to say, "Why have you brought a girl to the football?"

"Simon's on holiday," Chris said. "This is my girlfriend, Becky." The boys acknowledged Becky for a split second before launching into talk of their football team and the up-and-coming matches when they got back to school. They were clambering over the back of their seats to vie for Chris' attention. Chris chatted effortlessly with them, and Becky could see the total admiration in their faces when they looked at him (so it wasn't just her then), and she suddenly realised what an amazing teacher he must be. It was clear that these children adored him, and she sat watching their interaction in fascination as Chris chatted to them, listened to them, and made them laugh. He spoke with them as if they were adults and they raced each other to tell him stories from their holidays so far. When it came to kick-off, they begrudgingly turned around to watch the match, turning around every now and then to point out a particularly good pass or tackle, hoping that Chris would notice that *they* had noticed.

As Becky sat watching them it started her thinking, for the first time in her life, about having children. It was not something she had ever, *ever* considered before, and it was certainly not something she had ever wanted. Her main goal had only ever been to get a job within the care industry. Having children or a family was not something she had ever seen herself doing. In fact, after her own upbringing, she felt quite strongly about staying on her own and she had resigned herself to a life of being alone. Sitting there, watching Chris with the boys and the way they seemed to admire him, stirred something inside Becky that she had never felt before. She realised that maybe, one day, she might actually consider having children with Chris. If she was really honest, she realised, deep down she even hoped that maybe one day it would actually be a reality.

*

Tottenham won the match 3-2 and the crowd went wild when the final whistle blew. Almost instantly the crowds began to disperse from the stands and the two boys in front jumped out of their seats eagerly and wriggled their way along their row, pushing past people's legs to get to the end, where they waited impatiently on the steps for Chris and Becky to reach them. When Chris arrived, they followed at his heels up the stairs and towards the exit, still chatting away to him at a hundred miles an hour. Becky saw Chris turn and catch one of the dad's eyes over the crowd, nodding at them as if to say, *"I've got them,"* and the dad nodded back and smiled. Becky followed along at a slower pace, not caring enough to push through the crowd, instead she let it sweep her along and it wasn't long until she was outside the stadium and into the crisp cold evening. She spotted Chris and the boys through the darkness, standing waving at her to get her attention, and she walked over to join them, linking hands with Chris as soon as she got to his side. A few moments later the two fathers appeared, shaking Chris's hand and wishing them both a merry Christmas.

"Are you coming to the match on Boxing Day?" one

of the boys asked Chris, looking up at him eagerly.

"Billy, I've told you!" the taller of the two dads said in exasperation. "*We're* not going to the match on Boxing Day, we're going to your nan's!"

"But Daaad," Billy whined back. "I thought maybe if Mr. McNulty was going, you could go to Nan's without me, and me and Jack could come to the match with Mr. McNulty and Simon?" He looked at Becky pointedly as if to insinuate that she was not invited, and then turned to look longingly at Chris, who grinned down at him fondly.

The father shook his head and laughed.

"No! Leave Mr. McNulty alone! If *I* have to go to your nan's, *you* have to go to your nan's! You'll see Mr. McNulty at school next year."

Chris stood grinning as the boys' faces fell, and they glumly said goodbye before their fathers herded them off towards the main road. They turned and waved miserably at Chris as they walked away.

12

"You ready, beautiful?" – Chris.

The next day was Christmas Eve. Becky and Chris spent most of the day in bed, curled up in the sheets, chatting and laughing. They were going out in the evening to Chris' local pub. It was a tradition that Chris and his friends had kept up for years and he was bubbling over with the excitement at finally getting to introduce Becky to all his friends. Becky, on the other hand, was full of nerves. She had never been out on a social occasion like this before and being thrown into a group of friends like this was her idea of hell. She didn't say anything, though, knowing that Chris would insist that they didn't have to go if he had any idea how she was feeling. So instead, when the evening came, she threw herself into getting ready and tried not to think about it.

Chris was singing in the shower as Becky sat cross legged on the floor by her mirror applying her make-up. A little while later he came out of the bathroom, dripping wet, drying his hair with the towel as he walked. His phone had been beeping and ringing continuously throughout the day and Becky sat fascinated, listening as he had conversation after conversation, assuring everyone that yes, he would be out tonight, and that yes, he was bringing his new girlfriend. Word must travel fast. Chris took about three minutes to get ready and he sat on the end of the bed, his hair damp, watching Becky pick something to wear. She decided on a pair of skin-tight black jeans tucked into leather boots with a plain white t-shirt and a vintage Levi denim jacket. Her long hair looked beautiful as usual and Chris sat gazing at her, still bowled over by her beauty every time he looked at her. He stood up and wrapped his arms around her, feeling her relax against him as they embraced. He could feel her breath tickle his skin through his shirt and he could have quite happily undressed her right there and taken her back to bed, but his phone rang again, pulling them out of the moment. He grabbed his phone off the bed and answered it.

"Simon," he said, pausing to listen to the voice on the other end of the phone. "Of course I am... Yes, usual time in 'The Stag'," he said before pausing again. Becky saw a flicker of a frown cross his face, but it vanished before it could really register.

"Well, we are," he said, his voice level. He said goodbye and shook his head slightly as if confused. He looked over at Becky who was gazing up at him and he grinned at her when he caught her looking.

"You ready, beautiful?" he asked, and Becky nodded her head. She picked up the overnight bag that was by her feet and full of clothes for the next couple of days. They were planning on staying at Sue's tonight so that they could wake up there on Christmas morning. Becky also had the presents that she had bought for everyone buried in the bottom.

They headed out of the flat, turning off all the lights as they went. Chris scooped the keys off the breakfast bar and locked the front door behind them as they walked out into the freezing cold night, hand-in-hand. The cab Chris had ordered was waiting at the kerb, its headlights lighting up the otherwise empty street. They jumped inside, once again appreciating the warmth, and the driver pulled away as Chris gave him the address of the pub. Becky sat back in the seat and tried to ignore the butterflies that were in her stomach.

*

It wasn't long until the taxi pulled up outside of the heaving bar. To Becky, it seemed like there were hundreds of people stood smoking outside, huddled underneath the patio heaters, glancing over at the new arrivals. As soon as they stepped out of the cab, Becky felt as if she had been thrust onto the red carpet. The second they started walking towards the door, people started calling Chris' name and as they walked through the garden, dozens of people came over to say hello. Girls stood on tiptoes to kiss Chris on the cheek, and he shook people's hands, keeping his arm wrapped tightly around Becky's waist.

Becky herself was also causing a stir; the girls looked her up and down in distaste and the guys stared, blown away by her. She said, "Hi," meekly as Chris introduced people, and Becky felt completely overwhelmed, her face burning with embarrassment as she tried to remember all the names being thrown at her. They finally made it inside the pub and Becky was devastated to see that it was just as busy inside, and, in the light, it was even clearer to Becky that all eyes seemed to be on them. Most of the girls were looking at Becky bitterly, and Becky kept her eyes cast down, wishing she'd made an excuse to not come tonight, knowing that she didn't belong. After what seemed to Becky like an eternity, they eventually made it to the corner of the bar where Chris' friends were seated. Five or six tables had been pulled together and the group of people sat around, talking loudly between bouts of laughter. The table was filled with glasses, full and empty.

Another round of *hi*s and *hello*s ensued, but friendly this time, and everyone in the group smiled warmly at Becky. There was an almost equal mix of guys and girls around the table and each of them looked at Becky fondly as they introduced themselves. The girls, who were grouped together at one end, moved around on the bench they were sat on, trying to make room for Becky to fit in.

As she sat down in the space they had created, Chris insisted that they move around even more so that he could slide onto the bench next to her. He put his hand on her leg under the table and squeezed it reassuringly.

As Becky had feared, the instant that they sat down, all attention was on her. Everyone in the group wanted to hear how she and Chris had met and the table was filled again with loud voices as questions were thrown in their direction. Drinks were put down on the table in front of them as they told the story of how they met. The boys all laughed at Chris, and he blushed as they ribbed him for being so soppy, waiting outside Becky's interview for her, hoping she would turn up.

"When it's right, it's right," he said, holding his hands out and his face splitting into a grin.

"That's so romantic! I wish something like that would happen to me!" one of the girls next to Becky cried, slapping her hands on the table in front of her before sitting back in her chair with her arms crossed, pouting.

"You're engaged to the boyfriend you've been with since year eight!" Chris replied to the pretty blonde, who looked fondly over at a dark haired guy at the other end of the table; he winked at her.

"Yes, but that's so *boring!*" She sighed. "Your story is like something out of a film!"

Chris grinned and pulled Becky into him, kissing her head, causing her to blush. At this moment, Simon appeared at the table, and he looked stonily in Becky and Chris' direction.

"Where have you been?" Chris asked, looking up at him.

"Pool," he almost grunted in reply.

"Yeah and I smashed him!" a tall curly haired guy behind him said, slapping his hands down on Simon's shoulders.

"Hi! I'm Frankie," he said, leaning over Chris to shake Becky's hand, and she smiled up into his friendly face.

"Okay! Who wants a shot?" Frankie asked to a response of moans and cheers from around the table. Everyone leant forward to put money into a whip, and Chris held Becky's hand away from her bag as she attempted to get her purse out, smiling and shaking his head.

"My treat," he whispered, "for putting up with this lot!" Becky giggled and looked up at him from beneath her lashes, giving him a quick kiss on the lips. As they pulled apart, smiling, everyone around the table was whooping and laughing, and Chris nodded his head in a bow. Simon rolled his eyes and Chris caught him.

"What's up with you, miserable?" he joked, and before Simon could reply Frankie piped up.

"He's jealous!" he joked, although Simon did not look pleased. His eyes darkened as he looked over at Frankie.

"Bugger off," he said stonily.

"Not only has his best mate found someone better looking to spend his time with! He knows he will never be able to get a girl like Becky!" He cackled with laughter at his own 'joke' and winked at Becky before he headed to the bar.

The shots arrived and were drunk, conversations got louder, and laughter rang out around the table. As talk turned to other things and the focus turned to subjects other than her and Chris, Becky finally relaxed slightly and settled into her role as an observer. She sat quietly, watching the interactions between everyone at the table. It was obvious that they were a close group of friends, and it was clear they had grown up together. Becky wondered if she would have been part of a group like this if her father had never left and her life had been different.

Drinks continued to be put in front of her, although

neither she nor Chris had been to the bar yet, and she could feel herself starting to get tipsy. Everyone else seemed very drunk. Drinks were being spilt and debates were happening over the table as people pushed their luck the more they drank. Simon seemed to chill out more with each drink, and by the end of the night he was sitting next to Chris as they argued together with Charlie and Frankie about football, their voices getting louder and louder as they got more passionate.

"Are you bored with the football talk yet?" the pretty blonde who had spoken earlier asked Becky, nodding in the direction of the four boys, interrupting Becky's thoughts. She smiled and nodded her head.

"You just have to get used to it, Gary's football mad as well. He supports Spurs, too. He's desperate to get a season ticket so he can go to the matches with Chris and Simon, but he's been on the waiting list for years! Every year I pray he finally gets one so I can get rid of him every Sunday instead of him monopolising the TV all day!"

Becky smiled as the girl chatted away, and watched Chris and Simon argue with the twins out of the corner of her eye.

"...And then we could go shopping!" the pretty blonde finished with a flourish, and Becky realised that the girl had continued speaking and that she was expected to reply. She had not been concentrating and turned to smile and nod her head at her, hoping it was a good enough response.

"Are you spending Christmas with Chris and Sue, or is he spending it with you and your family?" she asked after a pause.

"I'm spending it at Sue's," Becky said carefully, not wanting to invite more questions. She motioned to the overnight bag under the table. "We're going to her house straight from here."

"Ahh, Sue is such a legend, isn't she! I used to go 'round there every day during the summer holidays when we were at school. Most mornings Chris would still be in bed when I arrived, and Sue and I would sit and have bacon sandwiches together before she went to work while I waited for Chris to wake up!" Becky zoned out again, half listening to the chatter whilst still watching Chris and his friends messing around. Chris seemed very drunk, his face was red and he was swaying in his seat. She had never seen him like this before and she sat watching him, entertained and full of love for him.

*

Time flew past surprisingly quickly for Becky, and it didn't seem long until the bar called last orders. Shortly after that, the lights came on and after a while the bar staff started to clean up around their tables. They were among the last to leave and the bouncers came over, begging them to go.

"Come on! It's Christmas! Let me go home!" one bouncer begged, which earned him a huge sloppy kiss on the cheek from a very drunken Frankie. It seemed to take forever for everyone to find their belongings, get their coats on, and finally make it to the exit of the bar. Once outside, the group started to disperse as they walked into the freezing cold night, and everyone said their goodbyes. Kisses and hugs were in abundance in amongst cries of, "Merry Christmas!" Cabs lined the street and the group got smaller as everyone jumped into the cars together depending on where they lived, and after the final few goodbyes had been said Chris, Becky, and Simon got into a cab together at the back of the queue.

Simon climbed into the front seat as Becky guided a very drunk Chris to the back door. Simon instantly started up a conversation with the driver, asking him which football team he supported, attempting to carry on the debate from the pub as Chris leant his head on Becky's shoulder and sat in silence. It didn't take long until they pulled up outside of Sue's house. Becky had to wake up Chris, who had fallen asleep, breathing heavily in her ear, and encourage him to get out of the taxi. She paid the driver, ignoring Chris' weak protests that he wanted to pay, as he unsuccessfully tried to find his wallet whilst staggering around on the pavement. Becky said goodbye to Simon and led Chris up the steps to Sue's front door. She fumbled around in his back pocket, searching for his keys. She eventually managed to get the front door open, and they entered the dark hallway. Being out in the cold air must have woken Chris up a bit and he started to fondle Becky's bum as he followed her through the front door. Becky had to slap his hands away, smiling to herself, telling him to *ssshhh*. They stood giggling like children as they took their shoes off. Becky could see a strip of Chris' face that was lit up orange from the streetlight outside which entered from the small window above the door. His eyes were on hers and she could see that he was smiling. She leant over and kissed the end of his nose, and he grabbed her, burying his head into her shoulder.

"I love you! I love you! I love you! I love you!" he whispered, a little too loudly, into her ear, and she pulled away from him, holding one finger over his lips, attempting to get him to be quiet.

"Shhhh," she said again, silently laughing, glancing upstairs, worried about waking Sue up. Chris pulled away and slipped into the kitchen to fill a couple of glasses with water. When he returned, he motioned for Becky to follow him, and they crept up the two flights of stairs and across the landing before entering Chris' room. Chris flicked the light on and as Becky's eyes adjusted to the bright light she looked around, taking everything in. Chris' room was surprisingly large, with bright blue walls and a wooden floor. It had a slanted roof with a double bed in the left-hand corner and a huge TV on a chest of drawers to the right.

Becky started to walk across the room, looking around, when she suddenly noticed two stockings hanging on the end of Chris' bed. One was a huge, red, dog-eared, knitted stocking with 'Chris' knitted across the top in white. The other was slightly smaller and brand new, which someone had had sewn 'Becky' onto in dark green felt. They both had presents in them, but Becky's was fit to bursting. She looked over at Chris and he was grinning at her.

"My mum," he said rolling his eyes, and before Becky could say anything he had closed the gap between them and lifted her up, all trace of his drunkenness gone. He flicked the light off as he laid her on the bed. He kissed her, pressing his mouth hungrily to hers, his heart suspended for that split second before her lips moved in response. As Becky was kissing him back, she noticed that there was a huge skylight in the slanted roof above them. She could see the stars through it as they slowly peeled off each other's clothes and made love in the early hours of Christmas morning.

13

"Merry first Christmas together." – Chris

Becky thought Christmas day was perfect. They awoke early in the morning to the sound of Sue tapping on the bedroom door. She opened it slightly and peeked her head around.

"Merry Christmas!" she whispered through the gap. "I've got tea here for you!"

"Come in, then." Chris spoke face down into the pillow, his voice muffled. Becky was relieved she had put one of Chris' t-shirts on to sleep in last night, as once again her face was burning with embarrassment. Sue did not seem at all fazed as she came in and put two steaming mugs of tea on the bedside table. She smiled at Becky before speaking.

"Breakfast is nearly ready, so get up – you've only got yourself to blame if you've got a hangover," she added, looking at Chris and winking at Becky. She left the room and Becky started to get up, but Chris grabbed her, pinning her back down on the bed. He kissed her on the lips.

"Merry first Christmas together," he said between kisses, making Becky smile.

*

They made their way downstairs, mugs of tea in hand. Sue was standing at the kitchen side, scraping scrambled egg onto plates. Tom was already at the kitchen table, in his usual spot, reading the paper and Becky smiled at him as she sat down. 'Let It Snow' by Dean Martin was playing softly in the background, and Chris bent down to kiss his mum on the cheek as he walked to the back door to call the dogs, who were running around the frosty garden, barking into the otherwise silent morning. They bounded over to the door when they heard him call and Chris slid the door open, allowing them into the kitchen. They leapt through the opened door, wagging their tails so hard they were practically vibrating. Chris crouched down on the floor and they clambered all over him, fighting each other to lick his face as Chris laughed. Sue glanced over disapprovingly but didn't say anything.

Becky watched Sue put plates of scrambled eggs and salmon down on the kitchen table and pop the cork on a bottle of champagne. As she was pouring everyone a buck's fizz, Chris sat down at the table next to Becky, kissing her on the cheek. The dogs, as if sensing they needed to behave or they would be banished to the garden again, quietly laid down on either side of Chris' chair.

They chatted over the table as they ate their breakfast while Sue passed around more glasses of buck's fizz. When everyone had finished, Becky got up and helped Sue clear the table, pausing for a moment to lean down and admire the huge turkey that sat in the bottom of the oven through the thick glass door. Once the table was cleared and everything was washed up, Becky and Chris went upstairs to wash and change before they headed back down to join Sue and Tom in the living room. Chris carried the packed stockings from the end of his bed with him and emptied the presents onto the pile now growing on the living room floor. Becky looked around the living room, seeing it for the first time. It was a large square room with a TV in the far corner and a huge fireplace taking up most of the back wall. There was a large sofa and two armchairs, but it was the enormous real fir tree in the corner of the room that took Becky's breath away. It was beautifully decorated with coloured tinsel, baubles, fairy lights, and a beautiful angel sat on top. Becky stared at it in wonder.

She had never had a Christmas tree before, she didn't

even own any decorations. Now, looking at this tree, she wondered why. It was just so beautiful. She wanted to take a picture of it so she would never forget how beautiful and Christmassy it was. Tom was sitting down in an armchair in the corner of the room watching *VH1* on the TV, which was playing classic Christmas songs. Becky wondered if that was the seat he always sat in, the same way he always sat in the same place in the kitchen. Chris guided Becky to the sofa and she sat down, her feet curled up underneath her. Chris crouched down in front of the fireplace, the dogs immediately joining him, lying at his feet as he started to build a fire. Sue came in from the kitchen and handed Becky a thick yellow drink with a cherry on the top. Becky looked at it, puzzled.

"It's a snowball," Chris said, seeing Becky look at it, confused. "Our Christmas drink – it's made of advocaat and cream soda. Try it!"

Becky snuggled down into the huge sofa, sipping the extremely sweet drink as she watched Chris crumple up old newspaper and fill the fireplace with kindling before adding logs. It didn't take long until the fire was roaring, and Chris joined Becky on the sofa, cuddling up next to her, enjoying the warmth it gave off.

Sue entered the room again, wiping her hands on the apron tied around her waist, a gesture Becky was becoming familiar with now, and conversation flowed over the Christmas songs playing in the background. They started to open their presents, picking a gift out of the pile one at a time. After a few minutes, Becky slipped off the sofa and ran up the stairs to grab the presents she had bought from the bottom of her overnight bag. She was so pleased that she had managed to wrap and name tag them all while Chris was watching football a couple of nights ago. She came back into the room and added her presents to the pile, causing Chris to look up at her quizzically. She knew he was wondering when she'd bought them; they had hardly spent a moment apart since the day they'd met. She smiled at his confused face and told him that she'd bought them when she went missing in the department store.

"I'd rather not have a present if it meant going through the worry I felt when I couldn't find you!" he joked, but he looked down at the pile of presents eagerly, nonetheless. Becky was extremely pleased with the gifts she had bought and was very thankful that she'd had the foresight to buy them, as present after present got pulled out of the pile for her, and they were mainly from Sue. There were dozens of small but thoughtful gifts. Face creams, pyjamas, books... Sue sat and watched, delighted, as Becky opened each gift; she was brimming with happiness – she would have loved to have had a daughter. She had enjoyed going shopping for Becky's Christmas presents after years of buying only for boys.

The pile of unwrapped gifts next to Becky got bigger and bigger and Becky's cheeks burned every time another present got pulled out of the pile for her. She was glad when her gifts for the others finally got picked. For Sue she had bought a large, leather-bound cookbook filled with recipes and space for your own notes and adaptations. Sue thanked her profusely and pored over it once it was opened. For Tom, Becky had gotten a bottle of aftershave which he opened looking surprised and pleased. He thanked her, speaking out loud for the first time that day. Becky was excited and nervous to see what Chris thought of the gift she had bought him and waited impatiently for it to be pulled out of the pile. Eventually it did, and the envelope was passed to him. She could see him looking at it, puzzled. As Chris opened the envelope, she saw his eyes widen as he read the 'Red Letter Days' voucher. *'Drive four of the world's most sensational supercars around a specially designed racetrack. With this high-octane driving experience you can take the wheel of the sensational Ferrari 360, the powerful Porsche 911 GT2, the classic Aston Martin V8 Vantage, and the fiery Lamborghini Gallardo Spyder...'* Chris' eyes shot to hers, his eyebrows raised.

"I got one for Simon, too, so you two can go together," Becky said, looking at him, her eyes flicking around his face, trying to assess whether he was as pleased as she hoped he would be. She had spent every last penny she had on these gifts. Chris grabbed hold of her and gave her a massive hug, squeezing her tightly.

"This is amazing!" he said while Sue and Tom looked on. "Thank you so much!" He kissed her on the lips and Becky grinned, feeling pleased with herself. Chris leant down to the now dwindling pile of presents and rooted around until he picked out a small, beautifully wrapped box. He passed it to Becky, and she looked at him with the same quizzical look he had given her, wondering when he had gotten the time to buy her a gift. She hadn't expected anything. She carefully unwrapped the gift, not wanting to damage the beautiful paper, and lifted the lid off the box underneath to reveal a beautiful gold charm bracelet. Becky looked at it then back to Chris who was looking at her intently, trying to read her reaction. She looked down again with a lump in her throat. The bracelet was beautiful, and the longer she looked at it, the bigger the lump in her throat grew. Each of the charms that were attached to the bracelet were so thoughtful. A small cameo for her love of all things vintage, a small dog that Chris touched with his finger, – "Scoobie," he said, smiling – a horseshoe, – "For good luck," – a beautiful golden heart with a diamond in the middle, a London bus, a little stiletto shoe, a 'C' and a 'B', and a golden disc with 'I love you' inscribed on it. Tears threatened as Becky held it out to Chris, asking him to put it on her wrist, which he did tenderly before looking up at her, their eyes catching instantly the way they always did. Sue looked on from across the room, getting a lump in her throat herself. The love that radiated from Becky and Chris was so touching, she felt as if she was intruding just by being in the same room as them. She averted her eyes and looked over at Tom who was watching her intently, as if reading her mind. She smiled and looked away. Was there nowhere she could look in her own living room?

*

After the presents were opened, Becky and Chris, wrapped up in jumpers, coats, and scarves, took the dogs out for a walk while Sue finished cooking Christmas dinner. It was a freezing cold day. The air was still, and the sky was thick with grey clouds. A layer of frost still covered everything in sight, even though it was now early afternoon. They each had a dog on the lead, and they held hands as they walked through the misty, deserted streets; it felt as if they were the only souls on the planet.

Once they were back at the house, the smell of Christmas dinner hit them as soon as they walked through the door. They followed the smell into the kitchen where Sue looked up approvingly at their timing. She had almost finished dishing up and the table was full to bursting with different dishes of food. The meal, as usual, was incredible. Once again Becky marvelled at what a wonderful cook Sue was. The turkey was like nothing she had ever had before. There were pigs in blankets, homemade stuffing, dozens of different vegetables, and gorgeous crispy potatoes, all topped off with a delicious gravy. They pulled crackers, wore paper hats, told jokes, and drank wine. Becky felt so content and at home, it almost brought tears to her eyes once again. She marvelled, not for the first time, at how lucky she was to find herself almost part of a family like this.

When the food was finished, everyone pitched in with the clearing up and it didn't take long until the table was cleared and everyone was back in the living room, stuffed and sleepy. Becky was curled up against Chris on the sofa as they watched a re-run of *Home Alone*. Becky must have dozed off, as she awoke with a start a while later when the dogs started barking at a knock at the front door. Sue got up to open it and the blast of cold air from outside came through the door first, followed by Simon, his face red from the cold, carrying a bag of presents that he dumped on the floor.

"I feel like shit," he announced as he threw himself into Sue's chair, thrusting his long legs out in front of him, running his hand through his hair at the same time. Sue walked in as he sat down and shooed him out of her seat, passing him the snowball she had made for him, which he looked at gingerly. He got up, taking the drink from her, and sat down at the other end of the sofa from Becky and Chris, looking paler than usual and obviously suffering from a hangover.

"You do it every year, you've only got yourself to blame," Chris said, mimicking Sue.

*

As the afternoon wore on, it became even darker outside, but it was cosy inside the living room with the fire flickering and crackling, casting a warm orange glow while the TV played quietly in the corner. Simon had gifts for Sue and Tom, but nothing for Chris. Becky asked Chris quietly if he had bought anything for Simon.

"We don't get each other presents!" He laughed as if it were obvious. Becky shyly handed the envelope to Simon with the 'Red Letter Days' voucher that she had bought for him. When Simon opened it, he looked over at Becky, taken aback. She thought it was probably the first time he had ever actually looked her in the eye.

"I can't accept this. This is too much," he said slowly, but Becky smiled at him, thrilled that he seemed pleased.

"I insist! I got the same one for Chris, and I know how much he'll enjoy it if you're there with him!" she said. Simon looked between her and Chris.

"I didn't get you anything," he mumbled, but Becky laughed.

"I don't expect anything! I'm just happy that you're both happy!" she said. Chris pulled her in closer to him and kissed her on the cheek.

"This is why I love her," he said while looking at Simon, and Simon looked a bit embarrassed.

14

3 Years Later

BECKY

"Although, now there were a few more hairs on his chest." – Becky.

I sat in my office, twiddling the wedding ring around and around on my finger as I waited for John, a severely autistic patient, to come in and see me. Although I knew that I shouldn't really have favourites, he's unquestionably my favourite patient. It was Saturday morning, and I was exhausted from working the night shift last night. I couldn't wait to get home. I had asked John to come by and see me at ten o'clock this morning, and it was now 9:55. I knew that he was hovering just outside of my office door – I could hear him muttering under his breath to himself and the shuffle of his feet on the carpet – but, as usual, he waited until his digital watch struck 10:00 exactly and beeped at him before he walked through the door.

"You wanted a meeting with me at ten o'clock," he said in his monotone, robotic voice. Not asking a question, more giving a statement. I smiled at him and told him to sit down. We had a brief chat and when we were finished I thanked him and told him that he could go. He looked down at his watch and then back up at me. "You said you would need me for half an hour… but it's only been twenty-three minutes," he said, and I sighed. I would have to fill the next seven minutes now. I should have known better, talked slower.

At precisely 10:30 he exited my office and I started to gather my things. My shift was finished, and I was desperate to get home. I knew Chris was at the flat waiting for me and I hadn't seen him since yesterday morning. Although I was exhausted, I couldn't wait to get back and see him. I still missed him so much every time we had to spend a night apart. I had a physical ache in my chest until we were together again. Just as I was about to leave, the phone on my desk started ringing. I contemplated not answering it, but I could see from the phone number flashing on the screen that it was Mark, the manager of the home. I sighed again. I knew what the call was going to be about, and I knew that the conversation was going to take a while. I really didn't want something else delaying me from getting home to Chris, but I picked the phone up out of its cradle.

I'd taken an autistic patient, Colin, out for the afternoon yesterday. Everything had been going well until we were sitting on the train on the way home. Colin was sitting listening to Steps on his portable CD player whilst looking out of the window. I had known the tantrum was going to happen the second I heard the irritating, upbeat singing stop through his earphones. Colin paused for a split second and looked down at the machine on his lap and it was then that I realised the batteries must have run out.

Colin started to get upset. At first it was just grunts of frustration, which got louder and louder until the grunts turned into screams. He started smacking his hands down on either side of him, hitting the seats in a rage. Other passengers on the train turned to stare at us as the outburst turned into a full-blown tantrum. I could literally feel the stares of the other passengers on the train burning into the back of me as I tried to console and distract him. I urgently tried to calm him down by pretending to fix the portable CD player, but this didn't work. As a last resort I turned to the train, staring at the other passengers imploringly.

"Excuse me! Does anyone have any double AA batteries? I'll pay for them!" I asked, hearing the panicked shrill voice coming out of my mouth but not recognising it as my own, petrified that Colin was really going to lose it. I was just about to give up hope when a teenage boy, covered in piercings and with dyed jet-black hair, approached me and dropped two batteries into my hand, smiling at me warmly. I didn't even have a chance to wonder where he'd got them from, and before I could offer him any money or even thank him he'd walked off again. I shoved the batteries into the machine with sweating, shaking fingers and the instant the music started playing again Colin was calm and silent. He continued looking out of the window as if nothing had happened. I breathed a sigh of relief as I sat back in my chair, praying that the batteries would last until we got back to the home. I entertained myself for the rest of the journey thinking of the iPod I would insist Mark bought Colin before I would take him out in public again.

*

After relaying the story to Mark over the phone and assuring him that yes, I had filled in all the necessary paperwork to record the incident, and that yes, I had filled all of Colin's carers in on what had happened, I put the phone down. I picked up my things and flew out of the home, waving goodbye to everyone as I left. Just as I reached the front door, I saw another patient I worked closely with, Oliver, who was extremely shy and barely spoke to anyone but me. He was hovering by the door, clinging on to the blue bouncy ball he took everywhere with him as if his life depended on it. I hesitated, torn between wanting to rush back to Chris and wanting to speak with Oliver. I knew that it always made his day when I did. I stopped in my tracks.

"How are you, Oliver?" I asked, smiling at him as brightly as I could. He nodded and smiled, his chin tucked into his chest, his fingers working the ball, turning it in circle after circle after circle. He wouldn't look me in the eye. "I'm just about to leave, Oliver. I'll be back on Monday morning, okay?" I said. He shook his head slightly, his eyes still fixed down, moving the ball in his fingers, faster and faster. "Okay, I'm off then, see you on Monday," I said, and he mumbled something under his breath that I couldn't quite hear. I leant in close, it sounded like 'I love you'.

"Do you love me, Oliver?" I asked, raising my eyebrow at him jokingly.

"Good," he replied before shuffling off.

*

I sat on the bus, hugging my overnight bag to my chest, and resisted the urge to put my head on it and go to sleep. My phone buzzed in my pocket. It was Chris, obviously. I rarely got texts from anyone else, and I only have his, Sue's, Simon's, and Mark's numbers programmed into my phone. Even after three years of being with Chris and us spending almost every minute of our spare time together, I still find it difficult to mix with other people.

I love my job. I adore the residents of the home – my co-workers leave me alone, which suits me, and I get on really well with the manager, Mark. I have my own office and can keep myself to myself, dedicating most of my time to the patients. I looked down at the message: *U r late! Where are you!!?? It's been over 24 hours since I've seen you . (Love you xxxxxxxxx)*

I smiled and quickly texted back: *On bus. Be 5 mins. Love you xxx*

I still loved Chris with every fibre of my being. He is literally my reason for living. My heart still lurched in my chest every time I saw him, and I could feel my adrenalin rising as the bus pulled up at the bus stop just down the road from the flat. I literally skipped off the bus and to the front door, fumbling with my keys in my haste to get the key in the lock and to be inside with him.

The door was suddenly pulled open and Chris was standing there, in the jogging bottoms he wore around the flat that hung off of his hips, bare chested, and with his trademark grin plastered across his face, meaning his dimples were visible. He looked achingly sexy. He still looked exactly the same as he did the first time I'd met him, although now there were a few more hairs on his chest and the hair that used to fall over his eyes had been cut shorter. I walked through the door and straight into his arms which he wrapped around me, kissing me on the top of my head.

"You look exhausted," he said, his eyes roaming my face.

"I'm knackered," I replied, smiling up at him, unable to conceal a yawn that escaped my lips.

He took my bag from me and led me to the sofa before walking into the kitchen to make me some breakfast. I leant back into the sofa, curling my legs up underneath me. I looked around the flat. It hadn't changed much from the way it was before Chris had moved in all those years ago. The only difference now is that it's packed full of framed photographs of us. I looked at the photo of us, mounted on the wall, from our honeymoon in Thailand and smiled. We were standing on a beach in Koh Phi Phi, the sea behind us and the sun just starting to set. Chris' skin was golden brown, and mine was even darker, and our hair was wet from the sea. We had an arm thrown around each other and the photo was taken just as we had looked at each other and laughed, capturing a perfect moment. We looked so young and happy, it still hurts my heart to look at it. Sometimes I cannot believe that it is actually me in the picture. Chris had loved Thailand. He had begged me to consider going back there to stay for a year after we'd returned from our honeymoon. "I could teach English, and we could travel!" he'd said, but I'd only been a year into my job at the home and I'd adored working there. I just wasn't ready to leave it.

"What are you smiling at?" Chris asked as he put his signature bacon and egg sandwich down in front of me. I hadn't realised how hungry I was until the smell hit me, and I picked it up gratefully.

"Thailand picture," I said through a mouthful of food, nodding in the direction of the framed photo. Chris' eyes followed mine and he looked at it too, a smile playing at his lips. I knew, like me, every time he looked at that picture it brought back the memories of the wonderful month we had spent there. I finished my sandwich and sighed. Chris looked at me thoughtfully.

"You want to go to sleep, don't you?" he asked, feigning disappointment and I nodded guiltily, smiling at him. "I'm at football tomorrow – you know that, don't you? You should make the most of me today," he continued, raising his eyebrows at me, and I laughed.

"Let me have a couple of hours sleep and then I'm all yours," I said, and he smiled. I carried my stuff through to the bedroom and dumped it on the bed. I peeled my clothes off and had a shower, standing for a while under the hot water. I towelled myself dry, put some pyjamas on, and just before I climbed into bed, I poked my head out of the bedroom door to glance at Chris who was sitting on the sofa, his feet up on the table in front of him, watching motor racing – possibly the most boring thing on TV. As I looked at him sitting there on the sofa, I couldn't face getting into an empty bed, so I climbed onto the sofa with him and laid my head on his lap. He leant over me and pulled a blanket up from my feet to my chin and within seconds I was asleep.

*

The weekend, as usual, passed way too quickly. We ventured out of the flat that Saturday evening to meet Simon and his fiancée Katie for dinner in Covent Garden. Katie is a beauty. Tall and slim with a year-round tan, piercing blue eyes, and long, jet-black straight hair that fell almost to her waist. Simon had met her two years ago on a night out and they had just recently gotten engaged after moving in together six months ago. If I'd thought Simon was difficult enough to get along with, I found Katie even harder. At least Simon's a bit more civil towards me now than he was in the beginning. Katie is very confident and loud, and constantly demands attention, meaning that she and Simon, who is the wildest person I have ever met, have quite a volatile relationship. Whenever we're out together, the atmosphere gets more and more tense the more they drink and they always end up bickering or arguing. Chris can sit back and watch, amused, but it makes me feel uncomfortable, especially as Chris and I never argue; I could not imagine us ever having anything to argue about. Tonight, though, it wasn't too bad, and we had a lovely evening. We enjoyed a gorgeous meal in a charming little tapas bar that Katie had heard of through some friends at work. We sat in the restaurant for hours, picking at different dishes and drinking jug after jug of sangria. When the meal was finished, we walked across the beautiful square to the 'Punch & Judy' for a drink. Every time I came in here and stood at the crowded bar or out on the balcony, it reminded me of the first time Chris had brought me here, and it still makes me smile every time.

The four of us stood out on the balcony tonight, making the most of the spring evening being slightly warmer. At the end of the night, we got the tube home and Chris and I walked hand-in-hand from the station to our front door. As we entered the flat Chris didn't even turn the lights on. He guided me across the living room in the darkness, his hands on my waist, and when we entered the bedroom he lifted me up and laid me down on the bed where we spent another blissful couple of hours making love into the early hours of the morning.

*

Chris and I slipped into a routine when we met, and it has always been the same even after we got married. I always try to work as many shifts as possible Monday to Friday to keep my weekends free to spend with Chris, unless it's during the school holidays when it doesn't really matter. Saturdays are always our day. Sometimes we spend it in bed watching films on the flat-screen TV that Chris had insisted we have mounted on the bedroom wall as soon as he'd moved in. We usually ordered a takeaway and moved to the sofa for the evening before going back to bed again later on. More often than not, though, we would spend the day out together. We would visit Camden Town, see a new exhibition at one of the museums, have lunch at a new restaurant or go for a picnic in Hyde Park, taking the dogs out with us for the day. Chris' love for the city was certainly infectious and I absolutely adored living in London now. Having someone like Chris to explore with just opened my eyes to all the wonderful places that had always been on my doorstep. Sundays mostly revolve around the football. When Tottenham played at home, Chris and Simon were usually at the match which meant I could spend the day with Sue at Borough Market wandering the food stalls, drooling over all the wonderful international foods. I would pick up bits and bobs for us to cook with during the week. Or some days, like today, I would get up early and make my way to Brick Lane, possibly my favourite place in London, to go vintage shopping.

*

I picked up a cappuccino as I got off the tube and took a quick walk to 'The Old Truman Brewery' where there is usually either a vintage or crafts market for me to wander around. This morning, though, it had been turned into a food hall. I walked up and down the stalls, picking up the odd small portion to nibble off a stick or out of a napkin. Chris was planning to get the tube here after football to meet me for dinner, so I didn't want to eat too much.

I wandered back out onto the street, picking up the pace as I approached Brick Lane and all the glorious vintage shops that it holds. I loved being here on a Sunday; the streets were lined with people selling their own second-hand goods, meaning there were always great bargains to be had. Sometimes there were street performers that enhanced the vibrant atmosphere of the street even more, and I always found myself walking along the street with a smile on my face. I spent the next few idyllic hours rummaging through vintage and bric-a-brac shops, and I was content and exhausted by the afternoon. I looked down at my watch – the Tottenham match had finished half an hour ago so I should expect a call from Chris when he was off the tube any time now. I walked into the garden of 'Fuse', a huge bar at the end of the street that has a big outdoor garden crammed full with picnic tables. I bought a cider and sat myself down, shopping bags scattered around my feet, and dedicated some time to my second favourite past time while waiting for Chris to arrive – people watching!

*

Chris called not long after I'd sat down, and shortly after he came strolling into the garden looking pleased with himself – which I knew meant that Tottenham had won. He went to the bar and bought a beer for himself before joining me on the bench. We chatted away and I filled him in on my day of shopping, showing him the items out of my shopping bags, and he filled me in on his day of football, explaining the match in great detail, his hands moving around animatedly as he spoke. After enjoying a couple of drinks, we headed back out onto the street, famous for its Bangladeshi curry houses, and picked the busiest restaurant. We went in and sat down at a table in the corner, pulling our chairs in nearer to each other and linking our legs around each other's under the table. The evening passed as the time always does when I'm with Chris: too quickly. All too soon we were back on the tube heading home again, another weekend over. As we entered the flat, I walked straight through to the bedroom and dumped my shopping bags on the floor. I fell back onto the bed, laying down to rest my aching feet. I knew it wouldn't be long until Chris crept up beside me, and, sure enough, a few minutes later he appeared, his hands roaming over my body as he planted kisses along my neck until I turned my face to him so our lips could meet. We ended the weekend lying in the dark, in the afterglow of our lovemaking. Truly, completely, and utterly in love.

15

BECKY

"The M6 motorway runs from Junction 19 of the M1 at the Catthorpe Interchange near Rugby via Birmingham, then heads north passing Stoke-on-Trent, Manchester, Preston, Carlisle, and terminates at the Gretna junction, Junction 45. It is just short of the Scottish border. It becomes the A74 motorway which continues to Glasgow as the M74. It is the longest motorway in the United Kingdom." – John.

The next morning, I kissed Chris goodbye before jumping out of the car at the entrance to the home. Every now and then when my shifts work out, Chris could drop me off on his way to work so I didn't have to get the bus. Sometimes during the school holidays, Chris would come in with me for the day and spend time with the patients or accompany me when I took patients out. Obviously they all adore him, especially when he comes in and organises football matches in the home's huge back garden – although the excitement usually gets too much for some patients and more than once it's ended in tears. But today, though, Chris sped off, beeping at me before turning the corner and driving off out of sight. I turned from the road once he was gone and made my way into the building.

*

Oliver was standing by the front door again, in exactly the same place I had left him on Friday, chin to chest, fingering his bouncy ball.

"Morning, Oliver," I said, and he shyly turned his head away before muttering a very faint, "Hello," back at me.

I grabbed a cappuccino from the machine in the

hallway before heading to my office and unlocking the door. I had another Monday to Friday week this week, which meant I had a whole weekend with Chris to look forward to.

I turned my computer on and threw myself into my paperwork, hoping I could get it all done this morning, leaving myself the afternoon free to interact with the patients. A few hours later, as I filed away my last behaviour report, I looked up at the clock, pleased when I realised that it was only just past lunchtime. I left my office, glad to finally be out of there, and I headed downstairs towards the kitchen.

The home is set up like a huge house, and the staff and patients move around freely. I's a privately run facility, meaning that most of the patients' families pay for them to live here, with only one or two special cases being funded by the government.

There was one patient, Nick, who was here voluntarily. His family pay for him to be here as he is more comfortable here than he is in the outside world. He has a mild form of Downs Syndrome, and he is quite capable of looking after himself if he so wished, but he loves it here and doesn't want to leave. He thinks that he is smarter than everyone else and is always up to mischief. He especially loves the attention from the nurses and other female members of staff. He genuinely believes that he is in a relationship with Geri Halliwell from the Spice Girls. I would often walk into a room to overhear him telling other patients how he had just gotten off the phone with her.

"I've just got off the phone with my girlfriend, Geri Halliwell," he would say loudly in his Bristolian accent, always using her full name. "She's in America at the moment so she can't visit, but she should be back by Christmas." The other patients ignored him, never taking any notice, and the doctors and nurses were split between letting him carry on with the harmless fantasy and trying to get him to snap out of it. I thought it was pretty innocent, and as he enjoyed his fantasy life so much, I let him get on with it when we were together. I was unlucky enough to be with him once or twice when she appeared on the TV, or when a song of hers came onto the radio.

"That's my girlfriend. That's my girlfriend, Geri Halliwell," he would repeat over and over again, smacking his lips together and smiling. I would smile and nod, chuckling to myself.

Nick was in the kitchen when I entered, and he watched as I flicked the kettle on and pulled a packet of cup-a-soup out of one of the cupboards.

"That's my girlfriend Geri Halliwell's favourite. Cream of mushroom. She just loves it," he said, and I shook my head smiling to myself as he wandered off into the adjoining common room. I boiled the kettle and poured my soup into a large mug before following Nick next door.

I spotted John, who, as usual, was sitting on one of the sofas, hunched over his laptop. I wandered over to say hello. I looked down at his laptop screen when I reached him and as always it was filled with barely eligible, tiny, coloured font. John is *obsessed* with roads. He carries his laptop with him everywhere he goes, and he uses it to record every single piece of information he learns on any road, motorway, or highway, as well as anything to do with roads, motorways, or highways. He records all this information into one Word document saved to his laptop, which is now well over a thousand pages long. The bar along the right-hand-side of the screen is only about a millimetre in size. Every day he uses a different coloured font, so the document is just a colourful mess of information.

Some of the other patients were sat around the TV watching a police traffic program, and the narration was a steady stream in the background: *"…The man, caught doing one-hundred-and-eighty miles per hour on the M6 in the west midlands during this sixty-five mile car chase in January, almost outpaced the police helicopter in the stolen vehicle…"* John was typing away furiously, I could hear his robotic voice muttering quietly under his breath, and his eyes were fixed intently on the screen, fingers tapping away, flying across the keyboard.

"The M6 motorway runs from Junction 19 of the M1 at the Catthorpe Interchange near Rugby via Birmingham, then heads north passing Stoke-on-Trent, Manchester, Preston, Carlisle, and terminates at the Gretna junction, Junction 45. It is just short of the Scottish border. It becomes the A74 motorway which continues to Glasgow as the M74. It is the longest motorway in the United Kingdom." He continued on and on to himself, hesitating on words, but forcing them out as if having to relieve himself of all the information he knows about this road until he has said everything out loud.

I looked down at his typing and saw that he was documenting this police chase in today's colour, blue, which was a lot better than yesterday's colour, yellow, which was almost illegible on the bright white screen. I knew this information would be committed to his memory forever now, ready to be brought up in the future the next time the M6 was mentioned.

*

I spent most of the afternoon in the common room, in amongst the madness that fills it every day. I still loved every minute. Towards the end of the day, another carer named Karen entered the room. She was being followed very closely by another patient, Harry. Harry is obsessed with Karen and follows her everywhere. I'm sure that he thinks that Karen is his mother, like the way you read in the papers that a duckling was adopted by a mother dog in amongst her litter of puppies, or how a calf will be adopted by a horse that has lost its foal, but they grow up happily never knowing any different. The love that radiated off Harry for Karen (and only Karen!) is plain to see. Sometimes I wonder if it's love or obsession. It's certainly a thin line.

Harry, like many autistic people, is obsessed with his and his loved one's daily schedule and timings. I started listening to their conversation as they entered the common room, thankful that it was Karen and not me that was the object of his affection.

"What have you got in your hand?" he asked Karen repeatedly in the same monotone, robotic, almost whiny voice that John uses. Karen was strolling through the common room, with Harry shuffling along behind her, closely at her heels. I could see her debating whether or not to tell him what it was, and I could literally see the thought process running through her head as she tried to think of an excuse before the pause went on for too long. She sighed as she answered him.

"It's my car tax information, Harry, I've got to tax my car when I finish work," she said. Harry stopped dead in his tracks, and I could see the appearance of panic on his face as he started stammering, shutting his eyes tightly on each word.

"But, but, but, but," he stammered, before the words could explode from his mouth in quick succession, "but, but you never told me you had to tax your car today! That wasn't in your plans! You said you were working here at the home with me until four-thirty, then home, dinner at six, then shower, watch TV, then bed! You did not mention getting your car taxed!" I felt sorry for Karen and I could see the exasperation on her usually patient face.

"I know, Harry, I've only just remembered that it needed doing, okay?"

Pause.

"No," he said. Karen sighed.

"I went to the toilet earlier without informing you, Harry, was that okay!?" she said, catching my eye. She raised an eyebrow at me and smiled. Harry looked up at her dismally.

"No!" he cried, genuinely dismayed. "What time!?"

16

CHRIS

"Have you heard of the Cradley Heath Secondary School?" – Paul Marsh, Headteacher.

"Come on, guys, I need your eyes and ears for a second, please!"

I was stood outside on the school pitches, attempting to get a group of year eleven boys to play a decent game of hockey. It was a losing battle, and not just because it was the last lesson on Friday. In year eleven, due to the GCSEs approaching, the boys and girls were split into different groups for PE. I had the group of boys lined up on the gravel hockey pitch and one of my colleagues, Tim Smith, had the year eleven girls next to us on the grass football pitch. The boys were not at all interested in listening to me talk about 'field player with goalkeeping privileges' while their hormones were running wild and the girls were parading around half naked on the football pitch next to them. If I hadn't been so exasperated with them all, it would have been funny.

Tim Smith should never have been allowed to become a PE teacher. He was the most competitive person I had ever met and everything he does or teaches he expects to be met with 110% concentration and effort. His passion is football, and he adores our school teams – but he is hated by every one of our competitors. When our team plays other schools and he's refereeing, he could be so blatantly biased that I was embarrassed to be associated with him. He would turn a blind eye to fouls from our team, lengthen injury time to help us get last minute goals, and I had even seen him give our team a penalty for absolutely no reason at all, oblivious to, or not caring about, the angry cries from pupils, parents, and teachers from the other school. The fact that Tim had been given this group of fifteen-year-old girls, who were not even remotely interested in sport, let alone football, was comical.

The group of boys and myself had made it out to the pitch first. As we were walking away from the changing rooms, I could hear Tim screaming into the girls' changing rooms, ordering them to hurry up, getting more and more frustrated with each second that passed. Eventually the girls started to saunter out, their arms linked, laughing, chatting, flicking their hair over their shoulders, and wiggling their bums as they walked past the group of boys. They'd pulled their socks up to their knees and they wore their white polo shirts tied up under their bras, flat stomachs on show.

Tim stormed out behind them, clutching a handful of colourful bibs, red in the face already. When they arrived on the pitch, he split up the group, issuing bibs to half the class. The girls squealed and jumped up and down when they were put into a team with their friends, and moaned, argued, and pouted when they weren't.

Ignoring their protests, Tim sent them out onto the pitch, and after a brief talk where he barked orders at them as they giggled and whispered to each other, the ball was placed down on the centre circle and he blew the whistle to start the game. Immediately he started screaming at them as if their lives depended on this match.

"Lucy! LUCY! Keep your eye on the ball! Cheryl just ran straight past you! Go on, Sam! Pass it! *Pass it!* Why did you do that? SHE'S ON THE OTHER TEAM! Rachel! One, two! *One, two! For God's sake!* Tiffany, TACKLE HER!"

After a while, one of the girls who had been

wandering around aimlessly near the halfway line suddenly cried out, causing all the girls close to her to turn to see what was happening. She crouched down and started rummaging around in the grass frantically. The girls around her stopped what they were doing and ran over to her. They too dived onto the floor and started searching around in the grass. Hannah, one of the sportier girls in the group, jumped on the abandoned ball and dribbled it up the pitch. She smacked it into the net, causing the goalie, who had been looking down at her nails, to jump out of the way to let it in.

"Lauren, you're supposed to save the ball, for Christ's sake! Why did you move out of the way? You're the goalie!" Tim yelled. He turned furiously in the direction of the group of girls who were still on the floor. He strode across the pitch, his face contorted with anger, to see what the commotion was.

"WHAT THE HELL IS GOING ON?" he screamed. I thought he looked close to a nervous breakdown.

"Joanne has lost one of her earrings, Sir!" came the reply.

*

I glanced down at my watch and was filled with relief to see that it was finally the end of the lesson. I thanked God it was the weekend. I dismissed the boys, who instantly ran off in front of me, racing each other towards the changing rooms. They attempted to push each other over onto the gravel, showing off in front of the sauntering girls who were walking behind them, pretending not to look. I picked the pile of bibs and cones up off the pitch and headed in the direction of the sports hall. I was joined by Tim, who looked angry and defeated.

"I don't know why we bother," he said, and for once I agreed with him. I'd been thinking the same thing for a while now. I'd left my position at the primary school where I'd originally worked eighteen months ago after being offered a job teaching the secondary school students.

Initially, I was filled with excitement about the move. There were more extracurricular activities for me to get involved in, and I was asked to help coach the school's year ten and eleven football teams – both of which were entered into a school league. They also played in several yearly tournaments. Unfortunately, it just hadn't turned out how I'd expected.

When I'd been at school, I'd loved sport more than anything. My friends and I had played for the school football team as well as our Sunday league teams – we couldn't get enough. But the boys here were just not interested, and it was starting to get me down. I didn't feel as if I was making a difference to any of these pupils, and I missed the enthusiasm that the primary school kids had for PE – before they had the worry and distractions these older boys did, like looking cool and worrying about the opposite sex.

Tim and I entered the sports hall, which was really more of a big corrugated shed, which held two sets of changing rooms and a tiny office for the staff. I dumped the bibs and cones back into the store cupboard and sighed at the pile of hockey sticks that had been thrown into a chaotic pile just inside the door. I listened to the shrieks and yells of both sexes coming from the changing rooms, and I breathed another sigh of relief that it was Friday and I would soon be on my way home to spend the weekend with Becky.

I had looked at the weather during the afternoon and was pleased to see that it was supposed to be nice this weekend. I was thinking of suggesting to Becky that we drive down to the coast for the weekend, just the two of us. We could take the dogs, go for some nice walks...

My train of thought was interrupted when one of my colleagues, June Anderson, (who I'd always thought resembled Mrs. Trunchbull from the film *Matilda)* poked her head out of the little PE office, clutching the phone to her chest as she called to me.

"I've got Mr. Marsh on the phone – he wants to see you in his office before you go today," she said, and I sighed once again. Mr. Marsh was the head teacher, and I just did not have the energy for another conversation filled with his excessive enthusiasm for our sports teams right now – all I wanted to do was get home and wrap my arms around my wife.

I collected my things and entered the main building of the school, heading in the direction of Mr. Marsh's office. I walked through the crowded halls in amongst cries of ,"Bye, Sir!" and, "See ya' Monday, Mr. McNulty!" I managed to avoid the kids that flew past either side of me, all rushing to get outside and be free of school for the weekend. I didn't even have the energy to tell them to stop running in the corridors.

As I approached the head's office, a small room situated next door to the school cafeteria, I braced myself for another long chat about the year eleven football team. When I arrived at the door, I took a deep breath and knocked before entering.

Paul Marsh was sat behind his desk, talking agitatedly on the phone. I guessed that he was talking to a parent, and I was glad that it was him and not me. He looked tired. His grey pinstripe suit looked too big for him, and his hair looked thinner. He looked as if he needed a holiday – but then, didn't we all. When he noticed me at the door, he signalled for me to sit down on the chair opposite him, which I did while I waited for him to finish his conversation.

A few minutes later, he said goodbye before putting

the phone back down in its cradle. He paused with his hand resting on it for a second, staring at a point on his desk, before he sat back in his chair to look at me.

"Chris," he said, before falling silent, and I instantly became alert. I realised that this was not the usual jovial man who bent my ear about football.

I looked at him, my mind working overtime, wondering where this was going, trying to think if I'd done something wrong.

"I've got some news," he finally continued after a pause. He leant forward and rested his elbows on his desk, letting out a huge sigh. I could feel adrenalin start to rush through me as I wracked my brain, trying to guess what on earth he could be talking about.

"Good news for you... Not so good for me, I suppose." He trailed off and I stared at him, wondering why he was talking in riddles. I stayed quiet, watching him until he spoke again.

"Have you heard of the Cradley Heath Secondary School?" he asked, finally looking me in the eye. I paused and thought for a second before I slowly shook my head.

17

BECKY

"A sob escaped my lips," – Becky.

For the first time since I'd found out that my mother had died, I felt completely panicked and out of my depth. I was in the flat, pacing around the living room – which was not an easy feat in this tiny space. This tiny space! This flat is just way too tiny! I didn't know whether to sit and wait for Chris to get home from work, or whether to run away and not have to face him. I screwed my face up, desperately trying to hold back the tears that were threatening.

I was panicking, *really* panicking. My heart was pounding. I glanced up at the clock. Chris was due home soon. If I didn't want to face him, I would have to leave now. I could say that I had been called into work – that would give me some time to think, some time to be on my own. But I had never lied to Chris before, and I didn't want to start now. I looked down at the pregnancy test on the table and tears welled in my eyes as I stared at the two blue lines staring back at me. Informing me that I was pregnant. I felt short of breath. This could not be right! We were always so careful! I was on the pill and religious at taking it… How could this happen?

A sob escaped my lips as I sat down on the sofa and held my head in my hands. I separated my fingers and glanced again at the white test sitting on the dark wood in front of me.

I tried to suppress the panic that started creeping over me and to think of other things, when suddenly I remembered something from when Chris and I had first met. I'd gone with him to watch a football match and a couple of his students had been there, too, back when he had taught at the primary school. I'd sat fascinated that day, watching the interaction between them all, and I suddenly remembered a fleeting feeling that I'd had. I had wondered, although only for a moment, what it would be like to actually start a family with him. I'd pushed the thoughts and feelings deep down, though, and hadn't given it much thought ever since. I'd always known that things would take their natural course one day if it's what we both really wanted – when the time was right.

The reality of the situation hit me again. The time was not right! We were too young! The flat is rented and the size of a shoe box! We both love our jobs and Chris loves his social life – this could not be happening at a worse time. I lowered my head further into my hands, and, as the emotion became too overwhelming, I finally let myself cry.

*

I had cried myself out. My face actually hurt from all the crying and my throat felt raw. I decided I'd get in the shower. I would wait for Chris to get home and break the news to him then. That was the right thing to do. Then we could make a decision on how to move forward on this together. I glanced at the clock again – he was already over an hour late. I hid the pregnancy test and got in the shower. I stood with my face under the steaming water, attempting to wash the traces of tears from my face. I knew it would break Chris' heart if he knew I'd been crying.

*

By the time I was out of the shower, a layer of calm had settled over me. I got dressed and sat on the sofa. Chris was nearly two hours late. I couldn't even bring myself to text him. I didn't want to communicate with him until he was here in front of me so we could deal with this properly. I hadn't even looked at my phone since I'd gotten home. I wondered if he'd been trying to ring me. I knew he would be worried if he had and hadn't been able to get through.

It was starting to get dark outside, and I sat in the darkness with no lights on. Just me and my thoughts.

18

CHRIS

"This really could be a dream come true." – Chris.

I shook hands with Mr. Marsh and thanked him for his time. He had certainly given me a lot to think about. I was excited. Really excited. But I tried not to let it run away with me. I had to think of Becky, too.

Cradley Heath was an award-winning private boys' school known for its quality sports students – many of which leave to have professional careers in football, rugby, and athletics. The school also gives scholarships to up to six boys a year who are particularly gifted but cannot afford the tuition fees.

They were looking for another PE teacher to join their team to work with the year ten and eleven boys, getting them prepared for their GCSEs. I was told that exams were taken very seriously at Cradley Heath, but none more seriously than PE. I spent a long time in Mr. Marsh's office that evening, and we talked in depth about the school itself and what they were offering me. We looked at the school's website, which was full of photos of state-of-the-art facilities and there were pages and pages of information on the triumphs of the school's football and rugby teams.

This job would be a dream come true for me. This school and its students represented the exact kind of place that I wanted to work at, and it was exactly the type of place I'd hoped I could teach in one day. This just seemed way too good to be true. It felt like too much information to process.

Mr. Marsh told me that I had to think long and hard this weekend as he needed an answer either way from me by Monday. If I did decide to take up Cradley Heath's offer, he would need to arrange cover for my position here as Mr. King (Cradley Heath's head teacher) wanted me to start work there in the new term, straight after the Easter holidays. Mr. King had extended an invitation for Becky and me to visit the school over the weekend so we could meet him and be shown around. It also meant I could discuss the job and contract with him in further detail. I was thrilled at the thought, and I left Mr. Marsh's office with butterflies in my stomach, heading home to tell Becky the news.

*

I walked towards the car park, the thoughts in my head whirling around. The school was deserted now, all the children were long gone and mine was the last car in the staff car park. Excitement bubbled away inside me, but I kept reminding myself that I shouldn't get my hopes up just yet. It meant we would have to move – leave the city and relocate to Oxford. There were a million reasons why this might not work out. Firstly – Becky. She adored her job as much as I adored mine – if not more. She lived for it, and she had worked so hard over the last few years to get to where she was now.

She would not even remotely budge when I'd begged her to go back to Thailand for a year after our honeymoon. She had been adamant that she didn't want to leave the home. Now we were only a couple of years down the line from then, and I was sure her feelings couldn't have changed that much in that amount of time. Secondly – my mum. She would be completely and utterly devastated if Becky and I moved away. She and Becky were as close as two people could possibly be without actually being mother and daughter. Quite often I would turn up at my mum's after football to find them deep in discussion around the kitchen table, or I would phone Becky when I left work to discover that she had finished early and was with Mum walking the dogs, or that they were out shopping somewhere. It would kill her if we moved away. *Move away?* How could I move away from here? Becky and I loved living in London, could we really leave the city? Would we get bored? Simon was getting married soon, and I knew it would push him over the edge if I left town. There were dozens and dozens of reasons why I couldn't accept the job… but I knew. Becky was the only one that mattered. If she was willing to come with me, nothing else would stop me. This really could be a dream come true.

19

BECKY

"I had the flutter of excited butterflies in my stomach." –
Becky.

Chris was nearly three hours late. It was completely
unlike him. It was typical; it had to be tonight when I
needed him the most but wanted to see him the least. In
another situation it might have been funny how he always
manages to give me exactly what I want.

The living room was completely dark, and I had cramp
in my feet from sitting so still for so long. The thoughts
running around my head were exhausting me.

*

Somehow, without even noticing it, my feelings had
started to U-turn while I'd been sitting here and another
side to this reality hit. This was Chris' baby. Our baby.
Sue's grandchild. A real family. I shook my head, as if it
would help to clear my thoughts. I still had an
overwhelming feeling of being out of my depth, but this
was now joined by a protective feeling. It was as if the
realisation that this was a real baby, that this could be the
start of Chris and I having a real family, had pulled me
out of the shocked state I was in earlier, and now I was
filled with thoughts of what the future might be like if we
actually *had* the baby.

I pictured us renting a bigger place, or maybe even
buying somewhere. Decorating a nursery… I wondered if
it would be a boy or a girl and whether it would look like
me or Chris. The thought of having a little mini-Chris
filled me with joy. My tears had completely dried up now
and I had the flutter of excited butterflies in my stomach,
rather than feeling like I had a huge burden on my

shoulders. I tried to imagine Chris' reaction when I broke the news. But for the first time ever, I had absolutely no idea what to expect from him.

*

My senses were heightened from spending so long sitting in the dark. I heard Chris' car pull up outside the building and his light footsteps as he jogged down the steps in his trainers to the front door. The door opened and he walked in, flicking on the light and calling out my name as he did so.

"Becky?" he said before catching sight of me sitting on the sofa. It took me a moment to register the bag of Thai takeaway that he held in one hand and the bottle of champagne in the other. I looked up at him, blinking in the light, my mind running at a thousand miles an hour.

Does he know? How does he know! Does this mean he's happy? That we're going to keep it? That he's not upset? That I don't have to break this news to him?

But he looked just as confused as me. I watched his face change as he registered me sitting alone in the living room, in the dark, with a puffy red face. That's when I realised with a sinking feeling that he obviously didn't know about the baby. There was no way he could know. I still had to drop this bombshell. This had all happened in a split second and before I knew it Chris was beside me on the sofa, holding my face in his hands asking me what was wrong. As I looked into his eyes, which were flicking back and forth between mine, I was hit with such an intense feeling of love it took my breath away. Seeing him finally, I now knew. I wanted to have this baby. So, so much. I opened my mouth to speak, and the words tumbled from my mouth one after the other as if I had no control over them.

20

"What do you think?" — Becky.

The night passed in a blur of emotion. Chris held Becky's face in his hands and watched the tears spill out from her eyes and roll down her red, blotchy cheeks. Becky, who thought she had no tears left, found herself racked with sobs again and again as the stress and emotion of the evening took over. She couldn't remember afterwards how she'd actually broken the news to Chris, but she would never forget his reaction. She watched his face completely light-up as she told him that she was pregnant, his eyes glittery with excitement. He pulled her against him, and Becky sat with her head against his chest as he rocked her back and forth, kissing the top of her head until the sobs subsided. When she finally pulled away and looked into his face again, they sat back and talked well into the night. Chris asked how Becky was feeling and she told him everything. The shock, the worry, the fear that they were too young, that now was not a good time – but then she explained the feeling of calm she'd had at the thought of them actually having a child together. Chris sat and listened carefully to every word she spoke, holding her hand, taking everything in.

Becky glanced at him. He hadn't actually said anything either way, yet. She realised she still didn't know what his thoughts were. "What do you think?" she finally whispered. Realising, though she didn't know why, that she was scared of his answer. She was unable to meet his eyes – instead she fiddled with the corner of the cushion that was on her lap, as if it was the most fascinating thing she had ever seen.

"I want to keep it," he said excitedly, sounding more certain than she had ever heard him before. Becky's heartbeat quickened and her eyes jumped up to meet his.

"But," he continued, staring into her eyes, causing her heart to fall through the never ending black hole that had once been her stomach, "*I* want to do whatever *you* want to do." Becky's eyes brimmed again and she whispered her reply, eyes cast down, shocked at what she was about to admit.

"I want to keep it, too."

Chris leant over and cupped Becky's face in his hands and all of a sudden Becky was sobbing again, wondering once more how it was possible that she had any tears left, then she was laughing and sobbing, and Chris started sobbing, and excitement bubbled around them as they sat on the sofa, holding each other, laughing, with tears running down their faces.

*

It was the early hours of the morning, and Becky and Chris sat wrapped in blankets on the sofa. Becky was exhausted from crying and had a throbbing headache, but she was too scared to take a painkiller, not knowing if it was safe to do so with the baby. Chris got up and put some of the Thai food he'd bought earlier onto a plate for her and began to heat it up in the microwave. Once it was warmed through, he placed it on her lap, ordering her to eat with a smile.

"You're eating for two, now!" he said, and Becky smiled at the old cliché. "So," he continued after Becky had eaten a few mouthfuls, "I, errr… had some news of my own tonight." Becky looked up, instantly alert as she remembered the bottle of champagne that Chris had held in his hand as he'd walked through the front door. She looked up at him quizzically with a mouth full of food.

Chris slipped onto the sofa next to her, pulling the blanket around so it covered both of them as he started to relay the story of his afternoon. Becky listened, filled with pride and love for him as he spoke of the potential job offer, and she listened as he told her of the invitation to go and see the school this weekend, if they wanted to.

"We won't be able to make it there tomorrow, now, though," he said, glancing up at the clock. "It's so late and you need your sleep. We should go to a doctor tomorrow to get this confirmed," Chris said, waving at the test that now lay on the table again.

Becky laid her hand on top of his. "We're going. We'll call first thing in the morning to confirm and will drive up there early. The doctor can wait until Monday. We can get a few hours' sleep now and have an early night tomorrow to make up for it."

Chris raised his eyebrow at her last remark and Becky laughed. She pulled her hand away and put the now empty plate on the table in front of them. Chris picked it up and walked to the kitchen to rinse it under the tap.

Becky stood up and brushed herself down before giving Chris a kiss on the cheek as she walked past him, heading towards the bedroom, exhausted by the evening's events, but filled with a joy she hadn't known was possible.

*

Chris stood at the kitchen sink, his head spinning from everything that had happened that day. The curl of excitement in his stomach at the prospect of the new job was unfurling. Becky's reaction was not what he had expected. She'd listened intently and not given anything away, but it hadn't been the point blank 'no' at moving that he'd thought it would be. And the baby! He was still numb with the shock of it but the happiness that had filled him when he'd heard the news still overwhelmed him and he couldn't get the smile off his face.

He put the plate away and turned off the lights, following Becky into the bedroom where she was just getting into bed, pulling the covers up over her. He looked at her for a second and they both smiled at each other when their eyes caught. Chris climbed into the bed and slid up next to her, kissing her on the mouth as he rested his hand on her flat stomach. Becky smiled under his lips, and he smiled, too, looking down at her before they cuddled up, whispering to each other in the darkness, talking about their future.

21

"Let's do it!" – Becky.

Becky sat looking out of the window as Chris drove the car out of London. It was a lovely, warm spring day and she watched as the scenery turned from the hustle and bustle of the busy city to rolling green fields and postcard pretty villages as they headed towards Oxford. The radio was on quietly in the background and Chris hummed along, tapping his fingers on the wheel as he drove. Becky looked over at him, surprised at how relaxed he seemed. He had gotten up early that morning to phone and let the school know he was free to visit. Mr. King had been delighted and had given Chris directions, arranging to meet in the early afternoon.

Chris had brought Becky breakfast in bed, kissing her face and running his hand across her stomach once again, causing her face to almost break in two with a smile. She sat and ate her breakfast propped up against the pillows, watching him as he got ready. He ironed his suit and Becky smiled when he entered the room wearing it, admiring how handsome he looked. She rarely got to see him this smart because they both wore their own clothes to work. Seeing him dressed up reminded her of their wedding day. Becky got up out of bed and walked over to him, barefooted in her pyjamas, to stand on tiptoes to give him a kiss.

*

They were nearing the school. The drive hadn't taken nearly as long as they'd thought it would and they'd only been in the car a little over an hour when the sat-nav started to tell them that they were close. Becky put her hand on Chris' knee and squeezed. He looked over at her, flashing a smile. A little while later they pulled into the grounds of Cradley Heath School, butterflies in both their stomachs. It was a magnificent red brick building that seemed to go on forever surrounded by beautiful, perfectly manicured grounds. They drove onto an immaculate gravel driveway that led to a large car park surrounded by a varnished post and rail fence. Chris parked the car before getting out and taking in the surroundings.

"It looks like Hogwarts." he joked, gesturing to the grand building, and Becky realised that even though he looked completely calm and cool, he was obviously nervous. She chuckled at him and walked over to clutch his hand.

"You're going to be great," she said, and Chris grinned at her. Chris and Becky walked hand-in-hand towards the impressive building, following the signs to the reception. Their heads moved from side-to-side as they attempted to take everything in. Pristine tennis courts sat in fenced cages in front of them and a gleaming running track spread out across a field to the side. Becky could hear the shouts and whistles from a football match being played nearby, although she couldn't see where. As they approached the main entrance, both of them realised that the building was even more beautiful than they had originally thought. It looked like a grand five-star hotel with the beautiful driveway and huge pillars on either side of enormous glass front doors.

They entered the huge, surprisingly modern reception, walking across gleaming marble floors and staring up at the high ceilings. Their footsteps echoed with each step that they took. Once inside, it finally started to feel a bit more like a school. There were huge wooden shields lining the walls with names and dates inscribed on small metal plaques, recording dozens and dozens of different sporting triumphs. Huge glass trophy cases were filled with gleaming cups and medals in each corner, and there were dozens of beautiful sports photographs lining the walls in amongst photos of people receiving numerous awards.

It was quiet in the reception, with it being a Saturday, and they approached the smart, friendly woman who stood behind a grand oak desk. Chris grinned at her, and Becky could see the woman blush slightly when she met his eye. Becky didn't mind, she was used to the reaction that women had to Chris' smile by now.

"Hello, I am here to see Mr. King. My name is Chris McNulty, and this is my wife, Becky," he said, and the receptionist smiled at them both, offering them a seat before picking up the phone and speaking into it quietly. Becky sat down and Chris wandered around the huge room, peering into the trophy cases and gazing at the pictures that lined the walls.

After a while, Becky became aware of quick footsteps coming from a corridor around the corner and an older gentleman appeared in the hallway in a flourish, wearing dark blue jeans with a white shirt and dark blazer. On his feet he wore shiny polished brown shoes. His hair and beard were silver, and he had a huge smile to match his sparkling blue eyes. He looked every inch the headmaster, and Becky could not help but smile up at him, liking him instantly.

Chris turned around, and, before he could even speak, the man had caught up with him, slapping him on the back and took his hand, thrusting it up and down. "Hello!" he boomed, and his voice echoed around the huge room. The receptionist behind the desk watched them, an amused smile playing at her lips, obviously used to his enthusiastic presence. Before Chris could answer, the man had turned to Becky with his arms wide and he strode towards her as if she were an old friend.

"And who is this?" he exclaimed as Becky stood up, smoothing the skirt of her grey suit down before she was embraced in his arms. He hugged her so tightly for a fleeting moment Becky was actually worried for the baby. He stood back and Becky could see the surprise and amusement in Chris' eyes.

"Welcome, welcome, thank you so much for coming on such short notice! What a pleasure it is to have you here!" he cried, and Becky cocked her head slightly at Chris and he raised his eyebrow at her over Mr. King's shoulder. "You must be Becky," he said, turning on his heel, "and you must be Chris!" Chris walked over to Becky and slipped his arm around her as the man spoke, smiling.

"My name is Dave King, please call me Dave, and welcome to our school. I am so pleased to have you here! I've heard such great things about you!" Chris didn't have time to wonder who he had heard these great things from, as before he knew it they were being whisked off on a full tour of the school. There was never a dull moment. Dave did not stop speaking and he regaled them with stories of the school and its pupils, followed by his raucous laugh as they walked through the corridors. He showed them the state-of-the-art classrooms, the dining room, the staff's individual offices as well as their communal staff room, and then he really found his stride and started talking about the school's sports department. Chris' eyes were wide with excitement as they strolled through huge indoor gyms, the indoor sports centre, badminton courts, and a room filled solely with brand new trampolines.

"I can see you are itching to get out and see our football pitches," Dave said to Chris before winking at Becky. She smiled back at him, filled with fondness for this kind man. They walked out the back door of the sports centre and Dave casually threw his arm about, pointing at outhouse buildings as they passed.

"Dance studio, indoor swimming pool, another gym," he said, and Becky could see the excitement mounting on Chris' face as they hurried along behind, desperately trying to keep up with him. As they rounded a corner, more sports pitches came into view.

"Hockey pitch, netball courts, rounders pitch, and *football pitches*," he finished with a flourish as Becky and Chris hurried along the path, past the netball pitches to a huge sports field where there were two immaculate, full-sized football pitches side-by-side. Chris' eyes followed the direction Dave was pointing as he continued talking: "And my pride and joy, our new, full-sized, floodlit stadium! It was finished just last year. It seats three-hundred people and has the capacity for two-thousand!" Chris' stride grew as he hurried to catch up, and he started firing questions at Dave who was more than happy to answer. They chatted away to each other, hardly pausing for breath, and Becky followed behind, looking around at the beautiful countryside that lay just beyond the school's grounds, only half listening. She would have been quite bored by their chat if Chris' excitement hadn't been so infectious. Dave took them inside the stadium for a tour and Chris' eyes were almost popping out of his head. Becky knew that he was envisioning himself stood on the sideline, cheering his team on.

They exited the stadium through a different door and carried on walking through the acres of land that the school seemed to own. They passed another athletics field that held long jump sand boxes and more sprinting tracks. After a while they started heading back towards the main school building, and Becky noticed rows of neat cottages lined up adjacent to the school that she hadn't seen earlier.

"Ah, so you've spotted our teacher accommodation!" Dave said, smiling, and Becky jumped guiltily, feeling like a naughty school child. She had tuned out of their conversation and let her mind wander, thinking of the baby that she had not had much time to think about so far today. Luckily Chris spoke straight away, diverting the attention away from her.

"Teacher accommodation?" he asked.

"Yes, yes. We offer accommodation to our teachers and their spouses, if required," Dave replied flippantly. Chris tried to process the information but couldn't think of a response before Dave spoke again. "Let's go and get some lunch, shall we, and we can talk about all the nitty gritty bits in detail!"

*

There was a late lunch waiting for them on platters when they arrived in Dave King's huge, beautifully decorated office. The three of them sat together eating delicious sandwiches and homemade cakes while Dave filled Chris in on what he could expect as a member of staff at Cradley Heath. The package and benefits that were being offered were wonderful, and Becky tried to hide how shocked she was as Dave told Chris everything that was included. After they had eaten, he took them outside and showed them around one of the school's cottages, explaining that Becky and Chris could choose to live here on site if they wanted to.

By the time Chris and Becky left a few hours later, with the promise that Chris would call on Monday to let Dave know his decision either way, they were both exhausted. They sat in silence as Chris reversed the car across the car park and even as they continued down the gravel driveway towards the main road. Chris' mind was racing and the excitement that had started on Friday evening was now an even tighter ball in his stomach. His mouth felt dry, and for once he didn't know what to say.

"What are you thinking?" Becky asked when they reached the main road, interrupting Chris' thoughts. He couldn't answer. Too many things were flying around in his head. He knew for certain that he wanted this job and that he would be more than willing to move here, he would even be willing to leave his mum and Simon, as long as Becky was happy to come with him.

The package that the school had offered Chris was like nothing he had ever imagined. His jaw had nearly hit the floor when Dave told him the starting salary. It was almost as much as both he and Becky were earning now put together! On top of that, they were offering him and Becky one of the cottages on site for an amazing subsidised price. For a large two-bedroom cottage on the school grounds they would be paying less in rent than what they paid at the moment for the tiny flat back in London. Chris pictured Becky and the baby in the new house, he pictured them all being able to walk out of the front door and into the rolling fields that surrounded the school.

"What are *you* thinking?" he replied, a smile playing at his lips as he took his eyes off the road for a split second to glimpse at her face.

"I asked you first!" she said, laughing, and the car went quiet for a second before she spoke again. "I loved it. I think it's perfect for you and I think you should take the job," she said, and Chris sat there, stunned. This was not what he had been expecting.

"You'd move here?" he said, unable to keep the exhilaration out of his voice, and Becky laughed. The sound made Chris' heart hurt in his chest. He kept flicking his eyes from the road to her face.

"If you were moving here of course I would move here!" she said in her sing song voice, and Chris tried to process the information.

"But what would you do about your job?" Chris asked, knowing that this was the big question. He glanced at her again and saw her shrug her shoulders out of the corner of his eye.

"I will be absolutely devastated to leave. But things are changing. We're having a baby," she said matter-of-factly, and they both smiled at the words. "So, I'm going to have to take some time off anyway. The flat is too small, we'd have to move somewhere bigger, and the cottages are so beautiful...' she trailed off. She turned to face him, and she could see the excitement plastered all over his face. He didn't know what to say, and silence hung in the air for a moment before Becky spoke again.

"Let's do it!" she said, turning in her seat to look at him, feeling excited herself. Chris' face broke into a grin and they both laughed, driving along in the dusk back towards London.

22

CHRIS

"You will never know how much I appreciate it." – *Chris.*

On Monday morning, I made my way into school earlier than usual and I handed in my written resignation to Paul Marsh. He looked across the desk at me and smiled a sad smile, shaking his head.

"I will be so sad to see you go, Chris," he said. "I knew once you'd seen the place you wouldn't be able to say no. Was it the new stadium that did it?"

"The stadium is amazing. The whole school is. I absolutely love it. I can't tell you what an amazing opportunity this is for me. Thank you so much for being so supportive, you will never know how much I appreciate it," I said sincerely, and Paul smiled warmly at me, nodding his head and sitting back in his chair to glance over my hand-written resignation.

Shortly after, I walked through the corridors, heading back towards the sports centre, and I saw things about the school that I'd never noticed before. It desperately needed a lick of paint and the corridors looked dull, cramped, and boring compared to Cradley Heath's. I felt a thrill at the thought of starting there as a teacher next term. Living in a proper house, being able to get up in the morning and walk across the field to work instead of driving through grid-locked, rush-hour London traffic. I don't think I'd ever felt happier as I crossed the playground and entered the small sports office, preparing to tell my colleagues the news.

23

BECKY

"I had broken the news that I would be leaving in a few weeks." – Becky.

I'd never felt as depressed and sad as I did at that moment as I walked up the path towards work, knowing I had to hand my notice in. I couldn't be happier for Chris, and I was truly excited at the thought of us starting this next chapter in our lives, especially as we now had a baby on the way. But the thought of leaving my job left me feeling completely desolate, and I didn't know how I was going to bring myself to tell Mark as I walked in the front door and headed towards his office.

As soon as I sat across from him I promptly burst into tears, before the words even had chance to come out of my mouth. Mark was completely shocked to have me weeping in his office and passed me a tissue whilst trying to figure out what on earth was wrong. I *never* cried! I blamed it on the pregnancy – I'd cried more in the last few days then I had in my entire life!

I told Mark the entire story, including the news about the baby. I felt as if I needed to give him a better reason for leaving the job I adored than just Chris getting a new job. Mark listened, lending a sympathetic ear, and by the time I left his office just over an hour later I felt much better. I had officially handed in my notice, and I would work my remaining rostered shifts which finished a couple of weeks before Easter and the end of Chris' term. Mark offered me any shifts I wanted after I'd left on an ad hoc basis, even after the baby was born.

"We can keep you on the books to use as cover, and if you give me an idea of any hours you want to work in the future at any point I'll try and sort them out for you. Even if you want to come down for a few days a month, that's fine, you can obviously stay here in the staff accommodation if you wanted to, just let me know," he said, and I smiled up at him as I thanked him. I wondered if the rumours were true that he had feelings for me. He did always seem to go out of his way for me and he always helped me in any way he could, but I'd always hoped that it was because I was good at my job, rather than for any other reason.

*

I spent the rest of the morning in the common room with John. I had broken the news that I would be leaving in a few weeks and now I was trying to coax some conversation out of him. I had the whole day set aside tomorrow to take him out, so I asked him where he would like to go. As usual he wanted to go for a drive, and he was busy planning a route around central London that he wanted to do by car. I knew it would be a nightmare, though, with the traffic, pedestrians, cyclists, and constant queuing at traffic lights. I knew that John would be impatient with the constant hold-ups. He preferred to be on the move, maximising the number of roads we covered in the time we had.

"How about we take a drive to up to Oxford?" I suggested. "I can show you the route I will be driving up to my new house? It's a nice journey."

He thought for a second, and I could see him weighing the idea up in his head.

"Yes. We could take the A40, then the M25, then the A40 again to Oxford," he said, dragging out every syllable of 'Oxford'. I smiled; I didn't question if he was right, he usually was. I knew that offering to use a sat-nav would bring out a meltdown. He hated the constant interruption of the voice giving instructions on where to go, especially when it contradicted what he was saying. Once, I'd had to pull the car over onto the hard shoulder of the motorway to calm him down when he'd really lost his temper. He'd banged his fists down on the dashboard in complete frustration when the sat-nav told me to exit the motorway a junction before he wanted me to.

I was making a mental note to call Chris when I got into my office to tell him I needed the car tomorrow when Karen came through the front door. As usual, Harry was following so closely at her heels he was almost tripping over her feet. Karen looked around the common room before spotting me. She headed over in my direction and I noticed she looked tired.

"Karen was angry with me today," Harry stated matter-of-factly, and Karen rolled her eyes up towards the ceiling.

"I'm not angry with you Harry," she said in a voice that I recognised, the strained voice you get after a long morning or afternoon of taking patients out of the home.

"Where have you been?" I asked, smiling.

"We went to visit Maureen today, didn't we, Harry?" Karen said, looking at him fondly.

Maureen had worked in the kitchen here since the home first opened over forty years ago. She was a lovely woman who was adored by everyone. She had retired two weeks ago at the age of sixty-eight and had been on holiday with her husband since then. I reminded myself that I needed to send her a card before Chris and I moved.

"Harry and I went to the shop to pick out a nice card for her today. Then we went to Costa to grab a coffee. I went to the toilet while Harry wrote in the card, and I didn't even think anything of it when he handed the envelope back to me, sealed. It wasn't until we were sat around Maureen's kitchen table and she nearly choked on her piece of cake while reading the card that I realised I should have checked it. The card read: *'Dear Maureen, I will miss you. I hope you don't die soon. Kind Regards, Harry Jacobs'."*

I threw my head back and belly laughed. I rarely ever laugh in public – Chris is usually the only person who causes me to really laugh out loud, but I was laughing so hard my eyes were watering. Karen started laughing too, and Harry looked at each of us in turn, smiling but confused. A few other patients were looking in our direction, but I just couldn't stop myself, I laughed and laughed and tears streamed down my face. There was a split second as I was laughing when I nearly crossed the very fine line into sadness and burst into tears at the thought of not being a part of this anymore.

24

CHRIS

"Well, that's actually not the only news we've got." –
Chris.

I sat outside the care home in the car, pulled up on the kerb with the engine still running, watching Becky walk down the path towards me. She looked tired. I could see faint shadows beneath her eyes. Her whole face lit up, though, when she saw me waiting and her pace picked up until she reached the car. We grinned at each other through my window as she walked around to the other side of the car and jumped into the passenger seat. I leant over and gave her a kiss.

"How did it go?" I asked, staring at her face, knowing that she would have had a difficult time handing her notice in today. She sighed.

"Not too bad. I got really upset, though." My eyes flew to hers, Becky rarely admitted to being upset and she definitely didn't let other people see it.

"I'm okay!" she said. "I think it must be the hormones."

I frowned at her. I hated the thought of her being upset, but she smiled at me reassuringly. We chatted as we drove to the doctors, both full of excited nerves. We had an appointment just after six o'clock and my stomach was tied in knots with the anticipation. I just wanted to hear a doctor say the words and confirm that this was really happening, that we were having a baby. Becky seemed just as distracted and fidgety as I did, and after a while the conversation slowed down and then stopped. We settled into a companionable silence as we drove, with the radio playing softly in the background.

*

It was almost dark by the time we left the doctor's surgery hand-in-hand, both smiling. The doctor had confirmed that Becky was indeed pregnant. I squeezed her hand as we approached the car.

"Do you want to go somewhere for dinner?" I asked as we got into the car. "Your choice?"

"I think we should go to your mum's..." Becky replied, and I felt a sinking feeling in my stomach. I had put telling my mum about our move to the back of my mind. I was absolutely dreading breaking the news to her.

"Why don't we do that another night?" I said. "We'll go out tonight, just the two of us, and celebrate. She won't be expecting us tonight now anyway, so there probably won't be enough food," I trailed off, lamely.

"I texted her earlier and told her we'd be there for dinner at around eight o'clock," Becky said casually, looking out of the window so I couldn't see her face. "We've got to tell her, Chris. It's only six weeks until we move, and we've got so much to do between now and then. It's not fair to her to keep her in the dark."

"Okay, okay," I said, knowing that she was right. I turned the engine on and swung the car around, dreading the hours ahead. I felt like a naughty child that had done something wrong as I started driving towards my mum's house.

*

"My darlings!" Mum cried as she opened the door, arms flung wide, ready to embrace Becky the second we walked through the door. Becky stepped straight into her arms and hugged her back, smiling widely. When Mum let Becky go, I stooped down to squeeze her, too. Seeing how happy she was that we were there made me feel even guiltier. Was I being selfish wanting to move away? I started to panic, but I took one look at Becky as she stepped into the kitchen and thought of the news we'd just received at the doctors, of the big house and the extra money, and I knew that we were doing the right thing.

I followed them both into the kitchen where my mum was starting to pull a huge chilli out of the oven, letting a blast of heat out with it as the oven door opened. Becky was leant back against the kitchen side, chatting to her, looking utterly gorgeous in a pair of dark blue jeans and a tight grey jumper. Her beautiful long hair was tucked behind her ears. I dragged my eyes away from her and sat down at the table. The dogs came flying over to me, clamouring for my attention.

"Alright, Tom?" I asked. He was sitting in his usual spot at the kitchen table with a pile of newspapers open in front of him. For once, though, he didn't have his head buried in them; he was looking at Becky, intently.

"She looks different," he said, nodding in Becky's direction. I was startled. I looked back at Becky again. She looked the same as usual.

"What do you mean?" I asked, genuinely confused. He looked me in the eye for a few seconds, and was it just my guilty conscious or did his look say, *'I know your secret'*? He shrugged and focused back on his newspaper again. I stared at him for a few moments before Becky interrupted my thoughts, leaning over me to lay the table.

"Papers, Tom," she said, smiling at him, and he picked the pile up and put them down behind him, out of the way. Becky flashed him her beautiful smile whilst positioning place mats and cutlery down in front of us.

There was a flurry around the table as Mum shooed the dogs away and put a giant bowl of rice in the centre, followed by huge plates of steaming, homemade chilli. Becky sat down opposite me as Mum came over with a bottle of red wine, plonking glasses down in front of each of us.

"Here you go, my dear," Mum said as she leant over to fill Becky's glass, but Becky leant forward and covered the glass with her hand.

"I'm okay, thanks, Sue," she said. My mum paused for a split second, looking at her, then at me, and then back at her.

"You're pregnant!" she cried, and I felt as if someone had drenched me in cold water. I could see the look of complete shock register on Becky's face and we looked at each other, startled, instantly giving the game away. "Oh my God, you are, aren't you? Oh my God!" my mum cried, and to my horror and amazement she burst into tears. She grabbed Becky in a bear hug, almost dragging her off the chair, and Becky blushed red with embarrassment. Tom thumped me on the back, wearing a big smile that crinkled the skin around his eyes.

"When did you find out?" my mum managed through her tears, dabbing her eyes with one hand and reaching out over the table to squeeze my hand with the other. For a split second I thought I was going to cry! Becky relayed the story and finished with us going to the doctors this evening.

"When's your first scan?" Mum said, now wiping the tears from the corner of her eyes with her apron.

"In about seven weeks," Becky said, smiling, looking over at me, and I swelled with pride.

"Well," Mum said, suddenly sounding determined, "what are you going to do about the flat? It's too small, you're going to have to move somewhere bigger – with another room. And Becky, what are you going to do about your job? Have you spoken to them about maternity leave? You should look online and see what you're entitled to. Obviously, I'll help with baby-sitting."

She droned on and on and I couldn't fathom how a mother's mind works. She was rattling off things that hadn't even crossed *my* mind yet. I realised that she had stopped talking and was looking between us expectantly, presumably waiting for some answers. Becky shifted uncomfortably in her seat and looked at me. I cleared my throat before speaking.

"Well, that's actually not the only news we've got."

25

BECKY

"Sometimes facts are depressing." – John

Sue took the news a lot better than Chris and I had expected. As I listened to Chris tell Sue and Tom about his new job, I wished I was sitting next to him so that I could give him an encouraging squeeze under the table, letting him know I was there. But as I was sat opposite him, I just sat quietly, watching him as he spoke. He explained everything, the job offer, our visit with Mr. King, the house, the extra money.

Sue listened to the news and didn't speak until Chris had finished. I noticed Tom staring at her closely while Chris was talking. He didn't take his eyes off her for a second. I wondered, not for the first time, if there was something between them. I was pulled from my thoughts when Sue finally spoke.

"Oh, Chris, I am so proud of you. What a wonderful opportunity," she said, trying to hide the sadness in her voice as she welled up again. "Congratulations." She got up and walked around to his seat and Chris stood up to give her a massive hug. Tom's eyes followed Sue and stayed on her as she stood at the end of the table. She turned to me and rested a hand on my shoulder.

"So, you've actually handed your notice in?" she asked, staring at me, concerned. She knew how much I adored my job and how much it meant to me. I nodded at her. "How are you feeling, my love?" I shrugged my shoulders, feeling the now familiar prickly feeling behind my eyes that meant I was close to tears. I blinked them away and smiled, pausing for a second before I spoke, praying that my voice didn't break. I hated all the emotion that seemed to be pent up inside me at the moment.

"I'm very sad," I said carefully, "but it's the right thing to do for now. Mark will keep my job open for me and I can go back any time I want."

"That's lovely of him," Sue said.

"It is and it's nice to know that it's there. Hopefully I can get something sorted once the baby is born, perhaps do some work there for a few days a week during the school holidays while Chris is off. We can come down and stay here for a few days, and I can work at the home while Chris and the baby spend time with you guys and his friends. I am sure it will all work out okay." Sue smiled at me and nodded her head, thinking.

"You haven't told Simon yet?" she asked Chris, and he shook his head, looking sheepish. "That boy is going to be furious!" she said and chuckled. She started picking the plates up off the table. I stood to help. "No, no, you sit down, my dear!" Sue cried.

"Sue, I am pregnant, not disabled! I am not having any of this special treatment for the next nine months! I am more than capable of helping to clear the table!" Sue pulled a face and looked at Chris for support, but he held his hands out and raised his eyebrows, as if to say, *'what can I do?'*. I laughed as he got up and started helping, too. The four of us moved around the kitchen, avoiding each other and the dogs, who were under our feet, following Chris like a shadow, as we moved everything from the table to the dishwasher.

Sue was talking about the move and everything else that was going on, and it finally hit me that this was *really* happening. We had both handed our notices in and Sue had been told. There were no other major hurdles now. There was no turning back. It *was* happening. We were moving!

I was lying in bed, feeling exhausted and guilty. Chris had woken up early this morning and taken the bus to work, leaving the car free for me to take John out for the day. Although I didn't have to be at work until lunchtime, I had still offered to get up and drive him in, but he brushed it off, telling me I needed my sleep. I was glad I had finally relented because as soon as he'd left, I managed to fall straight back to sleep and I didn't wake up until my alarm went off at nine a.m.!

I eventually dragged myself up out of bed to shower and get ready, trying to understand how I could still feel tired when I had slept in so late. As I left the flat, I scooped the keys off the breakfast bar and grabbed a banana to eat on the way to work. I knew that Chris would scold me if he thought I wasn't eating enough.

I was looking forward to the afternoon ahead, getting to spend time with John and the drive up to Oxford. As I suspected, John was waiting in the common room for me with his laptop tucked under his arm when I arrived at the home just before midday.

"Hello, John!" I said, smiling at him as I entered.

"I will be ready to go at twelve o'clock, as requested," he replied. I looked down at my watch; we had just over five minutes until it was twelve o'clock. It wasn't long enough for me to do anything else, but I knew it would only cause an issue if I told him that I was ready to go now. I sat down and watched the TV for a few minutes until I heard his watch bleep to signal midday. I jumped up before he could say anything, and we headed for the door.

"Have you got your driving licence?" he asked.

"Yes, John."

"You should have it on you at all times whilst driving. Even though it's not the law in the UK, *I* think that it is just sensible."

"I agree, John."

*

The drive was lovely, and it was a beautiful day for early March. The sun was out, and everything looked brand new as we drove out of the city. The fields on either side of the motorway were a lush green and the sky was crystal clear and blue. I rolled down my window once we got out of the city and breathed in the beautiful outdoor smells that you just don't get in London, not even in the parks.

John seemed relaxed today, and, as usual, he gave me a running commentary for the entire journey as he frantically typed away on his laptop, which he had precariously balanced on his lap while I drove. Whenever he saw any new road works or a roundabout or a service station that he hadn't seen before, the information would immediately get entered onto his Word document in today's font colour: blood red. I learnt some interesting new facts from John during the afternoon: the Denham roundabout on the A40 is sponsored by Buckinghamshire Golf Club, and the Headington roundabout is a hamburger roundabout and was given this name because it resembles a cross-section through a hamburger when viewed from above. I even learnt some interesting trivia regarding the 'Welcome Break' near Oxford.

"It was opened on the nineteenth of July, 1998, by Anthea Turner. It was the last services to open on the M40. Before that, the M40 originally held the record for the longest major road that did not have any services," John stated quickly while glancing up from his laptop.

I quite enjoyed listening to him, although sometimes the conversation could turn quite gloomy.

"Did you know," John said (this is how he starts a sentence every time he has a new fact to tell me), "the number of car accidents that occur in the UK every year is around forty-thousand."

"No, I didn't know that, John," I replied, and he paused before continuing.

"There are far more accidents than that, though. Those forty-thousand are the ones of a serious nature."

"That's depressing."

"More than three-thousand-five-hundred people are killed annually in these accidents, and more than thirty-thousand are seriously injured."

"That's even more depressing!"

"Sometimes facts are depressing," he said, staring out of the window.

*

When we arrived an hour and a half later, I drove into Cradley Heath's car park so John could have a look at the school. After a few minutes of sitting on the gravel looking up at the gorgeous building, I could see that John was already bored and had zero interest in seeing anything now that we were parked; he just wanted to be back on the road. I swung the car around and headed back the way we'd come.

I looked at the building and the grounds in the rear-view mirror as I drove off, and smiled to myself. I could not believe that this would soon be mine and Chris' new home.

26

CHRIS

"What I am offering you is a business opportunity." –
Edna.

Those final weeks in London flew by. It seemed as if so
much had happened since the news about the baby and
my new job. Everything had happened at once. Becky
and I had been back to Cradley Heath twice, firstly so I
could officially sign my new contract, and secondly to
pick up the keys to our new house. It was a beautiful, red-
bricked cottage with big windows and a slate roof. It was
surrounded by a wooden post and rail fence which
enclosed the large front and back gardens. There were
flower beds all the way around that were full of colourful
flowers, in which beautiful forget-me-nots bloomed
thanks to the early spring we were having.

Becky and I walked around the house hand-in-hand,
running our fingers across different surfaces and giggling
like school children as we marvelled at the size of it in
comparison to our flat. The front door opened into a
spacious living room, which then led through to a large,
bright kitchen. Our bedroom was upstairs and had huge
windows that looked out over the farmland behind the
school fields. There was a smaller room next to it which
would be the nursery. It looked out over the school's
sports pitches. It was perfect, and I couldn't wait to move
in and make it our own.

*

Things became even more interesting for us a few weeks
later when Becky and I visited Edna, the owner and
landlord of the flat, to officially hand in our notice. I had
never actually met Edna before – Becky had notified her

over the phone that I would be moving in shortly after we'd first met, and it had not been a problem. I suspected that she must have guessed we were planning on leaving when Becky asked if we could meet with her face-to-face.

Edna only lived a couple of tube stops away in a huge house that must have been worth a fortune! It was like walking into a beautiful old museum. We followed her through gleaming, wooden-panelled hallways to a huge, airy living room where we sat down on antique furniture. There was a huge bay window that took up almost the entire wall, which looked down onto the immaculate tree lined street below. Crisp white net curtains blew in the breeze.

Becky explained our situation to Edna, who was a beautiful, elegant old lady, and she listened whilst pouring cups of tea (into china cups, with silver spoons, using a teapot! I felt like I was sat in Claridge's). I could hear the strain in Becky's voice as she explained our situation; I knew she was worried about letting Edna down after everything she had done for her when she was young. Edna sat and listened, stirring three sugar lumps into her tea as Becky spoke.

"So, we're happy to keep on paying the rent as long as you need us to, or until you find a new tenant, we're not asking for any special favours. I appreciate everything you did for me, letting me have your flat in the first place," Becky finished, and Edna continued stirring her cup, the silver spoon making a clink against the side of the teacup, over and over again.

"Now, don't you worry at all," she said finally. "You have done yourself proud, young lady. When you first moved into that flat, I expected there to be missed payments, late payments, a whole heap of trouble. But you have never once let me down. Now, I am not getting any younger, and I have a sister down in Cornwall who, unfortunately, is very ill. Since I lost my husband, she is all I have left. So, although my heart will always be here in London, and it breaks my heart to say it, I am planning on selling my properties here and moving down to help take care of her." She paused, and I wondered where she was going with this. I could see Becky's brow furrow slightly, meaning she was just as confused as me. We caught each other's eyes briefly before Edna continued. "I was planning on offering the flat to you young people to buy," she said, pausing again. "I'll lay the offer on the table anyway, and give you both something to think about." Her blue eyes were flashing, and I sat forward in my chair. She immediately had my interest.

"I understand that you are moving," she said, "so don't look at me like I'm losing my marbles. What I am offering you is a business opportunity." She chuckled as she laid paperwork out in front of us and started pointing at the different sheets. "This is how much the flat is worth. There are three evaluations from different estate agents for sale prices, and if you look at these, this is how much each agency would advertise it to rent for." She handed me the sheets of paper and I stared at the figures. "This is how much I would want for it," Edna continued, scribbling down an amount in long floaty handwriting across a pad on the table. My eyebrows shot up into my head. She couldn't be serious. It was almost a third less than the amount she could get for it if she put it on the market. On top of that, the amount the estate agents said they could rent it for was a lot more than we were paying now. Edna watched my face closely, smiling. "You're a clever boy, and you are obviously doing the maths. What I am putting to you is this: if you wanted to buy the flat at this price," she pointed towards the pad she had written on, "as a thank you for being such consistent tenants for the past ten years, it's yours. I understand that you are moving now, but as I'm sure you are aware, you could rent that flat out in a heartbeat. With the price you would be paying on a mortgage at the price I am offering it, and with the rent that you could be earning, you would be making a nice little profit each month."

Becky and I sat in stunned silence.

*

Edna had been amazing, and she told us we didn't need to give her a definite answer straight away. Our rent on the flat was paid until the end of April and we assured her we would let her know either way before then. We had confirmed that it was an offer we would love to take up – we just needed to look into mortgages before we could confirm. Mortgages! All of a sudden, everything in our lives seemed very grown up. My new job, our new house, a baby on the way, and now we were discussing mortgages!

Later that day, I sat on the sofa in the flat with a calculator in one hand and a pen in the other. Paperwork was strewn everywhere, and I sat doing some sums. It was Sunday evening the week before Easter, and tomorrow would be the start of my final week at work. Becky's last day in the home had been yesterday, and so far she was coping with it better than I had expected.

I looked over at her. She was walking around the flat wearing baggy jogging bottoms with a tight t-shirt that showed off her still flat stomach. Her hair was piled up on top of her head, but some strands had escaped, framing her beautiful face. It reminded me of how she'd looked the first evening I came back to the flat with her, after she had gotten changed out of her interview clothes.

Becky had been a woman on a mission since finishing work yesterday, and she was already over half-way through packing the entire contents of our flat. Cardboard boxes labelled with Becky's handwriting in thick black marker pen were piled up in every corner. *'Chris clothes', 'Becky clothes', 'books', 'photos', 'kitchen'.* Becky's clothes boxes seemed to be taking up most of the space and as I looked at the growing pile, I wondered how it had all fit in this tiny flat in the first place. Becky caught me looking at her and winked at me, the marker pen held between her teeth as she sellotaped a box shut. I jumped up off the sofa to grab her.

She squealed and tried to escape from my arms, wriggling and laughing. I dragged her over to the sofa and sat her down next to me. "Look," I said, pointing to my workings out. Becky leant over the coffee table to look down at my writing. As she did, her t-shirt rode up slightly, revealing a strip of her tanned back. I slipped my hand through the gap and rested my palm on her warm skin as I spoke.

"This is what our incomings and outgoings have been for the last few years, both of our wages coming in, with rent, bills, etcetera, going out." I moved the hovering pen from one page to another. "This is what it will be from now on, with my wages coming in and the money we pay towards the cottage, blah, blah, blah, going out. Now," I moved the pen to the bottom of the page, "if we were able to get a mortgage on the flat on my one wage alone – which shouldn't be a problem with my new salary, and if we used our savings for the deposit, we may actually be able to buy the flat! From what the estate agents are saying, there should be no problem with renting it out almost straight away! Which means that, from now on, with the extra money we make from rent, we could be earning more a month than we did when we were both working full time! You will be a kept woman!" Becky looked at me and raised her eyebrows. I knew that being a kept woman was not something that she had ever aspired to be, but I still felt proud of our situation. Working hard for all these years had finally started to pay off.

We discussed everything in great detail. Our lives seemed to be full of important conversations and big decisions at the moment, and I longed for it all to be over. I just wanted to finally be in the new house so we could relax and get settled. Although everything had happened quite suddenly, it felt as if we had been waiting to move for ages now. I kept telling myself that we only had this last week to get through and we would finally be in our new home. My stomach lurched at the thought.

Because Becky had finished work a week earlier than me, she was planning on making a few trips up to the house over the next few days to take as many boxes as possible in advance. Then, at the weekend, Simon and I would drive up with the final bits and the last of the furniture in a van Simon was borrowing from one of his work colleagues. All the loose ends seemed to be tying themselves up and it was really starting to dawn on us that we were really leaving London in under a week's time. I looked around the flat. It already looked bare, with everything packed away in boxes. I closed my eyes. Just five more days.

27

BECKY

"I love you so, so much." – Chris.

Friday arrived. Our final day in London before the move. I was in the flat, taping up the last of the boxes, feeling exhausted. I had not stopped all week. I had driven to the cottage and back three times, and although it was tiring the journeys had been worth it. I had managed to take a big chunk of our stuff up already, meaning we would only need to make one trip tomorrow.

I loved being in the cottage. During my visit a couple of days ago, I had scrubbed indoors from top to bottom, wanting it to be perfect for when Chris and I arrived on Saturday. I opened up every door and window, letting fresh air flow through the place, bringing in the gorgeous, summery, outdoor smell that always seemed to be in the air in Oxford. It was a smell I already loved. When I took a break from cleaning, I sat and ate the sandwich I'd made that morning while I sat on the cottage doorstep. I watched the children streaming out onto the different playing fields in their coloured bibs and listened to the shouting and the shrill whistles of the teachers. In that moment, I was certain that we were going to be very happy here.

*

That evening, Chris came home from work later than usual. He'd warned me that he might get 'dragged' to the pub for a few goodbye drinks as it was his last day. I hadn't expected him to be home before midnight, but I could hear him fumbling for his keys on the doorstep not long after nine p.m. I was curled up on the sofa reading a book (the TV had already been boxed up, much to Chris' distress).

I smiled up at him as he walked through the front door, and I could tell he was more than a little bit drunk. His eyes were glazed over, and he swayed slightly where he stood. He grinned at me and leapt across the room and onto the sofa, sliding up next to me, nuzzling his head into my neck and wrapping his arms around me, trapping the book between us, not giving me a chance to put it down.

"Our last night here," he mumbled into my skin, and I smiled sadly. I loved this place so much. Knowing that we were going to try to buy it made me feel slightly better. It would be nice to know, at the back of my mind, that we always had the choice to come back here if we wanted to.

When I was lying in bed at night I would sometimes allow myself to look way into the future. I imagined that one day we would have enough money to keep this place empty, maybe in a few years when I was working again. I imagined us living between both London and Oxford. We could be in Oxford during term time, and I could look after the baby. We would be able to watch Chris giving lessons out on the sports field from the garden. Chris would be able to pop in and see us during his free periods and lunch breaks. I imagined us spending weekends walking around the countryside, perhaps we could even get a little dog. Then, during the school holidays, we could stay in London in the flat. We would get to spend proper time with Sue and Tom, and Chris with his friends. I could work at the home and Chris or Sue could look after the baby. It would mean that he or she would get a chance to grow up in the city as well as the country.

Although I was worried about all this change, and it still hadn't really sunk in yet, I was so excited by it all. I felt that, finally, life had really come right for me. Now, when I looked back at my life before I had met Chris, I realised how lonely and depressed I was and how resigned I had been to spending my life alone. When I compared it to my life now, I still could not believe how much had changed and how lucky I was. My life was filled with love and people and things to look forward to. I still couldn't believe that it had happened to me.

Chris pulled away from our hug and grinned at me. I put my book down and put my arms around his neck. We cuddled for a moment longer before kissing each other, still with as much desire and passion as we had that first time outside Leicester Square tube station.

"I love you so, so much," Chris murmured.

"I love you, too."

28

CHRIS

"Happy moving day." – Chris.

I woke up on Saturday morning wrapped around Becky's naked body. She was fast asleep, and I was about to snuggle back down into our bed for the last time when I realised that my phone was vibrating on the bedside table. It must have been what had woken me up. I moved away from Becky, who for once didn't stir, and grabbed the phone. It was Simon calling. I looked at the time: 7:20a.m. I answered in a whisper whilst slipping out of the bedroom and into the now almost bare living room.

"Simon?" I asked, my voice croaky, genuinely confused – Simon was not a morning person.

"Chris?" he snapped, his voice shrill. "Are you up? I'm coming to yours. I've had a row with Katie. I'm fuming, mate. I'm sick of her. I don't even know why I bother, and you have to choose this weekend to move. I am so *angry*! I can't be bothered with her anymore, I really can't." He kept on and on and I rubbed my forehead as I listened. As much as I did not want to deal with this right now, I really needed Simon's help with moving the last of our stuff today. He'd borrowed a van from one of his work friends, and we were planning on driving it up to the house together with the last of mine and Becky's stuff. Once unloaded, Simon was going to drive it back tonight. It'd work out perfectly, but I didn't want Simon being in a foul temper and ruining the mood today for me and Becky. He was still ranting in my ear, not even stopping for breath.

I looked through the bedroom door at Becky's sleeping figure under the duvet and thought, not for the first time, how lucky we were that we had such a great relationship. Although, deep down, I think that Simon thrived on all the excitement and drama that Katie gave him. I realised suddenly that he had gone quiet on the end of the phone and was probably expecting an answer. I managed to mumble that yes, of course he could come over.

He must have been just around the corner as I could hear him stomping down the steps to our front door soon after he had hung up. Before I could get to the door to open it for him, he was banging on it with enough force to wake the neighbours. I yanked it open, filled with frustration.

"Simon," I hissed at him through gritted teeth. "Becky's asleep! Why do you always have to be so damned loud?"

He stormed past me, ignoring my comment, and threw himself down on the sofa, dragging his hand through his hair as I stared at him frostily. Moments later, Becky appeared at the bedroom door, now dressed in a set of pyjamas, her hair all wild around her face. She looked like a little girl standing there and I walked over to her and put my arms around her, running my hand along her stomach as I kissed her on the nose.

"Morning, baby," she said sleepily. "Morning, Simon."

Simon grunted at her, and I shot him a warning look. He just about managed to mumble, "Morning," back. Becky walked into the kitchen, paused for a moment, and then turned around slowly to look at me.

"We haven't even got a tea bag! Everything's packed. I'll pop down to the café and pick us all up some breakfast," she said.

I felt like I hadn't even woken up yet and I couldn't think quickly enough to argue with her. Simon was typing away furiously on his phone, presumably carrying on the argument with Katie via text message. I followed Becky into the bedroom where she was pulling on a long coat over her pyjamas. I slipped my arms around her waist.

"Sorry, babe, you know what he's like, he's had a row with Katie again. Are you sure you want to go now? Wait for a minute and I'll go instead."

She turned and smiled at me, stepping on tip toes to kiss me on the lips.

"I'll go, I won't be long. I'll bring you something nice back," she said, and I followed her as she walked into the living room. I squeezed her hand before she walked out the front door.

"Happy moving day," I said, and she turned and grinned at me as she walked out into the fresh air. Even with her make-up free face and bed hair she still looked perfect.

"Happy moving day!" she replied, grinning, and I could see that the smile was still on her face as she turned and ran lightly up the steps to the pavement. I turned back to Simon, who was rolling his eyes at us.

*

Becky arrived back about half an hour later with a breakfast bap each for me and Simon and a bacon roll for her herself. There were also three large cardboard cups of steaming hot tea and a large carton of orange juice. She took off her coat and sat down on the floor next to me, eating quietly while Simon and I talked and I attempted to calm him down. This was the third time now that he was 'definitely one hundred percent going to call off the engagement' with Katie and move back in with his parents.

A little later when the food was finished, Becky got up, cleared everything away, and went off to the bedroom to get dressed. I glanced at the time. It was nearly nine o'clock. I had really wanted to be dressed by now and have the van packed with the last of the things, but Simon was still in full flow, furiously telling me over and over again the details of the argument from the night before. A little while later, his phone started to ring.

"It's her," he spat, putting the phone down in front of him where it sang its tune and vibrated its way around the table as we both sat and stared at it. Just before it rung off, Simon grabbed it and answered it with a curt, "What?"

He got up and stomped to the front door in two strides, flinging it open and slamming it shut behind him. I could hear him rowing out on the street outside. I let out a deep frustrated sigh and went to the bedroom where Becky was fully dressed and slipping her shoes on.

"Babe, I'm so sorry," I said. "I wanted this day to be special and he's ruining it."

Becky put a finger over my lips to shush me.

"It's okay, we've got the whole of tonight alone together in our new house," she grinned. "Help me put some of these smaller boxes into the car and I'll head up there now. You and Simon can follow on whenever you're ready, and I can start some unpacking while I'm waiting for you." She smiled at me and I pouted at her, but nodded in agreement.

29

BECKY

"See you soon." – Becky.

Simon was storming up and down the pavement outside the flat, still arguing into his phone during the whole time Chris and I loaded the car. We managed to get quite a lot of stuff in and Chris closed the door, looking satisfied. All that was left inside the flat now was a couple of large boxes and our furniture. It would all fit comfortably into the van that Chris and Simon were driving up in.

"Okay," I said, picking my handbag up off the pavement as I turned to face Chris. "I'll see you in a few hours."

He was staring over my shoulder, frowning at Simon. He shook his head and looked at me.

"I love you so much!" he said, pulling me into a bear hug and kissing me sloppily on the lips. "Sorry we're going to be a later than you, but I will be as quick as I can."

"Don't rush!" I smiled up at him. "I'll start unpacking, and I might even pop to the supermarket to get some stuff in for tomorrow." Sue and Tom were coming up for the day tomorrow to see the school, our cottage, and to help us unpack. Chris and I were going to cook a Sunday roast for them. I was really excited about it. It was impossible for us to have people over for dinner in the flat as there was just no room and we had nowhere to seat them. It seemed really grown up to be able to have Sue and Tom over for dinner for once!

I kissed Chris on the lips once more and walked around to the driver's door. I opened it and looked at him over the roof of the car before I got in. He looked so forlorn standing on the pavement looking at me. I laughed and smiled at him, and he smiled back.

"See you soon, love you," I said as I got in and closed the door. I knew he said, "I love you," back even though I didn't hear him over the slam. I pulled off down the road and beeped my horn at him as I drove around the corner. I saw him raise his hand and wave in the rear-view mirror, just before he was out of sight.

*

I put the radio on and settled down for the drive. It was another beautiful day. The sky was clear, and it felt like it was going to be hot. I thought of us having our dinner out in the garden tonight and the thought made me smile. I still didn't feel as upset as I had expected to be. I was beginning to feel quite excited now. I think Simon coming in and disrupting our morning had thrown me, but it had meant that I hadn't dwelled too much on the fact that we were finally leaving. I almost started to feel guilty, I felt as if I hadn't said goodbye to the flat properly! I berated myself for being so stupid. We were hoping to buy it soon anyway, so I would be able to see it whenever I wanted.

I smiled to myself as I drove past the different parts of the journey that John had pointed out and commented on all those weeks ago. I missed him and the other patients already. I wondered what they would be getting up to over Easter. I wondered which member of staff would be taking John out. I wondered if he would like them. I wondered if he would miss me, if he was even capable of missing me.

I was deep in thought as the scenery streaked past the windows, and it wasn't long before I started to see signs for the exit I needed to get off the motorway. I glanced into the rear-view mirror and moved over towards the slow lane.

30

Becky didn't even feel the impact. A seventeen-year-old boy driving his father's Porsche came speeding down the inside lane at over one-hundred miles per hour. He had been drinking the night before, although he hadn't felt drunk when he'd got into the car that morning. He had taken the car from his parents' driveway without his father's permission.

He had been showing off to his sixteen-year-old girlfriend who was sitting in the passenger seat, still wearing her clothes from last night, without a seatbelt on. She died instantly on impact and the driver died shortly after whilst still on the scene. Post-mortem results showed that he was nearly three times over the legal drink-drive limit.

He had put his foot down as he sped past Becky, undercutting her as he passed the side of her car. Becky had moved over, not checking her blind spot. The Porsche hit Becky's car so hard it flung straight into the air and landed back on the road, upside down, skidding across two lanes and smashing into the central reservation.

*

When the ambulance and fire brigade arrived at the scene shortly after the accident and saw Becky's car, they didn't expect to find anyone alive inside. Nearly an hour later, after intricate work had been carried out to release Becky's body from her seatbelt and the mess of crumpled metal, the fireman who finally managed to pull Becky's body out of the tiny gap that had been cut below the window sobbed with happiness when he realised that the beautiful young woman was still alive and, miraculously, didn't seem to have a scratch on her. She was unconscious, though, and he screamed for the paramedics who came running over, a look of complete shock on their faces.

It wasn't long before Becky was in the back of an ambulance, sirens blaring, lights flashing, flying off down the empty motorway, leaving the scene of the crash, and the miles of queuing traffic that had now built up, behind.

31

CHRIS

"She's alive." – Nurse.

I resisted the urge to close my eyes, sigh, and rub my temples. Simon and I were stuck in gridlock traffic on the motorway. This morning had been a complete disaster and I was starting to get a headache. I had loaded the van almost entirely by myself whilst Simon had continued arguing on the phone, still storming up and down the path outside our flat, oblivious as I struggled back and forth.

When everything was finally loaded and ready to go, I closed the door to the van. Seeing that Simon was still mid flow in his argument, I walked in and took one last look around the flat, which was now completely empty. I'd like to say it looked bigger now that everything had been taken out, but it didn't. If anything, it looked smaller. There was dust floating in the air and I could see it dancing around in the square of light penetrating in through the bedroom window. I saw strands of cobwebs hanging like ghostly shrouds up in the corner of the room that I hadn't noticed before. It was deadly quiet.

I felt a sudden wave of sadness wash over me as I looked around our home. I remembered the first time I had walked in here with Becky, how natural it had seemed. I smiled and turned to leave, suddenly wanting to get on the road, to be on the way to Oxford to be with her.

But now, nearly two hours later, we were still stuck in the van. The late morning sun was high in the sky, and it streamed in through the windscreen, making it almost unbearably hot. Both Simon and I had our windows down, but the front of the van was filled with the fumes from other people's cars. Although we literally hadn't moved an inch in over an hour, people were still sitting with their engines on, much to Simon's infuriation.

I had never actually seen such gridlocked traffic before. Simon was moaning and I could feel my patience wearing thin. My headache seemed to be getting worse with every second that went by. I wondered if Becky had got caught in this traffic and I worried that she would be bored, stuck in the car on her own. I pulled the phone out of my pocket with the intention of texting her, but every time I started to type, Simon would launch into another tirade against Katie and eye the phone in my hand, making me feel guilty. So, I slid the phone back into my lap to concentrate on him again. I'm sure he does it on purpose. He was always demanding my attention, especially when it came to Becky.

Finally, he seemed to wear himself out and he slouched back in the seat, huffing and puffing and grumbling about the traffic, albeit a bit more quietly. I wiped a bead of sweat off my forehead with the back of my hand and reached down to grab the phone from between my legs.

I jumped out of my skin, as it started ringing the second I touched it and I frowned as I looked at the number I didn't recognise flashing on my screen.

"Who's that?" Simon grunted at me, and I shrugged my shoulders in reply. I was about to let it go to voicemail when I suddenly realised it might be someone calling from Cradley Heath. I cleared my throat.

"Hello," I answered, turning to smile at a small child who was pulling faces against the window of the car next to me. I wrinkled my nose and poked my tongue out at him, causing him to smile in delight. When the voice on the other end of the phone spoke, I was hit by such an abrupt, painful surge of adrenalin that it took all the breath out of my lungs. I sat struggling to breathe as I received the news that changed my life.

*

You always hear people trying to describe what it's like when you go into shock, either in books, on TV, or in films. But nothing can ever, ever prepare you for when that moment happens to you. I completely fell apart as I received the news from the hospital of Becky's accident. As I listened to the call, it was as if I had floated up out of my body and was looking down, witnessing a call between strangers.

The first few hours after the call were a complete blur. Everything seemed to be in fast-forward around me while I sat motionless and unable to breathe in the middle of it all. I tried to fight the hysteria that was creeping into my body, threatening to take over. It was all I could do to concentrate on breathing and not being sick. I kept thinking over and over *it must be a bad dream, it must be a bad dream, it must be a bad dream.* The thought that anything bad could happen to Becky, the thought that she could die, was like being about to die myself.

After I'd been cursing Simon all morning, I thanked God he was there with me to take control of the situation. When he realised what had happened, he was out of the van and around to the driver's side door in an instant, helping me get out. My legs couldn't take my weight and I literally had to lean on him for support as I made my way around to the other side of the van and slumped back onto the passenger seat. I could see the amused looks on the faces of people in other cars watching us, most likely wondering what on earth was going on in the middle of this standstill traffic. Fighting back tears, I pushed my fingers into my eyes until I saw nothing but sparkles.

*

"She's alive," the nurse on the phone had said. "Unconscious, and there are no obvious broken bones as far as we can tell." She'd said they should know more by the time I arrived. Becky had been taken to a local hospital that I'd never heard of. I have no idea how Simon managed to find it. I can remember him talking frantically on his phone, barking at people. At one point I realised he was on the phone to my mum, but the thought of speaking with her made me feel nauseous. I didn't want to see or speak to anyone except Becky.

I could hear Simon talking but the words seemed to evaporate before they penetrated my brain. It could have been another language he was speaking. All I could think of was *Becky, the baby, Becky, the baby, Becky, the baby.* Through my shock I had somehow managed to tell the nurse on the phone that Becky was pregnant. She had paused for a moment before saying she would inform Becky's doctors, but that split second of silence had sent an icy wave through me.

*

The van finally hurtled into the car park of the hospital and Simon flung it into the nearest space, narrowly missing a red Fiat Punto in the spot next to us with a 'Princess on Board' sign in the back window. I yanked open my door and leapt out onto the concrete. I could barely stand up and my knees buckled underneath me as my head started to spin. I paused for a second, leaning against the van for support. I took a deep breath and looked around, disorientated. Simon was by my side in an instant and managed once again to help me, physically holding me up as we headed towards the hospital entrance. I tried to stay calm as Simon explained the situation to the nurse on reception, who looked at me sympathetically. I just stood, looking on stupidly, afraid to speak or even think. I just needed to see Becky. I concentrated on my breathing and told myself it wouldn't be long. We would be together soon.

We seemed to be filling out forms and following protocols for an eternity before I eventually found myself sitting in the waiting room, my head in my hands. Simon didn't say a word. We sat in silence, and that was fine by me. I listened to the blood pumping in my ears and concentrated on breathing in and out, in and out.

*

I don't know how much time passed before a stressed looking young doctor hurried into the waiting room. Once again, I became acutely aware of how different reality is to what is portrayed on TV or in films. Usually you see the concerned next-of-kin leaping to their feet in anticipation at the sight of a doctor approaching. But I couldn't move. I sat frozen in the chair, staring at him as he called my name.

"Christopher McNulty?" he announced, looking up from a clipboard. I stared at him for a few seconds, still unable to speak. Thankfully, Simon stood up, drawing his attention to us. The doctor headed over. "Do you want to come with me somewhere more private?" he asked, not giving us a chance to reply. He turned on his heel and rushed down the corridor, his shoes clip-clopping on the shiny white floor. Simon held the top of my arm to steady me as we followed him down the corridor and into a tiny, dark room. We sat down and I took a deep breath, hoping my voice wouldn't fail me.

"What's happened? Is my wife okay?" I managed, my voice full of tears, on the verge of breaking. The doctor looked up at me and I looked into his stressed face, seeing lines around his eyes that shouldn't be there on a man so young. He introduced himself as Dr Barratt.

"Mr. McNulty, your wife was involved in a serious road traffic accident earlier today. It seems that her car was hit by another car that was travelling at around one-hundred miles per hour. The car your wife was driving flipped and landed upside down with your wife trapped inside..." I couldn't breathe. I listened to the information as if it were for someone else. I could see Simon out of the corner of my eye, staring at me, concerned.

"The two passengers in the other car involved in the accident both died at the scene. Your wife, however, was pulled out of the wreck still alive. Miraculously, there does not seem to be any severe damage to her body physically, in terms of bones and spine, but your wife *is* in a coma. It seems she has taken a fairly substantial knock to the back of her head. Thankfully, there seems to be no major damage to her skull. She has already had CT scans and X-rays to sections of her brain to try and find out if there is going to be any lasting damage, but we will need the swelling on her brain to go down before we can see the full extent of the damage. Your wife was originally taken to intensive care, but she has already been moved down to one of the wards as she is breathing on her own – a very positive sign for somebody in a coma. She is obviously unable to eat or drink on her own, so she is receiving nutrients and liquids through a vein or feeding tube so that she doesn't starve or dehydrate. She also has a catheter as she will not be able to go to the toilet, so do not be alarmed by this when you see her." He paused again. I wasn't sure if he was waiting for me to speak or ask a question. I felt like a small child again, not knowing what was required of me. Before I could speak, though, the doctor continued, his voice low, "Now, one of the nurses informed me that you were aware of your wife's pregnancy..." He paused and I braced myself, knowing in that split second what was coming. "I am very sorry to tell you, Mr. McNulty, that, unfortunately, your wife has lost the baby. There was some bleeding after she was brought into the hospital and after a pelvic exam and an ultrasound, I'm sorry to say there is no heartbeat. I'm so sorry."

That is when emotion finally took over. I broke down and cried.

*

There was so much more that the doctor told me that afternoon, much more information that I just couldn't process. All I wanted was to actually *see* Becky with my own eyes. Touch her, be next to her. At long last the doctor finished speaking and stood up. Simon and I followed him out of the door and through the hospital.

We walked through the cramped corridors and into the small ward that Becky was on. It was dark in there. The only light came from small individual lights by each bed. It was surprisingly empty. Simon stopped at the entrance, giving me a nod and attempting a smile as I walked away from him, following the doctor, my eyes adjusting to the darkness as I walked through the centre of the room between the rows of made-up beds that lined each wall. We walked past a couple of elderly patients lying in their beds, their curtains pulled back, looking out into the silent room.

Becky was at the far end of the room on a bed in the left-hand corner. The curtain was drawn around her. My heart was beating uncontrollably in my chest as I approached her. I just didn't know what to expect. I was starting to have trouble breathing again and felt light-headed and sick. The doctor was speaking to me, but the words came as if from underwater and I didn't hear a word he said. He gestured to the corner of the curtain, gave me a sad smile, and strode off back up the ward, towards the door where Simon was standing shifting from foot-to-foot, looking uncomfortable.

I watched my hand reach out in front of me and pull

the curtain back as if it were someone else's, and I stepped through the gap, my breath catching in my chest as I saw her. Before I knew it, I was kneeling on the floor next to her, her hand in mine. My body relaxed slightly. I had expected to see blood, bruises, stitches – but she looked perfect. A wave of relief washed over me and I started to cry, tears of relief and almost happiness. The thoughts that had been rushing through my head, the horrors of what I had been expecting to see were all irrelevant. Here she was. Not a scratch on her, lying in bed, looking as if she was asleep. She actually looked okay! She had a brace around her neck and a drip going into her left hand, but apart from that, you wouldn't have known she had been in an accident. I clutched her right hand between mine, pressing it against my face and kissing it.

Yes, she was unconscious, but she would wake up. She was breathing on her own and that was a good sign (the doctor's words popped into my head unexpectedly, all of a sudden, getting through to me). Yes, we had lost the baby and it was devastating. But as upsetting as it was, we *could* have another baby. Things could have been so, so much worse. Becky was alive, that's all that mattered. I kissed her hand again, squeezing it as I stared at her. She was going to be okay, I just knew it.

I understood the seriousness of the situation, I wasn't stupid. I knew that Becky was in a coma, and they couldn't guarantee when, or even if, she would wake up. But I just knew she was going to be okay. I knew she would wake up soon, I felt certain. She was strong – always had been. I suddenly became so thankful and aware of everything good in our lives. I realised more than ever before how lucky we were to have each other. I wiped the tears from my eyes with the back of my hand and resolved not to cry any more. I was just so overwhelmingly thankful that Becky was still alive, I didn't know what to do with all the emotion that filled me. I knew we were going to get through this. I had no doubt. Now that I could see her, see what she had managed to survive, I knew we could get through anything. It was just a case of waiting for her to become conscious. Then everything would be okay. I stroked her face and whispered to her, telling her that she was going to be fine. That she would wake up soon and we could carry on with our lives.

I felt exhausted. I had no idea what the time was. I pulled a chair over from the bed next to us and moved it in as close to Becky's bed as possible. I laid my head down on the mattress next to her shoulder and looked at her beautiful face. She looked so peaceful. I willed her to wake up.

32

"If I were you, this is where I would want my wife to be."
– Dr Barratt.

Sue and Tom arrived at the hospital a few hours later to find a groggy Chris in the exact same position at Becky's bedside, still clutching her hand. Sue was beside herself with grief and looked as if she had already lost weight with the worry. Her usually rosy, red face was white and gaunt, and she sobbed into Chris' shoulder by Becky's bedside. Tom stood silently in the corner like a statue, not taking his eyes off Sue. Simon, who had walked in with them, stood behind him, for once blending into the background, not the centre of attention.

Sue sobbed and sobbed, blowing her nose on an endless amount of tissues handed to her out of Tom's pocket. Chris managed to smile at her as he tried to reassure her and relay as much information as his spinning head would allow, desperately trying to put a positive spin on everything, trying to be strong. Sue wailed as she heard the details of the crash and finally fell into Chris' arms, crying uncontrollably when he told her about the baby. He held onto her while she cried, glad that he felt stronger now – he could not have coped with this a few hours ago.

Eventually Sue sat down in a chair that Tom had brought over from the empty bed opposite. She sat down and clutched Becky's hand, her thumb moving back and forth across her skin, staring at her. The whole family waited in silence as it started to grow dark outside.

*

At seven p.m. the doctor returned looking, if possible, even more exhausted. He approached the group sitting around Becky's bed and informed them all that visiting hours were over and that they would have to leave the ward. Sue laid her hand on Chris' shoulder before he could argue and smiled and nodded at the doctor, who looked relieved when they didn't put up a fight. They all left the ward in silence and followed the doctor, blinking as they exited the dark ward and entered the bright corridor.

"We'll be in the waiting area," Chris said, his voice worn. "If anything happens, if anything changes, you come and get me." The doctor looked as if he wanted to argue with Chris, as if he wanted to tell him to go home and get some sleep, but the look on Chris' face must have told him not to argue and he nodded before turning away. Sue clutched Chris' arm as they walked together back towards reception and the waiting room. Simon and Tom followed behind in silence.

The waiting area was also surprisingly quiet when they entered, and it was more pleasant than Chris would have expected. He certainly hadn't noticed it on the way in. An exhausted mother sat in one corner, looking as if she was about to fall asleep. She leant her head back on the wall behind her as a young boy played a game intently on a mobile phone next to her, wriggling around in his chair with his tongue poked out in concentration. There were two toddlers playing with a pile of coloured toys in the corner of the room, chattering back and forth to each other and giggling, their grandmother watching them intently, a smile on her lips. An old Indian couple sat opposite her, hand-in-hand. The woman was dressed in a beautiful sari, the man in a brown tweed suit. He had a large patch over his eye. He looked up and smiled at Chris as he walked past, and somehow Chris managed to smile back at him.

Sue sat down on a bench in the corner and Chris sat down heavily next to her. All of a sudden, he felt utterly exhausted. A moment ago, when he had been at Becky's side, he could not have even thought of going to sleep, but now he felt as if he had been drugged and he desperately wanted to just close his eyes. He leant his head on Sue's shoulder and she reached her hand around and clasped his face, kissing him on top of his head. That was the last thing he remembered before he fell into a deep and exhausted sleep.

*

Sue sat awake for the entire night. Patients and visitors filtered in and out of the hospital while she gazed around her. She listened to staff gossiping behind the reception desk in the small hours of the morning when it was quiet and there was no-one around, and she watched the cleaners moving slowly back and forth between rooms. Chris' head was now in her lap, and he slept like a little boy, dead to the world. Both of her legs had gone dead, but she didn't move for fear of waking him.

Simon had fallen asleep in the chair opposite them, his legs thrust forward into the walkway, spread wide, taking up a huge amount of room. His arms were folded across his chest and his head had fallen backwards. His mouth was wide open, and a quiet snore escaped his lips. Tom sat next to him, ramrod straight. He was wide awake and looking around intently as if he were on guard. A few times during the night Sue's eyes had met Tom's and he had raised his eyebrows at her questioningly, asking if she was okay. Sue had nodded back at him in return.

In the early hours of the morning, almost as soon as the sun started rising, the hospital started to get busier. At around six a.m. a couple with a screaming young baby rushed in through the double doors and over to the reception desk. The baby's piercing cry cut through Sue and seemed to reverberate around the room. But still, Chris did not stir. It roused Simon, though, who looked around, blinking and confused, and Sue literally watched as the events from yesterday came back to him. She dreaded the moment this happened to Chris. Dreaded the moment when he woke up and had to face the reality of what had happened.

*

Chris stirred a little while later, and, for a split second, he wondered where he was and why he was so uncomfortable. It took a moment for the events from yesterday to hit him. It was painful, like a punch in the chest, and suddenly everything came flooding back to him. It was overwhelming, and Chris sat up quickly, his head spinning, feeling faint. He realised that he hadn't eaten in over twenty-four hours, and it pained him to remember Becky curled up on the floor next to him yesterday as they ate their breakfast on the floor in the living room of the flat. It seemed like a lifetime ago.

All eyes were on him as he frantically scanned the waiting room and reception area, looking for a doctor.

"Tom has already asked the nurse if someone could come and speak to us as soon as possible. He said someone will be along shortly," Sue said soothingly, resting a hand on Chris' arm, and he looked at her as if just realising she was there. Simon stood up uncomfortably, not looking anyone in the eye.

"I'll go get a drink and try and find some food," he mumbled before walking off. The thought of eating repulsed Chris, but he knew he had to try. He wanted to be strong and alert and able to deal with the day – he would force food down if he had to. He sat back in the chair, feeling groggy. He rubbed his temples, resisting the overwhelming urge to just run through the hospital and back to Becky's bed.

Simon returned a while later, balancing steaming cups of tea and four plates of hot bacon sandwiches on a tray.

Chris didn't argue as a plate was placed in front of him, and he forced a sandwich down even though he couldn't taste a thing. He tuned out the small talk as his mum and Simon discussed how surprisingly nice the hospital food was – all it did was cause a lump in his throat and he had to concentrate on swallowing. Chris did feel better after eating, though, and his hands felt less shaky. He sat back in the chair and closed his eyes. He willed something to happen and sat wishing someone would come and give him some more information. Fear was creeping into his chest again, and he was finding it hard to breathe.

He must have dozed off again as he jumped awake with a start a little while later when he heard his name being called. He leapt up out of the chair to see the same doctor from yesterday standing in front of him. For a fleeting moment he wondered if the doctor had been there all night, but looking closely he did seem to look slightly fresher than when Chris had seen him last.

"Mr. McNulty, can I have a word?" he asked, signalling with his arm towards the corridor leading to the room they had spoken in yesterday.

"Is everything okay?" Chris asked, hearing the panic creeping into his voice.

"Yes, no major changes, I just wanted to discuss some options with you, if that's okay?"

Chris relaxed slightly and tried to calm himself. His heartbeat was thumping in his ear. He nodded and looked down at Sue, who smiled up at him encouragingly. He followed the doctor again along the same route that they had taken yesterday, and, before he knew it, he was back in the same dark room, in the seat at the desk opposite him. Chris realised guiltily that he couldn't even remember the doctor's name. The doctor cleared his throat and started speaking, instantly having Chris' attention.

"Becky is doing well today. She is still stable and breathing on her own, which, as I mentioned yesterday, is a good sign. I just wanted to go through some of the details of your wife's condition with you again, Mr. McNulty, as I guess that yesterday is probably a bit of a blur to you.

Now, as you know, your wife is in a coma. There are several factors that can cause someone to go into a coma, for example a stroke, diabetes, an alcohol or drug overdose, or a head or brain injury. If someone suffers a severe head trauma, the impact can cause the brain to move back and forth inside the skull. The movement of the brain inside the skull can tear blood vessels and nerve fibres which can cause swelling on the brain. This swelling presses down on blood vessels, blocking the flow of blood, and, with it, oxygen to the brain. I think, from the investigations that we have carried out on Becky so far, this is what probably happened to her. I would guess that her head was thrown around quite severely when the car she was in flipped, and this is how she has sustained a large knock to the back of her head. As I'm sure you are aware, there are different levels of coma that people can be in, and they differ greatly. The good news, as I've already mentioned, is that Becky is already breathing on her own. Also, overnight it has been recorded that Becky has twitched and moved involuntarily, which is a very positive sign for someone in a coma. After some testing from myself and my colleague this morning, it seems that Becky does respond to stimuli with an increased heart rate, and although there is no movement as of yet, this is very positive."

The doctor paused to look at Chris, who was leaning forward in his chair, taking everything in.

"Most comas don't last more than two to four weeks. Recovery is usually gradual, with patients becoming more and more aware over time. Some people come out of a coma without any mental or physical disability, but most do require at least some type of therapy to regain mental and physical skills. They may need to relearn to speak, walk, or even eat. In some cases, patients do not recover completely. Now, if you don't mind me saying, I feel quite positive for Becky. The signs we are getting from her so far in less than twenty-four hours are all positive." He paused again and ran his hand through his hair, a gesture that reminded Chris of Simon, and it instantly made Chris warm to him.

"My colleague and I were discussing your wife this morning, and as she has coped so well so quickly without the need of intensive care, which is highly unusual for a coma patient, I hope you don't mind that we have made some enquiries on your wife's behalf. There is a hospital in London, called the West Park Hospital, which has the largest brain centre in the south of England. It is one of the country's leading private treatment centres, dedicated to the care of patients suffering with complex brain disorders. Sometimes they take on NHS patients. So, on the off chance, I phoned them this morning and explained your wife's situation and they have said, with your consent, they would be happy to take over your wife's care. It means that Becky would be getting the best treatment possible. They deal with complex brain conditions and have the leading specialists in the country. They offer full care, and they have a huge rehabilitation centre. If I were you, this is where I would want my wife to be."

33

CHRIS

"Becky is a very, very lucky young lady." – Carl Matthews.

I instantly took up the doctor's offer of moving Becky to the London Brain Clinic in West Park Hospital. I couldn't believe how quickly the wheels were put in motion and how smooth the transfer was. The day after the doctor first mentioned it to me, Becky and I were transported in an ambulance back along the motorway to London. My mum and Tom followed behind in my mum's car and Simon followed them in the van. They had all spent another night with me in the waiting room.

The service we received from West Park Hospital was impeccable from the moment we arrived. Becky was immediately stretchered out of the ambulance and taken to her room. I was taken through to a large, beautiful office and introduced to Becky's new doctor, one of the consultant neurologists. He was a tall, handsome man with a head of thick, jet-black hair and a pearly white smile. He looked as if he had stepped off the page of a glossy magazine. I cringed inwardly as I shook his hand, realising that I was still wearing the same clothes from Saturday morning. I hadn't even looked in a mirror since then, let alone washed myself or even brushed my teeth. I felt scruffy and embarrassed sitting opposite him in his expensive suit with his large, gleaming oak desk between us.

He introduced himself as Dr Carl Matthews and he radiated confidence, instantly making me feel like Becky was in the best hands. He was fresh faced and alert – the polar opposite of the exhausted doctor we had left behind this morning. He had already read all Becky's notes and seemed to be familiar with all her information. We talked for a long time and not for one moment did I feel under pressure for time or rushed in any way. We covered a lot of the same information that I had already gone through at the other hospital, but Dr Matthews sounded a lot more positive and confident that Becky was heading in the right direction.

"From what I can tell," he said, glancing down at the notes in front of him before looking back up at me, "Becky is a very, very lucky young lady and is showing all the right signs that she may be heading towards coming out of her coma. Younger people do always have a better chance of recovering from comas, and from looking through her notes so far, there have been several recorded instances of her twitching and making other involuntary movements, which is exactly what we should be hoping for. The main thing you can do for her at the moment is to stimulate her as much as possible. Be near her and talk to her. The experience of being in a coma differs between each person. It also depends on how deep the coma is. Some people are able to remember events that happened around them while they were in a coma, while others do not. Most memories are likely to relate to the period when the person is emerging from their coma, as I think Becky is now. This is why I think that it is important for Becky to have people around her at the moment, talking to her. Perhaps play her favourite music. Some people have reported feeling enormous reassurance from the presence of a loved one."

I nodded my head. I didn't plan on leaving Becky's side anyway. I wanted her to know I was there with her every second.

*

Later that afternoon I was sat in Becky's new room,

clutching her hand and talking to her quietly when my mum and Tom arrived. The hospital was based about forty minutes away from my mum's house. It felt strange to be back in London again. Even though it was only a couple of days since we had left, it felt like a lifetime ago. My mum was insistent that I should go home to have a shower and get a change of clothes, but I didn't want to leave Becky's side. I point blank refused to leave and we argued back and forth, my temper thinning. Only when one of the nurses assured me that she would not be left alone for longer than twenty minutes at a time did I finally relent and follow my mum out the door. I felt completely panicked at the thought of leaving Becky on her own. My mum put her arm around my waist and guided me out of the room and down the corridor towards reception. The thought of being away from her for the next few hours was horrible. I kept imagining her waking up and me not being there, or something happening while I was gone. I knew I would never forgive myself if anything happened, and I kept torturing myself, desperate to be back by her side again.

We left the hospital and walked out into another scorching hot day. I shielded my eyes from the bright sunshine overhead and followed my mum across the car park, squinting. I was genuinely shocked when I realised there were people walking along the pavement adjacent to the car park. An older couple were chatting, laughing and holding hands as they walked. A boisterous group of teenage boys in shorts and t-shirts with sweatshirts shoved into their backpacks ran towards the park, screaming and shouting at each other. A group of mums wearing sunglasses and pushing pushchairs chatted as they walked lazily behind them.

I stared at them all in bewilderment. How could all this still be happening? How could people just be getting on with their lives? How could the real world just be continuing around us while Becky was lying in a hospital bed, unconscious?

*

I sat in the back of my mum's car as she drove through the city with Tom sat wordlessly in the passenger seat. After what seemed like a lifetime, we were finally back on familiar roads. The car was quiet, and I watched out of the window, desperately wishing we were moving faster, wishing that everyone would just hurry up so I could get this over with and be back with Becky as soon as possible. The car finally pulled up outside my mum's house and I jumped out immediately. I followed her up the steps to the front door, hurrying behind her, desperate to be as quick as possible.

It hit me like a physical blow, almost taking my breath away, when I realised that Becky had been with me the last time I walked through this door, vibrant and happy. My throat was constricting, and I had to concentrate on breathing, telling myself to be strong, that I couldn't think like that.

As the front door opened, I realised with a shock that the hallway was piled up with the boxes and pieces of furniture from our flat – all the stuff that had been in the back of the van the day of the accident. I realised that Simon must have dropped it all here and I remembered that he'd had to give back the van to his work colleague, as promised. It startled me again that normal life was just carrying on while I was going through this living hell. I felt guilty – I hadn't spoken to Simon at all or thanked him for everything he'd done. I pushed the thought to the back of my mind, telling myself I would call him when we were in the car on the way back to the hospital.

The dogs appeared and approached me solemnly from the kitchen. It was as if they knew something was wrong.

My throat started to feel tight again as Toby pushed his nose into my hand.

"Stuart's been feeding and walking them," my mum said, and I suddenly felt overcome with guilt. It hadn't once crossed my mind to worry about them while we had all been sitting in the hospital. I stopped for a moment and stroked both of their heads, and I wondered as I looked at them if they were wondering where Becky was. The thought almost triggered tears again so I moved past the boxes and ran up the stairs, leaving my mum and Tom standing in the hallway at the bottom. I could hear them murmuring to each other when I was just out of earshot, but I didn't catch what they said.

I threw off my clothes as I entered the bathroom, having to pause when I caught sight of my reflection in the mirror above the sink. I had to stop and stare at myself for a second. I wondered how I could possibly look the same after everything that had happened. I felt as if there should be something different about me, something to show what I had been through. But I looked exactly the same. I turned away and put the shower on.

*

I felt a million times better when I was out of the shower and wearing fresh clothes. I shoved my feet into some trainers that were still in the wardrobe in my old room, and I threw a couple changes of clothes into an overnight bag. I ran back down the stairs and into the kitchen where my mum and Tom were sitting at the table in silence, their hands wrapped around mugs of tea. My mum stood up the moment she saw me enter and scooped her car keys up off the table in front of her. I was thankful that she seemed to sense the urgency and my need to get back to Becky as quickly as possible. No words were even spoken as I followed her out of the front door and down to the car.

*

I was a nervous bundle of energy on the journey back to the hospital and sat in the back seat sweating, just wanting to get back to Becky so I could begin to relax again. The anxiety I felt being apart from her at the moment was like nothing I had ever felt before.

34

CHRIS

"I prayed that her eyes would open." – Chris.

Two days later I sat in my usual position, next to Becky's bed, clutching her hand. She had an arterial line inserted into an artery in her arm – a very thin tube which was attached to a monitor to measure her blood pressure and the concentration of oxygen and carbon dioxide in her blood. She had an Electrocardiogram, also – round, electrode pads placed on her chest. They were linked to a monitor, which was monitoring her heart rate and rhythm. It beeped regularly and constantly in the background, a constant reminder that we were in the hospital. It was a sound that I loathed and wanted to be away from. She also had an intravenous drip inserted into a vein in her hand so that her fluids and medication could be given. She had been at the London Brain Clinic for two days now, and as much as I hated seeing her surrounded by so many tubes and machines, it was wonderful here.

The hospital itself was a beautiful, old stone building with ivy growing all over the walls, surrounded by stunning grounds. Becky had a large private room that I was allowed to stay in with her overnight on a small camp bed in the corner, which meant I hardly ever left her. The walls were painted white, the floor was tiled in large, shiny white squares, and everything was crisp and clean. There was a huge window against the back wall of Becky's room that overlooked a large park and children's play area. Every day the sun streamed in through the window, lighting up the already bright room. During the day I would open the window and the smells of spring would waft in, filling the room with the sweet aroma of blossom, cut grass, and suntan lotion. The evenings were getting lighter and sometimes it was warm enough to have the window open quite late.

The park outside the window had been constantly busy, probably due to it being the Easter holidays, and I sat and listened to the screams of the children running around and playing, dogs barking as they ran back and forth, making the most of the boiling hot spring we were having as I sat and talked to Becky. I talked to her constantly and never ran out of things to say. I told her how we first met, of holidays we'd been on, of our wedding day. I talked about her patients in the care home and retold funny stories that she'd told me over the years. I talked about my new job in Oxford and the new life that was waiting for us when she got better.

Earlier that morning I had spoken to Dave King on the phone. I had left Becky for a few minutes and taken my mobile outside the hospital. I walked around the garden as I explained what had happened. I was due to start at Cradley Heath in a week's time. Dave had been understanding and offered his sincerest apologies at what had happened, but I could tell by the underlying frostiness in his voice that he was not happy that I was not starting work at the beginning of the new term as planned. All the friendly joviality that had radiated from him when we'd met was gone. He told me he would arrange cover for the first week or two of the new term but asked when I thought I would be ready to start. I told him honestly that I didn't know. It was just a case of waiting for Becky to wake up. I sensed that he didn't understand why Becky being in hospital meant that I couldn't go to work but there was no way on earth I was leaving her.

When I came back, I sat back in my spot next to Becky and told her how the conversation had gone, thinking out loud, wishing more than anything in the world that she could reply to me. I didn't let myself think about how much I missed her. Even though she was here with me, I missed speaking with her, listening to her, looking into her eyes, seeing her smile, and watching her move around me. I missed the feeling of her touching me, holding my hand, resting her head on me. I sat clutching her hand all the time, but it just seemed so empty. I wished she would just squeeze my hand back – something, anything to let me know she was there. But, so far, there was nothing. Sometimes I could see Becky's eyes moving beneath her eyelids and I would sit and watch them flick back and forth, holding my breath. I prayed that her eyes would open. I would stare at her, the air trapped in my lungs, willing them to open, but the movement would slow down and eventually stop and her eyes would be still again, leaving my heart heavy. I wondered if she had been dreaming or if she had been aware of what was happening and was trying to fight her way back to consciousness.

*

The days passed one by one and there were no changes. The initial improvement Becky had made after the accident seemed to have slowed down, and although she still twitched and her eyes still moved under her eyelids, physical exams by Dr Matthews hadn't gained any real reaction from her yet. I watched every day as he checked her movements, reflexes, and her responses to painful stimuli by pressing on the angle of her jaw or into her nail bed. He tested her reflexive eye movements and sometimes squirted water into her ear canals to observe the eye reactions. He explained to me as I watched in distress that he wanted to see if her eyes would move in the direction of the water in her ear or the pain, or even better if she would react with movement or noise.

I didn't care. I hated watching it and I stood with my fingernails digging into the palms of my hands, fighting the urge to tell him to stop. As soon as the examinations were over, I would be back at Becky's side, her hand in mine, attempting to comfort her.

35

BECKY

"It irritates me." – Becky.

I can hear voices. I can feel people moving me around in my bed. It irritates me. I think I was dreaming but I can't remember the dream now. I try to tell whoever is touching me to get away, but I can't speak.

*

I must be in quite a deep sleep because I don't want to wake up. But the noises in the flat are confusing me, I keep thinking I can hear people and there is a beeping noise that I can't place.

*

Something weird is happening. It must have been a dream, but it felt very real. It felt as if cold water splashed into my ear. In fact, I can feel a tiny drop of water rolling down my neck. I try to wipe it away, but my arms feel heavy. I try to move onto my side, but I can't. I drift back into sleep.

*

I'm having weird dreams! They feel so real. It's as if there's a man in my room, talking.

"Her eye slowly deviated towards the ear where the water was injected."

"What does that mean?" A frantic voice. *"Does that mean she's awake? Becky? Becky?"*

I'm so angry. Are these people in my flat? I need to wake up.

36

BECKY

"You've been in a coma, don't try to talk." – Dr Carl Matthews

I was disorientated. I heard a voice saying, "You've been in a coma, don't try to talk." But that's all I wanted to do. I was so angry! Of course I haven't been in a coma, I've been asleep! Who is this in my flat? I finally started to drag myself out of the deep sleep I'd been in. I tried to rack my brain; where had I been last night? I felt as if I'd been drugged. I couldn't put my finger on it. I was probably just exhausted from working late again. Having two jobs is killing me.

"Becky, can you hear me? If you can hear me, please open your eyes." It seems weird, but I hadn't thought of that. I tried to open my eyes, but it was strange. It was as if I had forgotten how to do it. I really had to concentrate. Was I hung over? The voice kept talking and I felt like telling it to shut up. I just wanted to open my eyes. I began to feel alarmed. I tried to sit up, but I felt like a dead weight. That's when I really started to panic; I *must* have been drugged!

"Becky, don't panic. I'm a doctor, my name is Carl Matthews. You're in hospital. You've been in a coma, and you're waking up. Do not panic, relax everything, and just concentrate on trying to open your eyes – only your eyes. Don't worry about anything else right now." The fear was like nothing I had ever experienced before. My heart was beating wildly in my chest. What on earth was going on? But the soothing voice did fill me with a degree of comfort and reassurance, and it made me want to listen. I relaxed my body and concentrated on trying to remember how to open my eyes.

Suddenly, like the light bulb moments you see on cartoons, I remembered how to function my eyes and I slowly peeled them open. The scene I saw before me petrified me. I was not in my flat. I had opened my eyes to a brightly lit white room with a doctor peering down over me, saying my name. There were tubes coming out of my arm and a machine next to my head beeping, (I recognised that beep?) and the beeping was getting faster.

"Becky, well done! You are doing really well. Stay calm, you are safe," the doctor said, and I recognised the gentle voice as my eyes slowly started to focus. He was leaning over my bed, close enough that I could see his face, but not too close that I felt threatened.

For a split second, I forgot my fear as I looked into his chocolate brown eyes. He was a beautiful man: tall, dark, and handsome. His concerned face stared down at me, his eyes boring into mine. I tried to remember what had happened last night. I could remember walking home from work. I hadn't been drunk. I could remember putting my key into the door of my flat, walking in, going straight to my bedroom, being utterly exhausted and getting into bed without brushing my teeth. Then nothing.

My mind suddenly snapped back to reality, and I realised with a shock that there were more people in the corner of the room that I hadn't noticed at first. It looked like a family, a mother, a father, and a son. My eyes flicked from the doctor to the family; it looked as if the mother and father were physically holding the son back, as if he wanted to run at me. Had he beaten me up? I wanted to know who they were, and suddenly I remembered my voice. It was as if a switch had been flicked and all of a sudden I could remember how to speak.

"Who are they?" I asked. But my voice didn't come

out in the confident, firm, authoritative way I had meant it to, it was more of a croaky whisper.

"What did she say? What did she say? Becky?" the son said, straining forward as if to get at me, each of his arms being held back by the mum and dad. The doctor held out a warning hand to him and he stopped straining, turning his head to the side to try and hear us talk.

"Hi, Becky, my name is Dr Matthews, and that is your husband in the corner with his family. You have…"

"Husband?" I snapped, absolutely furious. My voice felt sore and foreign in my throat. "I'm not married. You have me mixed up with someone else. What the hell is going on?"

37

CHRIS

"It made me go cold." – Chris.

After praying for Becky to wake up for every single second of every single day since the accident, the reality of it actually happening was awful. I watched as she struggled awake, Dr Matthews literally coaxing her back into reality, with my heart in my mouth. I was elated that she was finally waking up, but mortified at how awful it was watching someone you love struggle and panic and be so confused. I desperately wanted to be the first person she saw when she opened her eyes, knowing it would reassure her and wanting her to know I was there, but the doctor had ordered me to stay back, saying she needed space and mustn't be crowded. As soon as she started to speak, in a low murmur that I couldn't hear, Dr Matthews turned to the three of us with a look of shock and confusion on his face, instantly causing me to panic. He told us we had to leave and ushered us out of the room. My mum and Tom were on either side of me – there was a hand pushing into the small of my back and a hand on the top of my arm. I was being pulled and pushed in the direction of the door, but I had no idea whose hand was whose. The doctor was blocking my view of Becky as he helped herd me out of the room. I knew he was talking to me, but his words fell upon deaf ears once again. I was oblivious to what was being said as I struggled to look over his shoulder at Becky. I desperately wanted to see her, to look at her properly for myself, as if needing proof that she was finally awake. It felt like an eternity since I had seen her.

When our eyes finally met, it me made me go cold. It

was only for the briefest split-second before I was ushered out of the door, but it was like looking into the eyes of a complete stranger. It wasn't just that Becky was bemused – it was more than that. It was not Becky I was looking at. Not my Becky. I couldn't bear the thought of the look we'd shared, and I couldn't understand it; I was completely haunted by what I'd seen. Within seconds we were outside the room and Dr Matthews snapped at one of the waiting nurses outside.

"Jane, can you get Dr Ford in here, please." His voice was tense for the first time since we had met. The nurse nodded and scuttled off. She half walked, half ran down the corridor and around the corner, out of sight. Dr Matthews closed the door on us with no more explanation. Dread folded around me like a cloak.

38

CHRIS

"I think she is quite curious to meet you." – Dr Carl Matthews.

I couldn't believe what was happening. I felt like I was back to the day of the accident again. Not knowing anything, filled with uncertainty and fear, but if anything this was even worse than before. The staff here were so attentive; rather than being left to sit in the waiting room on our own with our thoughts, we were now sitting in a private room, being given regular updates by one of the nurses. It meant that every half an hour or so one of the nurses would come into the room, causing my heart to jump into my throat, but each time there was no news.

Becky had woken up at around four o'clock in the afternoon. It was now nearly eight o'clock in the evening. I was trying so hard to stay calm and to not get upset or frustrated, but it was testing every part of my patience. I tried to think of anything but the look Becky and I had shared. I must be overreacting. I tried to think of anything but the coldness and the strangeness of her eyes. But I couldn't. I thought about it over and over again, driving myself insane.

*

It was ten p.m. and my mum had dozed off. The sound of her heavy breathing coming from the corner of the room was the only sound I could hear. Tom sat without a sound like a ghost, wide awake, his eyes flicking between me and my mum, watching over us both. I sat in silence, staring out of the window into the darkness. I had watched the sun set out of the window as the day turned into night. The sky had lit up, a mixture of beautiful colours. Fiery rays of red, pink, orange, and yellow had streaked across the sky as the sun melted into the horizon. With every moment that went by there was a change in colour. After a while, there was a strip of violet and grey among the fiery colours of the sun, then a deep blue took over before it finally turned to black as the night pushed its way through. I stared out into the night. It was as dark and empty as the thoughts in my head.

*

My heart leapt as the door opened a while later and Dr Matthews finally appeared. For once he didn't look like his usual immaculate self. His gleaming head of hair, which usually didn't have a hair out of place, looked wilder than usual and he had slight shadows under his eyes. He still looked remarkably handsome, though, and all it did was emphasise his dark eyes and smoky black lashes. Somehow being tired made him even more good looking. He seemed weary when he entered, and I got the feeling he couldn't look me as directly in the eye as he usually did. My mum startled awake as he came in and sat down heavily into a chair opposite us, sighing loudly. It felt unfamiliar to have him sitting in this room with us now, and for some reason I wanted him to take me to his office to talk to me there. I wanted the big oak desk between us like we'd had before.

I started to panic, and those few seconds that I waited for him to open his mouth and speak felt like a lifetime. Every muscle in my body was tense, it was a physical reaction, fight or flight. I didn't know what to do with all the adrenalin that was running through my body. I felt like running away, as if not hearing whatever it was that Dr Matthews had to tell me would mean that it wasn't actually happening. He cleared his throat.

"Mr. McNulty," he said, still avoiding my eye. I had been 'Chris' earlier, now we were back to 'Mr.

187

McNulty'. "As you saw, this afternoon Becky came out of her coma, which is excellent, positive news. Unfortunately, this seems to have brought with it a new problem. Becky seems to be suffering from a severe form of memory loss. As we have discussed, the accident your wife had did not cause any apparent brain damage, but after spending some time this afternoon with her, I am quite confident that she has something called Retrograde Amnesia. Retrograde Amnesia is a partial or total loss of memory of events before a traumatic event. This memory loss can consist of a few minutes or hours, or up to several years. However, new information can still be processed, stored, and recalled. The loss of memory may be temporary or permanent, but goes beyond ordinary forgetfulness. The physical changes in the brain that are the cause for this amnesia are still not known. Retrograde Amnesia targets the most recent memories first. The more severe the case, the further back in time the memory loss extends. This pattern of destroying new memories before older ones is called Ribot's law, and it's caused because the neutral pathways of newer memories are not as strong as older ones that have been strengthened by years of retrieval.

"On a positive note, amnesia patients do retain their personality and identity along with their implicit or procedural memory. This is because skills and instinctive physical memories – for example, riding a bike or driving a car, – are stored separately from episodic memories.

With regards to the types of treatment on offer, many different amnesia patients fix themselves without being treated, and there are many ways to cope with memory loss if that is not the case. One of these ways is occupational therapy, where the patient will learn to develop the memory skills they have and try and regain those that they have lost by finding techniques that help retrieve lost memories. This can include strategies for organising information to remember it more easily-"

I interrupted the doctor mid flow, completely confused and not able to keep up with all the information he was telling me.

"What does this mean for Becky? How severely affected is her memory, then?" I snapped, the room starting to spin around me. I knew that my voice sounded hysterical, but I didn't understand why he was waffling and confusing me when I just wanted to know the facts.

"Becky thinks she is nineteen," the doctor said, finally looking me in the eye. I stared at him. The room was silent, and I almost laughed. I could feel hysteria creeping into me again. This was just way too much information for me to take in after everything else that had already happened. How much can one person physically take?

I thought once again about how wonderful it would be if I could get up and run away. I just wanted to be away from all of this, to come back and for everything to be back to normal. The doctor started talking again, pulling me back to reality.

"The implication of this means that, right now, Becky has no recollection of you at all. In fact, she doesn't seem to be able to tell me about anyone close to her."

"She wouldn't," I snapped. "Becky lived alone when she was nineteen and she had no family around her."

"I see," Dr Matthews said before falling silent. There was an awkward pause. I rested my head in my hands.

"Is this for real? Does stuff like this actually happen?" I said, knowing that it was a stupid, almost childish question, but I couldn't help myself.

"Unfortunately, yes. It's not common, but it does happen."

"Is she going to get better? Will she ever be back to normal?" I asked, not knowing if I even wanted to hear his reply. Dr Matthews sighed.

"There is no way of knowing. It depends on the severity of each individual patient's condition. Sometimes people are lucky and get their memory back relatively quickly, whereas there are others who have never regained their memories back, and they are forever left with a gap in their memory. It really does depend on each individual case and there is no way for us to know what is going to happen with Becky at the moment. After testing this evening, it seems her learning abilities remain excellent, and, surprisingly, she has taken the news of what has happened to her remarkably well. I don't think she's gone into denial. I've spoken to her in great length, and she seems to understand what has happened to her and it seems that she has almost come to terms with it, which is remarkable. Some people can be in denial for a huge period of time, and, I believe, although it isn't proven, that this can actually hinder the patient getting their memory back." He paused, as if trying to figure out what to say next. "The thing that Becky seems to be struggling with the most at the moment is the fact that she's married. Now, this is understandable – in her head, she's a single nineteen-year-old girl. Trying to get her head around being a twenty-six-year-old married woman is a huge adjustment for her. I was also obligated to tell her about the loss of her baby, which was another huge shock for her. Obviously, as she has no recollection of the pregnancy and no emotional ties to it, she's taken the news in her stride."

I stared open mouthed as I tried to process all the information that Dr Matthews was telling me. He paused for a few seconds before continuing.

"I think she is quite curious to meet you and speak with you herself, and I'm sure she has hundreds of questions for you. I know that it's late, and that you're probably desperate to see her, but I think it's best that we wait until tomorrow. Becky and I spoke about it briefly, and she is happy to meet with you then. I certainly think this is a good idea, and that we should give her tonight to herself. Don't worry too much, Mr. McNulty, she will be monitored very closely overnight. She has already had a small amount of physio this afternoon and she will again in the morning. Her muscles have been still for quite a while now, so this is an important part of her recovery." Dr Matthews paused, as if he was concentrating on what he was going to say next and I waited, knowing that I wasn't going to like whatever it was he had to say. "I am aware that you've been staying in Becky's room with her overnight up until this point, but under the circumstances I'm afraid we're not able to allow this anymore without Becky's consent…"

Tears stung my eyes once again and I knew I was going to break down. I dug my fingernails into my hand and prayed I could hold it together until Dr Matthews had gone; I didn't want to lose face in front of him any more than I already had. My mum laid her hand on my arm, bringing me back to reality.

"Come and stay at home tonight, Chris. Get a good night's sleep and be ready for tomorrow," she said encouragingly, and for once I just couldn't be bothered to argue. The doctor looked relieved.

"I think that's for the best," he said. "Becky is aware that you have been here for her the whole time, she seemed very bewildered by it. Go home get some rest. Come back tomorrow lunchtime and we will go from there. Take it in your stride for now, Mr. McNulty; hopefully Becky's memory will start to come back soon."

39

BECKY

"Telling me things about myself that I just can't fathom being true." – Becky.

I opened my eyes, and for a split second I didn't know where I was. Then the events from yesterday came crashing back to me. I lay awake in the dark. There was nobody in the room with me. I looked around. It was quite cosy; the curtains were drawn and the room was filled with a reddish glow as the light from outside tried to get in. The machine I was attached to was still beeping steadily next to me. I laid my head back into the pillow and tried to understand everything that had happened. I found it very difficult to believe that this time yesterday I'd been in a coma and now I was lying in bed, feeling absolutely fine. How could that be? I resolved to ask the doctor more questions today. The only thing that felt really strange was my body. It felt so weak. I wiggled my toes and even they hurt slightly. The physio said it was because I had been so still for such a length of time and my muscles hadn't been used.

They say I'm twenty-six. Twenty-six! And that I'm married, and I was pregnant. It's as if I've woken up in someone else's life. I can't imagine how any of it could have happened. I've never wanted to get married, and I have certainly never wanted to have children. There is a part of me that still thinks they must have gotten me mixed up with someone else. I felt delirious, as if they'd put me on drugs or morphine, and none of it seems real. I still felt tired. Should I really be so tired if I'd been asleep for the past two weeks?

*

The doctor came in a little while later, flashing a smile at me, looking like an advert for toothpaste as he pulled a chair up next to my bed.

"How are you doing today, Becky?" he asked, looking genuinely concerned.

"I'm okay," I said carefully, and, to my surprise, I could feel my cheeks blush slightly. I'm sure he noticed, and he smiled even more, although slightly awkwardly.

"You're doing remarkably well, Becky. Can you remember the conversations that we had yesterday?"

"Yes, I'm pretty sure I can remember everything from yesterday," I answered, not wanting to meet his eye. He looked thoughtful.

"You still don't remember anything at all from when you were around the age of nineteen?" he asked again, and a sudden burst of unreasonable irritation jumped to the front of my mind, but I managed to control it. I felt like screaming, *"I am nineteen!"* at him, but I took a deep breath and stopped myself.

"No," I replied. We sat in silence for a while.

*

I had a busy morning, with a steady stream of people coming in and out of my room talking to me, testing me, and asking me questions. By lunchtime I was exhausted again, and I wondered if it was normal to feel this tired. When I asked Dr Matthews, he smiled.

"It's to be expected, Becky, you've been through a lot." I couldn't tear my eyes away from his face when he smiled.

He sat down with me when we were alone in the early afternoon and told me that my 'husband' was in the hospital and desperate to see me. I felt completely exhausted and nervous, but excited at the same time. Who was the man I had chosen to marry? I still couldn't get my head around the fact that I had been married at all.

I'd never been one of those girls that longed for a relationship. I was quite happy on my own. I wondered what he looked like and what kind of person he was. I looked at the doctor as he spoke, and found myself hoping it was someone like him.

*

I tried to hide the disappointment on my face when my 'husband' walked into the room later that afternoon. He was nothing like I had expected. Dr Matthews held the door open for him to walk through and watched me intently for my reaction.

"Becky, this is Chris," he said. I noticed a look of irritation flash across Chris' face when the doctor introduced him, and it put my back up. He walked over to me quickly, his eyes boring into my face, wearing an expression that I can't describe. It was pure admiration, almost like a dog looking at its owner. He looked at me as if he worshipped me, and it instantly put me off him. Tears were brimming in his eyes as he approached me, and he advanced so quickly – before I knew it, he was beside my bed, reaching out as if to hold my hand. I snatched it away, disgusted, and he looked as if he'd been slapped. I saw him looking at me in shock and disbelief. I didn't care, I stared back at him defiantly.

"Becky," he said, recovering himself. He sat down in the chair next to my bed that Dr Matthews had been sitting in earlier. He didn't seem to know what to do with his hands, and eventually he put them in his lap. "I'm your husband… Chris," he said, and smiled at me. When he smiled his whole face changed, slight dimples appeared in his cheeks and his eyes lit up. I could see how some people may find him attractive, just not me.

"You're not my type," I blurted out without thinking, and he grinned, a huge smile that took over his entire face, and once again I found myself seeing how people could find him attractive. It made him look very warm and handsome. He paused for a second and looked down at the hands in his lap. When he looked back up at me the smile was still there on his face and his eyes looked watery.

"That's what you said to me the first day we met," he said.

*

It was definitely the strangest day of my life. Well, the strangest day of my life that I could remember. The love that Chris had for me radiated off him as he sat with me that afternoon, and it made me uncomfortable. He was so awkward around me, and he just didn't know what to do with himself. I kept firing questions at him, hungry for information.

I wanted to know everything, but he kept stuttering as he talked, so desperate to impress me. He wanted to dwell on how we'd met, our wedding and our honeymoon, holidays we'd been on and his friends and family, but I wasn't interested in any of that. Especially after he told me I'd worked in a care home for people with learning disabilities. I've always wanted to do that! That's my dream! I can't believe that it's true and that I'd actually managed to achieve it. It broke my heart that I couldn't remember it. Sensing my interest, Chris regaled me with stories of the patients I'd looked after and I sat rapt, listening to everything he said, completely engrossed. I wished I could remember it, and hoped that the memories would start coming back to me soon. At the moment, though, there was still nothing.

"Do they know I'm in hospital?" I said. "Will I still have a job? You know, if I can remember again?" I asked.

"Well, no, you've actually left the job now-" Chris replied, and I interrupted him mid-sentence.

"What? Why?" I couldn't get the words out quick enough. I was genuinely confused. Why would I leave the job that I've been desperate for since I'd been at school?

"Well," Chris said, spluttering over his words, "because you were pregnant, for one, and because I was offered a new job teaching at a great school in Oxford. We were actually leaving London and moving to Oxford the day you had the car accident."

"So basically *I* had to give up a job that *I* loved to follow you, because *you* got a new job?" I said, staring at him, my lip curling in disgust, and for a split second I could've almost felt sorry for him. He cringed at my words and opened and closed his mouth, not knowing what to say.

"You didn't mind, you wanted to come with me, you were happy for me..." he trailed off, looking around hopelessly, "...and because of the baby."

"I don't even want kids! Not only was I having a baby I don't want, but I'm gave up a job that I love so you can follow *your* dreams? That doesn't sound like much of a marriage to me," I snapped. I knew I was being unreasonable and even a little bit spiteful, but I felt a streak of hatred for this man sitting next to me. He thinks he knows me so well. He sat next to me, telling me things about myself that I just can't fathom being true. I can't imagine giving up my dream job to follow a man and have a baby! That sounds like my worst nightmare.

I felt completely frustrated and I had an urge to scream, but I sat in stony silence, slightly enjoying Chris' obvious discomfort. I couldn't wait for him to leave. I knew that this wasn't his fault, but I still couldn't help feeling a huge resentment towards him. As soon as he left later on that day, and once Dr Matthews was back in the room with me, I felt relaxed again.

Later that afternoon, I threw myself into my activities. Firstly, occupational therapy, although the stuff I was doing with them didn't seem to help me in any way. It was mainly exercises to learn how to retain new memories and organise information, but I didn't have an issue with that! I could remember everything since I'd woken up, it was just the huge chunk before that that I couldn't remember. After occupational therapy came physio. I was absolutely desperate to be up and walking around, and I couldn't believe what a slow process it was. I was doing exercises in bed first of all to strengthen my arms and legs. I would be allowed to try to get out of bed in the next couple of days. I hated lying there, having people serve me, and I felt hugely embarrassed about the catheter. I knew I would be able to walk to the bathroom that adjoined my room. It was only about six feet away, but Dr Matthews insisted that I wasn't to move yet, saying it would be better to take it slowly. For some reason, it was him that I felt the most embarrassed in front of.

*

"Absolutely not!" I forgot myself and almost shouted at Dr Matthews, anger burning inside me. If I could have stamped my foot, I would have! I was so angry I could hardly get my words out. The cheek! Dr Matthews had the decency to look sheepish and embarrassed, and it reminded me that it wasn't him that my anger should be directed at; it was Chris.

Chris had sent Dr Matthews in to ask if he could stay in my room with me overnight! Apparently he'd slept in here every night while I'd been unconscious, and wanted to carry on! I could barely get my words out as I was in such a rage to put my foot down and say no. How *dare* he? I felt such an intense hatred for him at that moment, I would have been happy to never see him again. As if I would want some stranger to stay in my room with me overnight! The absolute audacity of him!

40

CHRIS

"When Becky was nineteen, she was a very angry, closed young woman."– Sue.

"Mr. McNulty, I understand where you are coming from, and I totally sympathise with you, but the hospital is in a difficult situation now and I have to stand by the patient's request. You have only seen Becky once since she's woken up, and as far as she's concerned you are a complete stranger to her. I cannot allow you to stay in her room against her wishes," Dr Matthews said gently and sensitively. We were sat in his office and my cheeks burned with embarrassment. The fact that I'd had to ask permission to sleep in the same room as my wife filled me with anger, and if that wasn't bad enough, I was now being told 'no' like a naughty school child. I squeezed my temples and battled to fight the tears that were very close to spilling over. All the determination I'd had to stay strong was slowly slipping away. I felt as if my whole life was falling apart in front of me.

Before all of this had happened, I just hadn't understood how precious life is. Since the accident, I felt as if I was walking over a frozen lake with the ice creaking and cracking beneath my feet, and now, since Becky had woken up, I felt as if I'd plunged through into the icy water and was suffocating. Trapped underneath, unable to breathe, looking up at the surface. Without realising it, a tear escaped and fell down my cheek, and I brushed it away angrily, thanking God my mum was outside and couldn't see me fall apart. That is what it felt like. I felt as if I were literally falling apart. All these thoughts were running through my head, and I finally gave in to all the emotion. All the resolve I'd had so far not to cry disappeared. I didn't care that I was in front of Dr Matthews. I put my head in my hands and sobbed and sobbed.

*

I lay in bed in my old room at my mum's house that night, feeling overcome with loneliness. I couldn't stop thinking about how my first meeting with Becky had gone. It couldn't have gone any worse, even in my worst nightmare. I couldn't even bare to think of the way she'd looked at me, filled with such anger and hatred. I couldn't get my head around it. I had honestly believed deep, deep down that if the worst had come to the worst and Becky really didn't recognise me, it was a given she would fall in love with me again. We were meant to be together. We were completely entwined in each other's lives. I knew her off by heart, and she knew me off by heart. How could she not have one tiny part of her that remembered me?

*

Over the next couple of weeks, things didn't improve for me. Not being able to stay at the hospital meant I had to make the time-consuming journey home every evening and back into the hospital every morning. This was made even worse due to me not having a car. Usually, my mum would drop me at the hospital and stay with me for the day, but on the days that she couldn't I had to make my own way in, meaning I had to get the tube, a train, and a bus to get to the hospital.

Every day, as I approached the main entrance, I would feel the familiar curl of fear in my stomach, and it got to the point where I actually dreaded seeing Becky. I would pray that she was in a tolerable mood. So far, she'd been very up and down. Some days she would sit there with a polite smile on her face, trying at least to be nice. I knew

200

she couldn't wait for me to leave. The only thing she was interested in talking about was her old job. I was constantly worried that I would run out of stories to tell her and that she wouldn't want me in there anymore. Other days she seemed so angry and stressed she would just snap at me constantly. It wore me down so much I would leave the hospital feeling completely desolate.

If that wasn't bad enough, I had Dave King on my case, frequently asking when I would be starting work. I had tried to put him off and asked if I could start my new role the following term instead, whilst Becky was still in hospital. The line had gone very quiet and his voice, as cold as ice, had informed me that the only way they would be able to accept that was if I was signed off by a doctor. Luckily my local GP, Dr Moran, signed me off for a month with stress due to the circumstances. I put it to the back of my mind.

*

Becky was up out of bed, now, and walking around. She started off with short distances, but she was as determined as usual, and it wasn't long until she could go outside the hospital and walk around the grounds. She was usually with one of the physios, but once or twice I'd seen her walking with Dr Matthews. As much as I hated to admit it, I was jealous of how much time he got to spend with her, and how much she seemed to trust him. I can't say a word without her picking it apart, and she always seemed to be looking for the negative in absolutely everything I said or did. Somehow, she managed to put a negative spin on anything I had to say. But when Dr Matthews spoke to her, she would light up.

I was becoming more and more depressed by the day, and was finding it increasingly hard to remain positive. I continued praying that Becky's memory would start to come back, but there were absolutely no signs that it was going to happen. I didn't know how much more I could take. I still missed her so much. Seeing her every day and acting like strangers was making it even harder. The old certainty that I had felt, how sure I was that Becky would fall back in love with me, was slipping away day by day and I was beginning to realise that if her memory didn't come back soon, if she couldn't remember how she used to feel about me, this could be it. Our lives would never be the same again.

*

Although I would never admit it out loud, I was also jealous of the relationship that my mum had struck up with Becky since the accident. Straight away my mum seemed very understanding of Becky's situation and how she was feeling. It broke my heart that she was doing a better job of grasping it than I was. She actually seemed to have bonded with her, while Becky still looked at me like a pesky stranger.

Dr Matthews had suggested getting new people to come into the hospital to meet Becky, to see if interacting with them helped jog any old memories. Simon had popped in to say hello to her a few days ago when he'd given me a lift in one morning, but I could tell he felt hugely uncomfortable about the whole situation, and he didn't stay for long. Becky didn't recognise him, and she seemed as uninterested in him as she did with me. The next day my mum came into the hospital with me to spend some time with her. I had wanted to be there, too, but Dr Matthews suggested I let my mum go in alone, to give Becky some time with someone else unaccompanied. I knew that his suggestion was an order and I hated him for it.

I sat down in reception while I waited for my mum to appear. I stared out through the glass doors at another unseasonably beautiful day outside as I sat twiddling my thumbs. I expected my mum to appear, shaking her head in frustration and agreeing with me that Becky was hard work and negative, but she didn't. She came down a couple of hours later looking very pensive. I leapt up and approached her the second she came into view.

"How was she? What do you think?" I asked, hating the desperate, whiny tone that seemed to be in my voice all the time now.

"I feel very sorry for her, Chris. She's just a confused young girl in her head. Give her time, I reckon." she said, looking up at me, a thoughtful look on her face.

"What do you mean, give her time? How much time? Why doesn't she know me, Mum? Surely she should remember me by now? And even if she genuinely doesn't remember me, surely she should just fall in love with me again? She fell in love with me once, why can't she fall in love with me again?" I fired the questions at her, everything I was worried sick about, unable to stop, but she interrupted me with a wave of her hand while I was mid flow.

"Because she is a totally different person in her head now, Chris," she said, her voice calm but firm. "When Becky met you, she was a very lonely twenty-three-year-old woman. She had been on her own for such a long time I think she was finally ready to open-up and meet somebody. I think you were lucky that you met her when you did. It was just the right time. When Becky was nineteen, she was a very angry, closed young woman. She'd been on her own, fending for herself since she was sixteen! She didn't want a man in her life, she didn't want anyone in her life. You know that. I think even if the two of you had met when she was that age it would have been a different story and you wouldn't have ended up together. She just didn't *want* people in her life then, she shut them out. She didn't trust anyone, and she didn't

203

want to get close to anyone, and you've got to remember that *that* is how she is feeling right now – made a thousand times worse by everything that has happened now with all of this. She's woken up in that teenage frame of mind, to be told she has effectively lost the last six or seven years of her life. It's no wonder she's behaving the way she is. Just give her time, it's all we can do."

41

BECKY

"You two were literally like two parts of the same person." – Sue.

I pulled my eyes open and looked around. My heart was beating slightly heavier in my chest. It must be early morning, as there was light shining in from beneath the drawn curtains. I desperately tried to remember the dream I had just had. Every morning for the last few days I woke up feeling as if I had forgotten something – which I know is ironic since I have severe memory loss (I refuse to say amnesia). I would wake up feeling the way you do when you want to say something and it's just on the tip of your tongue. It was such a weird feeling. I was pretty certain that I'd never had dreams before the accident, so I wasn't sure if these feelings were normal or not. Every morning now I would wake up knowing that I had been dreaming all night, but never remembering what about. Sometimes I would remember small split-second flashes, usually of me working in a care home, or I would have flashes of people that I didn't recognise. The frustrating thing was that I didn't know if the dreams were memories – if I was dreaming about stuff that *had* happened, or if I was dreaming about stuff that people have *told* me that happened. Every morning I wracked my brain, desperately trying to claw back the dream before it floated off, never to be remembered.

*

My days in the hospital were surprisingly busy. Chris came to see me every day without fail, and I had to endure a few hours with him. I still had occupational therapy every day, even though I still didn't believe it helped me in any way, and also physio, which I have thrown myself into. I loved finally having all the tubes taken out of me and being able to feed myself and get up out of bed to go to the toilet. I couldn't believe how weak I was the first time, though, and I realised that Dr Matthews had been completely right about me not doing too much too soon. I would get out of breath and dizzy if I ventured too far and would be so thankful to be lying back down in bed again once I was back. I wondered how people who had come out of a coma after years and years felt. Their bodies must have almost wasted away.

*

To try and 'jog' my memory, Dr Matthews suggested I meet people that I knew from before and after the gap in my memory to see if it brought anything back. I felt hot with embarrassment when I had to admit to him that I hadn't really had any friends back then, and Chris confirmed that when we'd met I hadn't had any friends of my own. Dr Matthews asked Chris about any friends I'd made since he had met me, perhaps over the last few years, but Chris shrugged his shoulders and said that I didn't really mix with any of his friends' partners or have any friends that he could think of. He said I was close to his mum and my boss at the care home. Dr Matthews kindly skipped over the subject, looking puzzled, and said that seeing anyone at all that I knew before may help. Chris had nodded his head enthusiastically and said he would bring some people in.

During this exchange, another surge of hatred for Chris shot through me. The reason I didn't have any friends when I was younger was because I had always been so busy. Working two jobs and having a flat to pay for meant I never had the time to socialise – but surely if mine and Chris' life had been as wonderful as he is always trying to describe I would have a group of friends of my own by now? The acknowledgement that even up until the age of twenty-six I hadn't really been able to make friends made me really sad, and tears of humiliation stung at the back of my eyes. I felt ashamed in front of Dr Matthews.

A day or so later, Chris brought one of his friends up to my room to introduce us. Although I didn't let it show in front of Chris, I was incredibly curious to see if meeting someone else would bring any of my memories back, and I sat waiting with bated breath as a man entered my room behind Chris. He barely looked me in the eye, and he had his hands shoved deep down into his pockets as he mumbled hello. He was very handsome. His jet black, long, wavy hair fell around his strikingly handsome face, which was filled with gorgeous dark eyes and a sensuous but slightly cruel mouth. I gazed at him, desperate for some form of recognition to flicker within in me. But there was nothing.

*

The next person who came in to see me, in an attempt to help jog my memory, was Chris' mum. I was dreading it. I imagined her to be a whiny woman who would tell me how wonderful my life had been with her son, how I would eventually fall in love with him again, and how we would live happily ever after.

I was nervous as I sat waiting for her to come in that afternoon and I felt on guard. I was in the room on my own when Chris' mum knocked gently on the door before poking her head around. I caught her eye and instantly felt my guard go down. She just radiated warmth and love – in a good way, though, not in the needy way that Chris did.

"Is it alright to come in now, lovie?" she asked, still waiting at the door, and I nodded my head vigorously. She came over to the bed and looked around for a chair.

She pulled one over from by the window and sat down close to my bed.

"You've lost weight," was the first thing she said, casting her eye over me. "You need to get a few good meals down you, girl." I stared at her. There was something so familiar about her, although I couldn't *actually* remember her. As far as I was concerned, I'd never met her before in my life and she was a stranger to me. I just couldn't put my finger on this familiarity. We sat in silence for a while as I studied her face, trying to get my thoughts in order, until I realised that I hadn't said anything yet.

"What's your name?" I asked.

"Oh, I'm so sorry, dear! How stupid of me! I'm Sue!" she cried, and held out her hand to me. I took it and we shook hands. Sue squeezed my hand slightly and looked me in the eye. "It is *so* good to see you up and talking my dear. I've been so, so worried about you. Obviously, I wish we were sitting here under different circumstances. I wish you could remember me, and I *wish* you could remember Chris. But thank the Lord you're okay." She paused. "How *are* you?" she said, looking me in the eye. It seemed like a genuine question, and, all of a sudden I just wanted to get everything off my chest.

"I'm doing okay, I suppose. It's just horrible. I feel so frustrated all the time. Sometimes I just want to scream and scream. When I came out of the coma it literally felt as if I had been nineteen the day before. I can remember in detail going to work, being in my flat, going to bed. I just cannot get my head around how so many years could have passed between all of that time, and I don't know about it… This is the stuff from movies, not what happens in real life." I paused, taking a deep breath before continuing. The words flowed from me easily, as if they had been desperate to get out without me even knowing. "I'm trying really, really hard to be grown up about it all and just get on with it without causing a fuss. But sometimes I just wish I could close off from it all and not have to deal with it."

"You've always been like that. You've always been a very brave girl. Even when you were tiny. You used to talk to me a lot about your mum and those years," Sue said, and my head snapped around to look at her.

"Really?" I said sceptically, raising my eyebrow at her. I found this hard to believe. I had always vowed never to talk to *anyone* about my mum and my life while she was still alive. But something about this woman convinced me that she was telling the truth.

"Yes," she said. "Not in the beginning. Not for a long time, but eventually you opened-up to me about it. I think it did you good to get it all off your chest. I don't even think you talked to Chris about some of the stuff we talked about." I continued looking at her doubtfully, and she smiled at me, raising an eyebrow.

"Don't look at me like that, my dear! We were very close, you and I. You were going to be the mother of my grandchild. I love you like my own daughter," she said, and I suddenly felt ashamed. Because I had been through so much myself recently, I forgot that the people around me were going through horrible times, too. Sue had lost her grandchild.

"I don't expect you talk to me right now, you opened up to me after years of being with my son and after years of being a part of my life. You don't need to talk to me about anything at all, at the moment. I understand that I'm a stranger to you now, as much as it breaks my heart."

We sat in silence for a while as I wracked my brain for something to say, but I couldn't think of anything. The silence wasn't uncomfortable, though, far from it in fact.

Sue seemed happy sitting in the companionship of a quiet person, and neither of us felt the need to fill the silence. It was comforting having her in the room with me.

"I don't remember Chris," I said after a while. "Not at all. He seems to think I'm going to fall straight back in love with him somehow, but I just don't see how it's going to happen." I didn't know if I was speaking out of turn, but Sue sat back in her chair and sighed.

"You and Chris had a very, very special relationship, Becky," she said, and I raised my eyebrows once again. Was I about to get the 'Chris is wonderful' spiel that I had been expecting after all? "Honestly, lovie, you can believe what you want, but it breaks my heart that you may never know how good you had it. You were so lonely when you met Chris. You'd been living on your own for years, working constantly, never socialising, never mixing with other people. Then, bam! You two met and literally overnight you were a couple and you never looked back. You supported each other through everything, and you *adored* one another. It was plain for all to see. I have never, ever seen anyone as in love as you two, before or since, and I doubt I ever will again. Honestly, you would light up at the sound of each other's voices, you were completely and utterly in sync with one another. Sometimes being in the same room as the pair of you made me feel as if I were intruding, as if I was peeking in through someone's curtains, looking in on something that I shouldn't be. I would give anything to have had that at some point in my life.

"Don't disregard it all straight away. I know you're angry and confused, and I know, believe me, that Chris isn't handling this very well. It's very unlike him to have got himself in such a pickle. I think it's a testament to how he feels about you. He was so certain that you would know him, and he cannot understand how you can't. You two were literally like two parts of the same person. *I struggle to get my head around it all, so God only knows how he must feel... he doesn't talk to me about it very much, but I know it is absolutely breaking him. I'm worried about him...*" Sue trailed off and I felt a bit ashamed of myself. I resolved to try a little bit harder with Chris, and to try and put myself in his shoes. Sue went quiet. We sat like that for a while.

42

BECKY

"He was the kind of man I could have seen myself being married to. Not someone like Chris." – Becky.

I opened my eyes. A room – an office? A small room. The door is open. Is there someone outside? I desperately try to retrieve my dream, knowing that in a few moments it would be gone forever. I struggled to remember finer details but as the seconds slipped by the dream evaporated, and I was left with the usual empty feeling of frustration. I groaned out loud.

I'd been out of the coma for a couple of weeks now, and every morning I woke up utterly exhausted. Every night without fail would be full of dreams, and every morning I would wake up with the same feeling of unease, as if something was on the tip of my tongue, as if there was information or memories that were going to burst through at any moment. But they never did. They just faded away. Once I was up and about and carrying on with my day the feelings would subside, and by the time it was the evening I would convince myself I had over reacted, that I must have been thinking too much into it – until the next morning, when the same scenario would happen all over again. I knew it was wrong, but I hadn't told any of the hospital staff or doctors about my dreams or the feelings they left me with. It was something that I wanted to deal with by myself. I didn't want to build people's hopes up that my memory was going to come back, because other than those first few seconds every morning, my memory was still a complete and utter blank.

I tried to convince myself that it wasn't even anything

to do with my memory, perhaps it was because I had started dreaming now and these were normal feelings after you'd been dreaming during the night. For all I knew this could be how everyone felt when they woke up – because I hadn't been a dreamer before the accident, I had nothing to compare it to. I lay in bed for a while. Once the dream had gone my mind started to wander, and, as usual, I found myself thinking of Dr Matthews. He seemed to occupy a huge amount of the time in my head. I was trying not to admit it to myself, but I had to face facts and admit that I had a little crush on him. I knew it was completely inappropriate, but I just found everything about him amazing. The way he spoke to me, the way he looked at me – and it helped that he was devilishly handsome. *He* was the kind of man I could have seen myself being married to. Not someone like Chris.

I looked forward to every moment we spent together, and felt genuinely depressed on the days he wasn't in the hospital. I looked at the clock on my bedside table. He would be coming in to see me in about an hour's time. The thought gave me butterflies.

43

CHRIS

"You want to pull yourself together. For her sake." –
Sue.

Things were not getting any better for me, even though
Becky was doing really well. She seemed to be getting
fitter every day, although her memory was still the same.
She was still distant with me and looked at me filled with
disgust most of the time. Since I'd asked to stay in her
room overnight things had gone from bad to worse. She
remained polite but hostile towards me now. Thankfully,
she did still allow me to sit with her every day, but it was
obvious that she couldn't wait for it to be over and for me
to be out of the door.

With each day that passed I felt more and more scared
to look her in the eye, and I was constantly terrified of
saying the wrong thing; it didn't take much to set her off,
and she would unleash her anger on me. I would
tentatively ask her how she was feeling and ask if there
was anything she would like to talk about. She would
sigh, a long, drawn-out, exasperated sigh, and confirm
that no, there was nothing that she wanted to talk to me
about. She would tolerate me for the few hours I was in
the hospital, and each day the lump in my throat and heart
would grow heavier and heavier.

*

One day when I walked into Becky's room she was
sitting in a chair by the window, looking out over the
park below. It was the first time I'd seen her sitting there,
usually she was in her bed when I arrived.

"Hey," I said, more enthusiastically than usual. I don't
know why – as if this small change in routine would

make a difference. Becky's head flung around at the sound of my voice, and I could see the disappointment all over her face when she realised it was me. It pained me to realise that deep down I knew it was Dr Matthews that she had wanted to see, and a slight rage started to seep into my body. I'd had suspicions for a few days now that she had some kind of teenage crush on him. I'd seen the way she looked at him when he walked into the room – it was the way she used to look at me. I dragged a chair across the room to join her, and she looked at me with distaste as the chair scraped across the tiled floor, making a loud sound in the quiet room. For once, I didn't care. Anger continued bubbling inside me. I sat opposite her and looked out of the window at the dew-covered park outside. There was a tree covered in blossom that glistened and sparkled in the morning sun. I stared at the candy floss and rose pinks of each bud. We sat in silence. She hadn't even returned my greeting.

*

The stress and worry were starting to get to me to the point where I was beginning to feel really ill. I could see the strain in my face, and the dark circles under my eyes when I looked in the mirror. I was barely sleeping, and, when I did, I would always dream of me and Becky before all of this had happened. We would be back in the flat, at my mum's, or walking the dogs. Every morning I would wake up and have to face the depressing reality of what was really happening.

I'd stopped eating. It seemed such a trivial thing to do now. Food had no taste, and I never felt hungry anyway. I knew the weight was falling off me, but I didn't have the energy to care. My mum was worried sick, but she had stopped nagging me about it. We barely spoke at the moment. When I wasn't at the hospital, I would stay in my room, alone. I would lay on my bed and look up through the sky light, desperately trying to think of anything but Becky. Simon tried to get me to go out and spend some time with him and my other friends, but I couldn't think of anything worse than having to go out and socialise with people. The only person I wanted to be near was Becky. The old Becky.

*

A few days later, I walked across the hospital car park, filled with the usual apprehension. It was a gloriously crisp, clear morning. The sun was starting to rise into a brilliant almost crystal-clear blue sky. There were only a few fluffy white, almost cartoon like, clouds floating in the breeze. There was still a hint of early morning pink sky thawing out the frost that hid in the shaded spots beneath the trees that hadn't seen the sun yet. I felt relieved to get out of the balmy morning and into the cold of the air-conditioned reception. I stopped for a moment to talk to the receptionist who was sat behind the main desk. I desperately wanted to delay walking up the stairs, and actually having to face Becky and see what mood she was in.

The receptionists and nurses had long stopped flirting with me like they used to, and I'm sure I even saw pity and distaste in some of their eyes now. I wasn't surprised, and I didn't care. I knew I looked like shit. My hair needed a cut, and I hadn't shaved in a while, but I found those simple daily tasks so difficult and pointless at the moment. Whilst we were talking, a visitor entered through the main doors behind me and approached reception, letting in a warm blast of air into the cool reception behind me as the doors opened and closed. I said goodbye to the receptionist I'd been speaking to and made my way up towards Becky's room, filled with the usual trepidation and dread. For some reason today seemed even worse than usual. I had found it really difficult to muster up the energy to get out of bed this morning.

I rounded the corner to Becky's corridor and pulled in a deep breath, preparing myself, wondering what mood she would be in. I approached her door, and it was then, when I was only a few metres away, that I heard her laugh. Her joyful, sweet, musical laugh filtered out of her room and filled the corridor. I stopped dead in my tracks. I didn't know how it was possible, but that sound transported me back in time and flooded me with a thousand memories. I hadn't heard Becky's laugh in weeks and weeks – it seemed like a lifetime ago. I stood reeling. Hearing that sound brought so much back, everything that I was missing, and I felt a physical pain in my chest. Before I knew what I was doing I was creeping towards the door. I knew what I was going to see, as much as I didn't want to. Witnessing it with my own eyes was much worse than I could have imagined. Becky was sat up in her bed, her knees pulled up to her chest. She had her arms wrapped around them and she leant her chin on her knees, leaning in towards Dr Matthews who was sat on the edge of her bed. He had his back to me, and he was leaning towards Becky. The smile on her face was another physical pain to see. It was *Becky*. My Becky. The Becky from before. The Becky that I had almost forgotten. Her face was alight, her skin glowing, and she was raptly staring at the doctor. Her hair tumbled around her face and her eyes were alight as she looked at him.

I stood looking through the doorway, unable to drag myself away from what I was seeing as my heart plummeted. A shiver tiptoed across my skin and my hairs stood on end as a snake of jealousy coiled around in my stomach. My fists clenched by my side without me even being aware. Dr Matthews was chuckling quietly, and Becky could not take her eyes off his face. He leant back away from her, and she leaned in even closer, not wanting there to be a gap between them. He said something I couldn't hear. Then he reached out and rested his hand on her knee. She didn't flinch.

*

I felt nauseous by what I had just seen and from the knowledge that things were never going to be the same again. It was one of those moments in life that you think will never happen to you. Where you can pinpoint the exact moment that your life has been forced off course, as if the vessel that was carrying you through has exploded and your life may well have ended. When you know, for certain, that things will never, ever be the same again.

*

I turned and walked away from the doorway, and somehow made it back out of the hospital and into the car park. I was in a daze similar to how I'd felt on the day of Becky's accident as I'd received the phone call from the hospital. I felt as if I were in a bubble.

I knew before I left the hospital that I wanted to get drunk. I didn't know the area of town that the hospital was in, but I walked the streets and soon found myself inside a pub. I ordered a drink. It was about ten o'clock in the morning. The barman didn't even question me. I sat in the corner and drank and drank and drank. I was sick after a couple of hours. I sat crouched in front of the toilet until I'd thrown everything up. A sheen of sweat covered my forehead as I heaved again and again into the toilet bowl. After a while, when the cubical stopped spinning around me, I went back to the bar and started drinking again.

*

My phone kept ringing. My mum's name flashed over and over again on my screen. I ignored it. It wasn't until much later when Simon's name popped up on my screen

218

that I finally picked it up.

"Hello," I managed. Just speaking made me feel sick.

"Chris? Where are you?" he said. I couldn't tell if he was worried or angry. I didn't care. I tried to mumble a response, my mind spinning.

"What? What? I can't hear you!" he was saying. I exhaled.

"I'm in the pub," I slurred. "Come and meet me, we never go drinking any more. We used to. Drinking all the time… but not at the moment."

"What? Are you drunk? Where are you?"

"Good question," I said, and made myself chuckle.

"For God's sake Chris, where are you? I'll come and pick you up." We muddled through the conversation, and I put the phone down. I walked to the bar to order another drink, looking forward to having a drinking partner.

*

I opened my eyes. I wondered what was going on until the events from yesterday hit me. A thousand images flashed into my head. Being sick in the pub toilet. Becky's face as she looked at the doctor. Simon striding into the pub to retrieve me. The car pulling over for me to be sick at the side of the road as we drove home. My mum's anxious face as I stumbled into the house. Becky's face as she looked at Dr Matthews. His hand resting on her knee. My stomach lurched. I didn't remember getting into bed. I looked at my phone. It was 11:30 in the morning. Where had the last twenty-four hours gone? I attempted to get up but lifting my head made the room spin.

A little while later my bedroom door burst open and my mum stood in the doorway, looking at me in absolute disgust, her face filled with fury.

"What the hell are you playing at?" she barked at me. I had never in my entire life had a crossed word with my mum, but today I felt my patience wearing thin.

"Leave me alone," I said.

"Who do you think you're speaking to?" she snapped. "What do you think this is achieving, hey? Getting blind drunk and not telling anyone where you are? You better have a bloody good reason for this behaviour, Chris. I've been worried sick." I pictured Becky's face as she leant in toward the doctor, her smile radiating warmth and admiration. I closed my eyes, shut tight.

"Not now, Mum."

"Are you going to the hospital today?"

"No."

"What's happened, Chris?"

Becky's laugh. Becky's smile. A hand resting on her knee that wasn't mine. A look of admiration. A private moment between two people.

"Nothing."

"You want to pull yourself together. For her sake." My bedroom door slammed shut.

44

BECKY

"In a way, it was nice to have something that only I knew." – Becky.

Chris hadn't been in to visit me yesterday. There was no phone call to say he wasn't coming in, nobody had heard anything – he just didn't arrive. I wasn't bothered, though, it meant I got to go outside and sit in the sunshine for the morning – and, even better, Dr Matthews had joined me while he was on his lunch break. He sat next to me on the bench I was perched on. He made me laugh, telling me stories from when he was at medical school and the things him and his friends had got up to. When it was time for him to leave, I felt desolate.

"I'll pop in before I leave tonight," he said, turning to look at me before he walked off. Our eyes met, and after a second he looked away, guiltily. It was at that moment I wondered if he felt it, too. Was there something happening between us? I nodded and he walked off. I watched him until he was out of sight.

*

The following day there was no sign of Chris, either. After my morning physio session, I settled down into bed and watched a film on the TV. My mind wandered throughout, mainly wondering what time Dr Matthews would be in. I was startled some time later when there was a knock at the door.

"Come in," I called, puzzled. It wasn't Dr Matthew's knock. I wasn't sure who it could be. The door opened and it was Sue's head that popped around the corner.

"Hello!" I said, genuinely surprised and almost pleased to see her. I quite liked this lovely lady, and we'd chatted a few times since our first meeting.

"Hello, lovie, how are you doing?" she said, and I smiled at her.

"Fine, thank you. My memory is still the same, but I'm getting fitter and stronger in myself. I think we may even start discussions about me leaving the hospital soon," I said, leaving the unanswered question of where I would go after I left hanging in the air. Sue attempted a smile. She didn't seem like her normal, positive self.

"Did Chris visit you yesterday?" she asked, and I shook my head.

"Nope, haven't seen him today, either," I replied, probably too cheerily.

"Did something happen with you two?" Sue asked. I thought for a second before shaking my head.

"No, he was here the day before, everything was the same as usual," I said. Sue didn't speak. "Why?" I asked, and she shrugged.

"He's not himself," was all she said.

We sat in silence for a while.

"Becky, can I ask you a favour? Will you please try a bit harder with Chris? Please? Don't give up on him. He's slipping away. He seems depressed and I think he's giving up. Please can you give him something to work towards or look forward to? Maybe spend some more time with him or something?" Sue asked as she looked at me imploringly.

I fiddled with my bed sheet. Dr Matthews had actually mentioned a couple of days ago that it would be good for me to venture out of the hospital for a few hours at a time. It would be good to see if being out of the hospital jogged my memory, as well as building up my fitness. I had secretly been holding out on asking anyone, hoping that Dr Matthews was going to offer to take me out somewhere himself. But nothing had been mentioned. I told Sue and she looked at me desperately.

"Please can I tell Chris? Can I tell him that he can take you out somewhere for a morning or an afternoon? Or whatever you want? Please? Please give him a chance, Becky, he *is* your husband! You never know what might happen." I sighed but agreed. Mostly because a part of me was curious to see if going outside of the hospital would jog my memory at all. My dreams were still rife, and I still woke up every morning feeling as if there were memories just out of my reach.

For a split second I felt like telling Sue about them, opening-up and blurting it all out to her, getting it all off my chest. But for some reason I held back. I think, in a way, it was nice to have something that only *I* knew.

45

"The doctors have said that she can go out of the hospital a little bit now." – Sue.

Sue left the hospital after speaking with Becky feeling slightly better. She walked out of the air-conditioned hospital and into the warm afternoon. She scanned the car park for Tom who was sitting in the car waiting for her. It must have been almost unbearably hot inside the car, and she wondered why he didn't wait for her out in the fresh air. He always puzzled her. Tom saw her approaching and watched her as she walked to the car. She could feel the intensity of his stare even from across the car park. She felt even hotter, if that was possible. She opened the car door and got in, sighing and rubbing her eyes as she sat down. She was right. The temperature in the car was intolerable, and she instantly felt hot and sticky. She wound down the window and started the engine, filling Tom in on her conversation with Becky, who had finally agreed to let Chris take her out of the hospital for a few hours over the next few days. He looked thoughtful and nodded as she spoke.

"It will do the pair of 'em good," he said when she finished speaking, and he turned to look out of the window. Sue knew that that was all she would get from him on the subject, but as always, it was all that needed saying.

*

When Sue and Tom arrived home a while later, Sue headed up to Chris' room to fill him in on the news. But his bedroom was empty. She phoned his mobile, but once again there was no answer. She tried Simon, praying that they were together, but Simon said he hadn't heard from Chris all day, and he also couldn't get through. Sue started to feel uneasy. She had offered Chris a lift to the hospital earlier that morning, but he had point blank refused to go, saying he needed a few days away from there. Sue couldn't understand what was happening.

*

At two o'clock in the morning, Chris came home. He had switched his phone off in the end and everyone had been worried sick. Sue, Tom, Simon, and Katie were sat in Sue's kitchen with the dogs at their feet when the front door banged open and Chris came in, roaring drunk. Katie – who hadn't seen Chris since the accident – couldn't believe what she was seeing. Chris had lost a huge amount of weight and his clothes were hanging off his body. His hair was long and greasy, and his fluffy blond beard was unruly around his face. His eyes were bloodshot from the alcohol, too. He stopped at the bottom of the stairs, looking into the kitchen, his eyes trying to focus on everyone sat there. He ignored them all and walked up the stairs, not saying a word. The smell of alcohol that lingered behind him embarrassed Sue, especially in front of Simon and Katie, and tears threatened her eyes as she apologised for worrying them, trying to make light of the situation. The atmosphere in the kitchen, for once, was full one of awkwardness as Simon and Katie said their goodbyes before heading out the front door.

*

The next morning, Sue sat at the kitchen table as still as a statue, in silence, waiting for Chris to appear. The dogs could sense a bad atmosphere and lay quietly on their bed in the corner by the patio doors. It was almost midday. Tom sat quietly reading the newspaper. Sue waited as the minutes ticked by, just waiting.

A little while later she could hear noises upstairs and she listened as Chris got up and started to move around.

She eventually heard his footsteps on the landing and then coming down the stairs. *Thud, thud, thud.* Even his footsteps seemed slow and depressed. He walked into the kitchen, ignoring her and Tom sitting there. He stood at the sink and poured himself a glass of water.

"You stink," Sue said to Chris' back. He shrugged, not replying. He turned around as if to leave the kitchen without saying a word and it filled Sue with rage. What had happened to her son?

"Sit down here now, Chris," Sue said through gritted teeth, and even she was surprised at the severity and seriousness of her own voice. She watched as Chris paused for a split-second before turning back, sighing. He refused to meet her eye. She wondered if he was still drunk.

He sat down opposite her, and she looked at him closely, suddenly overwhelmed with sadness. He looked awful. The stern telling off that she had planned on giving him went out of the window as she looked at her worn down, depressed son, and she leant over the table and rested her hand on his. His eyes were focused on a spot on the table and he stared at it, unable to look at her. They sat like this for a while before Sue started speaking.

"I went and saw Becky yesterday," Sue said. Chris continued to focus on the table. *Becky's laugh, Becky's smile, Dr Matthews chuckling, a private joke, his hand on her knee.*

"She's doing well," Sue continued, "she was telling me that the doctors have said that she can go out of the hospital a little bit now. It'd be a good opportunity for her to see if being out in the real world jogs her memory, apparently. We wondered if you would be able to take her out one afternoon this week?" Chris shifted in his seat slightly, still focusing on the table.

"She asked for me?" he asked, and Sue could hear

hope creeping into his voice. She paused for a split-second before replying.

"Yes," she said, before hating herself. It was the first time she had ever lied to Chris, and almost instantly she felt a crushing guilt around her heart. But the change in Chris was almost instant. It was as if a brightness instantly came back into his eyes.

"Okay, yeah," Chris said, looking up at her and meeting her eye for the first time. "When?"

Somehow, he looked like a different person to the one who had sat down at the table a moment ago, and before Sue could reply he was talking as if to himself.

"Tomorrow? Maybe tomorrow. I'll phone the hospital now and see if we can do something tomorrow..." he said. He stood up, and Sue realised that all the anger and fury she had been feeling that morning and the telling off that she had planned on giving him for his behaviour over last two days had disappeared. She hadn't even mentioned it.

"Thanks, Mum," Chris said, and she looked at him as he stood in the doorway. He looked tiny stood there and it emphasised his now smaller frame; usually he would have taken over the doorway, but now he seemed to shrink into it. Tears welled in Sue's eyes at the sincerity in his voice, and she nodded at him and smiled.

"Can I borrow your car for the day tomorrow then, please? I want to take Becky somewhere nice," he said. Sue nodded again. Chris smiled for a split-second before he turned away. Sue realised it had been a long time since she'd seen him smile.

As Chris walked up stairs, Sue turned to look at Tom. He nodded at her, one curt nod. No words were needed. She knew he was saying that she had done the right thing and the guilt eased slightly. She just had to think of Chris' smile and pray to God that there would be many more. Surely once he and Becky spent time together away from all the distractions of the hospital, they could attempt to build some sort of relationship again?

The main distraction that was worrying Sue was Dr Matthews. She had realised very early on that Becky seemed to be holding a torch for him. It was still quite obvious. Becky always looked disappointed when someone entered the room and it wasn't him. She seemed to sit up and take note at the mention of his name, and when he entered the room she flushed. It was something that had been playing on Sue's mind for a while now. She had been making a conscious effort not to worry about it too much, but yesterday, when she was visiting Becky, just before she had left, Dr Matthews had entered Becky's room in a flourish. He was obviously surprised to see Sue in there. He had stridden into the room, pulling on his overcoat, obviously in a rush, and he'd stopped dead in his tracks, startled when he saw Sue sat next to Becky's bed. There was an awkward moment where no-one spoke for a few seconds, and Dr Matthews had the grace to look a bit sheepish. It was obvious to Sue that this was an unscheduled, non-work-related visit, and Sue looked from Becky to the doctor, holding his eye and not looking away, enjoying how uncomfortable they seemed. It was at this point that Sue wondered if the doctor wasn't holding a torch for Becky, too.

46

CHRIS

"Your mum's been so worried about you. Don't worry her like that again." – Tom.

I felt positive for the first time in weeks, probably the best I'd felt since Becky had woken up. I walked up the stairs after speaking with my mum and phoned the hospital to make arrangements to take Becky out. I literally felt lighter, as if a weight had been lifted off my shoulders. I had to think positively now. I was finally going to get to spend time with Becky away from the hospital. Just the two of us! We could go anywhere we wanted! I felt more energetic, and I even realised that I felt a bit hungry. I made the decision to push what I had seen to the back of my mind. Obviously Becky and the doctor were going to be close. They spent a lot of time together and he was helping her get better. I was probably being unjustly jealous and over thinking what I had seen. There was probably nothing going on! Becky had asked for me to take her out, and maybe this would be the start of good things for us. Finally.

I had a stinking hangover, and my head was pounding. I had planned to get back into bed and sleep for the rest of the day, maybe even sneak out for a few more drinks later this evening. I'd never been much of a big drinker before, unless out socially with my mates, but since seeing Becky and the doctor together, the numbness that drinking brought was the only thing I craved. It was even worth feeling hungover and sick constantly, at least it gave me something else to think about other than what was really going on. It also meant I had untroubled deep sleeps.

But right now, after speaking with my mum and knowing I was going to see Becky tomorrow, I felt like I needed to pull myself together. I got out of the clothes I had been wearing yesterday, which I had also slept in, and threw them in the washing basket. I went to the bathroom and turned the shower on full blast, turning it to the hottest I could take it before climbing into the scorching water. It burned my skin, but straight away my head started to feel clearer. I scrubbed myself from head to toe and washed my hair twice. I climbed out of the shower and stood in the steamy bathroom. I rubbed my hand across the steamed surface of the mirror and looked at my face. The hot water had brought a bit of colour to my cheeks, and I looked slightly better than I had for a while. I decided that I needed to start making more of an effort. I couldn't just give up, I needed to fight. I stood over the sink and shaved, and I made the decision to go and get my hair cut.

I got dressed and walked downstairs to the kitchen. My mum was hanging washing on the line out in the garden and Tom was sitting in the same spot he had been in earlier. He put his paper down and looked at me as I walked through the door.

"Your mum's been so worried about you," he said, his voice grave and his look stern. "Don't worry her like that again." I nodded at him, not able to reply, and he nodded back and picked up his paper. Through the small exchange of words, I felt as if I'd been thoroughly told off.

The dogs were in the garden, running in circles around the washing line, barking as my mum hung the clothes up, and I felt guilty for how little attention I'd paid to them recently. I resolved to take them for a walk this afternoon. I opened the patio door and called out to my mum, telling her that I was going to get my hair cut. She looked over her shoulder at me, and she looked so genuinely happy; I felt even guiltier about falling apart over the last couple of days. I turned and walked through the kitchen and out of the front door.

Once outside, I stood on the pavement. I paused for a second, realising properly for the first time what an amazing spring we were having. The air was warm and clear and smelt sweet. Women were walking around in summer dresses and men walked around with their shirt sleeves rolled up. Everyone wore sunglasses and it seemed that each person I saw had an air of optimism about them. I couldn't wait to wake up tomorrow and take Becky out on a day like this. My head was full of thoughts on where to go and what to do as I walked off down the road.

*

I felt tired when I got home that afternoon, but in a good way. I'd had my hair cut; I'd left it slightly longer than I'd been wearing it recently, and it was around the length that it was when Becky and I first got together. I don't know if I thought subconsciously that this may help in some way. At lunchtime, after my haircut, I had sat in a café and eaten a jacket potato for lunch while watching people walk past the window, my head whirring with thoughts of what Becky and I could do tomorrow. I decided to go to the supermarket and buy some stuff for a nice picnic. If the weather was like this again, it would be lovely.

I spent a small fortune on food. I bought everything that I knew Becky liked: chicken legs, quiche, pork pies, mini sausages and scotch eggs, pâté, olives, crisps and dips, and loads of different fruits. I stopped in at the local bakers on the way home and bought some fresh French sticks and an assortment of cakes. I was so, so excited; it felt as if I was preparing for a first date.

I packed a bag that evening with blankets and bottles of drink, and I sat and had dinner with my mum and Tom for the first time in what seemed like ages. Mum cooked a beef casserole and it tasted delicious. I wolfed down as much as I could, but the portion was nowhere near the size I would have usually eaten. Dinner was quieter than usual and not a lot was said. I think there was an air of anticipation, each of us was worrying how tomorrow would go. I helped my mum clear up the dinner things when we were finished before heading up to my room. I just wanted to be on my own. I brushed my teeth and got into bed, switching the light off and staring into the darkness, butterflies fluttering around in my stomach. I didn't think I would be able to get to sleep, but within minutes I was gone.

47

BECKY

"I read recently that more than three-thousand-five-hundred people are killed annually in car accidents in the UK now, and that more than thirty-thousand are seriously injured." – Dr Matthews.

It was getting late. I climbed into bed and switched off the light, falling back into the pillows with a sigh. Thoughts of tomorrow were running around my head – I was mostly filled with excitement at finally getting out of the hospital and going somewhere different, but my spirits were dampened by the thought of having to spend a whole morning alone with Chris. Sue had asked me to promise her that I would at least try and be positive, and for some unknown reason, I really didn't want to let her down. I was also dreading having to spend a whole morning away from Dr Matthews. I wished it could have been him who was taking me out rather than Chris – although I knew that that would never happen. All these thoughts were going around and around in my head at a million miles an hour. I didn't think I would ever be able to fall asleep, but eventually, finally, I did.

*

I was walking across a windy beach with Chris, hand-in-hand. We were wrapped up in hats, coats, and scarves with two dogs playing at our feet… Then it changed and we were down a busy street holding hands, I felt really, really happy, almost elated… Then it changed again, and we were in a restaurant, our table crammed into a corner. It was busy and people were moving around us…

*

It was a dream so convincing it kept me glued to the bed. I was in a sleep so deep that when I finally woke up, I had to lay there for a few moments, desperately trying to assess what was real and what was fantasy. As soon as I was fully awake the dream was already disappearing, and I felt more frustrated than ever before. My heart was beating faster than ever in my chest. The dream had seemed so *real*. There were actual feelings associated with it, as if I had actually been through everything that I'd just seen. I tried to claw some of the details back, but already it was retreating and vanishing from my mind. Now I was struggling to remember what the dream had even been about. I felt so frustrated, I could feel tears prickling my eyes. As the seconds passed, it all slipped away and all I was left with was the uneasy feeling that I was so used to at this time of the morning now.

*

A couple of hours later, I sat on the edge of my bed with butterflies in my stomach. The curtains were open, and, as usual, I stared out at the park outside of my window. There were some young boys playing football, and I wondered why they weren't in school. The sun was out, and I was itching to get outside of the hospital. I watched as a little white dog chased a ball across the field, flying past the makeshift football pitch, and I stared at it, a flash going through my mind, reminding me of a dream, but as soon as I tried to remember, it disappeared. A knock at my door distracted me. Hearing the two quick raps, I knew it was Dr Matthews. He strode into the room, followed by another young doctor who had mousey brown hair and a confident air about him. He smiled at me and shook my hand as Dr Matthews introduced us.

"Becky, this is Dr Warren. We have been discussing your situation, do you mind if I show him some of your results and paperwork?" he said, and I shook my head and smiled. Looking into his eyes made my heart skip. He smiled back at me and the doctors both moved to the end of my bed, looking at my charts and flipping through my files, instantly in deep discussion. I looked back out of the window, wondering about the dog and why it made me feel so strange. I was aware of Dr Matthews' voice talking about me from a few feet away; his soothing voice was so enchanting. My mind wandered, and I wondered how today was going to go. I psyched myself up for the day ahead and tried to think positively about Chris. I tuned back into the conversation the doctors were having.

"…sustaining a substantial knock to the head."

"Is it known how?" Dr Warren asked.

"Car accident," Dr Matthews replied. There was a pause. Dr Warren exhaled loudly before replying.

"What is it with bloody car accidents at the moment, Carl? So many of the serious head injuries I see are due to car accidents. It seems to be getting worse." Although I wasn't looking at him, I knew Dr Matthews was nodding his head before he replied.

"I read recently that more than three-thousand-five-hundred people are killed annually in car accidents in the UK now and that more than thirty-thousand are seriously injured," he said.

My head snapped around, completely of its own accord, to stare at the doctors, open mouthed. My body had reacted to something that I had no control over. I sat unmoving. I knew the colour had drained from my face and I stared wide-eyed at both doctors, wondering what it was I'd reacted to. My mind was racing, as if trying to grab at something, but I didn't know what. Once again, my heart was beating like mad. I felt as if I had no control over my mind – it was as if it was working completely of its own accord. I struggled to get my thoughts in order.

"Becky? Are you okay?" Dr Matthews asked, noticing my odd behavior, his eyebrows furrowed in concern. I opened my mouth to speak, but nothing came out, so I closed it again. I closed my eyes and frowned. How could I explain what had just happened? I leapt as a hand rested on my shoulder and I looked up at Dr Matthews standing next to me, his face etched with concern. Dr Warren stood behind him, looking puzzled and even slightly amused. I managed to stammer out that I was fine, while my mind raced. I tried once again to figure out what had just happened. I realised it was a similar feeling to the ones I kept getting in the mornings, right after I'd woken up. I also realised that I was sweating.

"You've gone very pale, Mrs. McNulty," Dr Warren said, and I cringed at the name.

"Please call me Becky," I said.

"Becky, you really don't look very well," Dr Matthews said quietly, his voice laced with concern.

"I'm fine, I'm fine," I said, trying to smile. And just like in the mornings, with the more time that passed by, my mind started to slow back down and my heart rate went back to normal. All of a sudden, I wondered what on earth had just happened, I felt silly and giggled, brushing it off.

"I don't know what came over me," I said as brightly as I could, and saw a look pass between the doctors. I pulled my face into a smile and sat that way until they carried on with their conversation.

48

BECKY

"It all seems very farfetched to me." – Becky.

Not long after the doctors had left, with Dr Matthews promising he would be in to see me when I was back later, I sat in the room still thinking about what had happened earlier. I opened the window, and the curtains puffed and billowed in the breeze that carried in the scent of flowers from the garden outside. It wasn't long until there was a tentative knock at the door, and I turned to see Chris pushing the door open. He looked as if he'd lost weight, but his face held a warm smile. I stared at him for a moment, trying to figure something out.

"Hey," he said, and the spell was broken. I attempted to smile at him as I got off the bed and followed him to the door. "Are you ready?" he asked, and I nodded. It was pretty obvious I was ready – I was sitting there waiting for him! I followed him down the corridor to the elevator and finally out to the reception. We walked through the double doors and out into the beautiful day outside.

We approached the car park, walking towards a path I hadn't been down yet, and I swiveled my head from side-to-side, taking everything in. As we approached the car, Chris took a set of keys out of his pocket. He hesitated before he put the key in the lock, and he turned to look at me.

"Are you okay with us going in the car?" he asked, and I looked at him, confused. "With the accident and everything I wondered if you would be a bit worried about getting in a car..." He trailed off.

"No," I snapped at him, exasperated. "I can't remember the accident. It doesn't bother me at all."

Everything he said frustrated me, and I knew that this was going to be a long morning.

"Okay... brilliant..." he stammered. I tried not to roll my eyes. He unlocked the car, and we got in. It was boiling hot inside. I tried to remember the last time I could remember being in a car. My eyes roamed around, trying to see if there was anything that triggered any memories, but there was nothing. Chris and I wound our windows down simultaneously and he turned to face me.

"So... Do you have any requests on where we go today?" he said, and I was taken aback. I had presumed that Chris would have a whole day planned for us and I wouldn't get to have any say in it. The question surprised me, and I wracked my brain trying to think of somewhere that I would like to go, but I drew a complete blank. I shrugged my shoulders, not looking Chris in the eye. He spoke again.

"Well, I'd obviously love to be able to take you out in the city, we used to have so much fun spending time together around London, but I thought it might be too hectic, and considering this is your first time out, I thought it would be best if it wasn't too stressful..."

"I'm not a massive fan of London, anyway," I said absent mindedly, bored by him already.

"Oh, you are! You had really learnt to love the city!" Chris said knowingly, and irritation flowed through me.

"Oh, really?" I replied, quick as a flash. "If I loved it so much, why was I leaving it to move somewhere different with you, then? Another thing that I supposedly loved that I was willing to give up so easily for you."

Chris didn't respond. He looked crestfallen, and I felt smug. He didn't respond and changed the subject hastily, convincing me even further that I was right and that he was lying.

"I've, er... packed a picnic... I thought we could go

for a drive? I was wondering about maybe taking a drive up to Oxford? It's where we were planning on moving to? It's so beautiful up there, we could drive up, find somewhere to stop and eat…" He trailed off uncertainly once again, and as I couldn't think of anything else I'd rather do, I agreed. He looked slightly more pleased with himself and turned the engine on, turning in his seat to look out of the back window as he reversed the car out of the parking space. A welcome breeze came in through the window once the car started moving. I was actually enjoying the drive. It wasn't long until we were on the motorway, and we drove along in silence with the radio playing quietly in the background. It was the first time I'd listened to the radio since the accident, and I didn't recognise anything at all that was being talked about or any of the music that was being played.

It was about halfway down the motorway that I started to get the slightly uneasy feeling. I couldn't put my finger on it. I felt as if I were having déjà vu. I felt as if I'd dreamt about this journey. It couldn't be a memory. If it was a memory I would just remember, wouldn't I? I wracked my brain while staring out of the window, drinking everything in, trying to figure out what was going on. We approached a roundabout and Chris slowed down, letting the traffic to the right of us go. I looked over at a little sign planted in the grass on top of the roundabout: *'This Roundabout Is Sponsored by Buckinghamshire Golf Club'*. I froze. Instantly going cold and once again my mind flashed a split-second image at me, showing me something, but then it was gone. I was starting to sweat again, feeling exactly as I had this morning; I felt a frustration that overtook my body. I felt like I was losing my mind. Chris must have noticed something, and he slowed the car down and looked over at me.

"Becky, are you okay? Do you want me to stop? What's up?" He fired the questions at me, and, as he spoke, the feeling started to pass and I was left with the horrible emptiness again.

"Nothing!" I almost shouted, and he looked taken aback.

"Should I stop?" he asked again, and I groaned. I actually groaned. The frustration at what kept happening to me and the fact that Chris had interrupted my train of thoughts, making me lose whatever thread had been in my head, as well as the fact that I was here doing this with someone I didn't like – that *all* of this had happened to me – was starting to get on top of me. I hated living in this horrible world of frustration and the not knowing.

"No," I said, my voice laced with hatred. Somehow, I didn't know why, I felt that this was all Chris' fault. He didn't dare say anything more and we drove on in silence. He glanced over at me whenever he could as I sat staring out of the windscreen. I tried to put my finger on what had just happened. A little while later he pulled off the motorway and drove into a service station. I looked at him questioningly.

"I thought you could do with some fresh air. Let's get out and grab a coffee or something," he said, yanking up the handbrake which gave off an angry creak. I got out of the car without replying. I knew I was acting like a petulant teenager, but all the resolve I had felt earlier about trying to make an effort with Chris for Sue's sake had gone out the window today. All that I cared about were these funny spells I kept having. I wished I knew what on earth they meant.

We walked in silence across the car park in the now searing late morning heat as we headed towards the main entrance of 'The Welcome Break Oxford'. Another flash hit me, quicker this time, and then it was gone. I shook my head, closing my eyes and groaning once again. It felt like I was being tortured. Chris slowed down and looked at me, alarmed, but he didn't dare say anything. I ignored the flash and strode purposefully through the double doors, trying to tell myself not to think about it. I put it down to it being the first time I was out of the hospital; it was probably normal for people to feel like this. And that is when I saw it. A small gold plaque mounted on the side of the wall, just inside the main entrance doors:

**This establishment was officially opened by
Ms. Anthea Turner
on 19th July 1998**

And that was it. Something in my mind clicked and hundreds and thousands of memories flooded my head at once. John! I remembered John! I remembered him telling me about this very 'Welcome Break' as well as the roundabout and other things I'd seen earlier! The flashes I'd been getting *were* memories! But it wasn't just memories that came flooding back, it was feelings, emotions, an actual attachment to someone, and the more I thought, the more I remembered. It was like throwing a stone into a pond – the ripples were getting bigger and bigger. As fast as lightening I could remember the home, the patients, the staff, Mark! My office – my office! It was the room I'd been dreaming about! I held onto the wall while these memories flooded my brain, it was as if someone had turned on a tap full blast and everything was spilling out at a thousand miles an hour.

I became aware that Chris was saying my name over and over again, but it came as if from somewhere else. I didn't dare concentrate on his voice for fear of losing everything that was going on in my head. But I knew that this was different from before. These were not fleeting flashes that I would forget as time passed or if I got distracted. These were real memories that weren't going to disappear. I could remember names, places, specific details, what my desk looked like, what people looked like and the feelings I had felt for them. The love that I had for so many of these people and the patients actually scared me, and I couldn't fathom how five minutes ago I couldn't remember any of them. I suddenly came to and realised where I was. A few people had stopped in their tracks and were standing around watching me, amused, probably wondering if I was going to faint. I turned and stumbled out of the main entrance until I was outside. I breathed in deep lungful's of air, wishing it wasn't so hot outside. Chris was by my side instantly, his hand around the top of my arm.

"Becky? Becky? *Becky?* What's going on?" he asked, staring into my face, and I yanked my arm out of his grip as I turned at him, almost snarling.

"I can remember!" I said.

"What?" he said, his face lighting up with hope and delight and love.

"Not you!" I spat at him, my lip curling is disgust. "My job, John, the home…"

"Becky, that's amazing!" he cried, enclosing the space between us as if he wanted to give me a hug.

"Get away from me!" I cried, and he looked at me in shock.

"What?" he said. "Why are you being like this, Becky?" he said, his voice rising slightly, and for once I thought I could sense a touch of anger creeping in.

"You!" I said, filled with absolute contempt. "This is all your fault! Everything! I can *remember* now, okay? I can remember how much I *loved* my job, those people, that home! And it was *you* who was making me leave. Leave to be a housewife, taking me away from my *dream*

242

job, and for what? So I could follow you? So you can follow *your* dreams? You're not even my type, Chris! I would have never, ever fallen in love with someone like you! You are a *hypocrite* and a liar! Always telling me how in love we were, how happy we were. It's *pathetic*. If you had loved me *at all* you would never have let me leave that job!" Chris had the good grace to look stunned, hurt, and almost a little bit guilty. He stuttered over his words, repulsing me even more.

"But you wanted to leave... It was your idea... You encouraged it..."

"I don't believe you!" I spat at him once again, and I turned away from him, looking out over the little picnic area beside the car park, trying to get my head together.

"Becky you've got to listen to me!" Chris cried, his hands open wide in front of him.

"No, I don't! I'm done listening to you Chris! I think you are a liar and a fraud! I don't know what is going on here, but none of it adds up! We were not as happy as you make out, so you're lying about something. I never wanted to get married or have children and then one day I wake up with no memory to be told that this is my life? The life that I supposedly chose!? It all seems very far-fetched to me!"

Chris was staring at me, his face a complete picture of hurt. I yanked off my wedding ring, something that I had been itching to get off my finger since the moment I had woken up. I threw it at him. It hit him in the chest and bounced off onto the floor. I heard it ping as it hit the concrete. I strode past him to the car, not even letting him speak, not caring if he found the ring or not.

"Take me back to the hospital, we are *done*!" I threw over my shoulder. "And I never, ever want to see you again."

49

BECKY

"Didn't he see that it was someone like him that I wished I had woken up to being married to?" – Becky.

I felt stressed and exhausted. It was the worst I'd felt since I'd woken up from my coma. Since I arrived back at the hospital after some of my memory had returned, there had been a trail of doctors in and out of my room.

"So you can remember specific details from one part of your life, in this case your old job – people, places, etcetera, – but, past that, you cannot remember any other people or significant events? Birthdays, Christmas', your wedding?" one doctor I didn't recognise asked me, and I glared at him. I had been through this a thousand times. Dr Matthews was standing behind him, and he rested a hand on his shoulder.

"I think that's enough for today, Nigel," he said gently, and a surge of love shot through me for this man. I looked at him gratefully and he nodded slightly.

I had been back for almost six hours and a continuous stream of people had been in and out of my room ever since – doctors, nurses, occupational therapists, and, worst of all, psychiatrists. I had been asked the same questions over and over again, and I felt physically and mentally exhausted. I got the impression that some of them thought I was lying, whilst others seemed genuinely baffled. Dr Matthews had mainly kept quiet and looked deep in thought. Eventually, after what seemed like an eternity, he steered the remaining staff out of the room and closed the door behind them, leaving just the two of us alone. Evening was starting to set in and there was a beautiful red sky outside the window. I stared out at it. I was still in disbelief at everything that had happened today. Dr Matthews sat on the edge of my bed, and we sat in a companionable silence for a while. I sighed a deep long, drawn-out sigh.

"How are you doing?" he said, and I looked at him, my heart hurting in my chest when we made eye contact. I knew he was asking me on a personal level, not a professional one.

"It's been awful," I said truthfully. He nodded and we went quiet again.

"I know you won't want to hear this," he said a while later, "but your husband has been in a right state down in reception today. Obviously, we couldn't let him up to see you against your wishes, but he-" I cut him short.

"I am never seeing that man again, Carl," I said, and he nodded.

"I know you feel like that now, but you have to see this from his point of view, Becky. It *isn't* his fault that this has happened to you. I know you think it is, but you've got to understand that it really isn't. He's going through a really, really awful time at the moment, too." I started to get angry. I hated the fact that he was standing up for Chris. Didn't he see that it was someone like him that I wished I had woken up being married to? Not Chris. At that moment, I was glad Chris was wiped from my memory, I felt like he deserved it.

"I don't want to talk about it," I said, the petulant teenager coming out in me again. I just couldn't help it sometimes. In my mind I *was* still nineteen-years-old. Well, until today. Now at least I had some proof that the last few years of my life had actually happened. Although I couldn't remember applying for or getting the job. The details were still hazy, and I had no understanding of why some memories had returned and others hadn't.

I closed my eyes and sighed, just wanting to lie down

and sleep and not have to think about anything that was going on. I opened my eyes to see Carl looking at me intently with a gentle look in his eyes. It was at that moment I knew for sure, without a shadow of a doubt, that he felt something for me, too. I wasn't imagining all of this. If this had been any other situation, I'm sure he would have leant in and kissed me. Time froze for a moment while we looked at each other and I didn't dare breathe. I could hear my heart thumping in my chest. Carl looked away, and as soon as our eyes parted the spell was broken. My heart sank but I tried not to show it. He stood up.

"I'm exhausted!" he said, and chuckled. "I can't imagine how you must be feeling. I'll leave you to get some rest – I'll be back first thing tomorrow, okay?" I nodded at him, not trusting myself to speak. We both paused for an awkward few seconds while he hovered between my bed and the door. He walked towards me, and for an uncomfortable moment I thought he was going to shake my hand. But, before I knew it, he was in front of me, and he bent down to kiss me on the cheek. His lips brushed against my skin, causing the breath in my throat to catch. It all happened in the space of a second, and, before I knew it, he was back by the door to my room, avoiding my gaze.

"I'll see you tomorrow, then," he stammered, and managed a weak smile – although he couldn't catch my eye – before he left the room. I sat frozen in place, still staring at the door, still able to feel the light brush of his soft lips across my cheek as if it had been burnt there forever. A stupid grin took over my face as I undressed and got into bed. I fell asleep with a smile on my face that night and had a long, deep, dreamless sleep.

50

CHRIS

"This is it. It's over. I just know it." – Chris.

I don't know how I found the inner strength to get me through the first few hours after mine and Becky's argument outside the 'Welcome Break'. I didn't understand how it was possible for one person to go through as much turmoil as I had been through recently. I drove my car down the motorway, staring straight ahead out of the windscreen. The scenery was a blur next to me as I desperately tried to think of something to say or do that would make the situation better. Becky sat with her body turned away from me, staring out of her window in silence. Completely unmoving. Considering the awful atmosphere inside the car, the drive seemed to be over relatively quickly, and it wasn't long until we were pulling back into the hospital car park. Before the car had even stopped moving, Becky had jumped out, slamming the door shut behind her as she ran to the reception of the hospital. I drove the car into an empty space as quickly as possible and ran across the car park, through reception, and towards the stairs after her. I was about half-way up the stairs to Becky's floor when I saw Dr Matthews up ahead. I knew what was going to happen and my fists clenched by my side in frustration. He held up his hands in front of him like a suspect giving himself up to the police.

"Mr. McNulty," he said, and I stopped in my tracks, my patience wearing very thin.

"What?" I snarled at him through gritted teeth. A nervous energy and an anger coursed through my veins.

"You can't go up there right now," he said, his voice

light and soothing. "Not right now. Can you wait downstairs?"

"Do I have a choice?" I threw at him, almost laughing. I knew I was on the brink of hysteria. The same thought kept going around and around in my head: *how much more can one person take?*

A while later, when I had calmed down slightly, I phoned my mum. When I told her that Becky had regained some of her memory, I heard the sharp intake of breath.

"Chris, that's wonderful!" she cried before I could tell her the whole story. That was the moment the tears started. I sat in reception with my head in the palm of one hand and I let the tears fall. I managed to explain some of what had happened through the tears and uncontrollable sobs that wracked my body.

"I'm on my way," she said. "I'll be there as soon as I can."

A while later, when my mum and Tom entered reception through the main double doors, I couldn't even bring myself to stand and greet them. I was still crying uncontrollably. Tears stained my face, and my nose was running. I kept wiping it with the back of my hand, beyond caring what I looked like. My mum sat down next to me and put her arms around my shoulders as I stammered the story out to her as best I could. When I finished, she sat back in her chair.

"I think you're looking at this all wrong, Chris," she said gently. "This is a good sign! She's got some of her memory back! This is exactly what we have been praying for! If she can remember one thing, she must be able to remember others eventually. Surely if we just keep going as we are, she *will* remember you sooner or later."

I shook my head, another huge sob building in my chest. I closed my eyes tightly.

"No, Mum," I said, my voice hoarse with tears. "This is it. It's over. I just know it." I started crying again, a quiet wail escaping my lips, and I stopped attempting to hold the tears back. I allowed the sadness to flood out of me and I wept until I had no more tears left.

51

CHRIS

"I hate you!" – Becky.

I woke up in my bed at home. I'd cried myself to sleep last night and I now had a crippling headache as well as feeling sick. I went downstairs and poured myself a large drink, thankful that my mum and Tom were not around. I noticed that the dogs were gone, and I guessed that they were out walking them somewhere.

I sat on my own at the kitchen table, knocking back drink after drink while switching between utter sadness and an all-consuming anger. It didn't take long for me to feel drunk. I sat on my own in silence with only my thoughts. I don't know how much time passed or how long I sat there for. I don't know at which point I decided to go to the hospital, but I knew I needed to see Becky. I needed to explain everything to her. I hated the way I was so unable to defend myself whenever she was angry with me, and she was *always* so angry with me. It was so hard to argue with someone who was so convinced that they were right. How could I ever explain our love to her? To someone who couldn't remember? How could I explain what we'd had? How could I even attempt it when she wasn't even willing to listen?

I'd stopped pouring mixers into my drink and I filled the glass in front of me with a couple of inches of pure alcohol, throwing it down my throat and wincing at the taste as I wiped tears away from my eyes. I made my decision and stood up. I walked out of the front door, not thinking or caring about anything. I just needed to get to the hospital and see Becky – I needed to try and explain everything to her. I needed one more chance to try and make her see my point of view. I wasn't going to leave until she listened to me.

*

I don't know how I managed to get from my house to the hospital in once piece. I was drunk. People were giving me filthy looks on the bus and I didn't care. I stared back at them, hating everyone I came into contact with. I didn't even realise that I hadn't washed or changed my clothes since yesterday morning, and I probably stunk of alcohol even though it was the middle of the day. All I could think about was seeing Becky and fixing this. I had to fix this.

I eventually found myself outside the hospital and I slowly walked across the car park. It was boiling hot again. I'd never known a summer like it. I squinted as I looked towards the main reception. Doubt was starting to creep into my thoughts – deep down I knew that this was not a good idea and that now was probably not the best time, but I was buoyed up by the alcohol, and adrenalin from my anger and hurt. I marched on.

It was as I approached the doors to the building, just as I could feel the cool air from the air conditioning hitting me even though I was still outside, when I heard Becky's laugh again. This time her laugh was mixed with someone else's, and I knew before I saw it that she was with Dr Matthews again. I spun around towards the sound and saw the two of them sat on a bench in the garden. Becky sat on her hands, leaning forward, looking almost childlike. Dr Matthews sat with his back leaning against the bench, one arm spread wide along the top, his other hand shielding his eyes from the sun as he watched her. They spoke back and forth before bursting into laughter again. I couldn't hear what was being said. Becky's laugh was joyful and sweet like summer birdsong and just as it had the last time I'd heard it, it made me feel like I was taking a bullet to the heart. Before I knew what I was doing, I turned on my heel and marched towards them, completely furious. A rage I'd never felt before completely took over my body and it felt as if it was boiling out of me. I strode towards the bench where they sat, and enjoyed the moment they both looked up and saw me. Becky's face was indignant and angry, Dr Matthews had the decency to look guilty, and I knew at that moment that I was right. He had a thing for Becky. For *my* wife.

They stood up as I approached and Dr Matthews walked towards me, his hands open in front of him, trying to tell me to calm down. Before I had any idea what was happening, I had lunged at him. I punched him hard in the side of the head, knocking him sprawling onto the grass. It was the most satisfying feeling I'd ever had, and I lunged towards him as he lay on the floor. Becky was screaming. I'd never heard her voice like that before and I could tell she was genuinely scared, but even that didn't stop me. All I wanted to do was kill this man who had been sitting on the bench in the sun with my wife. Laughing and joking and probably trying to turn her against me. I'd known all along there was something not right about the way he looked at her, and now it was confirmed. I lunged at him again, landing another punch to his face as Becky climbed onto my back, attempting to pull my arms away as she screamed at me. It distracted me slightly, and Dr Matthews took this moment to scramble to his feet. Becky dived in between us, her back to the doctor, facing me, her arms spread wide to protect him.

"What are you doing?" she screeched, tears of anger spilling over her eyes. "Get away from here, you *animal*! I hate you! I told you I never wanted to see you again! You're a *thug* and a *drunk*! Get away! *Get away!*" She was hysterical and I saw the doctor look at me smugly from over her shoulder. He dabbed a spot of blood off his lip, and I realised I had just played right into his hands. I looked at Becky's face. Her eyes were wild, and her chest heaved up and down, trying to catch her breath, but she stood defiantly in front of me. I took one last look at her. Our eyes met for a second and there was nothing. They were blank. She didn't know me. She never would. I turned and walked away from them both. I didn't look back.

52

CHRIS

"Increased irritability? Agitation? Anger? Violence?
Excessive displays of emotion? Uncontrollable crying?"
– Dr Moran.

I could hear people whispering outside my bedroom door. Sometimes I was aware of my door being opened and people talking to me. But I didn't care. I had returned to the hole I'd been falling into after I had first seen Becky and the doctor together a few days ago, and I just didn't care. I had tried at least. Really tried. I'd pulled myself together and decided to give it my all. I really had thought that deep down Becky would fall in love with me again. I believed that spending some time together outside of the hospital would do us the world of good. But after watching part of her memory return, I now knew. I *knew* in my heart that it wasn't going to happen. She was never going to allow herself to love me again, and after losing it outside of the hospital and punching Dr Matthews in front of her I knew that we were never, ever going to be together again. I was so certain, it felt as if my heart was being ripped from my body millimetre by agonizing millimetre.

Nobody understood what I was going through. My family and friends were angry with me, telling me to 'pull myself together', but they just didn't understand the agonising pain I was going through every moment I was awake. It was as if I had suffered a bereavement. Becky may well have died in the accident. In fact, I wished that she had. I could deal with the loss of her life better than knowing that her life was going to carry on without me in it. I started crying again. I couldn't stop at the moment. I knew I was pathetic, and it was embarrassing that I was carrying on like this. But I just couldn't help it. I didn't want to move, talk, smile, see people, or be seen by people. I felt as if I hated everyone. I hated people looking at me with pity, people looking at me in disgust, people just looking at me. They didn't know what this felt like. I doubted that there was anyone else who had ever walked this earth that had felt the pain that I was feeling. I was being tortured. I had been tortured for months now. I didn't know how much more of it I could take.

*

Once again, drink was the only thing that got me through the day. Other than Becky, it was the first thing I thought about when I woke up. It'd been a month now since I'd last seen her, a month since we'd driven up to Oxford and when I'd then gone to the hospital and hit the doctor. It surprised me how quickly you could become so dependent on something. At first, I would go and sit in a pub somewhere. I would stay for hours on end and drink on my own, but it didn't take long until the journey out of the house and having to be around people became too much. That's when I started buying alcohol in bulk from one of the local shops and storing it in my room. It was weird. It was the kind of thing you see scummy characters on soaps or in films doing, not real people in real life. I knew as I was doing it that I was falling into a stereotype, hiding alcohol bottles around my room like a tearaway teenager, but I failed to care.

All I knew was that drinking gave me the numbness that I craved. It was as close to being asleep while I was awake as I could be. I slept for eighteen hours some nights. Those were good days. I didn't have to be awake for as long and deal with the fact that that this mess was now my life.

Days had no meaning. Time had no meaning. Did life even have a meaning? What was the point of life? Nobody is happy forever. My mum lost my dad. Becky lost her mum. I've lost Becky. Life is shit and full of hurt. I didn't think it was possible to feel this sick, low, and hopeless.

*

There were days that I would wake up and the hole I was in didn't quite seem so deep. Maybe it was when my hangovers weren't too bad. Sometimes I would wake up and think about attempting to see Becky again. Perhaps try to build bridges, to try and become at least friends – that or just forget her completely and attempt to move on with my life. I couldn't remember the last time I'd spoken to Dave King, and I doubted whether I would even have a job anymore. Not that I really cared. It was the least of my worries in the grand scheme of things. Sometimes I looked back at how happy and naive I'd been before all of this had happened, and I hated myself for it. Did I really think that Becky and I were any different to anyone else? That we were really going to fall in love, be happy, and stay that way for the rest of our lives? When does that really happen to people? It doesn't. Why would we be the exception to the rule? When I did wake up and feel like trying to do something with myself, I would tell myself that I was going to pick up the phone. Phone the school, phone the hospital, phone my friends. My phone would literally be inches away from my face, but I still couldn't muster the energy to pick it up.

*

One day, I found myself sitting in the local doctor's waiting room. My mum sat next to me, fidgeting like a bag of nerves. I didn't know how she'd managed to get me up, dressed, and here – but, somehow, she had. I couldn't remember doing any of those things. I felt as though I had watched someone else do it. I could see the anguish on my mum's face, but I struggled to even care. Deep, deep down somewhere inside me, somewhere that I had lost touch of, I felt awful for thinking like that. But it was true. All I cared about was getting back home to have a drink – and, ultimately, fall asleep. Mum sat there wringing her hands together, staring straight ahead as I sat slumped next to her. I knew my face had a permanent look of disgust on it, and people stared at me when they saw me. I stared back at them, my eyes boring into theirs until they looked away. I suddenly realised I didn't actually know why I was in the doctor's surgery, but as with everything else, I didn't really care.

A little while later my name was called and I looked up, forgetting where I was for a moment. My mum stood up next to me, pulling me by the arm. Not even speaking to me. I dragged my heavy body out of the chair and across the room after her, wondering at which point walking had become so difficult. We entered Dr Moran's room. He was an ancient man who looked every inch the stereotypical doctor. He probably hadn't changed his outfit in fifty years. He wore a smart tweed jacket over suit trousers with rimless glasses perched on the end of his nose. His chalky white hair was combed over a shiny bald head.

Dr Moran had been my GP for as long as I could remember. I could remember sitting in front of him when I was young, proudly showing off my football injuries. I remembered sitting in this exact chair next to his desk, writhing around, itching and scratching like mad, covered in the chicken pox that Simon had given me when we'd started primary school. Worst of all, I could remember sitting in front of him not so long ago, with Becky's hand in mine, hearing the news that we were going to have a baby. My eyes stung at the thought, and I felt the familiar shortness of breath I was accustomed to every time I thought of me and Becky before the accident. I concentrated on not bursting into tears. I would save it for when I got home. Then I could get into bed, drink, and really let it all out.

It was quiet in the room, and I looked up and saw Dr Moran's shocked face staring into mine. I stared back at him. I realised that my mum was dabbing her eyes next to me. I chose to ignore it.

"Chris?" Dr Moran said, his voice full of genuine shock and concern. "What's happened?"

What's happened? I almost laughed. I smiled and shook my head, suddenly feeling as if I could laugh hysterically or burst into uncontrollable tears. *What's happened!?* Before I could even contemplate speaking, even attempt to get my thoughts in order, my mum launched into the story of the last few months – sparing no details. I actually hated her for it. It was bad enough that this was my life now, and that she knew, and Tom knew, and Simon knew, and everyone at the hospital knew. I didn't want other people knowing my business, too. That's when the pity looks started, and I didn't know how many more of those I could take. When my mum finished speaking, Dr Moran exhaled loudly and looked at me, leaning down over his desk.

"You've been through so much, Chris. It's not surprising that you're feeling this way. Feeling down or depressed after something as traumatic as this is completely normal. We are here to help you."

"Who is?" I snapped.

"Me," he said. "The other doctors here, the local hospitals and alcohol groups, there are people you can talk to."

"Well," I said, my voice full of contempt, "maybe if

all the doctors and hospitals were working to fix something that actually needed fixing like *my wife* instead of worrying about people who are sleeping 'too much', or drinking 'too much', and handing out antidepressant tablets left right and centre, then we wouldn't be in this position."

"Chris!" my mum cried out, absolutely horrified, but I didn't care. She was the one who had wanted to bring me here to talk about it – she would have to deal with the consequences.

"I understand how you are feeling, Chris," the doctor said.

"No, you don't," I growled at him through clenched teeth, my eyes screwed shut as I spoke, trying to fight off the headache that was creeping in above my eyes.

He sat back and thought for a second before speaking again. "Can I ask you a few questions?"

I didn't answer him. He tapped away on his computer and then started talking again. "Have you experienced any weight loss or malnutrition?" he asked, ignoring my silence. I shrugged, refusing to look at him.

"I think I know the answer just by looking at you," he said, his words annoying me. "Any insomnia or oversleeping?"

"Oversleeping," my mum answered for me, and I closed my eyes again in frustration. This was pathetic.

"Any unexplained nausea? Or a sore stomach?" Dr Moran continued. I stared at him in disbelief. How could I explain to somebody who has absolutely no idea what it feels like to feel sick in every part of your body, for every second of every day?

"Redness of face or cheeks? Numbness or tingling in your hands and feet?" he said, looking over his glasses at me. I didn't answer his pathetic questions.

"Tremors or shaking?" he asked again.

"Only until I've had my first drink of the day," I spat, and my mum started to sob next to me. I couldn't wait to get out of here.

"Increased irritability? Agitation? Anger? Violence? Excessive displays of emotion? Uncontrollable crying?" He pushed on despite my lack of responses. "Do you have trouble concentrating or remembering things? Do you try to avoid dealing with other people?" I looked at him and we locked eyes for a minute. I still didn't say anything. My mum was snivelling beside me. I wished she would stop. For a while that was the only sound.

"Chris. I'm afraid to say you seem to have developed an alcohol dependency, and I'm very sure that you are suffering with depression. These two things together, as I'm sure you are aware, are not good and you need some help immediately."

I tuned out from his words. My mum's crying became louder. Was I depressed? How do you know if you're depressed? Had this 'depression' snuck up on me so gradually that it now just felt normal?

53

BECKY

"Our feelings had never been spoken of. They just sat there being ignored constantly, the 'elephant in the room'." – Becky.

After everything that I'd been through, I finally felt like I was getting my life back on track. I hadn't seen Chris since the day he'd turned up and attacked Carl in the grounds of the hospital, and that suited me fine. Somehow, we'd managed to get away without anyone knowing what had happened and I thanked God every day that no-one else had been near us in the garden that day. Carl had brushed off his injuries when we eventually ventured back into the hospital, saying he'd tripped over on the gravel path. I thought it was an awful, see through excuse and my heart hammered in my chest, just waiting for someone to dispute what he said and ask him what had really happened. But nobody batted an eyelid. Several people made jokes about 'head injuries' and remarked at how he was 'in the right place', laughing at their own jokes. I laughed along nervously, bordering on hysterical. Carl had point blank refused to tell anyone or report what had happened, even though I insisted that he should. He shook his head and looked me straight in the eye as I'd argued with him.

"It would raise too many questions, Becky," he'd snapped, ending the conversation, and I knew deep down that he was right. I knew it would only open a can of worms and cause people to start asking questions. My mind started running in a million directions as he spoke, wondering if he was referring to the two of us. I knew he spent way too much time with me. Any spare time he had in the hospital was spent in my room or out in the grounds with me. Was he admitting that there was something between us? Or was I jumping to conclusions? I had lived on edge for days after it'd happened, expecting Chris to turn up, cause another scene, ruin everything for me. I jumped every time someone knocked on my door, but nothing had happened.

Eventually, as the cut on Carl's lip healed and by the time the bruise on his hairline faded, what had happened retreated to the back of my mind. I had a feeling I wouldn't see Chris again now. I guessed he would be too scared to come back to the hospital after what had happened, so I looked at the whole event as a blessing in disguise. It had certainly cemented how much I hated Chris, and it proved that all my instincts about him had been right all along. He was a horrible person, and I still couldn't understand how I'd ever married him. When he'd appeared that day he had stunk of alcohol, and it was quite clear that he was drunk. Looking at him had reminded me of my mother and I knew that I would never, ever associate myself with another drunk after the childhood I'd had. I drew a line under it in my mind. I couldn't remember Chris from before. There was no point in dwelling on it. I had been given a second chance now to start a new life without him, and I was going to concentrate on that.

*

I received my expected visit from Sue a few days after Chris had turned up drunk. She knocked on my door and walked into my room just as I was heading out to go to physio. I stared at her, shocked at how frail she looked, and for a fleeting second I felt guilty. Now that I had made my decision to never see Chris again, I didn't want to continue seeing Sue. It would just be too awkward, and even though I felt a connection with her I wanted to cut myself off from Chris completely. She didn't stay for long. She obviously didn't know about Chris turning up and hitting Carl. She seemed to think that the last time he'd been in the hospital was the day he'd taken me out and part of my memory had returned. For a moment I felt like telling her what had happened, telling her exactly what her son was really like, but I refrained, Carl's words still at the front of my mind.

Thankful that I had my physio session as an excuse to hurry it along, I eventually managed to end the conversation. I think as Sue said goodbye we both knew it would be the last time we saw each other. Her eyes filled with tears as she stood by the door, and I was surprised when she turned and embraced me. A long, hard hug that left me feeling embarrassed. Sue left after that, and I could hear her sniffing as the door closed behind her. I paused for a second, not wanting to follow her along the corridor, and also to give myself a moment. I was surprised, but seeing Sue upset made me feel upset. I paced my room for a minute, composing myself before I headed out of the door and down the corridor towards the physio department which was on the next floor up.

Just before I turned the corner for the stairs, I could hear Sue's voice racked with sobs. I stopped, wondering who she was talking to. Curiosity got the better of me and I risked a peek around the corner to see her in the arms of a tall, grey haired, bearded man who was shushing her and shaking his head. I knew I had seen him before and wondered who he was. Sue sobbed onto his chest. I couldn't draw my eyes away from them and stared longer than I should have. I watched as she turned her face up to his and they shared a few seconds of a passionate kiss. It seemed like such an odd thing to do. I pulled away, embarrassed to have seen them and not wanting to get caught. I turned to walk the other way down the corridor, taking the longer route upstairs. For some reason I couldn't get the kiss out of my head.

*

Everyone in the hospital had been absolutely amazing as usual since some of my memory had returned, and I had been receiving even more extensive amounts of occupational therapy to try and see if it would help retrieve any new information. So far, there was nothing. The feelings I'd been getting when waking up in the mornings – not being able to remember my dreams and the overwhelming frustration – had slowed down, too, and it had been almost a month since the last episode. I still had the occasional dream that I had to pull myself out of, and occasionally I woke up with the feeling of something being just out of reach, but generally I felt much better in myself.

*

I was aware that there had started to be serious talk of me leaving the hospital, and the thought of it both thrilled and scared me. The first time I had heard it being mentioned I was taken over by a blind panic. Where would I go? What would I do? I heard the words 'care' and 'social services' being thrown around, and I felt sick at the thought of leaving the comfort of this hospital (more specifically, Carl) and having to go somewhere else. I felt at home and secure here. I would never, ever go to Chris or his family – I would rather live on the streets.

It was actually Carl who came up with the answer unknowingly one day while I was sitting talking to him about my old job. I was deep in thought, trying to use the exercises that I had been given to slowly and thoroughly trace back through certain memories to see if it would release more. Somehow, we had gotten onto the subject of Mark, the owner of the home.

"I've heard his name mentioned before," Carl said. "Were you very close?"

I thought about it for a second. I tried and tried to remember if we'd been friends outside of work, if we'd socialised at all – but, as with everything else, when it came to remembering the information it was like running against a brick wall.

"Why don't we get in touch with him?" Carl had asked. "At the very least it will do you good to meet someone from your past to see if this helps trigger off any more memories, and he may have some suggestions on where to go next when the time comes. He may know more friends or other family?" We looked each other in the eye, and I felt the usual pain in my chest. I wanted this man so much. He looked down at the floor guiltily, confusing me. There were times when we would lock eyes for what seemed like an eternity and the electricity between us was completely apparent. Then there were other times when he would hardly meet my eyes. I knew he was going through some kind of internal struggle, and I didn't know if it was because I was 'married' or because I was his patient. I daren't ask him the question. Our feelings had never actually been spoken of. They just sat there being ignored constantly, the 'elephant in the room'.

It scared me to think of what would happen once I left the hospital. The thought of that being it and the two of us never seeing each other again took the air out of my lungs. I nodded in response to his question of trying to get in contact with Mark. Anything was worth a try.

*

Meeting Mark was possibly the strangest thing I'd had to deal with since waking up, because when he walked in, I actually *knew* him! I had a rush of emotion and familiarity. He was tall, quite tanned, and his mousey brown hair was starting to recede. He had a lovely warm smile that made me smile in response straight away.

"Becky!" he cried when he walked in, and I realised that I even recognised his voice. "You look amazing!"

I didn't think I did. I hadn't worn make-up once since I'd been in the hospital, and I couldn't believe how long my hair was. It never got straightened or styled, so it was always left to dry in a natural wave around my face. If it was too hot, which it seemed to be all the time at the moment, I piled it all up in a bun on top of my head or in a loose ponytail at the nape of my neck. He sat down next to me and stared at me, taking me in. I saw Carl's face darken slightly and I got a rush of pleasure. Was he jealous?

"I'll leave you two alone" he said, and Mark grinned and thanked him, completely oblivious.

I sat with Mark for hours and listen engrossed as he told me stories of the care home. Some things he told me I had already remembered. Some were stories I was hearing for the first time – stories that I had no recollection of. We chatted about the patients and the home itself, and he had even brought a laptop in with him to show me some pictures. My excitement flared and I couldn't wait to see them, I sat impatiently while the laptop loaded up, literally on the edge of my seat. Once it was on, he opened the files and we sat flicking through photo after photo. The further back we went through the pictures, the more and more I started popping up. I stared at my face, engrossed. I looked so *happy!* Mark paused slightly longer on each photo of me, and I leant into the screen, staring, drinking it all in. We sat in silence for ages, just the *click, click, click* of the button flicking to the next picture. I was fascinated. There were thousands of pictures, and I could have looked at them all day. There were photos of patients, Mark, other carers, us on trips, in the home, and in the garden.

Then there was a photo of Chris. He was standing in a makeshift goal in the big garden behind the home. Three patients stood around him, a look of elation on their faces as a football was just about to go through his legs. He was smiling. A beautiful, carefree smile that I had never ever seen before. It was amazing. It changed his whole face and there were dimples in his cheeks. I couldn't take my eyes off him. He looked like a completely different person. His hair was longer and blonder than it is now, and he looked fit and healthy – it made me realise how ill he looked now in comparison. Before I could take it in, Mark had flicked onto the next picture and then the next, suddenly clicking onto a photo of me and Chris together. We were in the background – the photo was actually being taken of two patients with Downs Syndrome grinning wildly and posing with their fingers in the peace sign. Chris and I were behind them. He had his arm around my waist, and I was leaning into him, staring into his face with such an intense look of love it almost took my breath away just to look at the picture. Chris was grinning and looking at something near the camera. He looked happy and proud, and everything in the way he stood, even though he wasn't looking at me, radiated love. I felt completely shocked, and I wished I'd never seen it. I moved away from the laptop slightly and Mark looked over at me.

"Had enough?" he asked, and I nodded. "What's up?" he asked, his brow furrowing slightly when he saw my face.

"Nothing," I said as brightly as I could. "It's just that's the first picture I've seen of me and Chris together from before the accident." All of a sudden, it seemed strange. Why hadn't Chris ever brought photos in to show me? Surely that would have been the most obvious thing to do?

"Oh, really?" he asked, and looked embarrassed. "Well, er, your doctor explained some of your situation to me before I came in. I don't know what to say, Becky. It's just the last thing I expected to hear. I mean, you and Chris, you were so... in love. I just can't believe you..."

"I don't want to talk about it," I said, silencing him. It was the last thing I wanted to talk about.

Mark closed the folders on the laptop and shut it down, snapping it shut and burying it back in his bag. I changed the subject and before long Mark was happily chatting away again, and I sat trying to listen to him, trying to put the image of me and Chris to the back of my mind.

That night, the dreams started again.

54

"I am sick of all this moping around! Get in the shower, we're going out." – Simon.

Chris had started waking up in a sheer panic almost every night, his heart beating wildly in his chest and a stabbing pain behind his eyes. His first thought would be to have a drink. It was a regular occurrence now for him to wake up in the night and take a swig out of the nearest bottle before lying back down on the bed, overcome with shame, but welcoming the nausea that took over him until he drifted back off to sleep again. Throughout the day he would have a constant headache. It wasn't unbearable and he almost enjoyed it, revelling in the pain and self-pity.

He wandered around the house, avoiding his mum and Tom. He couldn't remember the last time he hadn't seen his mum in tears. She seemed to cry constantly at the moment, and although he knew it was wrong, he just didn't have the energy to care. When he did leave his room, he moved around as if in a dream, never speaking to anyone. Even the dogs avoided him now, their heads low and their tails between their legs. They would slink off into a corner and lay down together, staring at him with confused eyes.

Chris had stopped going to the pub altogether now, and instead he just drank at home. Sue had tried to put her foot down and ban any alcohol from the house after their disastrous appointment at the doctors, but Chris had walked out after they'd argued about it and gone missing for two days. She was so relieved when he was home again, after fearing that he was lying dead somewhere, that when he did eventually come home she had given in, petrified he would go off again and that something would happen. Chris stayed in the house most of the time now. He was skinny and frail, his hair lank and thin against his head, and the shadows under his eyes were almost purple. Sue wondered how there could be such a vast transformation in a person in such a short amount of time. From time to time, she could hear him being sick in the bathroom upstairs and she often heard him crying in his room. Sometimes the wails would become hysterical, and it would rip her heart in two. At first, she had gone into his room to try and comfort him, attempting to slip a comforting arm around his shoulders, but he would shrug her off aggressively. The look on his face, a mixture of contempt, shame, and embarrassment, had made her feel like she was unwelcome and intruding. She had no idea what to do.

She had now taken to standing at the bottom of the stairs, waiting for the wailing to turn to sobs and the sobs to turn to sniffs until it eventually went silent. But that was the worst of it for Sue. She hated the silence, constantly on edge, fearing that he had fallen asleep and choked, or even worse – that he had done something stupid. She always left it as long as she dared until she could sneak into his room to check that he was still breathing. If he was in a deep sleep she would sit on the side of his bed, breathing in the stale air, staring into his face, trying to recognise her son from a few months ago. The confident, content, happy, outgoing son who had loved life – not this shadow of him. With each day that passed, Chris was slipping further and further away, and she feared that soon he would pass the point of no return and she would never get the old Chris back.

*

Simon was also struggling to watch his friend fall apart and he felt utterly helpless. The first time Chris had gone missing he had spent hours and hours attempting to find him. When he finally did, he'd half dragged, half carried him to the car and was mortified when he realised Chris had wet himself. Thankfully, he managed to get Chris home and unchanged without Sue noticing that little detail. The following day, Simon had tried to bring it up with Chris, had tried to get him to open-up about why he had suddenly gone off the rails, but Chris had point-blank refused to speak about it. Later that day he had gone missing again.

Things had got dramatically worse since Becky's memory had returned and she had lost her temper with Chris, telling him that she never wanted to see him again. Chris was continuously drunk now, and Simon just couldn't believe how desolate his friend had become. It was scary. He was watching Chris fall apart in front of his very eyes. He was constantly trying to spend time with him, trying to coax him to come out, to do something – anything.

"How about we go and watch Spurs play on Sunday?" he had asked one day as he sat in the kitchen with Chris slumped in the chair opposite him. He watched as Chris slowly lifted his head up to meet his gaze. He looked him in the eye, a look of absolute contempt on his face.

"Are you kidding me?" he asked, shaking his head "Why would I want to go and watch the football? What the hell is the point? I honestly don't know how we managed to waste so much time on something so pathetic. On a stupid *game.*" Simon sat there, opening and closing his mouth like a fish, not knowing what to say or how to handle the situation. He felt completely out of his depth.

*

"I am sick of all this moping around! Get in the shower, we're going out," Simon demanded the following Saturday. As usual, he was spending the morning trying to coax Chris out of his depressive state and not getting anywhere. Today, though, he had reached the end of his tether and he was sick of pussyfooting around after him. After ignoring Chris' protests, he stood by and policed him until he had showered and gotten dressed.

"If you're going to sit around drinking all day, at least we can do it in a pub with the football on," Simon mumbled once Chris was ready. Chris didn't reply. He just followed him out of the front door with a face like thunder as Simon waved goodbye to a worried looking Sue. Chris felt sick and heavy, as usual, as he dragged himself down the road after Simon. Walking was not a pleasant experience for him anymore. Somehow, though, Simon managed to get him on the tube and into a pub. They sat down at a table by the window. Simon plonked a drink in front of him and Chris started to drink, detached from everything around him. He looked around the pub, staring at all the happy faces. Simon, as usual, started talking to everyone surrounding him, and before long he was lost in different conversations and debates. Chris sat stony faced, not getting involved, just drinking everything that was put in front of him. By the late afternoon, Simon and Chris were both hammered. For once, Chris remembered what it had felt like to be drunk before the accident and for a while he almost felt as if he was enjoying himself. Perhaps it was because Simon was getting just as drunk as him and he had someone to share it with. They continued drinking at the same pace, and, as the afternoon wore on, they started ordering shots with each round.

The football matches finished in the late afternoon and the hordes of men that had been crammed into the bar to watch on the big screens started to thin and the evening crowd started to enter. Dressed up couples sat at tables in the restaurant area. Groups of girls in short dresses and high heels entered through the door and stood against the bar, glancing around. Guys entered in packs – obviously on the pull, and they stood to the side, eyeing up the talent. Chris and Simon were slowing down at this point and sat mumbling to each other in the corner. Simon's phone started to ring in his pocket.

"It's Katie," he mumbled incoherently as he pulled the phone out of his pocket and stared at the screen. "She's gunna kill me." He held up his hand to signal he would be a moment and he answered the phone whilst heading towards the door to get outside. Chris sat on his own at the table, looking around. For the first time in a few hours, the realisation that he was completely and utterly on his own hit him once more. He would never have his concerned wife ringing to see where he was ever again. He got up, needing a drink, and stumbled to the bar, feeling sick as soon as he stood, his head spinning. By now, the bar was heaving, and he stood waiting for the barman to come over and take his order. He tried to get his eyes to focus and was concentrating on not being sick when he suddenly realised there was a girl by his side, speaking to him.

"Hi," she said, smiling at him provocatively. Chris dragged his eyes to her face and stared at her. He saw her smile falter for a second when she saw his face. Chris' lip curled in disgust.

"What?" he growled at her. People who were standing nearby turned their heads at the tone of his voice to look at him. Chris looked the girl up and down. She was skinny and perched on top of a pair of extremely high heels. A revealing gold dress clung to her body and her eyes were heavily made up with dark make-up. She was the exact opposite of Becky.

"I…er… just thought I'd say hi…" the girl stammered, and Chris grinned at her sarcastically.

"*Did you?*" he said, mimicking her voice. The girl looked around uncomfortably, obviously looking for her friends. Chris leant into her and she leaned away from him, smelling the alcohol on his breath. He looked her up and down.

"You repulse me," he said when his eyes met her face again, and he watched as the girl's face dropped in horror and gasps came from the people standing around them. The shocked girl, who now stood in front of him with her lip trembling, was clearly fighting back tears. A young guy who had been watching from behind them pushed past the girl and stood in Chris' face.

"What's your problem, mate?" he asked aggressively, and Chris stared at him, unmoving.

"No problem here," he said grinning, holding out his arms in surrender. The guy didn't like the look of Chris close-up, and had turned to walk away when Chris mumbled, "I've just got no time for *tarts.*" The next thing Chris knew, he'd taken a blow to the side of the head that knocked him to the floor. It was at that moment that Simon re-entered the bar. He ran over, sobering up immediately as the man continued to punch Chris while he was curled up on the floor, completely unable to defend himself. Simon managed to drag Chris along the floor and out of the way while punches were still flying. A bouncer came striding over and dragged Chris from Simon's grasp, lifting him up and carrying him to the door like a rag doll. Simon followed behind, completely bewildered, having no idea of what had happened.

"What about him? What about him?" Simon cried, looking over his shoulder and pointing at the guy who had started the fight, but he had vanished off into the crowd.

Chris was struggling and writhing around in the bouncer's grip, screaming, "Don't arrest me! Don't arrest me!" He kicked and punched the air around him.

Once outside, the bouncer threw him to the floor with a look of revulsion on his face, as Chris was still screaming at him as if he were a police officer. It was at that moment that Simon knew Chris had lost his grip on reality.

55

BECKY

"The accident, the hospital, and Chris would all be behind me." – Becky.

Since his first visit, Mark came to the hospital to see me regularly. I loved his company, and he became the first real friend I'd had since waking up. I loved listening to him talk, especially about the home, and I swelled with pride when he told me what a fantastic job I used to do. It was on his fourth visit a couple of weeks after we 'first met' when he turned to me while we were sitting out in the garden.

"Would you consider coming back to work for us when you're out of here?" he asked almost shyly, and I turned to look at him, stunned and instantly full of excitement.

"Really? But would I be allowed? After everything that's happened? How would it work?" I asked, the words spilling from my mouth. Mark shrugged.

"We'd make it work. Everything would come back to you, I'm sure. You were always a natural with the patients," he said, and my cheeks blushed at the praise. He continued talking about how wonderful it would be to get me back to work. I couldn't wait to speak with Carl about it! Straight away my mind began to wander, and I started thinking of what it would be like to be out of here, working and independent.

Then the worry that had been on my mind for weeks struck me. Where was I actually going to go when I had to leave the hospital? I knew that it was something that was being discussed frequently now, and I knew that Carl was putting off discharging me, knowing that I had nowhere to go. It played on my mind constantly. Mark walked me back to my room and I kept my eyes peeled for Carl, not able to contain my excitement. I wanted to tell him about Mark's offer. We finally bumped into him when we reached the corridor that my room was on, and I wondered if he had been hanging around waiting for me. His face clouded over slightly when he saw me with Mark – ever since Mark's first visit, he has always seemed on guard around him.

"Becky," he said politely, and nodded at me professionally as he always does when we were around other people. "Mr. Robinson." He forced a smile in Mark's direction.

"Hello, doctor," Mark said cheerfully. "I was just speaking with Becky about when she leaves the hospital. I was telling her how happy we would be to have her back in her old position at the care home." I stood there grinning, looking from one to the other, faltering when the atmosphere became even frostier.

"That's a lovely idea, but I hope you understand as an employer that Becky has been through a huge trauma. She has still not recovered her memory fully-" Carl started, but Mark shook his head and waved his hand silencing him mid-sentence, and I saw Carl's face cloud over even more.

"I don't care about any of that! Becky will always have a job with us, whatever happens, for as long as she wants it – and obviously a place to live, too." I spun to face him.

"A place to live?" I asked.

"Yes, yes, of course! You can come and stay at the home until you decide what you want to do and where you want to go. You can stay as long as you want! We have a number of nurses and carers that live on site anyway. It wouldn't be a problem at all." Excitement exploded inside me. I had been worrying myself sick wondering where I was going to go when I was discharged, and now I'd been given somewhere – and somewhere familiar! I felt like jumping on the spot with excitement!

"Oh, Mark, that's amazing! Thank you so much!" I exclaimed, tears filling my eyes, and I threw my arms around him in a hug, causing him to blush.

"No problem at all, I'm more than happy to help!" he said into my ear as we hugged.

*

The next few weeks were a complete blur, and I was completely torn between being excited and petrified. I was itching to get out of the hospital and out into the big wide world, but I couldn't contemplate not seeing Carl every day. As nothing had actually ever been said between us, I didn't dare say anything for fear that I'd totally imagined the connection between us. Apart from the time he'd kissed my cheek, and the lingering looks we shared, I didn't actually have anything to go by.

I lay awake at night, tossing and turning, worrying about it before falling into stressful sleeps where my dreams flicked back and forth between Carl and, since seeing Mark's photo of us, of Chris. In the mornings when I woke up, I had started struggling with what was a dream and what was reality again. Sometimes I felt as if memories and feelings were attempting to rise to the surface, but I shut it out and didn't dwell on them. I didn't *want* things to change! Things were finally moving in the right direction, and I was excited about moving forward and getting on with my life. Chris had had his chance – I didn't want to start worrying about him now.

I kept the dreams to myself and tried not to think about them. But I constantly had the niggling feeling at the back of my mind again that there was something I had forgotten, as if there was something I needed to do. I would get split-second flashes that would stop me in my tracks, but they would be gone as quickly as they had come.

*

The date was set for my discharge. I would be leaving the hospital on the first Friday in August. Nearly four months since my accident. In some ways I felt like it had flown by, but in others it seemed like I'd been here forever.

Mark's visits became even more regular, and twice now he had picked me up and taken me to the home for the day. It was the most surreal experience of my life – even more so than waking up from my coma. Pulling up to the home in Mark's car was like arriving in one of my dreams, and my head twisted and turned from side-to-side trying to take everything in. As I entered the main entrance of the home, with Mark following quietly behind me, I ran my hand along surfaces, walking through rooms, automatically heading towards my office, the instructions surfacing from my unconscious mind without hesitation. I hadn't met or bumped into any of the patients on the first visit, as Mark said it was best not to push myself, so even though my curiosity was driving me mad, we waited until the second visit for me to go and interact with people.

Mark stayed by my side constantly, re-introducing me to the patients and staff. I remembered almost everyone instantly – the second I laid eyes on someone it was as if everything I'd ever known about them returned. It was exhausting and bizarre, and I don't think words can ever describe it to anyone who hadn't been through it.

I walked away that afternoon feeling as if I really belonged somewhere, and I couldn't wait to move in and be a part of it all again. It reinforced my feelings that I had made the right decision never to see Chris again.

With the dreams I'd been having recently, he seemed to always be at the back of my mind, but now I knew for sure that I was right and had been all along. I would never, ever have left this behind, and if he had loved me like he said he did, he wouldn't have expected me to.

In just over a week this would be my life; the accident, the hospital, and Chris would all be behind me. I just prayed that Carl would also be a part of it.

56

CHRIS

"Knowing that it was in my hands, that I could make the choice to escape this life, made me feel better than I had in months." – Chris.

I could feel myself being lifted. Roughly. There were voices. I thought I recognised them. I tried to open my eyes, but it was too much effort. I felt sick and dizzy, as if I'd been spun around too much. I struggled to awaken, but a woozy blanket of unconsciousness covered me and I slid beneath it, ignoring the hard uncomfortable surface I was laying on. The voices drifted further and further away until eventually everything was black.

*

I opened my eyes and instantly knew that something was wrong. I felt like shit – even more so than usual. There was something different; I attempted to lift my head up off the pillow and a searing pain shot through the side of my face. I almost cried out with the pain. I opened my eyes and realised that I wasn't in my bed. I was on the sofa in our living room. There were muffled voices coming from the kitchen. I managed to drag myself off the sofa, a pain shooting down my right arm as I did so. I crept over to the mirror hanging over the fireplace. My reflection shocked me. I had a huge, puffy, bloodshot black eye and a huge graze along the length of one cheek that looked deep and sore. There was dried blood all around the graze, down my cheek, and onto my chin.

I was no stranger to aches and pains recently, I was constantly falling over whilst drunk and I'd been beaten up whilst out in a bar with Simon in a few weeks ago. Not that I remember any of it. This is just what I get told.

But these cuts and bruises looked even worse than usual, and I was in a great deal more pain than I'd been in before. I looked down at my clothes, which were filthy, and I realised I couldn't remember putting them on. It could have been days since I'd last got changed.

I didn't even care enough to strain my brain to think about it. I knew the voices in the kitchen were talking about me and I wanted to sneak out without having to face anyone. I also desperately needed a drink. I crept as quietly as I could over to the tiny drinks cabinet in the corner of the room where my mum usually kept her sherry and brandy. I opened the cupboard door as quietly as possible, disappointment surging through me when I realised it was empty. I would have to sneak past the kitchen door and get upstairs to my bedroom to get to some alcohol now. I crept back across the living room floor, opening the door as slowly and silently as possible, but the voices from the kitchen stopped mid-flow and I knew I was busted. Sure enough, my mum flew out of the kitchen with Tom following closely behind her.

It all happened before I even had a chance to think. My mum covered the ground between us in a split-second and slapped me hard around the face. The pain that shot through my skull was excruciating and it took me a moment to realise that it wasn't her blow that had caused the pain, it was her touching whatever damage was there already.

"You stupid boy!" my mum screeched at me, completely hysterical, and I stood there in shock, wondering what on earth I'd done now. "You just don't care? You don't care at all anymore, do you?" she continued, on and on, screaming and shouting, her voice breaking with the strain. Tom stood in the doorway, watching but not saying anything. It was hard to defend myself when I didn't know what I had done wrong, so I stood in silence, wishing it was over so I could be alone and have a drink.

It didn't take me long to piece the story together. I had gone missing again. It was a stranger who had found me, unconscious in an alleyway. They had used my phone to contact my mum and she had begged them not to call the police. Instead, she phoned Simon, getting him out of bed in the middle of the night to go with her to collect me and bring me home. My mum continued to scream at me, tears streaming down her face with Tom's steely gaze still staring at me over her shoulder.

I didn't understand why she was going so mental, why this time was any different from before. Until she told me what I'd started mumbling while semi-unconscious in the back of the car as they drove me home. As she was talking, choking on her tears, I suddenly remembered what she was talking about. I had made a decision last night. I can't remember at which point or why, but I had decided that rather than carrying on like this I would just end it all. Kill myself. Go to sleep forever.

Even as I stood here, my face in agony from where I had presumably fallen onto it, and even as my mum stood in tears in front of me, the idea just seemed completely and utterly the right thing to do. It actually made me feel as if a weight had been lifted off my shoulders. I didn't have to carry on like this anymore. I could just kill myself and be done with it if I wanted to. The realisation that I *could* if I wanted to made me feel a whole lot better. All of a sudden, I actually felt a bit better in myself, like you do when you have something to look forward to. Knowing that this was in my hands, that I could make the choice to escape this life, made me feel better than I had in months.

I stood and took the abuse from my mum, not saying a word, and I knew that this was the closest she had ever come to hating me. As she finished screaming, she looked at me, willing me to say something, but my mind went blank. All I could think of was the little secret that I was harbouring now, and I stood stupidly in front of her, not knowing what to say. After a few moments passed, I daringly attempted to move past her towards the stairs without saying anything. She stood aside and I took my chance, moving past her and up the stairs as fast as my aches and pains would allow. I couldn't believe my luck. I didn't even have to speak!

I entered my room and felt around under my bed for a bottle of rum that I'd left there and took a hearty swig, wincing at the taste. I climbed into my bed, fully clothed, and closed my eyes, my foggy brain exploring the thought of suicide. Could I really do it? I doubted it. But it was a nice thought as I drifted off to sleep.

57

BECKY

"No-one can know about this."
– Carl Matthews.

Time was flying by, and my discharge date loomed, getting closer and closer until eventually I opened my eyes for the final time in the hospital. As usual, I had to wait for a few moments with my eyes closed tight, waiting for the fragments left over from last night's dream to disappear. Everything was quiet, and I looked around at the perfect room. Everything was immaculate as usual, and I remembered when I had first woken up surrounded by people, beeps, and machines. The room seemed so empty now. As usual I looked over towards the window. Morning light was creeping in around the curtains, causing the room to be filled with a warm glow.

I rolled onto my back, pulling the crisp white sheets up to my chin. This was the last morning I would ever wake up here. My new life started today! My stomach lurched at the thought. Mark was coming to pick me up at lunchtime, and I knew that there was no way I would be able to go back to sleep. I tried to keep calm and not succumb to the panic that had filled me over the last couple of weeks. Carl had still not acknowledged – except in a professional way – that I was leaving. It sickened me to think about it, and I had been off my food for the past week with worry.

I was seriously starting to panic that I had fabricated the whole situation in my head. If there had been anyone to talk to about it, I would have, but I just didn't know where to turn. Part of me was desperate to mention something to him when we were alone, and part of me was indignant and proud. I wouldn't show myself up by mentioning anything. If I had made this whole situation up in my head then fine, I would walk away with my head held high. Or that was the plan. I just had to get through the next few hours.

*

Not long after I'd woken up, my room was a flurry of activity. Doctors, nurses, physios, and therapists were in and out with piles of discharge papers, asking me to sign this and sign that. I was given tonnes of paperwork to take with me, and advice and orders were being thrown at me from all directions. I sat in the midst of it all, feeling completely out of my depth, worrying how I was going to remember everything. Finally, as late morning approached, the stream of people had slowed and then finally stopped, and I was left in the room on my own, sitting on my bed. There was a knock at the door. Carl's knock. My stomach instantly fell, and my heart started beating as if I'd just run a marathon. Even my hands felt instantly sweaty. I attempted to stammer at him to come in, but I seemed to have lost my voice. Carl entered tentatively, closing the door firmly behind him as he headed over to me, smiling. Looking into his eyes gave me such intense butterflies, I couldn't believe it was possible to fancy anyone as much as I fancied him.

He slipped his hand into his pocket, looking around the room and towards the door before pulling out a small black mobile phone. He shoved it towards me, gesturing at me to put it in my pocket. I grabbed the phone off him with my sweaty hands and shoved it hard into the pocket of my jeans.

"My mobile number is programmed into that, okay? I've got the bill covered. Text or call me whenever you can. But, Becky," he paused. "*No-one* can know about this," he said to me, looking me straight in the eye, and I felt as if he was looking into my soul. I nodded my head, unable to speak. I was full of emotion: elated that I hadn't been imagining the feelings between us, despair at the thought of leaving him today, and thrilled at what had just happened.

Carl turned to look at the door once more, cocking his head to the side slightly as if listening for anyone outside. He paused for a split second, and I could see him weighing up something in his mind. Then he pounced. He was next to me in a second, his hand on the back of my head, his fingers entwining through my hair, pulling me to him, his lips pressed hard onto mine. I could feel his stubble grazing my chin and heard a moan at the back of his throat as our lips parted and his tongue slipped into my mouth for the briefest of moments. I felt desire explode through my whole body, and I was thankful that I was sat on the edge of the bed – I don't think my legs could have held me if I'd been standing up. This all happened so quickly, and all too soon he was standing up by the end of my bed again, his face flushed. We grinned at each other like school children, and I desperately wanted to be close to him again, but a knock at the door bought us both back to reality.

"Come in," Carl called, his professional voice back on, and the moment was over. So fleeting, I would have wondered if I hadn't imagined the whole thing if not for the small, hard mobile phone digging into me from my pocket.

*

Leaving the hospital was a sadder experience than I'd expected, and I cried as I said goodbye to all the people who'd helped me over the past few months. Everybody had been wonderful, and all the staff that had worked with me since I'd been here had signed a 'Good Luck' card for me. I clutched it to my chest as I followed Mark out through reception. He walked ahead of me, carrying my tiny bag of possessions, out of the hospital and into the sunshine.

I climbed into the passenger side of Mark's car, attempting to listen as he chatted away about how he'd redecorated one of the biggest rooms on the staff corridor for me, but all I could do was look down at the one corner of the card that contained Carl's handwriting. Strong and bold, just like him.

'Becky, I wish you every happiness in the world and all the best in your future. Carl'.

58

BECKY

"I don't know what we're doing, Becky. I don't know what I'm doing. I'm risking my job, you know."
– Carl Matthews.

I was exhausted. After a hectic afternoon, the evening eventually passed and night-time finally arrived. I sat on my bed, alone at last. Mark had been so very sweet all day, but he was suffocating me already, constantly asking if I needed anything and popping his head around my door, frequently checking if I was okay. We had dinner that evening, sat around a table in one of the staff rooms. I felt too exhausted to throw myself into the deep end by eating with the patients today.

Once everyone was finished, I made my excuses and walked up to my room with butterflies in my stomach. I firmly told Mark I'd see him in the morning and ignored the crestfallen look on his face. All I could think about was the mobile phone currently stashed under the mattress in my bedroom. I hurried around the corner and ran lightly up the stairs, excitement creeping into me at the thought of hearing Carl's voice.

When I got into my room, I closed the door firmly behind me and flicked the small lock, breathing a sigh of relief when the outside world was locked away. I entered my small en-suite bathroom and turned the shower on. I brushed my teeth while examining my face in the mirror as the bathroom filled with steam. I still found it strange every time I caught sight of my reflection, and I stared at my aged face in wonder. It still seemed to me as if I'd aged overnight, and I could spend huge amounts of time staring at the changes in the mirror.

I showered and dried myself as quickly as I could, desperate to finally get into bed and dial Carl's number. I pulled the phone out from underneath the mattress, feeling like a naughty school child. I turned the light off in the bedroom, somehow feeling safer in the dark, and slipped beneath the bedcovers. It seemed to take me an age to figure out how to unlock the phone and for a moment I panicked that I wasn't going to be able to figure it out, until eventually the screen lit up and I managed to navigate my way to the phone book. There was one number saved. *CM.* My throat tightened, and I took a deep breath before pressing the dial button and holding the phone against my ear. It didn't even ring once before it was answered.

"Becky," Carl said, and it sounded more of a moan than a word.

"Carl!" I said, my face splitting into a grin.

"How are you doing?" he asked, as if we had this conversation every day, and straight away the conversation flowed between us, completely natural. I talked of Mark, the home, my new room, and we spoke about the hospital, his day, and the staff. Before I knew it, time had flown past and we'd been on the phone for over an hour. The line finally went quiet for a moment before Carl spoke, pulling me back to reality.

"I don't know what we're doing, Becky. I don't know what *I'm* doing. I'm risking my job, you know. I don't really understand what's going on between us." My heart felt like it had stopped beating in my chest.

"I won't tell anyone, Carl, you know I won't. I don't know what's happening either, but I know I can't just walk away and not see you again." I could hear the panic and desperation creeping into my voice, and all of a sudden I felt sick. Carl exhaled loudly down the phone.

"I know, me too. I can't wait to see you again."

Warmth spread through me, and excitement exploded in my chest. His words rang in my ear: '*see you again*'! We were going to see each other again! I felt tears fill my eyes and I suddenly realised how much this had meant to me. I don't think I'd realised how strong my feelings were for this man until that very moment.

"I can't wait to see you," I said, desperately trying to disguise the catch in my voice as I struggled to speak over the frog in my throat.

We talked for a while longer until eventually Carl said he was going to have to go. He had to be in the hospital for five a.m., and it was nearing eleven p.m. now. I clutched the phone tightly, saying goodbye and trying to sound as cool and positive as I could.

"Bye darling," he said, and I thought my face was going to split in two. It felt so grown up to have a man like Carl call me 'darling' and I swelled with pride, whispering, "Goodbye," back at him before the line went dead.

I shoved the phone under my pillow and laid down, feeling emotionally exhausted. The conversation had been a rollercoaster of feelings and passion, and I tried to replay every single detail over in my head before I fell asleep.

*

My dream was a tangled mess. It was as if I knew I was in the home. I dreamt I was waking up. My mind was filled with things that needed to be done today. But I was filled with a longing for it to be over so I could leave and get home. Flashes of Chris' face kept coming into my dream mixed with flashes of Carl's. The faces would merge together, and even in the dream I was confused. The dream changed, as they often do, and I dreamt of the car accident, a new regular occurrence in my dreams, and then my hospital room. People were filing in and out, but

I always felt as if I was waiting for something.

*

I woke with a start. What an odd dream! I'd dreamt about a car accident and a hospital. It was so detailed! I'd have to tell Chris when I got home, he loved analysing dreams! Shocked, I shot up in bed, my hand covering my mouth. What? What had just happened? But as usual, the feeling I'd just had was fading away and I sat struggling to deal with it. Reality had taken over. But, for a tiny moment, just a few seconds ago, I was in a different life. It had seemed so natural to think of Chris. I actually felt sick as confusion took over and I kicked the covers off myself, suddenly feeling boiling hot. I was covered in a sheen of sweat and my heart was racing. I tried to claw my dream back, or at least the feeling that I'd just had. I tried to make sense of it, the so natural thought about Chris. But it was gone. I stomped to the bathroom, tears of frustration building in my eyes, filled with the usual emptiness that settled over me after a night full of dreams.

59

BECKY

"I wasn't sure if I was learning everything as I went along, or just remembering what I had already known."
– Becky.

After a week of being back, I had thrown myself into life working at the home. It didn't take me long to get used to the way things worked and the systems that were in place. I wasn't sure if I was learning everything as I went along, or just remembering what I'd already known. Sometimes I thought I knew what I had to do before Mark had fully explained it to me, and it wasn't long before I was back into the swing of things.

I kept away from the other staff, feeling odd that they knew me and I didn't really know them. They all seemed to avoid me anyway, which suited me. I tried to ignore the now constant feeling I carried around with me that I was missing something. I put it to the back of my mind until nighttime, where once again I became terrorised by dreams.

The days flew past quickly, and I loved every second of it. I spent most of my time with the patients inside the home – I didn't feel confident enough to take anyone out by myself yet. I dreaded the evenings. Mark seemed to feel like he needed to constantly entertain me, whereas I was quite comfortable sitting in silence with the patients, watching TV or playing a board game, just biding my time until I could sneak off up to my room to speak with Carl. Even if he was on a late shift he would make the time to speak to me. It was the highlight of my day.

Our conversations had started steering towards us finding a time when we could meet up with each other, and I carried the thought around with me like a precious secret. I don't think I'd ever looked forward to anything as much in my whole life.

First, though, I had to approach Mark about my time off and I was dreading it. I knew he would ask me a million questions. I hadn't taken any time off so far. I'd worked all day every day, waving my hand dismissively if Mark told me to take some time off. I finally built up the courage and took my chance to bring it up over dinner that evening. The other nurses and carers were talking amongst themselves, discussing a TV program that had been on the night before. I leant over to Mark, clearing my throat.

"Mark?" I said tentatively, and he turned to look at me, instantly giving me his full attention. "I wondered if I could ask you a question regarding my days off?"

"Of course! What do you want to know?" he asked enthusiastically, launching into a speech detailing the hours I'd worked so far and how much time off I'd earned as he explained to me how he was keeping a record of everything. It amazed me how much he was able to keep in his brain and I didn't doubt for a second that he knew down to the minute what time off I was owed.

"I wondered if I could possibly take Monday off?" I asked cautiously, dreading the bombardment of questions that were sure to follow.

"Of course! What do you fancy doing? I can make sure there's enough cover so we can take the time off together!" he said, his face lighting up, and I stopped him dead in his tracks.

"Actually, Mark, I wanted to have a day off on my own. I haven't had one second to myself since the accident, and I'd quite like to go off for the day by myself..." I trailed off. Mark's eyebrows furrowed and he frowned at me, looking deep into my eyes, and I *knew* that he knew I was lying.

"Do you think that's a good idea, Becky?" he asked, and I tried to avoid his eye. "You said you weren't confident enough to take a patient out on your own yet, which is completely understandable. Are you sure you want to attempt going out in the city completely by yourself? You may feel okay in here where it's familiar, but being out in public is going to be completely different for you. The doctors said you need to take these things slowly and not push yourself. They also said you need to have someone with you while you were doing new things, just in case something happened…"

I felt my patience wearing thin, and I breathed in deeply before I replied, reminding myself that he only had my best interests at heart.

"I know what they said, Mark, but it's something I need to do for myself," I said simply. Mark raised his eyebrows, and once again I knew he knew I was lying.

Eventually he agreed that, of course, I could take Monday off, and he launched into lectures of the dos and don'ts of every detail in the outside world. From crossing the road, using public transport, dealing with people in shops, money, and maps. It was painful but I sat and listened, nodding when appropriate, making all the right noises while he waffled on, desperate to get upstairs and tell Carl that it was sorted. Only a few more days and we would get to spend time together, completely on our own, away from prying eyes.

*

I pacified Mark by joining him the next day when he went out for the afternoon. He finally swayed me when he said we could go to the shops for a few hours. He said it would be good for me to go with him to get a feel for being out of the home and out in the city before I attempted it on my own. It was purely the thought that I could buy some new clothes for when I met Carl that helped me to agree! Since waking up from the accident, the only clothes I'd owned were a few items that Chris had brought into the hospital for me originally, and I was sick to death of wearing them now. I didn't own a piece of make-up or have any products of my own. I'd only used hospital soap and shampoo for months. I got excited at the thought of treating myself, and I relished the thought of getting dressed up for my date with Carl on Monday.

I followed Mark out of the home, and instead of getting into his car we walked down the road to the tube station. Mark was chatting away as usual, and I smiled and listened to him whilst looking around, taking everything in, trying to work out if the scenery was familiar or not. Mark asked if there was anywhere in particular I would like to go to shop, and for a fleeting second I went to answer him as if my brain was aware of somewhere that I wanted to go even before I knew, but then the thought was gone. I said I would leave the decision up to him and he said we should head over to Oxford Street.

I followed him onto the train and then the tube, my eyes wide. I was shocked at how big and busy everything seemed, and I felt a little bit panicked and out of my depth. I stuck close to Mark's side. He kept a close eye on me, and I knew he was trying to work out if I would survive okay 'on my own' on Monday. I tried to look calm and cool whilst taking everything in.

I didn't like Oxford Street one bit when we walked up the steps from the tube station onto the huge main road. It seemed too big and open and busy. Chris' words appeared in my head: *you had really learnt to love the city'*. Well, I didn't believe that – this was not a place I could imagine 'loving' and I held onto that thought, using it as more ammo against him in my own head, convincing myself further that I was doing the right thing by pushing him to the back of my mind and ignoring my dreams and the flashes I kept getting.

Once we went inside the shops, though, an old instinct kicked in and I loved wandering around, picking out clothes. I automatically knew which pieces would look good and which wouldn't. I spent way too much money, and after only an hour I was struggling with shopping bags. I asked Mark if we could go into the huge Boots store that I could see down the road, and once we were inside I walked around, filling my basket with beautiful smelling shampoos, conditioners, and dozens of items of new make-up.

My eyes and hands seemed to know what they were looking for before my brain did, and I watched myself picking items up off the shelf without even needing to try them on. I also bought some hair rollers, nail varnishes, and a beautiful perfume. I was shocked when I reached the counter and realised I'd spent nearly two hundred pounds. Mark looked at me questioningly. I smiled sheepishly at him.

"I think I deserve to treat myself!" I said, and he smiled.

"That you do," he said, almost wistfully.

*

I felt completely exhausted again that evening, but in a good way. I managed to go up to my room earlier than usual, telling Mark that the afternoon had taken it out of me. I locked the door behind me and turned on the little radio Mark had found for me a few days ago and brought to my room. I hummed to the music, not knowing the song or the band, but enjoying the sound anyway. I opened my bags of new purchases and hung the items up in my tiny wardrobe. I put my new shampoos and shower gels in the bathroom and put my make-up and perfume on the small dressing table in my room, loving the fact that it was starting to feel more like my own.

I wished I had some nice pictures to put up to make the room more homely, and suddenly the photograph I'd seen of me and Chris popped into my head and I tried to push it away. I hated the feeling it gave me when I thought about it, and I hated the feeling I got whenever I thought of Chris – a mixture of anger and hate mixed with a guilt and sadness that I couldn't understand.

Against my wishes, though, my mind wandered, and I wondered where Mark's laptop was. I knew it would be somewhere in the home and that I could look at it if I really wanted to. I hated myself for thinking it, but something inside me wanted to feed some sick pleasure that was within me, deep down somewhere that I didn't have any control over. I felt like a drug addict or a self-harmer that knew what they wanted to do was wrong but couldn't help themselves. I walked over to the radio and turned it up louder, attempting to drown out my thoughts. I looked at the time and counted the minutes down until nine p.m. when Carl was finishing his shift and would ring me on his way home. As usual, I had butterflies at the thought of speaking to him.

60

CHRIS

"Knowing that they were there gave me something to focus on, something to think about." – Chris.

I laid in bed, barely moving. I hurt all over. Every part of my body physically hurt. I stared forwards, unmoving. My thoughts drifted, and, as they always did first thing in the morning when I wasn't drunk enough, they started to drift to Becky and our life before this whole mess. Tears escaped out of the corner of my eye and ran down my sore cheeks, one after another, a steady stream.

I lay still, enjoying the feeling, watching them trickle down my face in my mind's eye. The path the tears fell down stung, so sore from the salty stream that fell over the same skin every day. My eyes were constantly swollen and puffy now, and the only time my eyes felt comfortable were when they were closed.

I wondered what time it was, but I couldn't find the energy to look. I didn't know if it was morning, afternoon, or night. I sighed. A long, drawn-out sound, and hearing the desolate noise come out of my own mouth upset me even more and I squeezed my eyes together, forcing tears to spill out and trickle over my face. I tried to hold back the sobs that were threatening to take over my body. I missed Becky *so much*. My body started to heave, and I managed to turn my head into the pillow to cry as quietly as I could. I pushed my face into it, sobbing and sobbing while picturing Becky's face. The day we met. Our wedding day. Her asleep in bed next to me. Coming home from work to find her curled up on the sofa, reading a book. Sitting across from her in a restaurant. Holding hands as we walked the dogs. These torturing images played around and around in my head. I had no control over them. I knew that drinking myself into a stupor was the only way I would stop these images from haunting me, torturing me – that or ending it all.

For a second the sobs slowed down and a layer of calm settled over me. I hated myself for thinking it, but it was the only thought I could have while I was remotely sober that made me feel like I was in control. I had started thinking about it a lot. I tried to tell myself that it was just a thought. That it was just something people thought about when they were depressed, not something that I would actually do. But even so, I'd found myself thinking about how I would do it, where and when.

I'd even started collecting pills and burying them at the back of my wardrobe. I'd decided that taking an overdose would be the best way to go. No mess. It would be like falling asleep. After I had flushed the original packets of antidepressant tablets Dr Moran had prescribed me down the toilet in a defiant rage, I had now started squirreling them away. I took pleasure in popping them out of the packet one by one and counting how many I had. I added each individual pill or capsule and mixed them together in a little bag.

Whenever I ventured out of the house, which wasn't very often anymore, I would buy a packet of painkillers, too. I put them in my pocket and took them home to add to my growing pile. Sometimes I took the bag of pills out of my wardrobe and just looked at them. Sometimes I went days without looking at them. But knowing that they were there gave me something to focus on, something to think about.

*

I lay with my face resting on the damp pillow, hating myself for crying, but not being able to stop. I obviously hadn't drunk enough yesterday as my mind seemed a bit clearer than usual this morning. I could see Becky's face in way too much detail. Her beautiful brown eyes framed by thick, long, black lashes. Her smile that lit up her whole face when she looked at me. Her beautiful, thick, long, dark hair that was the envy of every girl that met her. Even the natural glow of her skin. She really was the most beautiful girl I had ever seen, and thinking of her perfect face caused me agony.

I moved properly for the first time since opening my eyes and managed to shift to the side of my bed, stretching my hand down underneath and reaching around for a bottle. I found one that had liquid in it and brought it up to my face. I hated myself for what I was doing. I hated my life and everything that had happened. I needed to escape from reality.

I gulped and gulped, ignoring the heaves that threatened as my body tried to reject the liquid, but I concentrated on keeping it down. I was a pro now at not wasting alcohol. I put the bottle down by the side of the bed and slumped back into the pillows, allowing the sickness and hazy blur to take over me. I must have dozed off. I woke again a while later, feeling sick. Becky was at the forefront of my mind again. I must have been dreaming about her. I could see her face so clearly. I felt like I was being tortured. I didn't want to see her face or think about her. I sat up at the side of the bed, bracing myself as the room started spinning.

My mind definitely felt too clear today. I looked down at my pale, skinny arms and hated myself as I reached for the bottle again. I wondered why I couldn't pull myself out of this. Then an image of Becky laughing with the doctor would appear in my mind and I would think of her leaving the hospital. Starting a new lift without me. I wondered what she was doing now. Who she was with. I vaguely remembered my mum telling me recently that

Becky was due to be discharged. I'd ignored her. Blocked it out. I didn't want to know.

I couldn't bear thinking of Becky doing things that I wasn't a part of. I would start wondering where she was going and who with. I didn't want to torture myself, but I couldn't help it. This turmoil was my life. All day. Every day.

61

CHRIS

"I was torturing myself." – Chris.

I was outside. The fresh air was making me feel sick. It was evening. I couldn't remember why I was outside or where I was going. I wracked my brain, trying to remember why I'd gotten up. It must have been something important for me to get up and make it all the way outside to the pavement. I looked around. I was down the end of the road. How had I got here? I couldn't remember what the reasoning was, but I presumed I needed to get more alcohol. I felt in my tracksuit bottom pockets and found that I did have my wallet on me. I'd walk to the shop and get some.

*

I walked out of the shop with a bottle of whiskey and a box of Aspirin to add to my collection. The lady behind the counter wouldn't meet my eye as she served me. She put the items in the white plastic bag and accepted my money, being careful not to touch my hand as she took it from me. I walked out of the shop without thanking her.

*

I didn't go home. I don't know why. I didn't want to be in my bedroom. I don't know if it was because my thoughts had been so much clearer and more vivid today. I wanted the distraction of being out of the house. I had to keep away from pubs or crowds. Pubs and crowds had got me into too much trouble recently. I walked forward aimlessly.

*

I somehow managed to get on a bus. I sat on it for a while, watching the city pass by the windows. But I knew where I was going. I got off the bus a mile or so away from Leicester Square and walked without thinking. I found myself walking to the pub where Becky and I had first sat and had a drink, the day I waited for her outside of her interview. I stood outside, staring at it. I couldn't bear to make my way inside so instead I stood out on the opposite pavement looking at the door. I remembered the two of us, nervous and full of excitement, walking through it and sitting together for hours and hours. Talking, getting to know each other, falling in love. I leant against the wall, feeling short of breath as tears threatened, my throat constricting.

I took the bottle of whiskey out of the bag and swigged from it, ignoring the disgusted looks from people walking along the pavement next to me. I stared them in the eye until they looked away. I took several large gulps of the liquid, thankful that finally I was starting to feel hazy, starting to feel numb. I stumbled away from the pub and up the path. Once again, not knowing where I was going, but heading that way anyway. I recognised where I was, and I realised I was walking down towards Leicester Square tube station. The alcohol was starting to hit me now and I felt the usual sickness, anger, and disorientation creeping into me.

It wasn't until I was a few metres away that I was hit with a pain in the chest that felt like a physical blow. The tube station. Where Becky and I had shared our first kiss. Where we had run to, laughing in the rain. Like a scene from a film. Where we had stopped and kissed. The most magical first kiss anyone could ever have imagined. I hated myself as I realised I'd known all along that this is where I was heading. I was torturing myself. But I didn't know why.

I couldn't stop myself from approaching the entrance. Staring at the wall we had leant up and kissed against. I stared at it, tears welling up, about to spill over. I choked back the tears, desperate to turn away. But I couldn't. My head started spinning, the alcohol was starting to take its toll on my frail body. An image of Becky and the doctor sitting in the garden together flashed into my mind and I could hear the sound of her sweet laugh when she was with him. I thought back to the two of us, so young, so besotted. Right here. Kissing against this very wall. The images swarmed around my head, and I suddenly felt faint. I struggled to breathe as the spinning continued and I closed my eyes, willing it to go away. I heard a moan escape my lips, and before I knew what I was doing I launched the half-full whiskey bottle against the wall of the station.

The bottle exploded, shattering into a thousand pieces as glass and liquid flew everywhere. What I had done suddenly hit me and I stared around, confused. I turned away from the station and walked away as fast as I could without tripping over, filled with anger and hatred. I wanted to get away from here. Away from the memories.

*

I was in a taxi. The taxi driver had wound his window down when I'd got in, and he kept glancing at me disgustedly in the rear-view mirror. I stared at him back. He had insisted I pay him up front. What did he think I was? A tramp?

The warmth of the car was making me feel sick, and I suddenly hated myself for throwing the whiskey away. I thought of the waste. I imagined the amber liquid running down the wall outside the station like giant tears. I liked the thought of that. Giant tears.

I looked out of the window and suddenly realised that we were not far from mine and Becky's flat, and, all of a sudden, before I knew what I was doing, I found myself talking, telling the driver to stop. Telling him I wanted to get out around the corner here.

It was dark by now and the streetlights were on, casting an orange glow over the whole street. I asked the driver to drop me off at the end of the road and I got out before he had finished speaking to me, not caring if I'd paid him too much money.

I was on our street. The street we had spent many happy years living on. We should have just stayed here. If we had never moved none of this would have happened and we would still be in our flat. Happy and in love. Our baby soon to be born. It *was* all my fault. Becky was right. I should never have made us move. Tears started again without me even realising it, and I headed down the pavement slowly, my heart hurting in my chest. My eyes were struggling to focus in the dark and through my hazy drunkenness.

It was a few feet away that I saw it, and my forehead crinkled in confusion. What was that sign outside our flat? I picked up the pace, straining my eyes, and it hit me like a truck, taking my breath away. It was an estate agent's sign, with an ugly red 'SOLD' sticker taped over the top. I felt even more short of breath than usual. I bent over double, concentrating on breathing, worried I was going to have a heart attack. I stared up at it in confusion. The flat could not be sold. How could the flat be sold? *We* were going to buy this flat, no-one else. This was *our* flat! This must be a mistake. I found myself right outside and I thundered down the steps, suddenly full of angry energy. I was at the front door in seconds, suddenly filled with a blind fury. I banged on the door, as hard as I could, screaming, overcome with rage.

"HELLO? HELLO?" I shrieked, hating the sound of my voice, but I carried on anyway. My voice was breaking with the strain, and before I knew it, I was punching the door over and over again, and then kicking it. Pain shot through my hands, arms, and feet but I kept on hammering away, throwing my entire weight against it. I knew I was losing it, that I looked like a wild animal, but I carried on. Punching, kicking, and throwing myself at the door, not knowing what it was I was trying to achieve.

There was clearly nobody in the flat. The lights were all off and it looked empty, but I carried on attacking the door anyway, until eventually, like a child worn out by a tantrum, I literally crumpled to the floor and cried with my head on my arms. I wailed and cried and was overcome with a pain that I didn't know was possible. It was an actual agony that words can't describe, it hurt every part of my body.

Not one person had come to see what all the noise was about, and I didn't know if I was thankful for that or whether it added to the complete and utter sadness and loneliness that engulfed me.

62

CHRIS

"It was ours." – Chris.

I woke up freezing cold, slumped against the door of the flat. The sun was rising. I must have fallen asleep and stayed in the same position all night. I felt awful. My hands were swollen and throbbing with pain. I scolded myself once again for throwing away the whiskey last night. I desperately needed a drink. I got up, feeling pain shoot from my hands and up my arms as I tried to stand, wincing when I stood on my feet. I couldn't wait to get home and drink until I passed out. I hobbled up the steps, tears as usual creeping out of the corners of my eyes and down my cheeks, as they did every time I woke up. I brushed them away angrily, hating myself. I looked up at the 'SOLD' sign again, and all the memories and emotions from last night flooded through me. Our flat. *Our flat!* I headed in the direction of my mum's. I would call Edna today. Find out what was going on. Tell her she couldn't sell the flat to someone else. It was ours. Mine and Becky's. An intense pain shot through my right foot every time it touched the floor, but I welcomed the physical pain. It was much easier to deal with than the pain that was in my heart.

*

The sun was fully up by the time I approached my mum's front door. I had a plastic bag with two bottles of vodka and a packet of children's painkillers. There was a dinosaur on the box and the tablets were multi coloured. I couldn't wait to add them to my stash. I hobbled up the steps and opened the front door. It was never locked anymore. Ever since I'd started drinking my mum always left the door open, never wanting me to get home without my keys and not be able to get in.

I walked in and straight away I could hear my mum and Tom's voices in the kitchen. I heard a chair scrape along the floor and my mum appeared in the hallway. I didn't want to face her today. Not today. I felt the lowest I'd ever felt. Sadness didn't even come close to describing it.

"Chris!" my mum screamed my name at me, and I sighed, wanting to cry. I turned to look at her, and the mask of anger on her face slipped and horror and sadness took over. "What on earth have you done? Have you been fighting again?" she said, and I shook my head. I felt like a child stood in front of her, my bottom lip quivering and tears threatening to spill.

I bit down on my lip, not wanting to cry, just wanting to escape to the sanctuary of my room and the alcohol. My mum eyed my hands and then looked at me.

"I haven't been fighting, Mum, honest," I said, my voice hoarse. I felt as though I had swallowed glass, lacerating my voice. I realised that it was the first time I'd spoken to her properly in ages, I couldn't even remember the last time. She looked taken aback and nodded at me.

"Oh, okay. Okay."

We stood opposite each other in an awkward silence. For some reason I wanted to give her a hug. But I knew that if I felt human contact right now, I would cry, and I didn't know if I would ever be able to stop. I turned away from her and went up the stairs, wincing with pain at every movement.

63

BECKY

"Desperately trying to decipher what was the dream and what was real." – Becky.

I was coming to realise that my dreams always seemed to be worse when I was stressed. So, over the weekend as my date with Carl approached, my nights were filled with tossing and turning. I would wake up in the middle of the night in a panic after dreaming about having a car accident, and I would be convinced that it was just a dream. I had to really remind myself that *that* part was true. Chris was constantly in my dreams now, and no matter what I dreamt of, it somehow seemed to link back to him.

Sometimes, in the place between sleep and being awake, I would yearn for him and would be filled with an intense longing that even eclipsed the way I felt about Carl. But as soon as I awoke the feelings would be gone. I would bury them down and ignore them, filling myself with hatred for him by thinking of everything that had happened since I'd woken from my coma: the lies, the drinking, and the attack on Carl.

*

Monday morning finally arrived, and I dragged myself slowly out of a deep sleep as my alarm started going off. I had been dreaming of an island, a beautiful sunny island. It had been so real, I can remember how it felt to be walking on the sand. At first, I assumed it was Carl walking along next to me, but it didn't take me long to realise it was Chris. I was happy it was Chris. I felt so happy in the dream, and I tried to remember why. We walked and walked, and then the beach changed slightly, it was colder and not so tropical and Chris and I were walking along with two dogs at our feet. I watched them run off in front of us and I realised I'd had this dream before. I tried to think within the dream, but then my alarm started going off and I struggled and struggled until I was awake, desperately trying to decipher what was the dream and what was real, hating myself and hating my dreams.

Reality hit and it suddenly dawned on me that I was finally meeting Carl today. The thought brought me back to reality, and the dream instantly faded until it was at the back of my mind. I tried to ignore it as I threw myself into getting ready.

*

I was too nervous to eat. I showered and deliberated over what to wear. It was another boiling hot day, so I eventually decided on a long, plain black dress with some high strapped sandals, loving how tall and grown-up I looked. I decorated my neck and ears with some gold jewellery I had bought, and I put some gold bangles onto my wrists. It was sweltering outside, so I blow-dried my hair and pinned it on the top of my head, not wanting to make myself hotter by having it around my neck.

I started peeling the wrappers off the make-up I had bought, and I started applying it for the first time since the accident. Once again, I watched amazed as my hands went back and forth, applying the make-up with an instinct I didn't know I had. It didn't take long until I stepped away from the mirror and looked at myself, pleased with the result. I looked so grown-up and sophisticated. I turned around, looking at myself in the full-length mirror, trying to come to terms with the fact that this was actually me.

I looked at the time with knots in my stomach. I was due to meet Carl in an hour. We had agreed to meet at

Waterloo train station, and I had studied the train map last night, desperate to make my way there on my own and not let Carl know how nervous I was.

With one last glance at myself in the mirror, I checked no-one was outside before putting my phone into my bag, along with my purse and a tube map. I took a deep breath and headed out of my room, praying Mark wouldn't want to talk for too long – I was so nervous, I just wanted to get on my way!

64

BECKY

"Not today! Not today! Please not today!" – Becky.

I stood at Waterloo train station with my heart hammering in my chest and my bag clutched tightly in my hands. I couldn't get over how huge the station was. Twenty or so train platforms lined one wall, and, next to that, two escalators took a continual trail of people underground to the tube platforms. I stared over the crowds as people swarmed around me like ants, running for trains or towards the underground, pushing past each other to get in the direction they were heading. It was a constant battle and I gripped my bag tighter, staring ahead, trying not to look panicked, praying that Carl would come into sight soon.

The walls that weren't filled with train platforms were packed tight with food and drink establishments. Each and every one had a huge queue of people outside, filling the station up even more and causing mayhem as people pushed their way through the queues, trying to get on their way. I stood staring, open mouthed, at the hive of activity. Everyone seemed to be either talking into their mobile phones or walking along looking down at their phone screens, bumping into each other, giving each other dirty looks.

There were people of all ages and races – people in work suits with briefcases, mums with pushchairs, and even kids in school uniforms. I stared at them as they casually strolled through the crowds, gossiping and laughing without a care in the world, and I wondered how they could seem so relaxed here. It petrified me! I wondered once again why on earth I had lived in London for so long, it was horrible and busy; I hated it and the way everyone looked so miserable. I longed for the quiet tranquillity of the home or the hospital as my eyes scanned the crowd, desperate to see Carl. I glanced up at the clock, he was twenty minutes late. The knot in my chest tightened and I closed my eyes, concentrating on my breathing, praying that he would turn up soon. I actually felt weak with relief when I finally spotted him walking towards me. His eyes were fixed on my face, and he was smiling confidently. I straightened up and attempted to smile back, suddenly realising how dry my mouth was. He seemed to fill the gap between us in seconds, giving me no time to prepare, and before I knew it he was stood in front of me, looking down at me appreciatively.

"You look beautiful." he said, and he leant down and kissed me on the cheek, his hand resting on the small of my back as he did so. Before I could speak, he looked around, scanning the crowd. He took my hand – as if it was the most natural thing in the world – and I followed him without question.

He headed to the escalators that were leading down to the underground and I didn't even ask where it was that we were headed. We stood on the escalator as it moved down, and we got squashed close together as more and more people pushed onto the moving stairs behind us. I was very aware that our bodies were pressed up against each other as we travelled down to the tube platforms, which were a maze of walkways, once again filled with people.

Carl marched confidently through them, though, and I followed, attempting to keep up. His head moved back and forth as he looked at the signs and maps, and eventually he turned a sharp left and we approached a platform with a tube already sitting with its doors open, beeping loudly, signalling it was about to leave. Carl squeezed my hand and pulled me slightly as he broke into a run and I followed him, petrified of tripping in my heels or on the bottom of my dress. We made it through the doors of the tube just in time, and it was surprisingly empty inside the carriage after the hustle and bustle from outside. As the doors shut behind us with a hiss, I realised it was quiet and calm inside.

There was a couple with matching long dreadlocks kissing loudly in one corner of the carriage, and a lone man with his head buried deep behind a newspaper. Otherwise, we were the only people. I felt flushed, and worried that my make-up would have smudged or my hair would have fallen out of place, but as I sat down next to Carl he stared at me, greedily taking me all in.

"Becky, you look stunning." he said, his voice breathy and low like I'd never heard it before, and I felt a chill of pleasure creep over my skin. I blushed when I saw the way he was looking at me. I had to remind myself that I'm not a shy teenager anymore, I'm a grown woman. I should be acting sexier and more confidently if I wanted a man like this to love me, but I couldn't think of anything to say or do!

I stared at him, attempting to take him in without being too obvious. It was the first time I had seen him properly outside of the hospital. He was wearing a pristine white shirt and suede jacket over some smart, dark blue jeans, and I was surprised to see he was wearing a pair of dirty white, worn in trainers. The shoes didn't match the rest of the outfit at all, and I stared at them. It made me realise once again that I had only touched the surface of knowing him, there was so much more to find out.

"What are you staring at?" he asked, and I jumped, feeling like a naughty school girl that had been caught misbehaving. I looked up at him and saw that he was smiling. Once again, my mind went blank and I didn't know what to say. I could feel a blush creeping up into my cheeks from my neck and all of a sudden I felt very hot. At that moment the tube slowed down, pulling into another stop, and I watched as more people got on, distracting Carl as he looked at them.

A group of teenage boys entered the carriage and stayed huddled around the doors, choosing to ignore the empty seats that lined the sides of the carriage, and I glanced at them over my shoulder, wondering what it was that Carl was staring at. I was embarrassed to see that they were nudging each other and nodding in my direction approvingly. I looked back at Carl and saw that his face had clouded over as he stared at the group of boys stonily, his gaze not leaving them until I presumed they'd looked away. I wondered, not for the first time, if he was acting jealous. But rather than the thrill I used to get in the hospital when he acted this way, today it made me feel a bit nervous.

We sat in an awkward silence until we reached the next stop, and I wracked my brains looking for something to say, wishing for the easy conversation that had flowed between us in the hospital. Just as I managed to build up the courage to speak, Carl stood up and held out his hand to me, and I realised we must be getting off at the next stop. I looked out of the window to see where we were as we started to slow down, and I read the 'Leicester Square' sign mounted on the wall. As I read the words, for a split-second I had a flash of memory or a dream, and I felt the usual dread settle over me that I felt when my mind started playing tricks on me like this. *Not today! Not today! Please not today!* was all I could think as I closed my eyes and tried to concentrate on what was happening here and now, not the niggling feeling that was creeping over me. This was stronger than usual, though, and I knew that this wasn't a dream that was trying to surface – it was a memory. It was something from my past, from before the accident. I felt it so strongly – even more so than the day at the 'Welcome Break', but I tried to bury it down, to think of anything else.

"Becky?" Carl said, and I snapped back to reality, seeing him standing with his hand held out towards me, gesturing me to get up as the tube slowed to a stop.

I jumped up guiltily from my seat, praying that he didn't recognise my behaviour from the hospital and realise that something was wrong. He looked at me, his brows furrowed, and I smiled at him sheepishly. Luckily the doors opened, and the next few minutes were taken up with getting off the tube and navigating our way through the station. I didn't dare look around too much for fear of seeing something that would trigger off another memory, and I followed Carl along, staring at his back, praying to be away from here. Thankfully it wasn't as busy at this station as it had been at Waterloo, and we had more space as we walked towards to the exit.

I felt relief wash over me when I could see daylight up ahead and I hurried along behind Carl and out into the open. Just as I set foot outside the station one of my shoes slipped from under me and I looked down and noticed there was glass all over the floor.

"Carl, hold on," I said, moving out of the way of the foot traffic flowing in and out of station as I leaned against the wall at the entrance, attempting to pick a piece of glass out from the sole of my new shoe.

"What have you done? Are you okay?" Carl said, and I looked up at him and smiled.

"Yeah, I'm fine, I just trod on some glass," I said, standing up straight to look at him. As I stood up straight, another flash hit me. This one was stronger than ever before, it literally took my breath away. I was filled with a strong familiarity as if I *needed* to remember something, and I looked around at my surroundings, panicked. The wall I had been leaning up against flashed into my mind and I stared at it, wondering what one earth could be happening. It was filthy and covered in graffiti. What was going on?

I stepped away, once again desperate to get away from here, and for the first time since I'd woken up from my coma I decided I wanted a drink, hoping that some alcohol would numb this horrible feeling that was creeping into me, threatening to take over. Carl was staring at me, confused, and I realised that if I didn't pull myself together I was going to ruin this. I had to concentrate on the here and now. I was on a date with Carl! This is what I'd been dreaming of for months! I couldn't let something get in the way now. I stepped away from the station, even though something was drawing me back, something inside me was *begging* me to go back, to think, to concentrate. I felt as if I wanted to turn around, stand exactly where I had just been, stop, think, remember whatever it was that was attempting to creep back up from my subconscious. But I knew now was not the time, I had to concentrate on Carl. Not on whatever was going on inside my stupid head.

I somehow managed to pull my face into a smile, and I slid up next to Carl, feigning innocence.

"Shall we go and get a drink?" I said, and Carl smiled, looking relieved.

"Sounds like a plan!" he said cheerily. "Let's go this way. We can walk over towards Covent Garden, there are some nice places over there." His words struck another chord and the niggly feeling started again but I ignored it, smiling and nodding.

"Okay, lead the way," I said, and followed him as he

walked away. I risked a glance over my shoulder, staring at the entrance to the tube station, wondering what on earth had just happened.

65

BECKY

"I wondered how long I was going to be able to keep fighting it." – Becky.

The feeling stayed with me as we walked away from the station and down towards Covent Garden. Carl took my hand again and we walked along, just like a normal couple. I tried to concentrate on that, on how good it felt to be on the arm of a man like this, to have people walk past us and assume we were together. I wanted to be able to enjoy it and relax, but the creepy, niggly feeling left over from what I'd just experienced wouldn't leave me. I concentrated on listening to Carl speak, nodding or answering him when appropriate, and I focused on not looking around too much. I was petrified of seeing something I recognised, something that would trigger me off. Everything seemed to be familiar here and I didn't understand it. I'd been fine on Oxford Street with Mark a few days ago, why did this have to be happening now?

It wasn't long before we entered an open square that Carl told me was Covent Garden.

"Have you been here before?" Carl asked looking down at me, and I shook my head.

"Not that I can remember," I said, still not daring to look around too much. I must admit it was lovely here. People strolled around in the sunshine, and everyone looked happy and relaxed. I could hear screams and shouts coming from around the corner and I wondered what was going on. Carl headed in the direction of the noise, but I knew instantly that I didn't want to go that way. My senses seemed heightened, and I knew that it wasn't going to take much to set these flashes off.

"Let's go somewhere quieter," I said, stopping in my tracks and literally tugging on Carl's hand. He looked at me, puzzled.

"Really?" he asked "There are some nice cafés around here where you can sit and watch the street entertainers. We could get a coffee or some food? It's really nice."

"Erm... I was thinking more like an alcoholic drink..." I said, embarrassed, and Carl looked at me and smiled as if he had just realised something.

"Are you nervous?" he said, only half joking, but he looked quite pleased with himself. I realised that this was the scapegoat I needed for my odd behaviour so far today, so I shrugged slightly and nodded my head, playing along. He laughed and turned around, heading away from the noise which was getting louder and was filled with children's laughs and screams.

I could hear someone saying into a microphone, *"Thank you for watching, ladies and gentlemen, boys and girls! Thank you!"* I hurried away from the noise, wondering why the voice kept going around and around in my head, and although we hadn't walked around the corner to see what was there, I had a feeling I knew exactly what I would see. I had an image in my mind's eye, as if I had dreamt about this very situation, or visited here before, and I knew deep down that if I'd walked over there, had seen it with my own eyes, confirming what I thought I would see, I would start to be flooded with memories the way I had before. I wondered how long I was going to be able to keep fighting it.

My heart rate slowed down as we walked away from Covent Garden and down to some quieter side streets. It didn't take long until we approached a quiet looking restaurant. We entered, blinking as our eyes adjusted to the darkness as we walked in after the bright sunlight from outside. It was dated and dark. The walls were blood red, and the furniture was made of dark wood. I didn't recognise it in here at all and it was relatively quiet. I could see that Carl was going to turn around to leave, presumably to find somewhere different and nicer, but I put my hand on his forearm.

"Let's stay here," I said, and I could see his mind ticking over for a second before he agreed. We approached the bar and Carl ordered his drink before asking what I would like. I thought for a second, trying to think of the most grown-up drink I could order. I decided that a glass of wine would be okay. The middle-aged lady behind the bar barely looked at us as she put the drinks out in front of us, and Carl pulled his wallet out and paid with a crisp twenty-pound note, not even acknowledging her.

I thanked him and picked up my drink, heading towards a table at the back of the restaurant, and we settled down at a secluded corner table. I sipped the wine, surprised at the taste, not really liking it, but instantly feeling a calming sensation as it trickled down the back of my throat. I took a few mouthfuls, appreciating the warmth in my stomach, and I already felt like the horrors of the journey here were declining in my head, and almost instantly I felt more confident.

I smiled at Carl, looking into his face properly for the first time. We stared deep into each other's eyes for a moment and the old connection was back. I felt like electricity was crackling between us and we both smiled and sighed in unison. I liked the tension between us, and I took another sip of my wine.

"Looks like we should have got the bottle!" Carl said, raising his eyebrows at me as he took a mouthful of his pint and I smiled.

"Are you trying to get me drunk?" I said, instantly cringing at my poor attempt at flirting. But Carl looked at me knowingly and I wondered where on earth today was going to lead.

*

Hours passed and we both carried on steadily drinking. All my inhibitions were gone, and we were getting along really well. It was starting to feel just as it had when we were alone in the hospital.

Carl was full of stories, and I sat listening to him, barely hearing what he was saying; I was more interested in watching his mouth move and the way his tongue moved over his lips. I fancied him so much. I laughed at his jokes and asked questions in the right places, and I felt as if I was doing really well, the perfect little audience for him. He'd ordered more wine and joined me in drinking it. I was way past tipsy now and was certainly feeling drunk. Ordering food in the late afternoon had slowed down my drunkenness a bit, but we carried on drinking long after the food had gone, and we were still sat in the same spot when the sun started setting and the temperature started getting cooler.

Through my hazy state I realised that I didn't have a clue how to get back to the home from here, and I knew I wouldn't be able to manage the tube by myself in this state. Carl was staring at me intently.

"What are you thinking?" he asked, and I looked at him, trying to get my eyes to focus, beginning to regret the last glass of wine.

"I've just made the executive decision that I'm getting a taxi home tonight! There is no way I can cope with the tube in this state!" I said. It went quiet for a moment, and I jumped when I realised Carl had put his hand on my leg.

"Why don't you come and stay at my place tonight?" he asked, and I looked up at him, shocked. The realisation of what he meant dawned on me and I felt

323

both petrified and excited. I started to stammer about work in the morning, but Carl cut me off.

"You said your shift doesn't start until ten o'clock tomorrow, I have to be at the hospital way before then. I can drop you back in the morning," he said, and I could feel his hand moving up my leg slightly underneath the table.

The butterflies in my stomach started playing tricks and I felt out of breath. I wished I hadn't drunk so much. I didn't feel like I could think properly at the moment. As I tried to gather my thoughts, Carl leant in and kissed me roughly on the lips and one of his hands slipped to the back of my head, pulling me into him. I kissed him back, trying to bat away the thought that I was out of my depth. The kiss stirred something inside me, though, and as Carl pulled away slightly from my face and whispered, "So?" in my ear, I heard myself saying, "Yes," before I'd even contemplated what I was agreeing to.

It was dark when we finally left the restaurant. Carl had a protective hand on the small of my back and I concentrated really hard at walking in a straight line. When we got outside, we stood on the kerb while he phoned for a taxi. He didn't take his eyes off me for a second, and the way he looked at me reminded me of the way a hunter looked at its prey. I gulped and tried to breathe deeply, filling myself with fresh air, desperately trying to sober up, telling myself that this is what I wanted to happen, but the cold air outside seemed to be making me feel more drunk and I steadied myself, concentrating on breathing, listening to Carl's authoritative voice as if from far away as he snapped at the taxi service. He eventually put the phone down and appeared at my side, thrusting his phone towards me.

"Do you need to ring Mark and let him know you're not going back tonight?" he said, and I felt panicked all of a sudden. I hadn't even thought of Mark! How was I going to explain my way out of this? I suddenly regretted the hasty decision to go back to Carl's, but, as if sensing it, he snaked his hands around my hips and clasped them together behind me. Feeling him touching me gave me the push I needed to pick up the phone and ring the home's switchboard.

I prayed that one of the nurses would answer so I could ask them to give Mark a message, but it was his voice that answered in its usual genuinely cheery way.

"Good evening, Fairview Care Home, Mark speaking," he sang.

"Hi Mark, its Becky," I said.

"Becky, are you drunk?" he said, immediately full of concern, and I wondered if it was that obvious. "Where are you? Who are you with?" He fired questions at me, and Carl's eyes narrowed as he listened, and he rolled his eyes, annoyed.

"Keep it short!" he mouthed at me, smiling like a school child. I attempted to smile back.

"Mark, I've got to be quick, just to let you know I've bumped into some old friends. I'm going to go and have a few drinks with them tonight and will probably end up staying at one of their places, so I'll be back tomorrow, okay? I'll see you in the morning, my shift starts at ten."

Mark started firing questions at me, and my drunken, fluffy head couldn't keep up with what he was saying.

"I can't hear you, Mark, I'm going to go, okay? I'll see you in the morning," I said, and hung up the phone while he was still talking, feeling terribly guilty. Carl, probably sensing this, took a step towards me and kissed me again, and this time I just accepted it.

I felt like I was spinning when I closed my eyes to kiss him, and, thankfully, he held me up as I stood there. The kiss seemed to go on forever. Our taxi finally arrived, and

I stumbled from the path and climbed through the back door, relieved to be breathing some fresh air for a minute. Carl told the taxi driver his address and I sat with my head back on the seat, wishing the spinning would go away, wanting to open a window to let some air in but not daring to move.

The journey took about twenty minutes, and I started to feel slightly better. We eventually pulled into a beautiful road lined with tall, white brick buildings surrounded by black iron gates. Leafy green trees lined the street, and there wasn't a soul in sight. Carl paid the driver and got out, holding the door open for me, looking at me expectantly. I realised that this was it. The moment I had been waiting for. I'd never suspected that this time would really come, especially not this soon. But now it was here.

I got out of the car, thanking the taxi driver, and looked at Carl who stared at me, smiling. He looked up and down the street and then turned to the door immediately in front of us, putting his key in the lock and twisting, pushing the door open into a beautifully decorated hallway. I followed in behind him.

*

We made love, but it wasn't what I'd been expecting. I was much more nervous than I thought I would be. I still felt drunk and dizzy, and was surprised at how rough and impersonal it had been. I felt as if I could've been anyone, that it wouldn't have mattered. The routine wouldn't have changed. Even as we were having sex, I started to get a feeling of guilt and I felt cheap. Hating myself for what was happening. I welled with tears, wondering how I could have got this so wrong. There was nothing loving about what was happening. I felt a yearning for something. I knew that something was missing. I closed my eyes. Shutting myself off. Praying for it to be over.

66

CHRIS

"I knew what I had to do." – Chris.

I walked up the stairs, knowing my mum was still watching, but I couldn't bear to turn around and see her face. I collapsed on my bed when I was finally in my room, and I let the tears take over. Almost instantly my body was wracked with sobs that physically shook me. I was howling. Long, drawn-out wails that just kept on coming, desperate for release. I buried myself face down in the pillow, which was already wet from tears and saliva, and I cried and cried, my face contorted with pain. I don't know how long it lasted, but eventually my body started to give up, and the huge sobs turned to whimpers. I lay on my side until silent tears drenched my cheeks as I tried to catch my breath. My head was pounding. There was a sharp throbbing pain above my eyes that made me feel sick.

I reached out for the plastic bag on the floor next to me and unscrewed the bottle of vodka, taking huge gulps of the disgusting liquid, concentrating on not throwing it back up again. I fell back onto the bed and waited for sleep to take me away.

*

Time passed. I don't know if I did manage to fall asleep, or if I just lay torturing myself for hours on end. I tried not to think of the flat with the 'SOLD' sign outside, but I did, and anger started to bubble up inside me. Why had Edna sold the flat out from underneath us? Why would anyone do that? That was our home. That was all I had left of Becky. How could anybody else live there?

Tears of frustration started welling up again as I got

more and more wound up. I drank more and more until I started to feel sick, but I ignored it and carried on, my head throbbing. I lay in bed with anger bubbling inside me, grinding my teeth together, almost growling. I suddenly sat up in a fury, the room spinning at the sudden movement as my stomach turned over. I was going to be sick. I opened my bedroom window and threw up down the side of the house, my body heaving, out of control. I waited for the heaves to stop and pulled the window shut with an angry slam, coherent enough to be annoyed at the wasted alcohol.

I looked around for my phone, desperately trying to remember where I'd last seen it. I would ring Edna now. Give her a piece of my mind. Ask her what on earth she thought she was doing. She *knew* we were going to buy the flat! I was getting wilder with each moment that passed, and all of a sudden the all-consuming anger that I'd felt last night when I was standing at the front door of the flat started to creep back into me. I pushed and shoved objects and clothes out of my way as I stormed around my room, searching for my phone. I opened and closed drawers, slamming them shut in frustration. If I couldn't find my phone, I would go to Edna's house. I could still remember where she lived. I would go and have this out with her, face-to-face. How could she be so stupid, so selfish?

Rage was taking over, and I stormed around my room like a caged, wild animal. I was about to yank my bedroom door open and go over to Edna's when I realised my phone was sitting on my bedside table, inches away from where I had been laying a few moments earlier.

I snatched it up and started punching the buttons, but the screen was dead. It must have run out of battery. Almost snarling, I groped around under my bed for the charger and plugged it in, taking a gulp of vodka whilst waiting for the screen to switch on. It seemed to take an age until everything loaded, and I studied the screen, trying to get my eyes to focus.

All of a sudden, messages started coming through one after the other, causing the phone to vibrate in my hand over and over again. I attempted to scroll through them, trying to get my blurry eyes to focus. A tiny little part of me wondered if there might be a message from Becky, but they were mainly from my mum and Simon, asking me where I was or telling me to ring them. They were dating back as long as a month ago, and I tried to remember the last time I'd switched my phone on.

The voicemail icon was flashing, too, and I'd had a text message weeks ago telling me my voicemail box was full. I pressed the button to listen to the voicemails and held the phone to my ear, anger turning to despair as message after message played.

"...Where the hell are you? Your mum's freaking out..."

"...Can't believe you've done this again. Ring my phone as soon as you get this..."

"...This is another message for Chris McNulty. Chris, this is Dave King calling again. Please can you call me as soon as you get this message? I need to speak with you urgently..."

"...Chris. It's Edna here. I hope you and Becky are both well. I haven't heard from you in a while and I'm starting to get pushed for time with the move down to my sister's. I wondered if you could give me a call back, please, so we can have a chat about the flat? I look forward to hearing from you soon..."

"... It's Simon again, where the hell are you? Ring me back when you get this message..."

"...Chris, it's Simon again. Ring me, and let me know where you are..."

"...Where are you, for God's sake? Ring me back..."

"...It's Edna, I was wondering if you would give me a call back as soon as possible, I've been trying Becky's mobile, too, but I haven't been able to reach her. As I'm sure you're aware, your rent only covers you..."

"...Just didn't know what to do, so I'll put the flat on the market and hope that you'll come back to me soon..."

"...Dave King again. Chris, I'm at a loss of what to do. Your doctor's note ran out a week ago and I haven't heard from you. I have no staff here. I thought you understood how important it was for us to have someone permanent for the year elevens' GCSEs..."

"...A letter confirming that your position here has been cancelled due to a breach of contract. We will hold onto the belongings left in your accommodation for one month. I'm sorry it has come to this. As I said, a letter will follow shortly..."

"...It's your mum again. Ring me back, I need to know where you are! Why do you keep doing this? Ring me as soon as you get this so I know you're safe!"

I felt as if I was underwater, struggling to breathe. The voices from the messages swam around in my head. It was too much information for me to take in. How had I made such a mess of everything? My job. The flat. All gone. What had I thought was going to happen? Did I think I would one day pull myself out of this hole I was in, get up and carry on with life? Buy the flat and go to work at Cradley Heath as if none of this had happened? Had I expected everything to just be there waiting for me when I was ready? How could I have been so stupid? It just hadn't occurred to me that the outside world and other people's lives were carrying on as normal whilst I was stuck in this misery. In this hell. To me it felt as if time had been standing still.

And now the flat was gone. Sold. I had nowhere to go

and no job to go to. And no Becky. I launched my phone against the wall. Taking pleasuring in watching it smash into several pieces which ricocheted off in different directions, eventually hitting the floor and sliding over the wooden surface and out of sight.

Tears were falling now, completely beyond my control, and I felt as if I couldn't breathe. My throat felt tiny, and I heaved in and out, trying to get oxygen into my lungs. Was I having a heart attack? I doubled over, pain soaring through my chest. My vision blurred and I knew I needed to be sick again. I turned around with blood pumping in my ears and a pressure building in my head whilst I tried to reach the window to be sick again. I couldn't make it that far, though, and I threw up over the end of my bed. I didn't know how it was physically possible, when a moment before I had felt like I couldn't even get air through my throat. There was nothing left inside my body to throw up now, and all I did was heave up frothy bile spotted with blood. I heaved and heaved, desperately attempting to breathe at the same time, a sheen of sweat covering my whole body.

I knew I had reached rock bottom, and at that moment I knew with absolute clarity why I had been squirreling away so many pills and tablets, and the reason why I had bought two bottles of vodka this morning instead of one. This was the final straw I needed to confirm the decision I had been pondering as I lay awake at night. I was going to end it all. Right now.

I started to cry. These weren't like the tears I'd been plagued with for the last few months, though, tears fuelled by anger and frustration as well as sadness. These were genuine, sorrowful tears that bubbled up and spilled out of me, causing me to wonder once again how I possibly had any tears left. I cried and cried, overcome with raw emotion and sadness, but the tears were softer now. They weren't wailing, painful sobs, they were more resigned, mournful tears. I was crying for myself, for everything *I* had lost. My home. My job. My beautiful, wonderful soulmate.

I knew beyond a shadow of a doubt that I couldn't carry on anymore, and I whimpered and snivelled as I picked up the bag of pills from the back of my cupboard. I added the new ones that I had bought last night and this morning, bringing my total up to a few hundred different tablets. I looked at them. The different shapes and sizes.

I thought of my mum sitting downstairs, aged and thin with worry. She was probably wondering what all the crashing and banging was about up here in my room. She wouldn't dare come up here to see, though. She knew I would shout at her until she ended up backing out of the room, turning away from me, upset. I cried even harder knowing what this was going to do to her. Then I thought of Simon, my dear wonderful friend who was like a brother to me. I thought of the two of us growing up together and the brilliant times we had shared. I was lucky to have grown up with someone like him. I put my head in my hands, sobbing continuously, desperately wanting to pick up the phone to say goodbye to him, to just speak to him one last time. But I knew I couldn't. I knew that he would make me change my mind, and nothing was worth having to live the rest of my life in this pain.

I tried not to think of Simon, and my mind flicked back to my mum. I thought of the moment we had shared earlier today when I had come in through the front door. I remembered how much I had suddenly wanted to hug her. How close we had been, stood right in front of each other, within touching distance. I could go downstairs now, wrap my arms around her and have one last hug. Perhaps lay my head on her shoulder. Maybe she would hold me like when I was little and tell me that there were other ways out. That everything was going to be okay.

But things were never going to be okay, and I knew what I had to do. Crying earnestly now, overcome with pain and sadness, I scooped a small handful of pills into my hand and threw them into my mouth like sweets. I chomped on them, wincing at the disgusting, bitter taste as I forced myself to swallow them, washing them down with swigs of vodka and fighting off the heaves that threatened in my throat. I carried on chomping and drinking, praying that I wouldn't throw up. Tears and snot ran down my face as I openly wept, desperate for a layer of calm to take over me as I waited for sleep, waited for it to be over.

67

It was Sue who found Chris early the next morning. She tapped on his door, waiting to see if he would acknowledge her. There was no answer. She was in two minds whether to go in or not, and she stood hovering by the door uncertainly, wishing she knew the right answer. She didn't want to walk in and catch him crying again. She knew he hated her to see him like that.

She almost walked away. She told herself she would come back at lunchtime. But at the last second, she decided to push the door open just a crack and have a peek to check he was okay. Just to put her mind at rest. She would take his wrath if he caught her looking.

She knew the instant she laid eyes on him that he was dead. The way he was laying back on his bed, his mouth wide open, his arms spread, his legs dangling lifelessly over the edge told her everything she needed to know.

Sue screamed. An animal noise that shocked even her own ears. Her legs collapsed from underneath her as she struggled for breath. She couldn't stand up, her body wouldn't take her weight, and she couldn't speak as Tom ran up the stairs behind her, climbing over her and shoving the bedroom door open. He looked down at Chris' lifeless body.

Tom's face was the confirmation that Sue needed. Her son was gone. She wailed again.

Printed in Great Britain
by Amazon